khanjar

khanjar

Woody James

For Elaine and Sophie

ACT ONE

CHAPTER 1.1

September 11 2002

AMSTERDAM

After making his way along crowded corridors and moving walkways, Salah arrived at the departure lounge for his flight to the UK. Having time to spare he wandered in and out of the duty-free shops; he liked the idea of saving money, avoiding duty on expensive goods, but was unable to decide what to buy. He thought of Maria and Janek, they more than deserved a gift; then there was Jas and, of course, his mother. He browsed and then hesitated; even at duty-free prices gifts could be expensive. Note to self: buy something when flying back to Dubai.

Still waiting for the announcement to board he made his way back to the departure lounge. After a short delay he was able to join the aircraft, find his seat and struggle like the other passengers to stow his luggage in the overhead locker. More and more passengers boarded; the adjacent seat remained unoccupied until, soon after the crew closed the aircraft's doors, a very large man arrived out of breath and sweating profusely.

Squeezing himself into the empty seat, he wrestled with his seat belt whilst apologising for causing a disturbance. After disappearing into the folds of the man's stomach, the belt was finally locked in place at full stretch. Luckily, he was in an aisle seat and some of his vast bulk could spill over. Even so, the man's body pressed uncomfortably against Salah's shoulder and upper arm. Salah realised he had some wriggle room on his window side but didn't want to give ground too soon only for the man to encroach further. Not wanting to complain and possibly cause bad feeling during the flight, he settled for a standoff.

As the plane began to taxi towards the runway, a flight attendant walked down the aisle checking seat belts. She told the man next to Salah to stow his computer under the front seat and fasten his seat belt. He replied that it was fastened. She asked him to show her. Somehow he managed to move the folds of his stomach around enough to reveal the deeply embedded belt. She looked alarmed but moved on down the aisle, presumably satisfied.

After take-off, Salah switched on the TV screen in the back of the seat in front of him and stayed on the flight tracking channel. The man in the adjacent seat who looked up from his laptop briefly interrupted his concentration.

"My name's Randy."

"Hi Randy, I'm Salah."

"Is this your first visit to the UK?"

"It's my first visit anywhere."

"Where are you from, Salah?"

"I live in Dubai."

"You're so lucky, what a great place to live."

"Yeah, what about you?"

"I live in Austin, Texas."

"What's that like?"

"Being black in America can sometimes be challenging but I never thought of living anywhere else. Good to meet you, Salah."

"Good to meet you too; I'm going to university in the UK to complete my degree."

"Sounds great; have a good trip."

Randy resumed what he was doing and Salah returned to flight tracking, occasionally glancing sideways at Randy who was peering at the laptop on his knees, deep in thought. Salah wanted to ask him what he was doing and wondered why he was going to the UK himself, but thought better of it. Instead, he tried to take a sneaky look out of the corner of his eye but it was impossible to see what was on the screen from a sideways view. He decided he wasn't that interested after all – just curious.

As the pilot announced they would soon begin to descend the

plane banked steeply; Salah suddenly caught sight of the English countryside and was amazed how green it was. In no time at all they were on the ground taxiing to their arrival gate.

The plane came to a halt; Salah and Randy stayed in their seats while others stood in the aisle trying to retrieve their luggage. Salah didn't mind, he was enjoying the moment, his first trip abroad. Randy managed to prise himself out of his seat and insert himself into the aisle throng. After much jostling he began slowly to inch towards the exit, creating a small space for Salah to leave his seat.

Salah quickly occupied the small space in the aisle and stood his ground while other passengers closed in around him. Somehow, amidst all the waving arms, he managed to drag his luggage out of the overhead locker, check he had everything and push his way forward. He didn't see any reason why those at the back of the plane should get off before him so he kept pushing and eventually joined those disembarking.

ENGLAND

The flight from Amsterdam to Manchester Airport was short and Salah was pleased to be close to his destination. The airport was much smaller than Schiphol but the flight had been full and a long queue formed at passport control. Not having to wait for luggage, Salah was among the first in the queue. He watched patiently as passengers in front answered questions from passport control officials, noticing that non-UK passengers, especially non-white passengers, were being asked more questions. When other officers arrived and opened more checkpoints the queue began to move a little faster.

It was soon Salah's turn. The officer was polite, but unfriendly, and took a long time checking Salah's passport. Salah was amazed how much information he required to enter into his computer. He told the officer he was coming to join the same university in the UK as the one he'd attended in Dubai. The officer looked suspicious, as if he didn't believe Salah, and asked him further questions about the course, the university, where Salah would be living, his transport arrangements and, particularly, when and how he would be returning to Dubai. Eventually the officer seemed to lose interest and allowed Salah to proceed.

As he was moving on he saw Randy again; he'd been way behind Salah in the queue and now he appeared at the adjacent checkpoint with a suitcase. Salah wondered how he had been able to collect his luggage so soon when others were still waiting for the carousels to start up. The officer took one look at Randy's passport, showed it to another uniformed officer wearing what appeared to be more senior rank markings, and Randy was waived through without further delay. The second officer saluted and shook hands. Salah was puzzled; who exactly *was* Randy and why was he getting VIP treatment?

Salah went straight to customs where he was asked to switch on his laptop, but his luggage wasn't searched. He was fascinated to see all his belongings exposed on the X-ray machine as his bag passed along the conveyor belt.

Although the University had provided details of where to look for transport, Salah felt out of his depth and a little apprehensive. Reaching an information desk he found himself behind someone with several items of luggage. Salah couldn't help overhearing him ask questions and it soon became obvious they were both travelling to the same university town. Salah interrupted to introduce himself and suggested that if they were going to the same place they could travel together in a taxi and split the fare – it might not cost any more than public transport. Hesitatingly, the other person agreed. Finding a taxi was easy; the driver was friendly and pleased to be hired for a long journey.

Salah told his new acquaintance he was from Dubai. Kees said he was from Holland and was coming to study civil engineering. Sure enough, Kees also realised they were headed to the same university. Kees said he would probably be in the UK for at least three years and was looking forward to it. He was arriving before the beginning of term to find somewhere to live. He didn't fancy university accommodation. Salah explained he was in the final year of a management course and that the University had offered him accommodation on campus; he thought this would be more convenient for an overseas student.

As they drove away from the airport, Salah asked Kees if he had flown from Schiphol before.

"Twice, yes; maybe three times. Why?"

"I was surprised at how many people around the airport had guns. Is that number of police and military usual in European airports?"

"No, it's probably because it's the first anniversary of the terror attacks on the Twin Towers. By the way, some of the terrorists came from Dubai and flew to America via Schiphol."

Salah was visibly taken aback. He didn't say anything, wondering if he looked like an Arab terrorist and whether this was why the passport officer seemed so suspicious. They chatted off and on for the remainder of the journey, mainly about their expectations of life in England and they arrived at the university sooner than expected. They parted company and politely agreed to keep in touch, although both thinking it not very likely.

Following his joining instructions, Salah made his way to the student accommodation office. He'd received an e-mail informing him that as an overseas student in his first year at the University he would automatically be allocated a room on campus. He was relieved but not surprised therefore to find that he had been allocated a room in a student hall of residence. After completing a registration form he collected the key to his room.

Salah made his way to Sharpe Hall following the campus map provided by the accommodation office. He soon found it and was pleased on two counts. First, Sharpe Hall was not far from the main University buildings and various facilities on the campus and, second, it looked newly built. He hoped everything inside would also be new.

He wasn't disappointed; everything looked in good condition and smelt clean. His room number began with a '2' and so he reasoned the room would be on the second floor. He climbed the two flights of stairs and used his laptop to wedge open the heavily sprung fire door at the top so he could drag his other bag through into the corridor. He passed several rooms with open doors until he found his room near the end. In passing, he noticed several other students in various stages of moving in, their floors strewn with cases, rucksacks, laptops and the occasional guitar.

Salah dropped his bag on the floor, placed his laptop on the desk and began to explore. As far as he could tell, there was nothing but individual rooms all the way back to the fire door (he later discovered that some were shared). He passed the same students again in reverse order with the exception of one who had closed his door. One or two smiled and seemed willing to make contact but Salah kept going as he was keen to explore further. Then, beyond the fire door on the other side of the stairwell and through another fire door, he found the kitchen.

He couldn't believe his eyes. In front of him in the middle of the kitchen was a long table surrounded by about a dozen stackable chairs. There was an upsized box of cereal, several packets of biscuits and two sliced loaves of bread lying on the table, presumably evidence of someone else moving in. Along the wall to his left was a row of nine fridge-freezers, one for each student; to his right was a run of nine lockable cupboard units and along the far wall were cookers and microwaves. Behind him fixed to the door was a large noticeboard with a number of pins; he quickly scanned the fire regulations.

Salah realised rather sadly that he would have difficulty making good use of all these marvellous facilities as he had little idea how to cook or even what to buy for food. He had always relied so much on his mother and the College canteen. He had managed to produce meals for his friends when they went camping but all that food had been provided. He decided he would check out where students could buy cheap food on campus as well as watch and learn from others. Thinking of other students made Salah realise the kitchen wouldn't just be a place to prepare food, cook and eat but be a social centre for meeting other students and making friends; he realised he would need to get his act together in the kitchen or it could be a lonely and hungry existence.

The door opened whilst he was musing and in came a student with his arms full of food and drink items. Salah didn't recognise him as one of those he had seen through an open door. He smiled and the other guy said hi.

"Hi, I'm Salah."

"Hello, I'm Hani; I'm from Jordan."

"I'm from Dubai."

"As-salaam alaykum, kayf haalak." *Peace be with you, how are you?*

"Alaykum as-salaam, al humdoolillah." *And with you peace, thanks be to God.*[1]

"I guess we both arrived at more or less the same time."

"Not exactly, I got here a few hours ago; I was hungry so I left all my stuff in my room and went to the shop to get some food."

"You are better organised than I am. Where's the food shop?"

"There's one by the duck pond, another in the student union building. I am not sure which is better. I've only been to the one by the pond; seems OK, not too expensive!"

"Can you cook?" asked Salah.

"Only simple stuff, nothing ambitious. Eat to live not live to eat, that's all. You?"

"Not really."

Whilst they were talking Hani was putting food away in his cupboard and fridge. He looked for his milk. There was no milk. He was sure he'd bought milk on his first shop. He figured either someone had stolen it or, maybe, he'd forgotten to buy some. He'd been warned that some students didn't hesitate to make use of other students' food. He looked for his shop receipt. No luck, he must have mislaid it or thrown it away.

Hani decided to go back to the shop to buy some milk and suggested he and Salah go together. Salah could find out where the shop was and even buy food if he wished. Salah was more than happy to join him and they set off for the duck pond.

The shop was instantly recognisable from its garish signage and

____

1. An English translation is provided for words in the Arabic language when they first appear. Thereafter they can be found in the Arabic English Dictionary at the end.

hoardings showing special offers and cheap deals on beer. Hani's task was easy – milk; Salah's less so as he wasn't sure what to buy. Hani suggested bread, breakfast cereal, jam, milk, some fresh fruit and salad items. On his way round the narrow aisles collecting these items, Salah noticed something familiar – hummus. Hummus didn't need cooking and was good with raw vegetables, which don't need cooking either, also good on pitta bread which, again, didn't need cooking. Salah figured hummus was a win-win and retraced his steps to find vegetables and pitta bread.

By the time Salah reached the checkout Hani had paid and was waiting patiently on the other side with his milk. They left together to return to Sharpe Hall. Salah paused to watch the ducks floating about. He thought them charming, serene and relaxing and decided to come and feed them sometime. Hani said that their serenity was an illusion as they were paddling like crazy below the waterline; they tasted very good too, he added. Salah winced; he couldn't cope with the idea of murdering a duck, even less with dismembering a dead duck for cooking and eating.

As they arrived back at Sharpe Hall they noticed almost all the lights were on and imagined more rooms must now be occupied. The noise level had risen considerably, also suggesting more students moving in. Hani and Salah put their food items in their fridges and cupboards and were about to return to their respective rooms when they saw that a notice had appeared on the back of the kitchen door. It was to inform everyone that there would be a short meeting at 9 pm in the kitchen for all students with the senior resident. Hani and Salah found this mystifying. Judging by the buzz of conversation around them so did the other students.

Hani and Salah returned to their rooms and began to unpack, putting their clothes, books and other possessions in cupboards, on shelves and in the other spaces provided. Their cases, rucksacks and bags fitted neatly under their beds. Rooms were well designed and equipped with an en suite bathroom that was small but adequate for their needs.

After unpacking, Salah sat on his bed and looked around, then he sat at his desk, switched on the table lamp and imagined himself at work. He was looking forward to starting the course and reflected on how lucky he was to be here – all thanks to Maria and Janek. Salah was aware more than ever that without Maria and Janek he wouldn't have had the opportunity to attend university in the UK. They had done so much for him, investing their time, effort and emotional energy as well as providing financial support. He and they had both needed to overcome many obstacles along the way to reach this stage and had become close.

They hadn't been looking forward to saying goodbye at the airport. Maria had insisted on driving him, helping with his luggage, making sure he had plenty of check-in time and waiting while he queued at the check-in desk. Looking back, Salah realised she had prolonged their time together. It was a big moment for Maria who felt she was launching Salah into the wider world. After holding on tight for a tearful farewell, Salah and Maria parted company and he passed through the automatic doors to the other side. This was the only time he had touched her; she was soft and warm and he liked the experience.

Maria had asked him to let them know when he arrived and would probably be thinking about him right now. He would send her an e-mail straightaway to let her know he'd arrived safely and to thank her and Janek yet again for their help, kindness and generosity. He pressed the 'Send' button and looked out of the window.

There was nothing to see except darkness. He wanted to shut it out quickly and drew the curtains. Suddenly he felt alone, not just alone but lonely. Thinking about Maria and Janek had reminded him of his mother; she was always soft and warm too. He wondered where she was and what she was doing. No amount of kindness from others could make up for being without her. Just before he left Dubai he had been told there was a new lead in the efforts to find her, but he wasn't optimistic. He thought this would only raise false hope like all the other so-called 'leads'.

Returning to his bed, he lay down and looked around the room. His eyes fell upon the one book on the bookshelf. Its title was *BLEVE*. He picked it up, opened it and found a Dubai College library insert with date stamps from several borrowings, the latest of which was his own. The date was from long ago and he was surprised the library hadn't contacted him for being overdue. Then he remembered Suhaila, one of the librarians, and his futile attempts at getting her to notice him. This added to his gloomy mood and he replaced the book. The subject matter might be relevant to his course but he had no recollection of packing it and no idea why he had brought it.

Salah decided to go back to the kitchen to find something to eat. He felt pleased with himself at having provisions and choices. The obvious starting point was to open the pitta bread and the hummus, maybe even with a raw carrot and cucumber. Other students were entering and leaving the kitchen. He guessed they were English. Perhaps he and Hani were the only two overseas students on the second floor. The others weren't very friendly but Salah didn't feel like being friendly either. Perhaps everyone was feeling ill at ease at being on unfamiliar ground and in unfamiliar company.

Having organised something to eat, Salah looked at his watch: it was 8.45. He just had enough time to eat his food and clear up before the meeting. All eight students had arrived in the kitchen by 9 pm. The Senior Resident, Max, turned out to be a student himself, a postgraduate student in the Business Studies Department working towards a Masters in organisational behaviour.

Max explained that the University had introduced senior residents to all student halls of residence, one for each floor, to provide an immediate pastoral link between students and the University. Their main role was to provide students with guidance and, if necessary, a helping hand. Senior residents were not required to be disciplinarians but were expected to try to moderate the most extreme cases of student excesses, especially those likely to lead to damage to people and property. Max invited questions. There were none and so he wished everyone the best of luck and added that he could be contacted by telephone, e-mail, Facebook or by knocking on his door, and he promised to post his contact details on the kitchen noticeboard soon.

The meeting over, everyone began to disperse. Salah said

goodnight to Hani and went back to his room where he suddenly realised how tired he was; it had been a long day. He'd travelled a huge distance, not just from Dubai to the UK, but from the life he'd left behind to his new life ahead. With that thought he went to bed.

CHAPTER 1.2

September 12 2002

Salah didn't sleep well; he'd felt strange and uneasy during the previous evening, strange because everyone and everything around him was unfamiliar, uneasy because he was lonely, homesick and feeling further away than ever from his mother. He was also troubled by the recurring guilty thought that he could and should have done more to find her when he had the opportunity. These feelings must have festered in his subconscious during the night causing him to be restless, tossing, turning and sleeping only fitfully.

Still in bed he reached down to the floor for his laptop. He sat up, switched on and clicked on Yahoo! Mail. There were new messages in his inbox. He skipped over those from his bank and one from KLM asking him to complete a customer satisfaction survey, then he opened the one from the Wankowskis:

'Hello Salah

Thanks for letting us know you arrived safely. Hope the flights and journey were OK. Your accommodation sounds great. Lucky to be in a new place with all those facilities and equipment. Everything is the same here. Do let us know if there is anything we can do for you. Best of luck. Sorry, no news about your mother yet.

Maria & Jan'

Salah was reminded again how lucky he had been to find Maria and Janek or, rather, that they had found him. Without doubt they rescued him from a bad situation, one with few if any good prospects. It was up to him now to make a big effort to take full advantage of the opportunities ahead. Getting out of bed would be a good start.

Sliding his legs out from under the bed covers, his feet found the carpet. Not being used to carpet, Salah enjoyed the feeling of comfort. He got up and turned towards his en suite bathroom. At least that's what the University called it. Initially, Salah was disappointed; there wasn't a bath and you could hardly call it a room. It was more of a cupboard, but he later realised the design was brilliant. In this tiny space there was a WC, a toilet roll holder, a wash basin, a glass shelf, a shower head, a shower curtain, a tiled floor, a small cupboard with a mirror and an integral light.

Salah looked in the mirror, checked for spots, played with his hair and showered. Drying himself, he returned to his bedroom to look for clothes; he was better off for clothes now than he had ever been, with inexpensive jeans and underwear from Dubai, shirts and trousers chosen by Maria and Janek who had also made sure he had warm indoor and outdoor clothes for the UK winter weather.

After dressing he went to the kitchen, decided on an easy breakfast, opened his fridge, grabbed his milk and poured it over some cereal. Still hungry, he refilled the bowl. Another student arrived and made tea and toast. Salah hadn't seen him before. He offered Salah tea, which was nice of him, but Salah politely declined, taking the rest of his breakfast back to his room.

He wondered about toast. He'd heard that all the British guys made toast in the mornings. It didn't look that appealing and the idea of burning bread until it was nearly black seemed a bit odd, but others seemed to like it and it might be more nutritious and filling than Choco Pops. Perhaps it was worth a try; sliced bread would be on the list for his next shopping trip.

Salah washed up, tidied away and went downstairs. On the way past the first floor landing he heard the sound of girls' voices. Hoping to catch sight of one or more, but failing, he fantasised about coming down the stairs at exactly the right moment to meet a pretty girl leaving the building. They would walk together, chat and who knows where it might go from there. But then most of them would be English girls and might not be interested in a half-Indian, half-Arab boy.

Arriving in the main area of the campus, Salah began to explore; he'd never thought of himself as having much of an interest in architecture but he couldn't help noticing all the University buildings had been built in different styles. He learned later that this was because the University had grown over time with building design construction and materials changing.

He noticed each faculty had its own building, often named after someone, perhaps a national figure, a benefactor or a distinguished academic perhaps. He imagined the buildings were also designed to reflect different needs; some faculties requiring laboratories, some lecture rooms, some workshops and others, large halls for heavy machinery and equipment. No wonder the buildings were so many different shapes and sizes.

At the centre of the main area was a quadrangle with large buildings along each side reached by a network of pathways with lawns and garden areas between, including many fine trees. Along one side was the main University administration building. This had obviously started out as a red-brick private house, now greatly extended.

Along the opposite side was the University library, by contrast, a huge modern building apparently consisting almost entirely of glass. Along another side was a multistorey tower looking rather like an office block. This was the Faculty of Commerce and Social Sciences and on the opposite side was an extensive, futuristic looking building housing the Faculty of Science and Engineering. Salah's department, the Department of Built Environment, was part of this Faculty, so he expected to be spending a lot of time in that building.

Having nothing better to do, he decided to explore the library. After walking up the steps he found himself in an empty entrance area with four lifts in front of him. To the side was a noticeboard showing what was available on each floor. On the ground floor and several underground floors were the stack rooms for storing books, manuscripts, media and artefacts. The accessible parts of the library were on the upper floors.

He pressed one of the 'Up' arrows and entered a lift. Salah was surprised when he reached level one and the lift doors opened behind him; it was one of those where you go in one side and come out the other. Having not been in one before he was amazed when the doors opened and revealed a vast expanse of floor area consisting of dozens of tables and chairs, people sitting and standing reading journals and magazines, multiple cabinets designed to display current and previous journals and several arrays of computers and workstations around the perimeter. He thought of the small library in Dubai College – what a difference!

Salah realised he couldn't see any books so they must be somewhere else. Picking up a library guide from a pile he saw spread out on a table, he discovered that books were located on the upper four floors and the leaflet provided a floor plan for each floor and zones for each faculty.

He decided to test the system, returning to one of the lifts and travelling to level four to have a look at the science and engineering books. Following the floor plan, he found the right zone and went to speak to a librarian to ask how to search for a title. The librarian asked Salah if he was registered; he wasn't, so the librarian asked him for his name and department, searched the University database and then issued him with a library card.

Armed with his new library card, Salah found a computer containing the library catalogue, sat down, entered his password and began searching. He couldn't think of a book to begin with but then came up with *BLEVE*, the book he accidentally brought with him from Dubai. He found the classification number and looked for it on the floor plan. He soon found the right shelves but finding the book itself was unexpectedly difficult; an entire shelf at least six feet long contained books with the word 'BLEVE' in the title. He never found the one he was looking for; someone must have borrowed it. Salah thought this an odd coincidence.

Salah wandered up and down the many aisles of shelves containing books on aspects of science and engineering, pausing whenever he saw a title of interest to pull out a book for closer inspection. As on level one there were tables and chairs around the perimeter for staff and students to study and work. He sat down and browsed the library guide, enjoying the quiet and finding the environment conducive to contemplation and study.

There were few people about other than library staff, but it would appear that some students had arrived at the University early like him. As Salah got up to leave he spotted someone dressed in an abaya and a hijab with her back to him, sitting at one of the tables reading. Unable to resist taking a closer look, he walked to the end of the aisle, turned around and walked back again to be able to see the person from the front.

He was both surprised and excited to discover it was Samara. They greeted each other enthusiastically. Samara was one of those Arab women who didn't like to shake hands with men. She didn't make a fuss about it, she just quietly indicated she preferred not to. Salah understood from previous experience in Dubai.

"Hi Samara."

"Hi Salah."

"Asalaam alaykum."

"Alaykum asalaam."

"Kayf haalek?" *How are you?*

"Tamaam, shukran." *I'm fine, thank you.*

"Al humdoolillah."

"This is a nice surprise."

"For me, too; when did you arrive?"

"I arrived yesterday. Where are you living?"

"Travis Hall."

"Is it OK?"

"I suppose so, it's one of the older halls; I hear the newer ones are better equipped. Travis is for female students and all those I've met so far are Muslims, which suits me."

"I'm in Sharpe, one of the newest. It's mixed, boys on the ground and second floors, and there are girls on the first floor. I'm on the second; I've already met a nice guy from Jordan, which is great."

"I expect you know it's Freshers' Week."

"Yeah, I wasn't going to bother much with Freshers' Week as I just wanted to arrive a couple of days before term to have some time to settle in."

"Really? But there are so many interesting things happening. I've just been reading this pamphlet by the Student Islamic Society. It looks interesting and I'm thinking of joining. They're holding a meeting tomorrow; why don't you come? It will help you be a good Muslim."

Salah was taken aback. He wasn't silly enough to think Samara was asking him on a date, but she *was* being very friendly. It would be fun to go to something with her although he was unsure about becoming involved in serious religion. He had avoided it until now. If it was anyone else he would probably have said 'No', but this was Samara.

"What a great idea! When and where?"

She explained.

"OK, see you there tomorrow. Bye."

Salah left Samara and walked away. He walked with purpose as if he had somewhere to go, something to do or someone to meet. In fact, he had none of these but wanted to portray a confident image. He didn't want Samara to notice he was really adrift, at sea without a paddle.

Reflecting as he walked about what had just happened, Salah was cheered by meeting Samara and happy to be doing something together. He couldn't help remembering all his previous efforts at getting to know her in the Dubai College, which had failed spectacularly. His mind flashed back to the day he first met her in the students' dining room…

"Hello Samara."

"Hello."

"Do you mind if I join you?"

"Not really," she replied half-heartedly.

"How are you?"

"OK, I suppose."

Salah failed to read the signals.

"Wouldn't it be nice if we became friends?"

"I don't see why – just because we were at the same College doing the same classes we should be friends – we don't even know each other."

"But we could get to know each other," suggested Salah. This was his best chance to get to know Samara. Chances like this didn't happen often and he wasn't going to give up now.

"I don't think so, Salah, my parents wouldn't like it; they warned me about boys."

"Tell me about your parents." Salah knew he was struggling at this point.

"Not now, Salah. I have to go, bye."

And that was the end of that. Salah was left alone, thinking about what could have been. It was all over so quickly. He wouldn't accept this setback as final. He would think of Samara's diffidence as shyness and feeling reserved. It didn't mean she disliked him. Her reticence was exactly what anyone would expect of a nice girl. Her parents were right to warn her about boys, as Salah knew only too well from some of the male conversations about girls he'd overheard or been involved in.

On another occasion, also in the dining room, Samara came over to Salah's table and asked if he was on his own. Salah asked her to join him. She sat down and after the usual pleasantries he said he would get something to eat and rejoin her. Looking back at Samara while he waited to be served, she was wearing a hijab as usual with some sort of top and trousers. Everything fitted her body closely and he was able to see what a nice shape she was. It was not the first time he had thought so.

Back at the table they engaged in small talk for while. Salah plucked up courage and told her what an attractive woman she was and then asked her if she would remove her hijab so he could see her with her hair.

"That's impossible, Salah." She got up immediately and walked away. He felt stupid and regretted asking.

Today she was different and he wondered what had changed. Perhaps going to the meeting with her would enable him to find out.

He wandered around the campus again to explore further; the campus was vast. He called in to the student union building, had a look around and studied the Freshers' Week notices on the information boards. One or two were mildly interesting but not enough to make him want to join any of the clubs, societies or activities on offer.

On his way back to Sharpe, he saw Khamis coming towards him.

"Hi Khamis. Asalaam alaykum. I was hoping I might see you around."

"Alaykum asalaam."

"Kayf haalek."

"Al humdoolillah."

Actually, peace was not with Khamis. In fact, he was his usual complaining self. Admittedly, he had reason to be upset. He'd just purchased a car, a sports utility vehicle, but not a Tiguan like the one he owned back home; that would have been too extravagant. Luckily, he'd found a second-hand Pajero in excellent condition and more affordable. Tragically, Khamis had neglected to familiarise himself with the University's parking arrangements and on his first trip to the campus he'd parked his Pajero in a space outside the main administration building. Leaving his vehicle, he went to tell his new friend Majid about it. Bursting with excitement, he hoped Majid would be similarly excited and keen to go for a drive together.

When they both came back to the space he'd parked the car, the Pajero had gone. Neither of them could understand why it had disappeared, even less why another car was now parked in the same space. Majid noticed that the names of some of the University's administrative staff had been painted along the lower part of the wall of the main admin building and suggested these were probably the names of those for whom the parking places had been reserved. Mysteriously, the name in front of the space where Khamis' Pajero had been parked was 'Secretary'.

The car now parked in this space was one of the latest top-of-the-range Mercedes. Khamis reasoned this must be the most highly paid secretary in history. He thought it unlikely his Pajero would have been removed to make way for a car belonging to a secretary.

Khamis and Majid decided to deal with their problem head-on and went into the building. The doors inside were all marked with labels, which didn't look helpful. However, there was a door marked 'General Enquiries' and one marked 'Information'. These looked more useful. Khamis wondered which was likely to be the best choice. 'Information' seemed most appropriate, so in they went. A friendly woman asked if she could help. Khamis explained he had lost his car. The woman looked puzzled.

"I think you've come to the wrong office; we provide information about the University."

Majid said, "OK, so we need information about the University; how do we find our car?"

"I have no idea; sorry, we don't provide that kind of information. You could try the enquiries office."

Khamis and Majid followed the advice and went to the enquiries office where a second friendly woman met them.

"Hello, the lady in the information office said you could help us. We parked our car outside this building and it's disappeared. Could you please help us find it?"

"I am very sorry, I think you are in the wrong office. You could try the estates office across the entrance hall. They deal with car parking on the campus."

Khamis and Majid left and went to look for the estates office. They soon found the door marked 'Estates', one of those doors that initially looks unhelpful. They went in and waited until someone got up from their desk and came over to them.

"How can we help?" asked a not very friendly man in a dark blue uniform, similar to that of a police officer looking very official and with an authoritative bearing.

"I've lost my car; it was parked outside the front of this building and now it's not there."

"Name?"

"Khamis Al Farsi."

"Just give me a moment… We don't have a car registered under that name."

"I only just bought it today."

"Did you register your car before bringing it onto the campus? All vehicles entering the campus are required to be registered and to show a pass, without exception. Where did you leave your car? What make and model is it?"

"No, sorry, I didn't. It's a silver Pajero and it was left–"

"Oh, I know that car; it's been towed to the pound. It was parked in the University Secretary's space and he was very annoyed. You'll have to pay a fee to have the car released."

"Did you say 'he'? Who is the University Secretary?"

"He is the most senior member of the University after the Vice-Chancellor."

Khamis was visibly shocked, realising he must have got the wrong idea about the role of a secretary in a university. Also, more importantly, he was worried about the fee to get the car back. Having paid cash for the Pajero he was now financially challenged and it would be a while before he received funds from home.

Salah listened to this story with interest, but not much empathy. Khamis was always complaining and, to be truthful, Salah was a little envious that Khamis had even been able to buy a car. But on reflection he *had* been helpful with lifts, even generous at times, so Salah felt he should be sympathetic and supportive.

"I am sorry you have had all this hassle. When will you get it back, do you think?"

"I don't know. I can't afford the £100 fee the estates office demanded. No fee, no car. I am waiting for money from home or from anywhere, I suppose."

"I wish I could lend you some cash but I've only just enough to manage. Maybe Majid could help?"

"Maybe; we'll see."

"I *can* afford to buy you a coffee, though. Shall we go for a coffee and catch-up?"

"OK, but I won't stay long."

Salah retraced his steps back to the student union building, this time with Khamis, and found the cafeteria. He bought two coffees, some biscuits and carried these over to Khamis.

"Thanks, Salah. It really is good to see you and I'm sorry if I've been a bit preoccupied. So, when did you arrive then?"

"Yesterday. I must say, it all feels very strange, I haven't really found my feet yet."

"I know what you mean, although things were going fine until this parking problem."

"Have you been here long?"

"This is my fourth day, actually. I wanted time to check out my digs before term start. Where are you living?"

"Oh, you're in digs."

"Yeah, the accommodation office was very good. They would have put me in a hall but I wanted to be able to get away from the University at the end of the day and at weekends, so they found a house in the town for me; I'm sharing with an Iranian, an Iraqi and a Syrian – should be interesting when you think what these guys have been going through in those countries."

"Funny you should say that. I met Samara earlier. She persuaded me to join the Student Islamic Society. Are you interested?"

"Maybe; I've got to deal with this car problem at the moment. Ask me again later, I might be interested, although I wasn't planning to get too involved in religion or politics."

"So you've seen Samara, anyone else from Dubai?"

"Not so far."

"Where are you living?"

"Sharpe Hall. It's great, everything's new. Come and visit as soon as you can."

"Will do, Salah."

Khamis ate his biscuits and finished his coffee. "Thanks for coffee and the invite, great to see you. I must go now and try to get hold of some money to pay this so-called fee – more like a fine if you ask me. See you around."

Salah watched Khamis leave and then decided to look for the shop he visited with Hani to buy bread. He found a sliced loaf so he could make toast and was attracted to some recently cooked chickens, still warm in plastic bags. He decided to try one and added it to his basket with another pot of hummus and a bag of salad.

Returning to Sharpe he called into the kitchen to put his bread away when he noticed a poster on the back of the kitchen door advertising a disco at the end of Freshers' Week. At first he thought he might go although it wasn't really his scene. It was likely to be too crowded and too noisy, hardly a good place to meet people – by people he meant girls. If you couldn't hear yourself there was little chance of hearing anyone else. Probably best to give it a miss.

He went to his room to have a think about what to do next. He decided it would be a good idea to visit his department. Retracing his steps to the central area of the campus, to the quadrangle he discovered yesterday, he found the Faculty of Engineering again and was pleased to be able to see inside this unusual looking building.

Following the signs and arrows pointing to the Department of Built Environment, he went through the glass doors to reception. Reception was an open-plan space with clusters of workstations, computers, scanners, shredders, printers, filing cabinets, telephone systems and, of course, people. Few were working at their desks. Most were moving around the office, chatting, carrying documents, opening and shutting drawers, conferring with someone else or speaking on the telephone. Such was the level of activity that Salah's arrival went unnoticed for several minutes. Eventually someone came over.

"I expect you're a new student; can I help you?"

"Hello. I've just arrived at the University. Do I need to register with my department?"

"No, we already have all your details but it's good to know you've arrived from... where was it?"

"Dubai."

"Oh, Dubai. Lucky you living in the world's favourite holiday destination."

"Yeah, but it wasn't quite like that for me."

She looked crestfallen as if she'd said the wrong thing. In a way she had, by making Salah realise he'd never had a holiday in his life.

"Someone suggested I should make contact to collect my timetable. Am I in the right place?"

"Hayley will help you; she's our admin assistant." She then shouted "Hayley!" at a deafening volume.

Along came Hayley, younger and prettier. Salah liked her immediately.

"Can I have your name, please?"

"Salah Al Munairi."

Hayley returned to her workstation, sat at the computer, clicked through several screens and printed a document, which she collected from the printer and brought over to him.

"Facilities Management?"

"That's me. Thank you very much, Hayley."

She smiled and seemed to hesitate. Salah couldn't help hesitating too. Nobody else was looking in their direction, but this didn't feel like the time or place for boy-meets-girl stuff, even if Salah could overcome his nerves, which he probably couldn't, but he knew he would remember Hayley.

"Bye."

"Bye, Hayley."

Salah left the department and the Faculty building in a state of confusion. Did something just happen? He wasn't sure. It would be disastrous to think it did and get it wrong if it didn't, but what if it did? He could miss out on something really great.

This confusion was made worse when accompanied by a sense of déjà vu. He couldn't help being reminded of all those futile visits to the Dubai College library trying to make contact with Suhaila. What a waste of time and so frustrating. He didn't want to go through that again.

He decided to share his problem with Khamis. Khamis had had girlfriends although, admittedly, they came and went. In fact, turnover seemed quite high. Still, Khamis was experienced, would understand and give helpful advice. Salah decided to change the subject, preferably to something less confusing and beyond his control, than 'girls'.

Feeling hungry it made sense to go back to the students' union for something to eat. Someone had told him he could expect to be able to obtain an inexpensive and nutritious lunch in the cafeteria. The advice was no doubt well intended, but Salah thought all the food looked bland. No doubt the University's caterers were making an effort to provide a varied international menu, with stir-fries, curries and the occasional Mexican item, but he could tell from their appearance and the cooking smells that the flavours would be disappointing, probably because of a lack of authentic ingredients.

After collecting a warm plate and some cutlery, Salah chose cottage pie with carrots and peas. He poured a glass of water, paid, and carried his tray to a table where he ate his food without enthusiasm. He couldn't identify the meat in the pie but finished everything on his plate. The food wasn't expensive and was probably nutritious, if boring. Salah doubted whether any of the cooks had ever seen a chilli, but agreed the meals were good value and portions were OK.

After lunch he decided he may as well visit the University Medical Centre and register. This at least should be straightforward. Not having his campus map with him he called in to the library where he had seen a large map of the campus. He located the Medical Centre. It was not close by but the walk would do him good.

Registration was easy but not in a good way. It should have taken a while but it took hardly any time at all because, in addition to personal details, the form required a lot of information Salah was unable to provide. He couldn't give any details of his current doctor or medical practice, he had no idea of his immunisation history, he wasn't even sure if he'd ever *been* immunised and had no recollection of any illnesses or of any medication received. All he could come up with was next of kin whom he assumed would be Maria and Janek, the wonderful Wankowskis.

He handed his form in to the receptionist who didn't pay much attention. She asked him to print his name in capitals after his signature and told him he would receive an e-mail to confirm his registration. The e-mail would also contain an attachment setting out the Medical Centre's opening hours and other necessary information, which he could print off if he wanted a hard copy.

Salah returned to Sharpe. Mulling over the day's events he felt better today than yesterday, not as lonely or out of his depth. He had enjoyed meeting Samara and Khamis and found it reassuring to have friendly fellow travellers within easy reach – friends with whom he could share his hopes, fears, feelings and troubles. He was pleased also to have visited his department to collect a timetable and to register with the student Medical Centre; both necessary administrative chores now out of the way. Looking back he began to realise that one of the day's experiences stood out more vividly in his mind than the others. It could be summarised in one word: Hayley!

CHAPTER 1.3

September 13 2002

Salah got up late and made a drink. The previous evening's feelgood factor seemed to have evaporated, so he returned to bed. The general silence on his floor suggested everyone else was doing the same although the occasional noise from downstairs suggested some of the girls were up and about.

When he awoke for the second time he was in a very different frame of mind. He was hungry and it was nearly lunchtime so he prepared simple food. He saw the cooked chicken in his fridge. He began to pull it apart and placed a leg quarter on a plate with some odds and ends from the bag of salad. Lunch looked quite appealing.

After clearing away he went back to his room remembering he had agreed to meet Samara at the Islamic Society meeting during the afternoon. Salah looked at his phone to check the time. Hoping there was still enough time to find the meeting place, he set off, following his campus map.

He arrived before Samara and waited briefly until they could go into the building together. They found the right room and sat down. A few seats were already taken and more students were arriving; it looked as if the meeting would be popular.

Salah liked everything he heard at the meeting. The first speaker welcomed new students saying the Student Islamic Society was open to all students, not only Muslim students. The main aim of the society was to create a better understanding of Islam by changing incorrect perceptions and stereotypes, also to promote a well-informed, tolerant and peaceful multi-faith community on campus. It also supports Muslim students with their religious observance and helps them with any problems they encounter whilst they are at the University.

Another speaker explained the Society aims to engender a feeling of brotherhood for everyone on campus based on the principal that Islam is not just about going to the mosque and saying prayers but a guide for all aspects of life. Imams are available for advice and guidance about homesickness, personal problems, financial problems, spiritual problems and eating and drinking problems. The Society regularly makes information available about the local mosques, including prayer times, also those at the University's prayer room.

The third speaker concluded by extolling the virtues of Freshers' Week and suggested all new students set themselves personal objectives for the week. He wrote down the following suggested objectives on a flip chart:

- Make a friend!
- Register with a GP at the University Medical Centre.
- Walk around the town and campus.
- Visit home department and check first week timetable.
- Join a society, club or organised activity.
- Get enough sleep.

Salah told Samara he enjoyed the meeting and thanked her for suggesting it.

"I enjoyed it too. Thanks for coming, Salah. I like the aims of the Society and the personal objectives seem so sensible. I shall definitely join."

"So shall I." Salah was pleased to tell Samara he'd already achieved two of the objectives, collected his first week's timetable and registered with the student Medical Centre.

"Well done, you're way ahead of me, Salah. Do you feel like a tea or something?"

"Why not? The cafeteria is just round the corner."

Samara asked for tea, Salah ordered a coffee. Picking up a packet of chocolate biscuits, he went to pay but Samara insisted on paying for herself. They sat down and began chatting. Salah couldn't believe his luck. This was her idea. Perhaps she would like to be friends after all. He felt tense; on the one hand he wanted to let her know how he felt about her but, on the other hand, he was worried that if he told her it would frighten her away.

"I'm not sure what I am supposed to do about making a friend," he said meaningfully, hoping this might facilitate the kind of discussion he wanted to have with Samara about their relationship. "Perhaps this is meant for students arriving on their own, students who don't know anyone?"

"You're right, Salah. We're lucky to be friends already. I thought it meant 'make a new friend'."

"That makes sense, Samara, I've already met a guy from Jordan and he could become a friend."

"Exactly."

"The last time we sat together was in Dubai and you were going to tell me about your family, but you had to rush off somewhere."

"I remember, Salah, but I must warn you we are not very interesting."

"I am sure that's not true."

"We are from Iraq. My father was a government employee, quite senior; all of a sudden he found his face didn't fit. He became worried because he knew of cases where others who fell out of favour were interned or suddenly disappeared; some may have managed to escape but he began to fear the worst."

"How terrible, Samara. I had no idea."

"Luckily, my father's work involved liaising with government people in other neighbouring countries. One of these kindly arranged visas for us so we were able to leave Iraq. This person also recommended us for refugee status, which was granted a year after we left Iraq."

"So, is it just you and your father?"

"No, my mother is also with us. I don't have brothers and sisters. My father has another wife who is still in Iraq. She refused to leave. As far as we know she is OK and still lives in the family home."

"Would you ever go back?"

"Never, it even makes me nervous when I see Iraqi names among the students."

"Sure, I can understand that, Samara."

"Now tell me about your family, Salah. I heard something in Dubai about your mother being missing. Is that true?"

"I am sorry to say it is true and she's still missing. There's quite a lot of effort going on to try to find her; leads come up from time to time but no luck so far."

"Do you mind me asking what happened?"

"Not at all, it's a long and complicated story but I'll try to keep it simple. I came home from the College one day to find that my father had died. At the time I didn't know he was my father as my mother had found it too difficult to tell me until after he died. He was also my mother's employer and a senior member of a very successful Emirati family. My mother and I were living in his villa. She was my father's housekeeper.

Two days later I came home from the College to find my mother had been sacked and evicted from the villa. There was a letter waiting for me from one of my father's brothers saying there was no longer a need for staff in the villa and asking me to leave as soon as possible."

"Oh, Salah, how terrible and upsetting this must have been for you. Were there any other family members to help when you became homeless and parentless?"

"No, 'fraid not, but I've had amazing help from wonderful people so in some ways I have been very lucky. As I said, it's a long story and I don't want to bore you. Perhaps I could tell you more another time."

"Whenever you like, you won't bore me, Salah, I would love to learn how you recovered from all this bad luck, but it can wait. Meanwhile, if you feel in need of a friendly chat any time, I'm always available."

"Thank you, Samara, that's very nice of you. I shall remember."

They got up and left together, both saying again how much they'd enjoyed the meeting and their chat.

"Can I walk with you then I'll know where you are?"

"That's very kind of you, Salah, but it's not necessary."

"Sure, but I would like to. Another time you can come and see where I am."

"OK, why not?"

Salah walked with Samara as far as Travis Hall and then back to Sharpe. There was a noticeable spring in his step; he felt more positive and motivated. Life seemed to have taken on a new purpose. He always felt good when being with Samara and now they were going to be friends. The Islamic Society meeting had exceeded his expectations and he was beginning to feel part of the so-called 'campus brotherhood'. This felt good too, and having already achieved some of the suggested objectives for Freshers' Week, he resolved to achieve them all.

CHAPTER 1.4

September 14 2002

Salah was up and about and heading towards the kitchen to make toast when he heard the ping on his mobile. It was a text from Khamis. He was pleasantly surprised, as he didn't receive many calls or texts; the Wankowskis seemed to prefer e-mail. He must have given Khamis his number in Dubai:

'Hi how's it going car back me Majid going town wanna come?'

Salah said *OK* but he would need a few minutes for breakfast and asked where to meet them.

Khamis replied...

'Go for it meet you in the Hall car park half an hour'

By this time Salah was already in the kitchen waiting for a toaster to become available. This was the downside of toast making. Everyone else wanted to make toast. There were only two toasters and eight slots for bread. When Salah's turn came he inserted two slices. Not having much time he applied spreadable butter and ate his first pieces of toast with a glass of milk. He quite liked it and decided to do it again, maybe with something else to spread. Another student was spreading peanut butter; he might let Salah try some another time.

Salah was grateful to Khamis for solving the first problem of the day. What to do? He was pleased to be meeting Majid and to be able to scope the town so he would know his way around in future whenever he needed to go there for something. Checking his wallet to make sure he had enough cash he went downstairs, quickly passing by the tantalising sounds of girls' voices on the floor below. Today was not the time for a chance meeting or a happy coincidence. Today, Salah was on a mission.

Khamis and Majid were waiting in the Pajero. Khamis pointed to the back seat. Salah got in and Khamis started the engine. It sounded noisy to Salah, but what did he know? He certainly wasn't going to make any critical comments. It was comfortable enough in the back and he would no doubt enjoy the ride. It took hardly any time to reach the town; Salah paid for a couple of hours' parking and they wandered into the main street.

They weren't interested in clothes shops, although they had a look around a couple of department stores like John Lewis and Debenhams. Majid was impressed. Khamis and Salah were not. They compared them unfavourably to the shops in the malls in Dubai. They found themselves outside Waterstones so they went in and checked out the management books. However much they would rely on the University library it was inevitable they would have to buy some books of their own when they received their module book lists.

For coffee shops they were spoilt for choice. There was Starbucks, Costa, Coffee Plus, Caffè Nero, Coffee One and many other possibilities in smaller outlets. For Salah, coffee was just coffee. Not so for Majid who fancied himself as a connoisseur and was adamant the only coffee worth drinking was Arabic coffee and that Sudanese was the best.

"If you can't drink Sudanese coffee you may as well forget it 'cos all the other coffees are rubbish."

"Where do you think we are going to find Sudanese coffee here, Majid?"

"We should try, it's worth it."

They were now outside Tesco. Salah said he wanted to improve his cooking skills and he would like a few minutes to find some ingredients.

"No problem, Salah. We'll all have a look around."

Salah found the curry section and picked up a packet of easy-cook rice. Careful not to be too ambitious, he knew he wouldn't be able to cope with cooking the way his mother did it, not at first anyway. So anything with the word 'easy' sounded about right. Further along the aisle he saw jars of jalfrezi sauce. They didn't say 'easy-cook', but according to the label all you needed to do was heat it up in a pan.

Now he needed to find some meat for the jalfrezi. Having little or no experience of cooking meat he looked for something already cooked but the only cooked meat he could find was thinly sliced in the deli. This didn't seem right for a jalfrezi. On the point of giving up he caught sight of a row of roasted chickens turning round in a hot cabinet. He asked for one of these and placed it in his basket.

He was nearly all set. The only things he needed now were yogurt, chutney and poppadoms. He went to the dairy section for the yogurt and then back to the curry aisle for the other two before adding all three to his basket. The others were waiting patiently at the checkouts while his shopping was scanned. He then packed his bag and paid the bill.

When he rejoined them, Majid asked what he had bought. They were impressed. Khamis asked if he could come to dinner. Salah wasn't sure whether he was joking but, actually, this suited Salah very well as there was something he wished to discuss with Khamis in private.

"Why not, Khamis? Consider yourself invited."

Majid's mobile rang and he walked away, quite a distance, presumably for privacy.

After the call, Khamis looked uncomfortable.

"Everything OK, Khamis?"

"Yep."

"You don't look OK."

"I'm fine, Salah, it's just that Majid is always having texts and calls. I know we all need privacy sometimes but he never likes anyone to be able to hear what he is saying. I did overhear him once in the house although he was speaking very quietly, *very* quietly. I would even go so far as to say furtively. It makes me wonder if something's going on."

"It's probably nothing."

"You may be right, Salah."

"I thought you said Majid lived on campus?"

"He did, but he didn't like it, said it was too noisy, so he moved into our spare room."

Majid returned, obviously preoccupied with something on his mind.

"Are we done? I really need to get back."

"We've still got plenty of time on the car park ticket."

"Sorry, Salah, but something has come up. I need to get back to the house. I thought we only came to have a quick look at the High Street."

"Fine, come on then, let's go."

Salah was happy with his shopping and didn't complain. They were soon back to where Majid and Khamis lived and Majid got out. Khamis continued on to Sharpe Hall and into the car park.

"You're here now, Khamis. Come in and have a look round. I can make you a drink."

"OK, Salah. Will do."

Salah and Khamis climbed the stairs. Salah paused on the first-floor landing and asked Khamis if he could hear anything. The girls' floor was more subdued or maybe some were out on the campus, but there was still the joyful sound of female voices.

"Looks as if you've landed on your feet, Salah."

"I'm hoping so, Khamis, we shall see."

They reached the top and Salah went into the kitchen to put his shopping away. At the same time he was able to show Khamis his fridge and the kitchen facilities in general. Khamis was suitably impressed. Salah filled a kettle and they went to Salah's room with mugs of coffee.

Khamis liked what he saw and wondered whether he'd done the right thing by going into private accommodation. Everything about Salah's room was new, clean, tidy, bright, smart and well organised. His house was almost the exact opposite and his kitchen arrangements were nothing like as good as Salah's.

"Khamis. There is something important I want to ask you about."

"OK, but I can't stay for long."

"Khamis, I need a girlfriend. Where can we find girls?"

"Are you sure you need a girlfriend, Salah, or do you need a friend with benefits?"

"What's a 'friend with benefits'?"

"A fuck buddy."

"I don't get it. What's a 'fuck buddy'?"

"You know, a friend with benefits."

"I still don't get it. So, tell me, what's a 'friend with benefits'?"

Khamis thought Salah a bit dim and lacking imagination, maybe not unintelligent but definitely ignorant about the ways of the world. He was unsure whether any good could come from continuing the conversation or whether to change the subject, but decided to do his best.

"*Friends with Benefits* is the name of a film where a man and a woman meet at work and realise they have much in common. They gradually become friends. They both have a history of failed relationships so they agree their relationship will only be physical and they will not allow themselves to become emotionally involved. They hope this will prevent disappointment, emotional turmoil and the misery of another break-up. This works for a while but, surprise, they begin to feel and act as if they are emotionally involved.

"So, Khamis, you seem to be suggesting something that is not likely to work."

"It depends what you want, Salah. Are you looking for sex or a wife? For the first, you need to find a girl who is also looking for sex; better, a girl who doesn't wish to become anyone's life partner or who isn't ready to do so. For the second, you need to find girls to date. The first doesn't require much emotional involvement, although that may happen. The second does."

"OK, Khamis, I get it. I have heard of this kind of thing but it didn't occur to me that people actually did this. I am not sure I could even get started."

"Of course you can. Some of us find it more difficult than others but basically it's all trial and error. You know, if at first you don't succeed, etc… The mating game is not an exact science. First, find a girl you like. Second, do some research. If you can find out about her then so much the better. It could help you decide whether she is likely to become a buddy or a keeper. You're looking for someone who would be fun to hook up with, cute, great to spend time with and up for sex. Is there anyone you can think of who might be a possibility?"

"I do like Samara. She's great and very cute."

"You *are* joking! Think about it, Salah. She's a Muslim girl. Is she a realistic prospect for becoming a buddy? Also, isn't she a member of your tutor group? Supposing it all goes wrong. Think of the embarrassment of having to meet this girl every time you have a tutorial. Why not spend more time in and around the student union building? Try to find someone who knows how to hook up, someone who has had a few flings, at least."

"I can't see myself asking any girl if she wants to be my fuck buddy."

"You need to get to know her a little, perhaps do some flirting, pay her some compliments and find out if she is available. This will let her know that you're interested. You will soon see whether she wants to hook up. You must make sure she understands you don't want to date, so don't arrange to meet every day. This could mean agreeing you are both free to hook up with other people. Try to find ways of making it clear that if either of you gets too attached the deal is off, unless of course, you fall in love with each other. The whole point is to just have fun, especially fun with sex in all its possible forms."

"OK, Khamis. I asked you for advice and I am grateful for it. I'm not sure I can do what you suggest but I shall give it a go."

"That's the spirit, Salah. Try not to get too uptight, there's a lot of luck involved."

"Whilst we are on the subject of hanging around the students' union, are you going to the disco tonight?"

"I hadn't thought of going, are you?"

"I haven't decided. It will probably be dark, noisy, crowded, hot and smell of sweat."

"If that's what you think, Salah, definitely don't go. I think I'll give it a miss."

Khamis got up to leave. Salah thanked him for the ride and for his advice. Khamis thanked Salah for the tea and biscuits.

"Don't forget to call me when you've made that jalfrezi."

"Of course not; we'll eat it together."

Salah accompanied Khamis to the top of the stairs and patted him on the back. Down he went and Salah returned to his room. He realised he hadn't had much to eat so far and it was lunchtime. He decided to make some more toast and to have it with hummus. This would be quick, easy and tasty – perfect, in fact.

Back in his room, Salah opened his laptop and Googled *Friends with Benefits*. He found a detailed description of the film and that it was available on YouTube for a small fee, also several Internet links on the subject with titles like 'Getting started with FWB', 'Rules of being FWB', 'How to make FWB last' and 'Trusted hook-up apps'. He would read some of these another time. First, he would watch the film.

Salah organised his pillow and got comfortable on his bed with his laptop resting on his knees. He found the film and pressed 'Play'. He watched it until he became more tired and then fell asleep.

Salah woke up with a start, taking time to realise where he was and what he was doing. The laptop was still resting on his knees; he was thankful it hadn't fallen to the floor. Having remembered some of the film but had missed too much to understand the story, he decided to watch it again without falling asleep.

The afternoon had passed and he felt in need of a drink. Back in his room with a mug of tea, he restarted his laptop, checked Yahoo! Mail for e-mails and then clicked 'Compose'. He would send a nice message to the Wankowskis:

'Hi

Thank you both for your message. I was feeling a bit out of my depth; was very pleased to hear from you. You can imagine how different it is here. I have met Samara and Khamis, which reminds me of Dubai. I am sure I shall make new friends and get used to life in the UK. Actually I have done quite a few useful things during Freshers' Week and feel very positive now.

Best wishes,

Salah'

He then went to the kitchen for more tea and something else to eat. Back in his room he thought about Jas. He hadn't thought of her much so far but he did now. All this talk of friends with benefits reminded him how much he missed her. She was his first girlfriend and their gentle romance had nothing in common with the kind of arrangements suggested by Khamis. He felt uneasy now about his chat with Khamis and more than a little guilty. She had said he would forget her when he was in England and would soon find someone else. He hadn't wanted to believe her at the time but, sadly, it was beginning to look as if she might have been right. Time would tell.

CHAPTER 1.5

September 15 2002

Salah was washing up and clearing away when Hani came into the kitchen carrying bags of shopping and sat down looking miserable, as if he didn't know what to do. Salah remembered Hani because he'd been so helpful when they first arrived. They exchanged greetings. Salah asked whether everything was OK. Hani said everything at the University was fine, but otherwise nothing was OK and probably never would be again. Salah realised something must be terribly wrong.

Salah knew what it felt like to be down and was wary of prying into Hani's troubles, having learned firsthand that having to explain things to well-meaning friends and others sometimes made problems feel even more overwhelming. Whilst he felt a strong need to be sympathetic and supportive, he decided to bide his time. Salah helped Hani unpack his bags and put his food away.

"Thanks, Salah."

"Would you like a drink?"

"Coffee would be great. Salah, have you got a minute?"

"Of course, Hani, is there something wrong?"

"I've had bad news."

Although there was nobody else around, Salah suggested they both go to his room where they could be more private. Hani agreed and sat down in the easy chair. Salah sat on his desk chair.

"Go on."

"We've just lost our home in Nablus."

"Hani, I am so sorry, but how?"

"The occupation, of course."

Salah had a vision of homeless people entering Hani's home,

taking it over and turning it into a refuge for themselves and other homeless people. He'd heard of such things happening, but didn't speak at first. Neither did Hani; there was silence for several minutes. Hani became tearful. It was awful.

"You must have heard about the war between Israel and Jordan, Egypt and Syria."

"Yes." Salah said 'yes', meaning he'd heard about it but didn't really know much about it.

"Well, Israel defeated the Arabs and then occupied the West Bank. Nablus is a town to the north of the West Bank, about 30 miles from Jerusalem. The Israelis then built a number of Jewish settlements in the area, sometimes taking over Palestinian homes or even blowing them up if they felt like taking revenge for some reason."

"This is so terrible, Hani."

"Yes, Nablus is my hometown. We have, or rather – had – a nice house. My father is the headmaster of the local school. My mother and two younger brothers are also there.

I have just heard from one of my uncles who lives nearby that two days ago, very early in the morning, a number of Israeli occupation forces Jeeps and a helicopter entered Nablus, surrounded houses and arrested people. Several of those were seriously hurt and taken to hospital. People were woken up very early. My brothers were on their way to school when the first explosions were heard.

The Israelis also stormed a number of villages around Nablus. There was resistance of course and many clashes, but luckily there was no armed confrontation between the IOF and resistance fighters. The Israelis seemed content with their arrests, especially of a high-profile Palestinian opponent of the occupation. Nevertheless, they still stormed neighbouring villages searching homes, vehicles and removing property."

"Hani, you must be so upset and worried."

"Salah, you haven't heard the worst. My uncle says there's now an Israeli military guard on our home and my family has gone. He doesn't know where, he's still searching."

Salah didn't know what to say. His immediate reaction was a strong feeling of déjà vu. Instinctively, he felt deepest sympathy for anyone arriving at their family home only to find their family gone. Needless to say, this reminded him of coming home to an empty villa with his own mother gone.

Although Hani would no doubt have been pleased by the extent to which Salah was able to empathise with him, Salah decided this was not the right time to tell him about his own troubles. Momentarily he was lost for words, his mouth tried to move but words wouldn't come. He felt powerless to do or say anything at all and he certainly couldn't offer anything that could make a difference. Fortunately, Hani filled the awkward space.

"I am not sure how much you know about my country."

"Not much, I am afraid; hardly anything at all. I know there is a river there where Jesus was baptised."

"That's a start. How do you know about that? I thought you would be a Muslim?"

"Yes and no. I have been a bit lazy about religion. I am gradually becoming more serious about it. I grew up surrounded by Muslims. I have attended a Muslim funeral. Some of my best friends are Muslims. I am thinking of joining the Student Islamic Society."

"So you are definitely not a Christian."

"No way. We could go to the local mosque together."

"OK, why not?"

Maybe Hani was just being polite; he didn't sound that keen on the idea. Salah was surprised their conversation had taken this turn. He wasn't sure why he'd suggested going to the mosque, having hardly ever been inside one himself. Perhaps he thought going to the mosque with Hani was something he could do to show his support when Hani was having such a bad time. Perhaps religion would be a comfort to him, maybe to both of them.

"Where were we?"

"You asked me what I know about your country."

"Oh yes. Well, it's complicated, Salah. I am not sure where to start. Palestine has a long history going way back to prehistoric times. Many different races and ethnic groups have lived there. Before the First World War, for a hundred years or so, it was part of the Turkish empire.

"The Turks were defeated and, after the war, Palestine, which included what is now Jordan, came under British rule. Then after a while it was split: west of the River Jordan was designated for Jews, east of the river for Arabs. The idea originally was for Palestine to become a home for Jews without affecting the rights of non-Jews already living there. The reality is that, from then on until today, there have been more or less continuous uprisings, rebellions, insurrections, civil wars, guerrilla wars and military wars."

"Thank you for explaining some of the background, Hani. I should have said earlier that I am aware violence has been taking place."

"Can you cope with a bit more history?"

"Of course."

"The Jews were committed to creating a Jewish state and expelled thousands of Palestinians and destroyed their villages. Arabs fought back to try to preserve the Palestinian nation, but thousands and thousands of Palestinians chose to leave their lands and homes. Most found refuge in Jordan, either by crossing the river or otherwise on foot, with whatever possessions they could carry. My family were also Palestinian refugees who went to Jordan. Now you can see why we call ourselves Jordanian, but it was not always so."

"I get it, Hani."

"I am afraid it gets worse and worse."

"Go on, I'm listening."

"Well… once the state of Israel was established the Israelis began to behave like a colonial power, absorbing by various means more and more of Palestine, eventually the whole of historical Palestine, evicting and expelling thousands more Palestinians.

"Needless to say, there were frequent clashes on the Israeli-Syrian and Israeli-Jordanian borders when thousands of Palestinian refugees tried to cross back to search for relatives, to return to their homes or to recover their possessions. It is estimated that Israeli forces shot dead between 2,000 and 5,000 people who were trying to cross back.

"When Israeli soldiers were killed Israeli forces rounded up villagers and blew up dozens of their homes. As many as 22,000 Palestinians were forced out of one town as a 'punishment'," he explained, using his hands to create the quote symbols.

"Hani, this is such a terrible story. Surely there are international agreements and laws designed to prevent this kind of thing happening."

"There are, Salah. Israel has been in direct contravention of international law, especially when Israelis began building settlements in the Syrian Golan Heights, the West Bank, and in the Gaza Strip. By 1977, around 11,000 Israelis lived in the West Bank, the Gaza Strip, the Golan Heights and the Sinai Peninsula.

"Palestinians have endured years of military occupation, theft of land, colonisation, ethnic cleansing, unlawful killings, detentions, blockades, abuses and restrictions on their movement. They have been subjected to widespread discrimination, a kind of apartheid, with Palestine itself now like a prison and, in some respects, more like a concentration camp. Their human rights, as well as international law, have been violated on a vast scale and yet Israel has never been held to account by the international community."

"Why not?"

"I am never sure but I think the main reason is that Israel has always had the support of America. You have been a great listener, Salah. Thank you. I hope I've not depressed you too much. I had better go and make some calls. Maybe I shall be able to find out what happened to my family."

"I wish you the best of luck, Hani. Please let me know how you get on."

"Will do. Bye for now."

Hani had been having increasing difficulty holding back tears. As he was leaving, Salah also became tearful. What had happened to Hani affected him deeply and his thoughts strayed towards his reasons for feeling so aggrieved. He realised that some of these were deeply ingrained, personal, and had nothing to do with Hani. They were about the disappearance of his mother and the way her employers had treated her.

For the first time he began to have ideas about seeking retribution and punishing those responsible for all the harm done. He realised Hani's grievances on behalf of himself and his countrymen were far greater than his own, but the principle of seeking justice for those who had been wronged seemed equally valid in both cases and he was motivated to try to do something about it.

Salah sat quietly for a while. He felt instinctively he should side with Hani by protesting in any way possible about the enormous injustice and violence that had befallen his family and so many other Palestinians and Jordanians. He felt also that any feelings of grievance should not only be directed towards Israel but also towards America for supporting Israel.

These thoughts caused him to reflect on what kind of person he was. For the first time he realised that life wasn't just about trying to be a good person, working hard and ploughing your own furrow. This was hard enough but also there were big issues to be addressed, issues affecting the well-being of countless people, including people he knew, even so far as affecting whether they lived or died. Someone had to address these kinds of issues.

Salah's feelings were sincere and his resolve strong, but he had no idea how to turn these into practical actions that could have any realistic chance of making a difference. He decided to leave his room and go outside for fresh air. The time with Hani had been so intense that Salah needed to clear his head and think how he should respond to what he had learned.

Strolling around the campus, Salah became increasingly tormented by the idea that having been made aware of Hani's dire situation it wasn't an option to do nothing. The immediate crunch point was how far he was willing to go to actually *do* something. What would something look like? Could he take any kind of effective action on his own? If not, with whom? And how would anyone know that his action was a protest against the injustices inflicted on Hani by Israel and its American ally? He wondered whether he needed to align himself with a relevant pre-existing protest group whose aims and objectives were already established and known.

Salah realised he was generating a greater amount of questions but few, if any, answers. He thought of discussing the matter with his friends but he needed to choose carefully. Khamis, currently his best friend, although an inveterate complainer, didn't look much like a protester or an activist. Salah needed an ally, preferably someone familiar with his situation, who had reason to have similar views and who had the time to think things through. But he was also very wary of sharing his secret thoughts and ideas with anyone, especially as any effective protest activities were likely to be controversial, have unintended consequences or even repercussions, some of which could be on the verge of illegality or even criminality. He thought about Hani on the way back to his room, then about his mother and then his mind flashed back several months to the day his own life began to fall apart.

CHAPTER 1.6

May 2002

DUBAI

The smell of flatbread warming in the oven was unmistakable. Salah was also aware of the tinkling sound of cutlery and plates as he gradually drifted in and out of consciousness. Realising his mother must be preparing breakfast, probably the usual Arabic dishes such as ful mesdames[2], laban[3], cheese and bread, he reluctantly rolled out of bed.

Still drowsy, he stumbled over the clothes on the floor and lurched in the direction of the bathroom. Looking in the mirror whilst relieving himself, he checked his appearance. No new spots – good!

After making his way to the kitchen, late again, he would have to rush his food. This would upset his mother, but she hadn't waited for him this morning. He just missed her as she had already left to start work elsewhere in the villa. She liked to begin her work early.

Salah didn't like to miss breakfast. On one occasion he'd got up so late he had no time to eat anything before setting off to the College and nearly fainted soon after arriving. This had also happened to some of his course mates. The extreme heat of the morning journey seemed the likely cause, but the College believed it was because of an empty stomach and there had been talk of providing breakfast for the poorest students and those living farthest away with long journeys.

Salah helped himself to food and ate quickly. He cleared the

---

2. Fava bean stew/dip
3. Yogurt

table, put the remaining food away in the fridge and returned to the bathroom for the daily ritual of washing himself and cleaning his teeth. He picked up yesterday's clothes from the bedroom floor, quickly dressed and left the villa. On the way out he looked for his mother; the villa was very large. By this time she could be anywhere so Salah left without being able to say goodbye.

He set off through the small side gate and walked the short distance to the main road where there was a good chance one of his friends would stop and give him a lift. Salah would be grateful for a lift with any of his college mates, but he quietly hoped the guy with the Porsche would be the one. Not today though, it was a Volkswagen Tiguan; this would do nicely.

"Hi Salah."

"Hi Khamis, thanks for stopping."

"Mafi mushkila." *No problem.*

"Asalaam alaykum."

"Alaykum as-salaam."

"Kayf haalek."

"Tamaam, shukran."

"Al humdoolillah."

Khamis was a good guy who lived in a very different world to Salah's. The main difference was wealth. Simply put, Khamis was surrounded by it and Salah wasn't. Even so, in spite of his considerable assets and good fortune, Khamis was one of the world's most accomplished complainers; almost nothing was right in Khamis' life.

"It's today, Salah."

"What is?"

"The meeting."

"What meeting?"

"You know, the meeting with the College about the student car park."

Khamis' current complaint was that the tarmacked road to the College only extended through the College gates as far as the main building and that access to the student car park beyond was via a rough, stony track. Khamis convinced himself this track was doing terrible damage to his vehicle.

He'd complained to the College authorities but felt frustrated when nothing was done. Gradually, he persuaded other students with expensive cars and 4 x 4s that something should be done and they eventually decided to confront the College together and insist on a meeting.

"That's great, Khamis."

Salah didn't really care but he liked Khamis and was grateful for the lift. He had learned not to become too involved in Khamis' problems; he had issues with something all the time. It would be a mistake and possibly very exhausting to get involved. Salah was hoping to be able to afford a car of his own one day. His mother had told him if he worked hard at the College he would be able to get a good job and buy one. He wasn't sure he was working hard enough.

They were fast approaching the big roundabout nearest the College, one of the busiest in Dubai. Khamis said that if you didn't force yourself into the circulating traffic you wouldn't be able to make progress and have to endure a cacophony of motor horns from those backing up behind you.

Although Khamis was a good driver Salah was always a little nervous at this point in the journey, especially as one of his friends was arrested by traffic cops and put in jail because he kept circumnavigating the roundabout in the inside lane. The poor guy had only just passed his driving test and was too frightened to pull over into the outer lane to turn off to the College. His licence was confiscated and it was several hours before he was released.

Khamis successfully negotiated the roundabout again this morning, turning off into the side road across the small area of desert surrounding the College. Passing through the College gates, he slowed to a crawl just before the stony track to the student parking area.

They both entered via the back entrance to the College through the coffee shop, before going their separate ways. Salah went to the College library, which should have been a good thing but, sadly, his interest in the library wasn't academic; it was Suhaila. Suhaila was a beautiful young Arab woman and Salah fancied her like crazy; he wasn't alone in having a crush on her as so did many other male students.

Suhaila was busy issuing books to a small queue of borrowers whilst at the same time managing not to engage in human contact. As well as having a distant manner, she had cultivated the useful skill of not seeing; all attempts at catching her eye were futile.

Not for the first time, Salah pondered how he might succeed in reaching out to her. He could move a book to the wrong shelf, pretend he couldn't find what he was looking for and ask Suhaila for help. He could ask her a question so she would have to speak to him or, now he had inspiration, he could simply borrow a book and then take it to her to be stamped at the issue desk.

He spent ages looking at shelves of books until he chanced across one entitled *BLEVE*. It had a picture of a massive explosion on the front, which looked vaguely interesting. He took it off the shelf and tried to look casual as he went over to the issue desk. Suhaila date stamped the book, scanned it into her computer and quickly turned away to do something else. Salah couldn't believe how quickly it was all over. He had missed his chance for sure.

Suffering from a terrible sense of failure and a high level of frustration, Salah left the library for one of the computer suites where he reluctantly worked through his English homework. This involved completing a series of English sentences containing spaces for missing words. A list of the suggested missing English words was provided. This was not as easy as it first appeared since there were more English words listed than were needed to fill the spaces. Some decision-making was therefore unavoidable and many decisions required an understanding of the English language which, as he realised, Salah would only achieve after a lot more work.

After taking almost three times as long as allowed for the task, Salah clicked on the computerised marking. The result was dire and the comment following the score, *Needs improvement*, seemed like a huge understatement. Feeling a failure once again, Salah went to the men's room to wash his feet before prayers.

Salah joined some of his classmates for lunch and participated in the usual student banter. Today it was mainly about sport and cars. He was glad it wasn't about girls again. He asked someone about the result of the student car park meeting but it was scheduled for later in the afternoon. He pretended to care. He couldn't decide between pizza and salad or curry and rice until he saw that pizza was cheaper.

The afternoon sessions were very average. There was nothing to get excited about in Occupational Health and Safety, which seemed pretty much like common sense. However, Salah did quite enjoy Fire Science; he thought fire and the reasons why things burn seemed intrinsically interesting, exciting and dramatic. He found the application of the principles of combustion in everyday life not only informative but also useful, and it contained some surprises, especially the idea that fires mostly go out of their own accord through lack of fuel and are not, strictly speaking, wholly extinguished by firefighters, as is the public perception. Salah looked forward to more Fire Science lectures.

Leaving the College for home there was no possibility of a lift with Khamis who was at the meeting. There was only a small chance that another student would be travelling home in Salah's direction and so he resigned himself to a long, hot walk. He set off slowly towards the roundabout hoping that someone would be leaving the College and going in his direction. No such luck. He continued along the main highway, sweating profusely, and wishing he had thought to refill his water bottle before setting off. After a long walk of several miles, he turned into the side road leading to the villa where he lived.

Passing between the villas he began to notice an unusual number of parked cars on both sides. Some were very large, others quite ordinary. Salah was inquisitive but it didn't occur to him that these cars had anything to do with what was happening where he lived.

He entered through the small side gate passing the fig trees on the way to the car port which, unusually, was also full of cars he had not seen before. He opened the back door and went into the kitchen. His mother, Aparna, was sitting at the kitchen table crying and sobbing, clearly in a highly distressed state.

Aparna wailed…

"Salah… I… have… ter…ri…ble news."

Her words were barely intelligible.

"Tell me."

"Salem has died."

Salah pulled his mother up towards him and held her close, as close as possible, both clinging to each other and crying together in shock and grief.

After the initial impact of his mother's 'terrible news', Salah realised how much he had been affected by his mother's grief. He cried because she was crying. He also felt sorry for his mother that he loved dearly, but Salah didn't really know Salem and he was not sure how to react to Salem's sudden death.

Calming down, Salah began to understand his mother would naturally be very upset, as she had always been on good terms with Salem. She thought he was a nice man and a good employer. She might also be wondering whether she might lose her job as housekeeper and possibly her home as a consequence of Salem's death. It was impossible to know what would happen to Salem's villa.

The stark realisation that life may never be the same again from that day onward now dawned on Salah, with an awareness that his own life might soon change in unwelcome or even unpleasant ways. He wasn't wrong.

His mother pulled away from him; she was still crying but had become more coherent.

"Salah, I am sorry, I should have told you this a long time ago. I am so, so, so sorry. I tried and tried to tell you but the words wouldn't come."

"Tell me what?"

"Salem was your father."

Salah's brain stopped working. He couldn't think, speak, move or react in any way. Since arriving home he had experienced in quick succession curiosity, surprise, shock, sadness, agitation, anxiety, fear and now panic. He just looked at his mother in disbelief and walked away.

Leaving the kitchen, Salah felt an irresistible urge to go and see Salem. He didn't normally venture outside his mother's simple accommodation near the kitchen and wandering around the villa felt like trespassing. But this wasn't a normal situation. Many people were congregating in the entrance hall, some waiting to go upstairs, some coming down. Salah could see through the big double doors that the *majlis* was full of people standing together talking in hushed tones.

Salah inched his way through the crowd, upstairs to the room where others were coming and going and entered cautiously, being unsure what he would find and about whether he should be there. After all, he didn't know if anyone else knew what he had only just discovered. As he hoped, he found himself in Salem's bedroom; a huge room with a thick carpet, a large bed, a number of heavily upholstered sofas and chairs, cabinets of various sizes and elaborate curtains, which had been closed.

His father, Sheikh Salem Al Munairi, aged 55, was dead, lying on his bed covered by a white sheet. Salah recognised Salem's son, Mubarak. Others were also present; Salah thought they must be close family members. Some seemed to find it difficult to believe the evidence of their own eyes and expressed regret they had not had the opportunity to offer Salem love, kindness, reassurance and hope before he died.

Salah felt a little more at ease when Mubarak reached out to him, guided him to his father's body and pulled back the sheet to reveal Salem's head. Salah was pleased to see how peaceful Salem's facial expression was and said as much to Mubarak. Mubarak agreed and they moved away, allowing others to view Salem's body and to pay their respects.

Feeling strange, uneasy and confused, Salah wanted to grieve but found it difficult. He didn't have a close relationship with his father, Salem and neither did he feel entitled to be involved as a family member because of his low status amongst others who were present. Nor did he wish to arouse curiosity about his relationship with Salem. Much as he tried to grieve, he couldn't help feeling so inhibited from expressing his feelings.

Mubarak stayed close to Salah and explained that funeral planning was already underway for the following day and Salah plucked up the courage to ask if he could be present at the mosque. Mubarak acted as if he was not surprised and willingly agreed. Salah thanked him and then excused himself saying he was going back to console his mother.

No wonder Aparna had been so unwilling to tell Salah anything about her past. Time after time he had asked the questions nearly all sons and daughters want to ask about their parents. Of course, Salah was puzzled that one of his parents was always absent, but he had learned not to be too pressing on the matter as this always upset his mother and then, if he persisted, she became annoyed.

Eventually, he assumed his father had once left his mother or died from an accident or ill health. In a strange way he hoped this was the case and that he had not been conceived as a result of a violent act or some other disreputable behaviour. Being born as a result of love or even just desire were better scenarios. Now all speculation had suddenly become unnecessary and he felt profoundly upset and angry that the moment of discovering he had a father was also the moment he lost him forever.

Salah rejoined his mother in the kitchen and noticed her eyes were very red from crying. He was initially lost for words. He felt like crying himself and increasingly angry towards his mother for not telling him about his father. Even so, he could see his mother needed comforting but he was fearful this might make things worse. Hoping to avoid triggering another outpouring of uncontrolled emotion and grief, which he found uncomfortable and embarrassing, he kissed her and put his arm around her.

He maintained a stoic face in trying to keep his own emotions in check and hoped his mother would do the same. She looked up at him. He'd never seen her so distraught. Without doubt she loved him and he loved her but that didn't mean he couldn't be angry with her. Judging the moment carefully he told her about his conversation with Mubarak and that he wished to attend his father's funeral tomorrow. She said she was too tired and upset to talk and went to her bedroom.

CHAPTER 1.7

Salah felt unusually tired after a night sleeping only fitfully. He attributed this to many interruptions from disturbing dreams. Salah couldn't remember what any of these dreams were about but assumed they related to the events of the previous day. Tired as he was he was up early to get ready to make his way to the mosque to join Mubarak and other members of Salem's family and friends for prayers and recitations.

According to Islamic Law and custom, a body should be buried as soon as possible. Salem's body had been washed three times by the male family members and covered in a clean, white sheet. It was then shrouded in three white sheets with the left hand resting on the chest and the right hand resting on the left. The shrouded body was then tied with ropes as per the custom, to be ready for the journey to the mosque.

Salah joined those following the body to the cemetery. This was a new experience. From the beginning he had been watching what everyone else was doing, anxious not to make a mistake. Only men were involved in performing the burial rituals and attending the burial itself. He felt upset for his mother and wondered how she was feeling about not being involved.

Salah watched as his father's shrouded body was placed in the grave on his right side, facing Mecca. His body was then covered with wood and stones and each of the mourners placed a handful of soil in the grave. Salah did the same at a respectful distance. No one seemed to take any notice of his presence or involvement. Finally, a small stone was then placed on top as a marker.

Those standing around the grave in their white, loosely fitting dishdashas seemed untroubled by the intense heat, unlike Salah who was now bathed in sweat. He left the burial party and wandered alone, deep in thought, going over and over in his mind everything that had happened following Salem's death.

On reflection, he was glad he'd taken part in the mourning, to have attended the mosque and assisted during the burial. Nobody had challenged his right to be involved and, in a perverse way, he felt that through being there he had established some sort of relationship with his father, more so in death than in life. This wasn't much of a consolation but it was something.

Salah's memories of being with Salem were few and far between and he struggled to bring to mind those few occasions they were together. It was Salem, of course, who, in a rare one-to-one chat, suggested to Salah that he apply to one of the local colleges for a two-year diploma course. According to Salem, if Salah worked hard he could progress to the parent university in the UK and obtain a degree. Salem had recommended one of the more practical, down-to-earth programmes such as Management, which, he argued, should help Salah get a good job.

Later, on another occasion, while researching possible courses, Salah had asked Salem what Facilities Management was about. He remembered how enthusiastic Salem had been. He listed the main subjects within Facilities Management and told Salah that when he graduated the prospects for employment would be very good indeed.

Salah's best memory, however, was the day Salah returned from the College as Salem was returning from his office. Arriving at the villa at the same time, Salem asked Salah to sit with him and tell him about the College and about his hopes for the future. Looking back, Salah wished he'd sounded more confident and ambitious. Salem had been very positive and encouraging and told Salah that if he worked hard and achieved a recognised qualification he would be well rewarded and have good prospects.

He had felt particularly close to Salem that day; he had been like a father to Salah and even allowed him to examine his *khanjar* to feel its sharpness. Salah remembered wishing they could spend more time together and wondered whether Salem felt the same. His thoughts returned to what else he knew about Salem. He realised it wasn't much, but from what he'd seen and heard, he'd formed a definite impression he could fairly be described as a self-made man.

Salah found himself alongside Mubarak and realised there would never be a better opportunity to find out about his father. As they both walked back to the villa, Salah told Mubarak he regretted knowing so little about Salem and his life. He said he had always assumed Salem had been very successful in business because of his apparent wealth.

Mubarak seemed happy to respond, saying his father was a very private man who worked closely with the Ruler on many aspects of national development. It was true he had been well rewarded but he lived modestly and was always a devout Muslim. Mubarak said he was very proud of his father's achievements and that he had led a good life.

Mubarak went on to explain that earlier generations of Salem's family had been close to the ruling family; his father and grandfather had been particularly close to the Sovereign who was a traditionalist, who viewed his responsibility as maintaining the status quo established by his family's dynasty. He was more or less insulated from most aspects of modern life, hardly aware of any rumblings of discontent. When pressure for change eventually forced itself on him he resisted on the grounds that all change was inherently undesirable, unnecessary and bad.

Salah had been unaware of this family history until now and thanked Mubarak for explaining it to him. He was astonished to learn that his father had been so close to the Ruler and asked Mubarak to continue. Mubarak explained that the present Ruler succeeded his father by acclamation. Considerably younger in mind than his father, he applied himself diligently from the time of his accession to improving conditions steadily of his people's lives. He lived in the present rather than the past and focused on the future.

Salem, who was of a similar age, had the same outlook

and instincts. Both could see ways of improving people's lives. Embracing this philosophy, Salem began to feel at one with the Ruler to the extent he could even read the Ruler's mind. He soon realised there were opportunities to help the Ruler achieve his goals for their country whilst at the same time achieving personal advancement and wealth.

Salah asked if Salem had been involved in the oil industry. Mubarak said the discovery of oil was definitely a factor in helping Salem achieve power, influence and wealth. Of course, neither Salem nor any of his countrymen could themselves have 'discovered' oil, nor could they have drilled a productive well or refined the products of oil and gas extraction. All these essential activities were carried out by well-established and highly experienced international companies on the basis of concessions awarded by the government.

The new business opportunities came about because the companies involved needed specialist equipment that had to be imported, equipment maintenance, accommodation, transport, catering for their personnel, specialist clothing providers, payroll management and other commercial, legal and technical support facilities.

Families that were already established and successful seized upon these opportunities: local entrepreneurs with government connections, especially those closest to decisions about contracts with the oil companies. Those able to read the Ruler's mind were best placed to benefit from these new opportunities and Sheikh Salem Al Munairi, head of one of the most illustrious families, didn't miss these opportunities. He kept close to the Ruler so he was almost always privy to where the next business opportunity would come from. Occasionally, the Ruler asked Salem for advice, which brought the two even closer together and enhanced Salem's status, also giving him greater influence and involvement in business opportunities to a wider degree.

Salah had been listening attentively, impressed with Mubarak's detailed knowledge of his father's life and work. Salah now understood how Salem had amassed his considerable wealth and that he had indeed become a self-made man, although he had much luck and help along the way to becoming 'self-made'.

Mubarak said his father was expecting him to assume responsibility for his business interests after he finished his education. He had expressed his wish on several occasions and had always encouraged Mubarak to take an interest in his diverse business ventures. Salem also told Mubarak he had discussed his future role in the family businesses with his brothers who were fully supportive, happy to advise and provide whatever help Mubarak needed.

Salah asked Mubarak about Salem's brothers whom he had just seen for the first time at the funeral. Mubarak said they were not business people like Salem but very senior and influential in their own ways. One was an ambassador, another was a senior member of the National Civil Defence and one was a senior ministry official. Salah was impressed.

They reached the villa and Salah thanked Mubarak for allowing him to be present during the day, for helping him understand what kind of person Salem was and how he had lived his life. Mubarak thanked Salah for coming, for his support and wished him well.

Salah watched Mubarak walk away and up the steps to the front doors of the villa. Salah continued to the back as usual. He wondered whether Mubarak knew they were brothers and wished he had the courage to ask him. Not having done so tormented Salah for a long time thereafter. He also reflected on how it happened that two sons of the same father were born with such great differences in social status, wealth and life chances.

CHAPTER 1.8

Salah and his mother ate their breakfast together in silence; there was none of the usual small talk about the day ahead. Salah was relieved they were both able to behave relatively normally, although the atmosphere was tense. He thought about breaking the silence but wasn't sure he wanted the conversation that would follow. He would have to make his mother aware of his anger over what she'd done, or not done, and at the same time tell her he still loved her. This would not be easy and not something for today.

Instead, he told her how much he would prefer not to go to the College. Aparna replied that there was nothing to be gained by staying at home. He wanted to argue with her but thought better of it. She was probably right. He helped her clear away the breakfast and returned to his room against his inclinations to collect the things he needed for College. Salah said goodbye to his mother, left the villa and headed off as usual to the main road, hoping as always to catch a lift.

He just missed Khamis; Salah caught sight of him going past at high speed. He wondered whether because he was later than usual this morning he may have missed his chance of a lift altogether. Luckily, Ziad was also late and saw Salah just in time, screeching to a halt a few yards past the junction. Salah ran towards the car and jumped in. He was excited to be riding in a Porsche, he'd been hoping for this to happen. He didn't know much about cars but he knew what everyone knew, that Ziad's Porsche was a super luxury family car with the high performance of a sports car.

The novelty of riding in a status symbol soon wore off when Ziad, friendly as ever after the usual Arabic greetings, asked Salah how he was. Salah replied he was going through a bad time because Sheikh Salem had died, that Salem's death had been unexpected and that his mother and he had experienced a terrible shock. He stopped short of telling Ziad that Salem was his father, he didn't want to answer any questions that might follow and neither did he mention the likely consequences for him and his mother. Ziad expressed his sympathies.

Ziad was one of the nicest students at the College, probably at any college anywhere, as he positively exuded nice-ness. Someone once said rather unkindly that he had a lot to be nice about. He was born into one of the wealthiest families in Dubai, living in an enormous villa high in a mountainous area overlooking the sea. He and his family enjoyed regular exotic holidays in their villas in some of the best locations. Ziad was good-looking, athletic, personable and hugely popular with other students, the College's teaching staff and, seemingly, everyone he met.

Ziad asked Salah if he could do anything to help. Salah gratefully declined. Privately and silently he wondered how different his life would be if he had a fraction of Ziad's wealth, but he thought it best to downplay his problems for now rather than allow a situation to arise where Ziad felt obliged to help. He told himself he was dealing with his problems, dealing with them in his own way.

The short journey to the College was soon over. Salah had been enjoying the comfortable ride and Ziad's company. He thanked Ziad and they went their separate ways; Salah, who was by now on autopilot, couldn't resist calling in to the library to see what Suhaila was doing. As usual, admiring male students surrounded her, as she was looking particularly attractive and wearing clothes that enhanced her figure. Salah wasn't in the mood; he couldn't have cared less this morning and regretted wasting his time.

Leaving the library, he made his way to the furthest of the newly built classrooms, a pleasant stroll along the new paths between the recently planted palm trees, the new water fountain and the rock garden. Recent attempts to 'green' the College campus were much appreciated by students, especially the palm trees, which also provided much needed shade.

More shade had also been provided by stretching an awning between the new classroom blocks. This covered a number of tables and chairs and a small street food outlet that soon became a favourite with students, especially the smokers. Most tables were provided with ashtrays and the College's no smoking rule had been relaxed for this area. Non-smokers found it harder to find a shady table.

Arriving at the designated lecture room, Salah scanned the faces of those sitting in the terraced rows, one of which was Samara. The male and female students tended to sit separately and Samara was with the girls. She was sitting near the middle of a row with several unoccupied seats next to her.

Salah took advantage of the fact that there were few available seats elsewhere and decided to sit as near to Samara as possible without actually sitting beside her. He considered her a very attractive girl and he wanted to try to get to know her better. He'd asked around to see if he could find out anything about her but the most he came up with was that she was from Iraq.

The lecturer arrived for the Risk Assessment session. Students called him by his nickname, 'Juicy', behind his back, of course. This puzzled Salah until he eventually asked someone 'why is he called Juicy?' The answer was 'because he keeps saying 'd'ya see? D'ya see?' when he's explaining something'.

Salah was enjoying the Risk Assessment module. It seemed to him a useful approach to a wide range of life situations and problems. The lecture was interesting enough; the only slight downside being that 'Juicy' set an assignment. The task was to research two computer models for risk assessment and then to e-mail a brief description of each to 'Juicy' within the next two weeks. Salah thought this needn't take long and would be relatively easily accomplished with the aid of the Internet.

The lecture over, students were beginning to stand up and work their way along the rows towards the exits. Samara could have moved in Salah's direction and, if he timed it right, be close enough for him to speak to her. But she didn't, she left the row by going the other way even though it was much further; Salah was crestfallen to say the least.

There was nothing for it but to grin and bear it, so he made his way to the covered area and bought a Coke and a chocolate biscuit. He looked for a table without an ashtray and sat down by the palm trees with other students. Smoke wafted across his nostrils from the smoking tables. He didn't know any of the others personally, but joined in their general chatter about the extravagant social lives of some of the better off students. One turned to Salah and said:

"Smart move sitting next to Samara."

"Yeah, didn't do me any good though, did it? She could have come my way when she was leaving but she went the other way; maybe it was to avoid me."

"Doubt it, more likely she didn't even notice you – couldn't care less about you."

"Thanks."

This may have been normal student humour but it added to his troubled state of mind and dented his self-confidence, which was already at a low point. He hoped it didn't show.

Salah left the table and made his way back to the main building. On the way he called into the men's washroom, which was crowded as usual at this time of day with students washing their feet in the hand basins in preparation for midday prayers. He was in awe of their dedication to their religion and felt inadequate himself by comparison. After waiting to relieve himself he made his way to the dining room for a quick lunch.

After lunch, Salah visited one of the computer suites to begin researching the **Risk Assessment** assignment, but he was too distracted by his problems at home to make any useful progress. Unable to concentrate, time slipped by without any purpose or progress until it was time for the afternoon session, the Surveying module.

This module was another of Salah's favourites. He particularly liked going out on location with the equipment for practical work and, here again, the subject involved applications of skill and knowledge to solve real-life problems, not just knowledge for its own sake. He also liked the fact that most of the practical tasks required at least two students to perform them and he enjoyed the cooperation and teamwork.

This afternoon he worked with Khaled again. He liked Khaled who was from Kuwait. All the Kuwaiti students were OK although they tended to stick together and be rather insular. Apparently, they had clubbed together and hired a huge villa not far from the College. Khaled had said that nobody could cook or wanted to, so they ordered and had delivery of their meals from the nearby Indian or Italian restaurants. Salah imagined they must have an easy life. The owner had insisted they hire a maid to keep the place clean so they didn't have to shop, cook or even clear up. It sounded too good to be true.

At the end of the session, Khaled said he wanted to leave the College promptly and asked Salah whether he had transport. Salah said he didn't. Khaled had a Toyota 4 x 4, not the big Land Cruiser model, but an attractive, robust SUV that was more than adequate for his needs, including the occasional off-road trip with his friends into the wadis. He even suggested that Salah might like to join them on one of their camping excursions as the Kuwaitis had more than enough vehicles, tents and other equipment to accommodate him. Salah was pleased he and Khaled were becoming closer as friends.

He thanked Khaled for his offer but politely declined as he said he wasn't quite ready to leave the College. They parted company and Salah watched Khaled walk off to the students' car park.

Salah had lied; he didn't have anything else to do. On the contrary, he couldn't wait to leave the College. It had been a lousy day. He had fallen out with his mother, he couldn't get his troubles out of his mind, he couldn't apply himself to the course, girls he liked didn't like him and, although he'd experienced kindness from friends, he didn't feel completely able to open up and confide in anyone. It would be too difficult, too embarrassing. He felt alone and now he *was* alone.

For whatever reason he'd declined Khaled's offer of a lift he would have to live with his decision, irrational though it may have been. If, deep down, he wished to be alone with his thoughts then this was it. He would have to make the best of things during the long, hot walk from the College, back to the roundabout and along the highway for several miles until he reached his home. At least he'd had the sense to fill his water bottle this time, unlike the other day. He wouldn't make that mistake again.

The heat was brutal and he began to sweat. Soon his clothes were drenched and becoming increasingly uncomfortable. Salah began to think of his mother and of how they could overcome the strain on their relationship caused by Salem's death and the revelations that followed. He wondered what she was doing, whether she was doing her work in the villa as usual. He wondered what would happen if she lost her job, what she would do and whether she might want to go back to India. She'd never said much about her life before coming to Dubai. Salah knew little about her early life and if she wanted to go back, what would he do?

Thinking about his mother made Salah realise he had been so wrapped up in himself he hadn't given any thought to her feelings over Salem's death. He didn't know whether she had loved Salem or whether she still did and he had no idea how his mother as a Hindu viewed his death. As far as he knew, family was the most important aspect of Hindu death rituals and yet, in Salem's case, she had not been involved. That must have been terrible for her. He decided to try to moderate his anger and be more sympathetic towards his mother.

Whilst Salah had been thinking he had also been walking, walking at a steady pace. He was now within sight of the turning from the highway into the side road leading to the villa. He was nearly home. Eventually he walked down the side road and arrived at the gate that opened into the front garden. Passing by the fig bushes and bougainvilleas, he carried on through the carport to the kitchen back door.

The door was open as usual. His mother wasn't around, probably elsewhere in the villa. Then he noticed her bedroom door was closed; she could be resting, no doubt still very upset and sleep deprived. Salah went straight to his room and then to the bathroom where he stripped off his sweaty clothes and turned on the shower. It was such a relief to be able to wash off all that sweat and to generally freshen up, ready to put on clean clothes. He realised how tired he was after the long walk in the heat and he flopped on his bed, exhausted.

He hadn't meant to go to sleep and was surprised when he awoke to find it was dark. He felt for his bedroom light switch and turned on the light. Then he noticed it was dark everywhere else in the villa. He was surprised his mother hadn't called him for their evening meal and guessed she must have fallen asleep too. Neither of them had enjoyed a good night's sleep recently. He put more lights on and went to her bedroom. She wasn't there; her bed was made but there weren't any clothes, shoes or towels around as usual and her wardrobe door was slightly ajar. Salah opened it further and found it empty.

He was at a complete loss to understand what was going on. He thought of going into the rest of the villa searching and calling for his mother but worried that Mubarak or one of Salem's other relatives might be in residence. He didn't want to be caught trespassing.

It occurred to him that his mother may have left a note and that he should check this out first before doing anything else. He returned to her bedroom and looked everywhere, then into the kitchen. He noticed an envelope on the kitchen work surface. She had left a note after all. He'd seen it earlier but in his near panic didn't attach any significance to it. This time he picked it up; it was unsealed with his name on the front. He tore it open and read the short, typed message:

'Following the death of His Excellency Sheikh Salem Al Munairi there is no further requirement for staff at his villa. Your mother has returned to India and you are to vacate the villa with immediate effect, taking all your belongings with you.

HE Sheikh Khalid Al Munairi'

CHAPTER 1.9

Salah looked at his watch continuously. It was still dark and he'd lost count of the number of times he'd checked the time. He'd hardly slept at all, still experiencing the same sensation since reading the letter, a sensation he'd never felt before; it was in his stomach, a combination of panic and generalised terror. He would never forget it and he longed for daylight.

Staying in bed was serving no useful purpose for he couldn't sleep. He wasn't even resting. Sliding out of bed, he was initially shocked by the quietness. He realised this was a contradiction but he was used to hearing the sound of his mother getting ready for work and making breakfast. He hadn't adjusted to the fact that she wasn't there.

He picked up the letter and read it again and again. Could it really be true that his mother had returned to India? How could this have happened so quickly? And why didn't *she* leave a note for *him*? If she was back in India there would be no hope of finding her. India was vast; he wouldn't know his way around in India for he'd never been there. Even if he knew where to look he would never find her. In any case, it was unrealistic to think he could organise a search. He simply didn't have the resources.

He went to the bathroom thinking he would feel better after a shower, then realised what he most needed was a drink. He went to the kitchen to make tea and returned to the bathroom. After showering and drying himself he decided he couldn't be bothered with breakfast and so he dressed and finished his mug of tea.

At first, Salah was doubtful whether there was any point in going to the College – on the one hand he couldn't pretend that life would go on as normal, but on the other hand he reasoned that if he did go he would at least be able to tell someone what had happened and he might even be able to get help.

Suddenly he had an idea. He wondered whether his mother knew the servants in the neighbouring villas and whether they knew her. If so, they might know a little or perhaps may have seen or heard something. He decided to go and find out before leaving the villa. At least this was something he could do.

Hoping they were also up early, Salah went from door to door and spoke with both neighbouring housekeepers. He learned that neither of them knew his mother, nor could they shed any light on what had happened to her.

By normal standards he was setting off for the College very early and didn't expect another student to pass by and offer him a lift. He tried to convince himself that the walk would do him good, which was probably true; it also provided useful thinking time, although his thought processes were not serving him well. Abject confusion and dread would be a good description of his mental state.

At this time he was avoiding the worst heat of the day but it was still very warm. Salah walked slowly, trying not to work up too much of a sweat. He made it to the big roundabout and crossed the road carefully but without difficulty; there was hardly any traffic this early in the day. He had now reached the side road leading to a small private track across the area of semi-arid desert surrounding the College campus. Finally he arrived at the main entrance and walked up to the back doors of the canteen where he usually entered the College building.

There was nobody to be seen. Obviously it was too early. After checking his watch he estimated it could take as much as an hour before anybody arrived for work. There was no avoiding a long wait so he sat patiently outside the entrance to the canteen. After just over half an hour the woman who ran the catering arrived with keys in hand. She unlocked the doors to go inside and locked them again behind her.

Twenty minutes later, Mrs Wankowski arrived. She noticed

Salah sitting on the ground outside the canteen as she drove past on her way to the staff car park. She parked and then walked back round to the canteen entrance.

"Hello Salah, you're very early today; everything OK?"

"Hello Mrs Wankowski. No… not really."

Salah was having difficulty; his breathing was becoming uneven, his eyes tearful.

The canteen lady unlocked the doors.

"Let's go in and have a chat, Salah."

"You can have a cold drink if you like," offered the canteen lady. "I've only just turned on the equipment. The hot drinks machines need time to heat up, sorry."

"Thanks, can I have a Coke, please?"

"I'll get these; I'll just have a glass of water, thank you."

"You can pay me later. I can't open the till either; I've only just switched the computer on."

Salah sat at a table. Mrs Wankowski came over with his Coke and her glass of water.

"Salah, you look as if you need help. What's the matter?"

"Mrs Wankowski, I've got trouble at home."

"I'm sorry to hear that. Would you like to tell me about it?"

Salah had always liked Mrs Wankowski and he felt he could trust her.

"My father died suddenly; it seems he had a heart attack. He was only 55. It's a bit weird, actually."

"Oh Salah, I'm really sorry. You must be so shocked and upset."

Salah was managing to stem the flow of tears, just.

"The weird bit is that, until he died, I didn't know he was my father. I didn't know him very well at all, actually, and certainly not as my father. My mother didn't tell me he was my father until after he died. I don't understand why she didn't tell me before; she said she was very sorry and she said she tried to tell me but couldn't. I tried to get her to tell me more but she wouldn't, so I still don't know how all this could have happened. Now I may probably never know."

"Why do you say that?"

"Mrs Wankowski, I've only told you half the story. When I went home last night there was no sign of my mother. I searched everywhere. Later, I found an envelope addressed to me containing a letter from one of my father's brothers. I'll find it for you."

Salah rummaged in his rucksack, found the letter and handed it to Mrs Wankowski.

After a few moments of reading, Mrs Wankowski said, "Salah, this letter is terrible, I don't know how anybody could be so ruthless and heartless. I am so very sorry to hear your sad news. Is there anything I can do to help?"

Mrs Wankowski was feeling affected by Salah's story, especially because he was so upset. She immediately regretted asking if there was anything she could do to help. It was a stupid thing to ask. The question wasn't 'Is there anything I can do?' There was *everything* to do. The question should be 'Where do we start?'

She suggested she could perhaps help immediately in a small way if Salah would like her to help him remove his belongings from the villa and store them temporarily in her office. She suggested they could do this straightaway. Salah jumped at the idea. He had been wondering all night how he could leave the villa without delay; he didn't want to stay there a moment longer than necessary.

Mrs Wankowski said she would need to make a couple of phone calls to let colleagues know she was leaving the College. She suggested Salah meet her in the staff car park in a quarter of an hour.

"OK, Mrs Wankowski. I'll be by your car."

Salah cheered up a little, feeling very lucky Mrs Wankowski had seen him outside the canteen and that she was willing to drop everything to help him. She must have other things to do or she wouldn't have come to work so early herself. He went to the men's room and splashed water on his face, hoping it would make it less obvious that he'd been crying.

When the time came they both left the College in Mrs Wankowski's car and drove to the villa Salah had been calling home. It took him hardly any time to collect his things together and put them in boxes. Everything he owned in the world could be fitted into two boxes. The pathos of the situation began to affect Mrs Wankowski increasingly and she became emotional. She didn't want Salah to see. Returning to the College, she suggested there was no need to take the boxes up to her office as they could remain in her car overnight. Salah was happy with that.

She couldn't help but ask him if he had a bed for the night; he said he didn't and she asked him what he was going to do. He said he was hoping one of his friends would know of spare accommodation somewhere, even if it meant sleeping on the floor. She said she hoped he would find somewhere.

It was time for lunch. Mrs Wankowski asked Salah if he would like to continue their chat in her office or go to lunch.

"I think I should go to lunch and try to see my friends about finding somewhere to sleep tonight."

Mrs Wankowski said she would stay in her office to get some work done and that he could come and see her again at any time, if he wished.

"Please let me know how you get on before you leave the College."

"OK, Mrs Wankowski."

She was left pondering Salah's sad news. She had always liked Salah. He was always clean and tidy although his dress sense was sometimes strange but no more or less so than other students living on restricted budgets. She liked his manner. He was quietly spoken and unfailingly polite, even when his work was being criticised. All things considered, Mrs Watts thought Salah a nice young man. As far as she could tell he seemed to get along well enough with other students, although she suspected that many of the wealthier students looked down on him because he was obviously poor.

It occurred to Mrs Wankowski that she and her husband had a spare room in their villa, although she wasn't sure how Janek would feel about having a student staying with them. She called him. As anticipated, Janek was somewhat taken aback by his wife's suggestion of having a student to stay and asked for time to think about it. She knew him well enough to be confident of his support even when he was uneasy about something. Janek rang back quickly and suggested they do it on a one-off trial basis. Mrs Wankowski said she wouldn't mention it to Salah if he were able to find somewhere to sleep that night.

Salah chose a curry. Not having had any breakfast he was very hungry. As he was paying for his meal and a Coke, he had a minor panic attack. The sight of the notes and coins from his pocket suddenly made him realise that money had always come from his mother and that, without her, he had no money except his meagre savings, which would only last a few weeks at most, even if he was extra careful.

As he was walking away from the till he caught sight of Khaled's Toyota going past the windows. He remembered how helpful and friendly Khaled always seemed and waited for him to enter the building. They exchanged greetings and Salah asked if Khaled could spare a minute. They found a table where they could speak privately.

Salah told Khaled the whole story since they last met, explaining that he had nowhere to live and asked him if he knew of anyone with spare accommodation, preferably somewhere cheap. Khaled said he was deeply saddened by Salah's news and the terrible situation in which he found himself. He couldn't think of any likely spare accommodation immediately and would ask around. He promised to catch up with Salah later, but probably not today. Salah felt Khaled's reaction had been positive but he was by no means confident he would be able to come up with anything and definitely not for tonight.

Salah doubted he would be able to concentrate during the afternoon lecture but he would do his best and arrived in good time for the Managing Physical Hazards module. Students were handed a set of module notes produced by the College, which looked interesting. He noticed the word 'BLEVE' in a section entitled *Storage of Liquids and Gasses* and wondered where he had seen this word before. He flicked through the rest of the notes with interest. He had little idea what happened in the rest of the lecture having been in a troubled world of his own for most of the time.

The session was followed by a period of private study. It was easy to squander and waste private study time and Salah often felt guilty for doing so. But not this afternoon; this afternoon he felt justified in not being able to think of anything but his own problems. He wondered who else he could ask about accommodation. Khamis or Ziad might be able to help but he hadn't seen them around and wasn't sure if they were even at the College today. He felt helpless, not for the first time, and decided the best course of action was to go back to Mrs Wankowski and tell her he thought it unlikely he would be able to find anywhere for the night.

"Come in."

"Hello Mrs Wankowski. I'm sorry to disturb you. I really don't want to cause you any more trouble but you said to let you know if I found somewhere for tonight. I have asked the person most likely to help; he said he didn't know of anything immediately but would ask around and that he would let me know later, but not today. There are two other people who might be able to help but they don't seem to be in the College. I can ask them when I see them, of course."

Without hesitation, Mrs Wankowski said that Salah could have the spare bedroom in her villa that night.

Salah was taken aback; he couldn't believe his luck and desperate as he was he hadn't considered this a possibility.

"Thank you, Mrs Wankowski. Thank you so much, I shall never forget your kindness."

She then rang Janek. No answer, he was probably driving. Janek rang her back when he reached home. Mrs Wankowski explained what had happened since they spoke earlier and told him she was on her way home with Salah.

She and Salah set off for the Wankowski's villa. Neither was completely comfortable with the situation; both finding themselves in unfamiliar territory. Grateful as he was, Salah was well and truly outside his comfort zone and Mrs Wankowski still harboured a small doubt about how Janek might react.

To break the silence she decided she would tell Salah why she came round to the canteen doors to speak to him in the morning.

"Salah, obviously this is not the time to mention this but the reason I came round this morning was to ask you to come and see me to talk about your English homework. We do need to have a chat sometime. Can I leave it to you to let me know when you feel able to discuss your College work?"

"Yes, you can, Mrs Wankowski. I was expecting you to say something about my English."

Mrs Wankowski had been gentle with him thus far but had made it clear his English was nowhere near good enough for him to be able to progress to degree level in the UK. He knew he needed to work harder and was now even more determined to do so.

ACT TWO

CHAPTER 2.1

September 16 2002

ENGLAND

Salah was surprised by the large number of students assembling in the main lecture hall of the Faculty of Science and Engineering, also slightly unnerved by the amount of noise. He took a while to realise that students from several programmes and courses had been asked to assemble in the same location for a welcome talk by the Faculty Dean.

Even allowing for the numbers present the volume of chatter seemed abnormally high and many students seemed restless, even agitated. After a while he spotted Samara sitting on the other side of the hall. Khamis must have been somewhere but Salah couldn't see him. The Dean appeared and the volume gradually subsided. He introduced himself as Professor Richard Farrar. He sounded genuinely welcoming and friendly, congratulating the assembled students on their choice of university and on their choice of subjects. He said how proud he was of the high ratings awarded to the University's Engineering Research and Teaching Programmes by the Quality Assurance Agency for Higher Education, adding that, in his opinion, the University's facilities for engineering were second to none.

Professor Farrar continued by extolling the virtues of engineering as a major contributor to national life, to the national economy and to society as a whole because of its applications in almost every sphere of human existence. He explained that all the engineering disciplines continue to develop at a fast rate and there are very good prospects for jobs for well-qualified engineering graduates. He added that this also applied to graduates following related subjects such as Facilities Management.

He then directed the various courses to their course leaders who would be waiting for them in designated lecture rooms. After advising all students to keep in close contact with their personal tutors and not to hesitate to raise any problems with them at an early stage, he wished everyone good luck with their studies and a happy and rewarding time at the University.

The Dean left the hall and the students resumed their chatter. Again, this became increasingly louder until enough students had left the hall for the noise level to subside. Salah joined the queue to leave. He still hadn't seen Khamis yet so he waited outside in the hope of catching him. While he was looking for him, Samara appeared in his view and she came over.

"Hello Salah."

"Hi Samara, how are you?"

"I'm fine thanks, and you?"

"OK, pretty good actually. What did you make of that?"

"I thought he was very good. I liked him."

"He was OK, but I wasn't thinking of him, I meant the students," he said.

Samara looked as if she didn't understand the question. "What about the students?"

"I was surprised how noisy they were and they seemed very restless; I wondered if something was going on."

"Oh, I see. Yes, they were and yes, they did. If you're going to ask me why I have no idea; have you?"

Khamis emerged from among those leaving the hall and on seeing Salah and Samara chatting came over to join them.

"Hi guys, what's up?"

"Just chatting, Khamis."

Khamis was suspicious; he thought Salah and Samara looked furtive and he wondered why they didn't want to say what they were chatting about.

"We've got time for a coffee before the first lecture. Shall we go to the cafeteria?"

"OK, Khamis, good plan." They made their way to the students' union cafeteria and joined the line for hot drinks.

Feeling refreshed, they made their way back to the lecture rooms. Arriving at the room for the meeting with the Facilities Management course leader they joined the other students waiting outside. Salah noticed as they approached the building that it was designed as a rotunda with eight lecture rooms built around a central concourse. Inside each lecture room, tiers of seats steeply banked faced and overlooked the presentation area at the front.

Salah, Samara and Khamis climbed the stairs to the highest level and took their seats. Looking down on the front they saw multiple screens of all types and other presentation aids. Suspended from the ceiling were several different kinds of projectors. Behind them were small windows high up in the wall at different levels and doors at the top of the steps on either side, which they assumed led to a room or rooms behind the windows.

On closer inspection Salah saw the word 'GALLERY' on the nearest door. Whilst they were waiting for the course leader, he couldn't resist the temptation to prise open the door and look behind it. There was a large, open, circular space with little windows into each lecture room and projectors set up ready to project.

Salah was impressed, very impressed. The lecture suite had been designed so that a technician could move quickly and easily between any of the eight lecture rooms to provide whatever kind of educational technology support a lecturer might need. Salah couldn't help comparing these amazing facilities with those in Dubai.

Jack Russell entered the lecture room and introduced himself. The Dubai students recognised him from his visit to their College earlier in the year.

"Hello everyone.

"My name's Jack Russell. I'm the course leader for Facilities Management. I should like to add my welcome to that of the Dean and say how pleased I am to see you all here. Congratulations. You've made it. This is what you have worked so hard for. I am particularly pleased to see so many female students have chosen Facilities Management and it's also a pleasure to welcome our overseas students from several countries.

"First of all, before we talk about the course, I'd like us to do a small exercise. We are going to divide into four groups and each group will go into one of the breakout rooms downstairs underneath the lecture room.

The task is to work in pairs and for each of you to interview someone and then be interviewed by that person. You will then come back to the lecture room and introduce each other. The interviews should discover the person's name, perhaps also their nickname, a few personal details and something distinctive about them that will help us remember them. I have allowed 15 minutes for the interviews. Then we shall do the introductions, which will take the rest of the session. OK, off you go."

Samara, Salah and Khamis decided not to interview each other. They agreed the exercise would be more useful for them if they both paired off with others. Samara and Simon got together, Salah and Paul, as did Khamis and Mike. Everyone was friendly and cooperative so they all managed to come up with personal details and a distinctive feature. They had enjoyed the process and, in some cases, may even have made a new friend.

Back in the lecture room, Jack Russell organised the introductions. They had the desired effect. Anyone who'd felt alone and anxious at the beginning had an opportunity to get involved in a way that forced them to become proactive, to meet other course members, to make a small presentation and to observe everyone else doing the same thing, all in a fail-safe situation. Nobody was judged and everyone could succeed in the task.

Jack Russell rounded off the session by thanking everyone for their participation and informed everyone that he would produce a list and a timetable of personal interviews so that he could get to know each student on a one-to-one basis. These would be posted on the student hub of the University's intranet and would take place over the next few days.

The Facilities Management students left the lecture room and joined the other students milling around in the concourse, either leaving or arriving for lectures. Salah and Khamis had nothing else on their timetable for that day so they loitered for a while, unsure what to do next. Samara joined them briefly then went her own way.

Khamis decided to go home and asked Salah if he would like to come back to his house for a drink and maybe a bite to eat. Salah was grateful to Khamis for coming up with a plan.

On the way back to Khamis' house, both admitted to feeling unsettled. It was the first day of the course and the warm-up exercise was fine but they didn't feel they had made a real start yet on their final year of study. Salah said he had another problem. After he collected his timetable from the office he was surprised to see how few lectures and tutorials take place during a week, much less than in Dubai. He was anxious about how much time he was expected to organise himself. Khamis agreed they weren't used to having so much time to fill but didn't necessarily see it as a problem.

Khamis skilfully reversed into a space as near as possible to his house. He then locked the Pajero whilst complaining about the problems of having to park in the street. Allowing for Khamis' propensity to complain about almost everything, it seemed a fair point. The Pajero was not high value but the road was narrow, cars were parked on both sides, and some cars had so much body damage it looked as if they had been used for stock car racing. It seemed only a matter of time before Khamis' Pajero would be on the receiving end of some unwanted body modifications.

They went through the garden gate, down the cobbled path to the front door. The door looked very old. Salah hadn't seen anything like it before. In the top half were two rectangular glass panels either side of a wooden central section. The glass was opaque with bevelled margins of brightly coloured shapes, not unlike a church window. The central section had a brass door knocker near the top and a letterbox near the bottom. Salah thought it beautiful, in a way.

Once inside he was surprised how dark the hallway was. It

had no windows of its own, the only light coming from half-open doorways to the rooms leading off. The tiled floor consisted of maroon and black interlocking squares and triangles, presumably ceramic of some sort, rather in the style of a giant chessboard. The general effect was attractive but sombre.

Khamis saw Salah looking around. "It says high up on the front wall that this house was built in 1910. Apparently, it has many original features; the hall floor is one, the front door is another and there are one or two original fireplaces. It says in our tenancy agreement that this stuff is of historical interest and we have to look after it."

"If you're used to our way of life it's difficult to understand how people lived in dark houses like this."

"True, Salah, but actually it's not too bad when you get used to it. Let me show you around.

"As you come in through the front door there's a small washroom in the corner on the right. Also on the right is a very small room; it's too small for another student so we don't use it much, just occasionally for the ironing board." Salah had a problem imagining Khamis doing the ironing.

"On the left is the main living room which is where I am. I found the house and arranged the lease, etc, so I get the best room. I don't see why I shouldn't. Second on the left is a smaller room but still a good size. That's Majid's room and as far as I know he's perfectly happy.

"The door at the back of the hall leads under the stairs to the kitchen; it's a bit small but we manage OK. We don't cook much and we have a fridge, a dishwasher and a washer-dryer.

"Up the stairs on the first floor are two bedrooms and a good size bathroom. Reza has the biggest room and Bassam the other. Up the stairs again, on the top floor, is another room that belongs to Karim. The upstairs guys tend to keep themselves to themselves, which is fine. Majid and I keep to ourselves, it all seems to work."

Khamis suggested they have coffee and think about finding something to eat. A search of the fridge and kitchen cupboards produced very little so they agreed to try the little take-away round the corner.

"I haven't tried it myself, Salah, but Majid says it's great, nice food and not expensive."

"Sounds good to me, Khamis, let's give it a go."

They walked down the road together. Salah was amazed at the long row of identical houses. Some looked a mess.

"Probably occupied by students," said Khamis.

"So many still have their curtains shut," said Salah.

"I expect they are still in bed; again, probably occupied by students," concluded Khamis.

They reached Annie's. Annie was an attractive, shapely, middle-aged woman with a warm maternal manner. The two happily regressed to their childhoods and wished they could have a cuddle.

"What can I get for you two boys? Everything is freshly made this morning. You look like you're used to this kind of food."

"We are, but we don't see it very often in this country. I'd like a portion of falafel, some hummus and pitta bread, please."

Annie placed two boxes on the glass shelf above her chilled counter, filled one and handed it to Khamis.

"I've added some salad, no charge."

"Thank you, Annie, that's very kind of you."

Salah asked for the same and he also received a free portion of salad in his box. They paid, thanked Annie again and promised to return another time.

Walking back to Khamis' house they remarked on the weight of their boxes and felt they'd had a good deal from Annie. In Khamis' room they wasted no time in getting their plastic forks out and diving into Annie's food.

"I'll just get rid of the debris and make us another coffee. By the way, how are you getting on with the mating game? You can tell me when I'm back from the kitchen."

"OK, Khamis."

Khamis returned with two mugs of coffee. "Well?"

"Thanks for the coffee, Khamis, and the lunch was excellent. Majid's quite right, Annie's food is delicious and a real taste of home… To answer your question though… this is embarrassing…

I *did* think about what you said and I found *Friends with Benefits* on the Internet."

"And..?"

"I put it on and after a while I fell asleep." Khamis looked disappointed. "But I have made progress with Samara." Khamis looked worried now. "After we spoke I began to see her differently. I now think we should just be good friends and I'm happy with that." Khamis looked relieved. "By the way, I've met another girl I like but it's still early days so I can't tell you anything. Watch this space!"

"Sounds like progress, of a kind. Good luck, Salah."

CHAPTER 2.2

September 17 2002

Salah dropped a tea bag into a mug and filled it with boiling water. Back in his room with tea and a bowl of cereal he realised he needed to get his beans in a row before the first real Facilities Management lecture. After quickly hoovering up his bowl of Shreddies, he showered, changed into his clothes and made sure everything likely to be required was in his rucksack. He went back into the kitchen to wash up by which time several other students had arrived and were leaning out of windows. Salah thought this unusual enough to go over and see what they were doing.

"We're egging the security guy's van," explained one, as if it was the most normal thing in the world. "It's harder than it looks. We've already used up more than a dozen eggs; have you any to spare?"

"Sorry, no. Surely you're worried about being caught?"

"Nah, they would never be able to tell whether it was us or the girls below. If we have to we'll say it must have been them."

"What have they done to deserve this?"

"Nothing, really, it's just a bit of a lark."

Salah cleared up his breakfast things and left the kitchen with mixed feelings. Whilst he could see the funny side of the egging he was glad they didn't ask him to participate.

Before leaving for his lecture, he couldn't resist going back into his room to have a look out of his own window. Although he didn't have the best view of the van it was good enough to see what a terrible mess it was in, especially the windscreen and bonnet, both covered in a mixture of egg whites and yolks. Amazingly, one yolk was actually intact on the bonnet and had almost cooked.

The walk to the lecture room block took longer today for some reason. Arriving in the nick of time, however, Salah looked for familiar faces but had to sit down quickly in the nearest available seat as the lecturer was about to begin.

On the screen was a graphic image displaying the main knowledge areas of Facilities Management. Salah had been looking forward to this moment; now the course was beginning for real.

The lecturer, Dr Sims, began by saying that Facilities Management (FM) is a new academic discipline. He went on to explain that the Institute of Workplace and Facilities Management (IWFM), which was formerly called the British Institute of Facilities Management, has developed and accredits a qualifications framework up to Masters degree level, which is aligned with European definitions and qualifications. He added that the University's FM Programme is accredited by IWFM and is therefore recognised throughout Europe.

Salah was pleased to hear this. He felt he had moved into the big time. By comparison, the Dubai College felt so much like school. Most of the time was spent in classrooms and lessons. Success, if it happened, only meant gaining access to another level of study, whereas here at the University he was trusted to organise his own time and learning activities. Success, when it happened, would lead directly to jobs and careers internationally.

Referring again to the image on the screen the lecturer explained that the programme itself would concentrate on four areas, Asset Management, Risk Management, Business Management and Operations Management, each module containing between three and six knowledge areas. Students would be assessed by a combination of examinations, coursework, assignments and projects.

At this point, Salah started to feel a little queasy. This sounded like a very heavy burden of assessment. Still, all students were in the same situation and he reasoned that the University didn't want people to fail their degrees, did they? That would be bad for the University's reputation, wouldn't it? Also, he must be capable of succeeding or they wouldn't have let him join the University, would they?

Salah wasn't completely reassured by his thoughts; they felt a bit too much like whistling in the dark. The lecturer asked if anyone wanted to ask a question. Samara put up her hand.

"Can you tell us how all the work we did in the first and second years fits into the structure you have just described?"

"Good question. Of course, I can tell you but it would take too long this morning. What I can say is that when you begin each module I am sure you will soon be able to see how earlier work relates. The programme is progressive, so some subject titles in the final year may be the same but they are delivered at a higher conceptual level. For example, if you studied Fire Safety in the second year, this will now be part of the subject delivered more broadly as Security. If you studied Managing People in year two, this will be part of what we now call Human Capital. Do you see what I mean?"

"I think so. Thank you."

"Any more questions? No? Then we'll take a five-minute break and then we shall begin work on the Business Management module.

Salah thought it very brave of Samara to ask a question and he wanted to tell her so. Most students got up and left the lecture room. Salah was looking for Samara when he caught Khamis' eye as he came over.

"Samara was very brave. I wouldn't have had the nerve to ask a question, would you?"

"No, Khamis, I wouldn't." Salah waved at Samara, encouraging her to join them."

"You were very brave, Samara," said Salah.

"I did feel a bit nervous, but I thought it was worth asking."

"Yes, that was very brave of you, Samara. Well done. We all benefitted from the answer he gave you." Khamis had decided to praise her too.

"Thanks, Khamis."

"Salah, shall we have lunch together after the lecture?" Khamis asked.

"Why not? If you're going back home we could go to Annie's again. We don't have to be back for anything this afternoon."

"Fine with me. What about you, Samara? Why not join us? We Emiratis should stick together."

"Thank you. Who's Annie?"

"Come with us and you'll find out."

"OK, I'm in."

Khamis, Salah and Samara sat together for the rest of the lecture, which was right up Salah's street. This module was going to discuss human capital, leadership skills, financial management, contracts and estate management. Salah always preferred subjects where what he was learning involved knowledge and skills that could be easily transferred to a wide range of real-life scenarios.

The lecturer finished on time just as a crowd of students could be heard outside arriving for their turn next in the lecture room. They were very noisy and some of their talk sounded angry. Salah wondered what they were so worked up about.

Khamis, Salah and Samara made their way down the stairs, out of the lecture room and through the waiting students, then out of the building towards the student car park to where Khamis had left his car. They bundled each other in the Pajero and set off for Khamis' house. Samara was particularly pleased to have an opportunity to leave the campus for a while. Khamis was fairly sure he would be able to find a parking place near his house; during the day many Primrose Road residents were either at work, attending colleges or the University. His prediction turned out to be correct.

Khamis' accommodation and living arrangements were new to Samara. Like Salah, she found the old house dark and rather depressing to begin with, although she did think Khamis had a comfortably large bed-sitting room with more space and character than modern rooms in halls of residence.

It was early for lunch so they sat around chatting for a while.

"Samara and I were discussing how noisy and restless the students were at the Dean's welcome this morning. Did *you* notice, Khamis?"

"I know what you mean. I wonder if it was anything to do with whatever's going on at the mosque. Majid said people there are very unhappy, something to do with an American visitor."

"Sounds controversial, although we know why Muslim students might be against it, but why would non-Muslim students be so concerned?"

"Good point, Samara, but there's a fair amount of anti-American sentiment about these days; they're probably more interested in the politics than the religious aspect."

Their conversation continued along the lines of, even if the student unrest is political there may still be a role for the Islamic Society, especially if the unrest gets worse. Samara and Salah said they would try to find out more.

"Our friend, Majid, says the Islamic Society is a waste of space, a well-intentioned but useless talking shop."

"Khamis, are we sure Majid knows what he's talking about?"

"Perhaps not, Samara, but who's for a bite to eat?" Khamis extolled the virtues of Annie's food for Samara's benefit.

"Hello boys. You liked my food; you've come back for more?" asked Annie.

"Hello dear, ladies first; what would you like today?"

Samara replied that the hummus and falafel had been highly recommended. Annie smiled, opened one of her little boxes and began to fill it. Is that all?"

"Yes, thank you."

"I'll give you some of my fattoush to go with it, no charge."

"That's very kind of you. Thanks, Annie."

"You're very welcome, dear. Have you boys tried my shawarma?"

"No, but could we have some today, please?"

Two more boxes were assembled and placed as usual on top of the glass-fronted chiller. Into each went a generous portion of shawarma chicken slices. The smell of spices was wonderful and very nostalgic.

"Is that all?"

"We'll have some fattoush too, please." Annie added their salads, closed the boxes and then placed all three boxes and plastic forks in a small carrier bag, which she gave to Samara. Khamis paid.

Back at the house, Salah asked Khamis what he owed him. Khamis brushed the question aside with a wave of his hand.

"Thanks, Khamis. I owe you."

"So do I."

"Forget it, Samara, please be my guest."

"Thank you, Khamis. I hope I shall be able to return the favour sometime."

Conversation died while forks were diving in and out of the lunchboxes. Samara was visibly delighted to be eating food so much like home cooked food and she was full of praise for Annie who, she said, had not been in any way overrated by 'the boys'.

Khamis collected the boxes and forks and took them away for disposal. Salah took advantage of his absence to tell Samara, confidentially of course, that he had met a nice girl and that he was going to try to get to know her and hopefully ask her out.

"That's such good news, Salah. I couldn't be more pleased. Which course is she on?"

"Actually, she works in an office at the University. I am not making any assumptions, just hoping for the best."

"Good for you."

Khamis returned and asked if anyone would like tea or coffee. There were no takers. Samara said she would like to be back to the University soon as she had planned to do some reading and preparation for tomorrow.

"No problem, I can give you a lift."

"Are you going back too?" Salah asked, surprised.

"Well, no, not especially." Salah was right to be surprised.

"It's OK, Khamis. Samara and I can catch a bus; they're very frequent this time of day."

"It's no problem."

"You're very kind, Khamis but, really, we'll be fine." Samara and Salah got up and looked for their coats.

"OK, if you insist."

"Khamis, I've still got that jar of jalfrezi sauce, you know, from when I went to Tesco, remember, our visit to the High Street? I promised to cook you a meal. I should have done so before now. Anyway, watch this space, it's going to happen."

"Looking forward to it, Salah. There's no rush."

Samara and Salah renewed their thanks and left Khamis. They walked along Primrose Road to the main street and waited at the bus stop. Chatting away during the bus ride, Samara realised how happy she was to have Salah as a friend. He was thinking the same thing. At one time he had romantic hopes and aspirations for Samara. Now he was glad to have a beautiful and intelligent Arab girl as a trusted friend with whom there could never be any complications.

CHAPTER 2.3

September 18 2002

Salah had been looking forward to the Managing Physical Hazards module which, according to the module description, would be about controlling the risks associated with the five main groups of workplace hazards: explosive, flammable, oxidising, gaseous and corrosive.

Salah accepted the general premise that it was a good thing to try to reduce the number of accidents at work. He could see this was good for corporations and for people themselves. He understood that accidents led to absences from work, reduced productivity and increased personal and corporate costs.

This morning was going to be about the storage of liquids and gasses. From the beginning in Dubai, Salah had become especially interested in explosives. He remembered noticing the word 'BLEVE' in last term's course notes. At first, he couldn't remember where he'd seen it before, but then he realised it was the title of a book he'd borrowed from the Dubai College library. No wonder he didn't remember, he'd only borrowed the book as a pretext for going up to the library issue desk to be close to Suhaila. It was purely accidental that it would relate to part of his course.

To say that Salah had researched or studied the topic BLEVE would be an exaggeration, but he had flicked through the pages of the book last term and again when he had realised he had brought it with him. He had also re-read last term's course notes and was reminded of one or two points that had caught his interest earlier. For example, he had been surprised to find that not everything boiled at 100 degrees centigrade like water and was astonished to find that some substances boil at temperatures substantially below room temperature. Salah had enough common sense to realise that if water, a liquid, is cooled it eventually becomes ice, a solid, and that if heated, it becomes steam, a gas, but whilst he'd grasped the concept that substances can exist in different forms, called states of matter, he didn't necessarily understand it.

Turning to the subject of this morning's lecture, Salah was not too astonished to learn that some flammable gasses used to provide energy could be stored as liquids. He remembered that a gas becomes a liquid when its boiling point is reduced. This can be achieved by increasing the pressure surrounding it. If this pressure is subsequently reduced the liquid becomes a gas again, and when a liquid substance becomes a gas it expands and requires more space. So storing a gas as a liquid is more convenient and efficient because it requires less space.

Salah had more or less grasped these scientific principles, although he didn't fully understand these either. But he was beginning to be able to imagine the circumstances that could produce a BLEVE (Boiling Liquid Expanding Vapour Explosion) and was therefore looking forward to learning more.

Arriving at the lecture, Salah noticed that Khamis was already seated so he joined him and they chatted briefly. The lecturer began by revising some of the principles already covered earlier in Dubai, in particular the scientific relationships between pressure, temperature and volume in relation to liquids and gasses. Salah felt good that he had at least turned the pages of the book on BLEVE and revised last term's notes. At least he had some idea of what the lecture was going to be about.

Then the lecturer showed a video of a BLEVE showing how a gas storage tank with a small initial leak became ignited. The tank's pressure relief valve released more gas to reduce the increased internal pressure caused by the heat. This gas also caught fire. The effect of ever increasing heat on the remaining liquid gas in the tank caused the liquid to boil. The boiling liquid produced more and more gas which expanded rapidly and increased the internal pressure further. Eventually the internal pressure was so great that the tank ruptured and a massive cloud of burning gas and liquid was released over a great distance.

Salah experienced a feeling of huge excitement over what he had just seen. He didn't know why or try to analyse why. He was similarly excited by the other videos the lecturer showed from real-life footage of actual BLEVES, in particular, the South Texas oil tank fire. In this case everyone thought that the firefighters had extinguished the fire but the tank shocked everyone by exploding in a deadly fireball.

Salah was amazed at the number of BLEVES that had taken place all over the world involving storage tanks, vehicles, trains and buildings. Towards the end of the session the lecturer suggested that students access relevant sites on the Internet to familiarise themselves with other BLEVES. He asked them to make their own notes to supplement their course notes and to prepare themselves for a question on BLEVES in the module assessment.

Salah arrived early for the Risk Assessment lecture and reviewed the notes he made earlier on the subject. The trickle of students entering the lecture room quickly became a crowd and Salah caught sight of Samara. He waved, trying not to look stupid. She didn't see him so he stood up. Samara then came over with another girl and sat next to him. She introduced him to the other girl and they chatted briefly until the lecture began.

The lecture consisted of a brief overview of the module's contents followed by a revision session on the five-step approach to risk assessment. The lecturer then gave advice about what's required to achieve a high grade in the module assessment. Salah noted that the quality of coursework would be particularly important, especially the practical work. This would be based on applying the five-step approach to risk assessment in the students' union cafeteria.

After the lecture, Salah and Samara chatted again briefly. She and the other girl were obviously keen to get away; they said they were going to 'chill'. Salah couldn't help thinking how things had changed since the Dubai College days when he'd tried so hard and so unsuccessfully to sit next to Samara. Now she was his friend for life. That was progress and very satisfying.

CHAPTER 2.4

September 19 2002

Today was the day Salah was scheduled for his one-to-one meeting with Jack Russell and he was quite looking forward to it.

He found Mr Russell's office and knocked on the door expecting to hear 'come in' or something similar. Instead, Mr Russell opened the door himself, ushered Salah into his office and pointed to an easy chair. This felt informal, even friendly, and Salah was immediately at ease.

"Hello Salah, thanks for coming. Five down, 15 to go."

"It's good of you to see us all individually, it must take ages."

"Actually, I enjoy it and, anyway, it's my job. First, you can call me Jack. Second, there's no agenda, we can talk about whatever we like. OK?"

"OK."

"OK. I expect you remember asking to meet me in Dubai when you wanted to talk about your father's death and then your mother's disappearance. You were worried that when you needed help it was difficult to find someone to talk to in confidence who wasn't also teaching you on the course. You looked at the University's website and found the helping services we offer students here but these were not available in the Dubai College. Is that right?"

"Yes, I was, and yes, that's right."

"Well, this is part of my role as course leader. I won't be teaching on the course but I shall be responsible for everything that affects students' participation and learning. You told me in Dubai you had found on the Internet all the different ways this University provides support for students. If you like I can help you access these services."

"Thanks, Jack, that's great. When I met you in Dubai I was in a bad place. My father had died suddenly and unexpectedly. I didn't really know my father before he died; in fact, I didn't even know he *was* my father. You can imagine, that was all a big shock, but I didn't feel able to grieve for him and felt very confused. Sometimes I felt guilty, sometimes angry. I felt aggrieved towards my mother because she didn't tell me about him and it seemed such a waste to have had a father and yet not know him until he died.

"After the funeral my father's relatives said they no longer needed staff in his villa where my mother and I lived. She was my father's housekeeper and was sent away, I don't know to where. I received a note telling me to leave as soon as possible.

"Although I had no reason to blame myself for anything I began to feel more and more guilty and angry after my mother was evicted from our villa. I was also angry towards my father's family for the way they treated my mother and me and angry with myself for not doing more to support my mother when my father died. I also felt guilty because I had been hostile towards her for not telling me about my father, although I always loved her and she loved me. I felt ever increasing guilt and anger when I realised I was unable to do anything to find her."

"Salah, please let me say before we go any further that I am so sorry you've had to experience these deeply traumatic and life changing events. I can well understand how you must have needed someone to talk with and how distressing it must have been to realise there wasn't anyone available."

"Thanks, Jack. I'm coping better now but sometimes, usually when I am on my own and feeling sorry for myself or homesick, it all comes back to me. I'm better when I am with my friends."

"Salah, I'm not a psychologist but I believe these feelings are entirely normal for anyone in your situation. You mentioned feeling angry more than once. Do you still feel guilt and anger now?"

"I suppose so, when I go over it again in my mind."

"I understand; would you like to meet one of our experienced student counsellors to talk things over?"

"Can I think about that, please? I have managed on my own so far."

"OK. Would you like to continue with your story?"

"So, in spite of everything I continued at the College. I didn't know what else to do when it all seemed completely hopeless. Then I had some luck. Mrs Wankowski, my English teacher, had been worried about my English. Looking back I think she believed that unless I made a huge improvement I would have no chance of progressing to England to complete my degree. She asked to see me to talk about my English and I told her what had just happened to me. She was very interested and concerned and telephoned her husband. They gave me a bed for the night and helped me move my few things out of the villa into her office.

"The next piece of luck was making friends with some Kuwaiti students who offered me a spare room in their villa. Mrs Wankowski and her husband, Janek, encouraged me to live with the Kuwaitis, which they thought would be better for me than staying with them. This arrangement lasted for the rest of my time in Dubai. I lived in a small room at the top of their villa and they didn't even ask me to pay rent. This helped me manage to live on my savings.

"The Wankowskis tried to get help to find my mother by seeking advice from influential Emiratis beginning with the College's Personnel Officer who contacted one of his friends in the Ministry of Labour. It is because of their amazing kindness that I suddenly went from nothing being possible to everything being possible. In short, they are the only reason I am here now."

"That's terrific, Salah, I couldn't be more pleased. I must ask, though… are you sure you have recovered from the effects of all these traumatic experiences? You have, after all, been on such an emotional rollercoaster."

"I am not sure what you mean by 'effects', Jack. I *do* still feel guilty and angry sometimes, wouldn't you? My mother still hasn't been found."

"I do understand, Salah. Is there anything you can think of that I could do to help? For example, are you sure you wouldn't like to discuss your experiences with a trained student counsellor, someone with insights into emotions and feelings and expertise with ways of coping and improving those coping skills?"

"I appreciate your support, Jack, I really do, and I have quite enjoyed telling you my story. But then, of course, I know you; I am not sure I would enjoy telling a stranger about my innermost feelings. Can we leave things as they are for now?"

"OK, Salah, that's fine with me, you can always change your mind at any time if you feel the need. Don't forget I am always here for you if you would like to chat. I am here to help. As I said, it's my job. Good luck with the course."

"Thanks, Jack."

Jack got up and opened the door for Salah to leave. When he'd gone Jack felt uneasy. As he'd admitted to Salah that he wasn't a psychologist, neither had he received very much training for his current role as course leader, which involved counselling students occasionally. However, during the course of his experiences of trying to be helpful, Jack had learned that the best approach when students had problems was to provide non-possessive warmth and temporary support whilst the students tried to solve their problems themselves. If this didn't work and clinical intervention became necessary he was in no doubt they should be left to the professionals.

To a greater or lesser extent, Jack also relied on his instincts and, today, his instincts told him that Salah could be in denial. He had told a good story but seemed over anxious to give the impression he was on top of things. Jack suspected that, deep down, Salah was in turmoil and that guilt and anger, which he had referred to repeatedly, were still present features of his state of mind. Jack decided to make a note of his thoughts and file them away. He would also keep an eye on Salah, from a distance of course.

Salah returned to Sharpe, thinking the meeting with Jack had gone well. He believed he'd acquitted himself OK and that Jack had been a good listener. Then he began to have second thoughts. He wondered why he was so eager to tell Jack a good story and refuse counselling. True, he'd made it to the UK, but nothing had changed; his mother was still missing and there weren't even any leads as far as he knew.

On reflection, there had been no need to make a good impression and gloss over the long and difficult process he'd had to go through so far. But he didn't feel comfortable talking about his current feelings and, maybe, he'd said too much already about his anger, especially as he hadn't been completely honest with Jack. In particular, Salah's anger these days was only partly about his mother and father, now it was much more about injustice generally, about Hani's family and the outrageous treatment of Palestinians. The last thing he wanted was to be referred to a counsellor with the risk that some or all of the true reasons for his anger would be revealed.

Salah tried to put these thoughts into perspective. Here he was beginning the final year of the course. If only his mother could see him, how pleased and proud she would be. Although Salah was fairly pleased with himself he also felt a heavy weight of responsibility. During the chat with Jack, Salah had re-imagined his story and in so doing reminded himself of all those whose support had helped him succeed, people such as his Kuwaiti friends, the College Personnel Manager, those well meaning officials in the Ministries, even Jas in her own way and, of course, the incredible Wankowskis.

Salah felt eternally grateful to Mrs Wankowski for pushing him to better and better standards. He remembered how hard he'd needed to work on his English. He always felt a little emotional when he thought of the extraordinary kindness of the Wankowskis and the sacrifices they had made and would no doubt continue to make. They and many other people had put their faith in him, he *must* succeed; there was no option, no ifs, no buts, no mistakes and no excuses.

CHAPTER 2.5

May 2002

DUBAI

Mrs Wankowski arrived at the College with Salah. His overnight stay had worked well and she was feeling good about herself and her husband for having done a good deed. She had told Salah that he could stay as long as he needed until he found his own accommodation and suggested they meet again at the end of the College day and then travel back together. They went their separate ways.

Mrs Wankowski was left wondering how best she could help Salah. Providing him with a bed for the night on a temporary basis may not be enough. To begin with, Salah had indicated he was desperate to find his mother but felt powerless to do anything. Mrs Wankowski could understand his feeling of helplessness as Salah had no resources of any kind. She realised she didn't know where to begin either, especially if Salah's mother had been returned to India. Surely it would be impossible to find someone in a country the size of India even if you knew where to look.

Then there was the problem of Salah having to live his life without either of his parents. She realised she needed help and decided to make an appointment to see the College's Head of Personnel, Yahya Al Maskari. Fortunately this wasn't difficult and she was soon in his office; he wasn't responsible for students but he was approachable and as a local Emirati he would understand local culture and institutions and be able to advise on how best to proceed.

The first thing she noticed was a picture of Yahya with the

Ruler of Dubai. They were both in military uniforms walking together past a row of soldiers standing to attention with their weapons in the present arms position. Mrs Wankowski asked about the picture. Yahya said it had been taken during one of the Ruler's inspections when he was a unit commanding officer. He was obviously very proud of the picture and of his military service.

Mrs Wankowski explained why she had asked to see him and told him of Salah's story as she remembered him telling it to her. Yahya relayed the story to Mrs Wankowski to assure them both he had understood correctly.

"So, Salah's father was a Sheikh and his mother was an Indian servant in the Sheikh household. The Sheikh, his father, died suddenly and then his family immediately got rid of his mother after the Sheikh's death. Is that it?"

"More or less, Yahya, but it's a bit more complicated. Salah only found out that Sheikh Salem was his father on the day he died. His mother hadn't told him. You can imagine how distressing that would be. Also, Salah received a letter from Sheikh Salem's brother immediately after the funeral saying his mother had returned to India and he should leave the villa without delay."

"So, Salah became parentless and homeless at the same time. Where is he living now?"

"My husband and I are giving him a bed for the night until he finds somewhere."

Yahya said he knew of the Al Munairi family and had heard of Sheikh Salem's death. He thought he'd met one of the Al Munairi brothers at some time but couldn't remember where, when or which one. He wondered whether he knew someone who knew the Al Munairis who might possibly be helpful. Then he realised it would be indecent and certainly frowned upon for anyone to approach one of the Al Munairis on a deeply personal matter whilst they were still grieving over the loss of Sheikh Salem.

He explained that Indian servants were not well treated generally and it was unsurprising that Salah's mother had been returned to India if she was no longer required. He accepted that in this case the situation had been handled badly, even brutally.

Yahya assured Mrs Wankowski he would look into the matter very carefully and let her know whatever he could find out. He realised the implications for Salah for whom this must have been a terrible experience. Yahya accepted the College had a responsibility towards Salah as one of its students. He said also, in addition to the College's duty of pastoral care, he would take a personal interest in the case and do his best to help. Mrs Wankowski said she was most grateful and how pleased she was that she had come to visit him.

Salah had enjoyed the safety and the comfort of the Wankowski's villa and quite liked their English food. Janek didn't say much although he wasn't unfriendly. But much as Salah appreciated the Wankowskis' kindness the homeliness of their villa engendered in him a profound feeling of loss; he missed his mother more than ever and felt very vulnerable without her. He wondered what had happened to her and vowed to find out. He felt guilty he wasn't doing more to find her but didn't think there was any point in searching in Dubai if she had returned to India and India was a vast country – he didn't know anybody in India.

After leaving Mrs Wankowski, Salah went to the College library, passing by the issue desk as closely as possible in the hope of catching Suhaila's eye. He thought he had failed as usual but then he saw a slightly fleeting smile. Perhaps she had noticed him after all. Was this simply wishful thinking? To Salah it felt like progress.

Salah wished to begin the process of finding his mother. He knew he couldn't do this on his own and would need help. He had seen a poster on one of the library noticeboards with '***NEED HELP OR ADVICE?***' in large letters. Here were contact details for the Student Information Service. He found a computer, sat down and searched the University's website.

He found that there were various ways of helping students with problems available from the University. As well as the Student Information Service, there was also the Student Counselling Services and a Multi Faith Centre. He also found that every student was allocated a personal tutor who would be independent of the course's teaching team. Salah wondered if he had been allocated a personal tutor. He decided to ask Mrs Wankowski that evening.

It was soon time to go for the next session of the Surveying module, which Salah was enjoying very much. As luck would have it he saw Khaled heading in the same direction. He hurried to catch him up.

"Hi Salah. I was looking for you earlier. How's it going?"

"Tamam."

"I wanted to tell you that I *did* ask around about accommodation but unfortunately no one came up with anything."

"That's OK, Khaled, thanks for trying."

"Well, actually I *did* have an idea that I wanted to run by you. I spoke to Ali and the other Kuwaitis and they wouldn't mind if you shared our villa. There are two small bedrooms right at the top. The maid uses one while the other isn't used at the moment. The rooms aren't brilliant because they are quite small – they get very hot and they don't have air conditioning. On the good side, you can walk out onto the roof and there's a great view."

"Shukran Khaled, that's fantastic. Thank you so much. Please thank the others."

"Afwan, Salah." *You're welcome.*

"I'm staying with Mr and Mrs Wankowski at the moment so I shall need to speak to them, I don't want to appear ungrateful. Shall we speak again tomorrow?"

"Sure, Salah. Let me know what you want to do. Shall we go to the lecture? I think we're going to be a bit late."

Salah was more than pleased with Khaled's proposal and wondered what Mrs Wankowski would think about it. The last thing he wanted to do was offend the Wankowskis. Another issue was money. This hadn't been mentioned yet in the chat with Khaled but it was going to come up at some point and he would have to pay a share of the rent for the villa. There would be a lot to talk about with the Wankowskis this evening.

Salah and Mrs Wankowski met up as agreed and went to Mrs Wankowski's car. Both had much to say to each other about the day's events but for some reason neither wanted to speak first.

Perhaps Mrs Wankowski was understandably preoccupied with the challenges of driving, especially the traffic congestion noise and other distractions when driving in Dubai. They arrived at the villa and made themselves at home. Mr Wankowski hadn't yet returned. Mrs Wankowski made tea and called out to Salah.

"How was today, Salah?"

"A bit mixed, really. I need to find out what happened to my mum so I went to the library to see if I could find someone to help me. I found Student Information Services on-line and there are several people in the University who help students with problems. These arrangements seem to be for students in the UK, including international students, but I am not sure whom to go to here at the College. By the way, there is mention of a personal tutor who is not part of the course teaching team. Do I have a personal tutor?"

"Well, yes. That would be the year tutor who looks after the second year students. His name is Dr Skyrme."

"How could he help me?"

"Good question. To be very honest I think it would be difficult for an expatriate member of the College staff to get involved without causing offence and possibly even more trouble. I think we really need a local person. Although we are providing a British standard of higher education at our College we must be aware of and abide by the local customs and culture."

"You make it sound very difficult, Mrs Wankowski, but I do see your point. I am the son of a Sheikh but in these circumstances I don't feel able to confront members of my own family about my mother's treatment. How much more difficult will it be for someone outside the family to do so? In any case, the family members will probably say that they have acted within their rights. They might even argue that they have acted reasonably. How can anyone argue against that?"

"Salah, it *is* going to be difficult but we must find a way to locate your mother. Certainly we are not as well resourced as our parent university but this College definitely has a duty of care towards you and our UK partner will not only realise this but also insist that we make whatever arrangements are needed to carry it out. Here's Janek; shall we ask him what he thinks?"

Janek arrived showing all the signs of having had a hard day. Understandably, Mrs Wankowski was more aware of this than Salah and felt that they should not spring anything on him as soon as he came home. She suggested they wait until after dinner to ask if he might be willing to help them. Salah read between the lines.

Neither Mrs Wankowski nor Janek lived to eat but were people who eat to live. Tonight it would be bubble and squeak. Salah was uneasy about the concept of bubble and squeak, but when the plate arrived he was happy to eat it with the fried eggs and baked beans. He left the bacon but not for religious reasons, he just didn't fancy it. Salah wasn't at all sure about religion. Of course, his default position was Islam because of his upbringing and he had observed some of the rituals from time to time, but he had not attended any religious instruction or even thought deeply about it.

Conversation during dinner had been casual and fairly superficial with the Wankowskis re-engaging after a period at work. Nobody came up with anything discordant, challenging or profound. By contrast, after dinner, Mrs Wankowski asked Janek if he would help her and Salah with the problems they had discussed earlier. Janek listened patiently to everything his wife said. He couldn't help noticing the worried look on Salah's face.

Janek was silent for several minutes, apparently thinking deeply. He then said he couldn't think of any reason to be optimistic about solving all the various problems presented. He believed that Western European thinking about what was right and wrong was not very helpful because Arab nations, societies, customs and cultures had evolved so differently. To this extent he shared his wife's view that they needed to enlist a helpful local person but it would need to be someone with good connections and influence with the powers that be. Janek said he was also troubled that wealthy aristocratic families might consider themselves to be above the law and therefore immune to any external influence.

At this point Mrs Wankowski interjected.

"Thank you, Janek. There is something I have been waiting to tell you. I haven't yet mentioned it to Salah. I hope you don't mind, Salah, but I went to see the College's Personnel Manager today to ask his advice. His name is Yahya Al Maskari. He was very approachable and listened carefully to what I told him, all in confidence of course. He said he knew of the Al Munairi family and had heard of Sheikh Salem in particular.

"It was obvious he understood how upsetting it is for Salah to be without his father and mother and was very positive about the College's duty to help in whatever way it can. Yahya promised to make discreet enquiries and to see if there is anything he can do on behalf of the College and personally."

"That's great, Mrs Wankowski. Thank you for taking this up for me. I didn't expect to be able to make much progress today, but you have. Thank you so much."

"I agree. This is a good first step but we mustn't build our hopes up too much, too soon," said Janek.

"Actually, I also have some news. When I first became homeless I told my friend Khaled and asked him if he knew of anyone with a spare room or other accommodation. He said he would ask around. I saw Khaled again today and he told me nobody had come up with anything. He went on to say he and the other Kuwaitis would be happy for me to have the small room at the top of their villa."

Salah was anxious, being unsure how this information would be received. He was reassured when Mrs Wankowski said that of course it would be better for him and much more normal for him to live with other students. She seemed enthusiastic about the idea of Salah moving in with the Kuwaitis. In fact, she couldn't think of anything against the idea. Janek agreed; Salah felt relieved and said he would let Khaled know and arrange a convenient time to move in.

Privately, the Wankowskis were relieved too. They were aware of the potential difficulties that could arise if one of the College's tutors appeared to be over identifying with a student. Even if this was not true, the perception that it might be true was all that would be needed to cause trouble for Mrs Wankowski and Salah, and possibly for the College as a whole.

CHAPTER 2.6

Salah was beginning to feel a little happier today, probably because he was aware now that he would get help to find his mother. Also, whist he was still enjoying the Wankowskis' kindness and hospitality, the awkward discussion about moving in with the Kuwaitis had happened yesterday and was behind him. He was relieved that, far from being offended or disapproving, the Wankowskis had been thoroughly supportive of the idea.

Hoping the Kuwaitis hadn't changed their minds he now needed to speak to Khaled. Luckily, he would be seeing him again this morning at the Surveying module. They had worked as partners on the fieldwork and Salah had the feeling they would both be happy for this to continue. Fieldwork took place outside the classroom, usually around the campus but sometimes even further afield; this provided multiple opportunities for a private chat.

"By the way, I have spoken to the Wankowskis and they don't have a problem with me sharing your villa. So if you and the others are still OK with it I could move in more or less any time. What would I have to pay for my rent?"

"Good for you, Salah, I am pleased for you. I'm sure we'll get along great. I haven't spoken to the others about rent. I've no idea. We can sort that out later. So, when would you like to move in?"

"I'd like to as soon as possible but I don't want to upset the Wankowskis; they'll be expecting me to have a meal with them this evening. What about tomorrow morning?"

"OK, but make it early. I shall need to be there to let you in and I don't want to be late for College; say 8 am?"

"OK, Khaled, will do. I expect Mrs Wankowski will help me with my stuff."

After the Surveying module, Salah returned to the main building, went upstairs and made his way to Mrs Wankowski's room. She had mentioned on their way back to the villa that she wished to speak to Salah about his English. He wasn't looking forward to this conversation and had successfully avoided it thus far. But today he decided against putting it off any longer and went to her room to see if she was free. They could discuss his progress with English and he could also take the opportunity to ask her about moving in with the Kuwaitis.

"Come in. Oh, hello Salah, I'm with another student at the moment. Would you mind coming back later?"

"OK, Mrs Wankowski. When would be good for you?"

"Say half an hour?"

"Fine."

Half an hour later, Mrs Wankowski was gently reminding Salah that if he wished to progress to the final year of the course at the parent university in the UK he needed to clear two hurdles: one, he must achieve a level of English acceptable to the university; two, he must achieve an examination result that places him in the top tranche of students to be sure of Ministry of Higher Education funding. This was only available to the best students on a quota basis.

She said she was ill at ease speaking to Salah in these terms, feeling the timing was unfortunate to say the least. She realised how very upset he is about his mother and his current circumstances were far from satisfactory. She expected he was having great difficulty applying himself to his academic work. Even so, these issues had to be raised and improvements agreed. It was not so much his spoken English, which was quite good, but his written English that required improvement. It was currently well below the standard needed to be reached by the end of the academic year.

Salah listened and nodded enthusiastically. He knew he needed to improve his English and would have to spend more time on it. He agreed to submit more written work for Mrs Wankowski to critique. She said she would allow him a little more time but she would then be tough with him for his own sake. She would not allow him to avoid the issue.

"Thank you, Mrs Wankowski. I realise that this is for my own good. Now can we speak about my move into the Kuwaitis' villa?"

"Of course, Salah."

"I told Khaled that you and Mr Wankowski are OK with me sharing the Kuwaiti villa. He said I could move in any time. We talked about tomorrow morning. Would that be possible, do you think?"

"I don't see a problem, Salah. I can give you a lift and help you with your things. I assume you know where it is. What time do you need to be there?"

"Khaled would like me to come early so he's not late for College; would 8 am be OK?"

"It's OK with me, Salah; I am always up early."

"That's great, Mrs Wankowski, thank you again and again. I shall always be grateful to you both for helping me at such a difficult time. Really, I shall never forget you and Mr Wankowski."

"Salah, we are both pleased to have been able to help. We shall miss you but you are doing the right thing. Life will be much more normal for you from now on. We shall be close by if you need any more help from us, whatever that might be. We can talk more this evening at home."

"That's very kind. Thanks. By the way, would it also be OK if I make my own way back this evening? Khamis and I are going to compare notes and work on our Risk Assessment assignments."

"Of course, Salah. See you later."

Yahya arrived at his office, sat at his desk and considered his priorities for the day. This caused him to reflect on the assurances he'd given Mrs Wankowski yesterday about looking into the problem of Salah's mother. He'd promised to take a personal interest in the matter, which of course he would, but to start with he didn't know where to begin.

Then Yahya had an idea; he would contact the Ministry of Labour. Presumably if Salah's mother had been working in Dubai she would need to have obtained a Labour card. To obtain a Labour card she would have needed a sponsor. He reached for his *Directory of Government Ministries* and began to browse the list of Ministry of Labour Departments until he reached the Labour Card Department.

Someone 'phoned back within a few minutes.

"We've made enquiries about your problem family and have found some information in-house. Assuming the family name is Malik, we can confirm that Aparna Malik's Visa and Labour Cards were cancelled. The reason given was because she had returned to India. We have no information about why or how she was returned yet. I've asked a colleague to check airline passenger lists to see if she was on any flights back to India on the day her Visa and Labour Cards were cancelled. These arrangements are usually coordinated. I shall contact you again if we have further information."

"Thank you, you've been very helpful. I look forward to hearing from you again soon."

There was a knock on the door.

"Oh Yahya, you're busy; it can wait, it's not urgent."

"Come in, Mrs Wankowski, I'm not in any hurry. How can I help?"

"Well, I just wanted to update you about Salah, the boy we spoke about recently. He was staying with Janek and I until he found his own accommodation; I am not sure whether I told you. Anyway, he has been lucky and was offered a room with Kuwaiti students who have a villa and he's just about to move in."

"Thank you for telling me. As it happens, I just spoke today with someone senior in the Ministry of Labour. We discussed Salah and the urgent need to find his mother. Regrettably, I am unable to report much progress at the moment but it's early days and several people are trying to help us. I can say that Aparna Malik's Visa and Labour cards were both cancelled. The reason given was 'Returning to India'. The person I spoke to is now checking flight details."

"I see, so she wasn't an illegal immigrant worker."

"It seems not. But as I am sure you've heard, Indian servants are often treated very badly; she could be anywhere, even out of the country by now. Her sponsor was Sheikh Salem Al Munairi and her employment seems to have been above board, but we don't know yet how she came to be in Dubai or how Sheikh Salem found her.

"There are many problems. Women are contacted by agents in India and lured by the promise of attractive jobs in the Gulf Countries. The women pay the agents a commission fee for finding them a job. They are then trafficked overland to Dubai, which is the main hub of the racket. These women are 'bought' by agents and enter Dubai on Visit Visas, they are then sold to local employers or trafficked onward to other Gulf Countries; they don't usually possess official documents and so are vulnerable to exploitation and are also unable to seek help from official bodies. There's little chance of escape."

"So, you're saying that if she came through an agent she may have been handed back or even sold back to the agent who supplied her. Then she may have been sold to another employer locally or even trafficked to another country. I suppose this is the worst-case scenario as it would then be impossible to find her," Mrs Wankowski said, trying to ascertain the situation.

"I'm afraid so, it's not going to be easy."

"Thank you, Yahya. I am sure you are doing your best. We must of course make every effort to find Salah's mother but I also have other worries. I believe his mother was giving him a small allowance from her wages. Obviously this is not happening now, so I wonder how he is going to be able to afford rent, clothes, books and food. And, in the long term, if he is successful this year academically and qualifies for progression to the final year of the course in the UK, how is he going to cope financially with everything that would involve?"

"I see your point, Mrs Wankowski. I find myself at a loss. As far as I am aware this College has no arrangements for supporting students financially, whatever the circumstances. You could approach the Ministry of Higher Education but I am not very optimistic they can help. It is my understanding that the Ministry will be happy to pay his fees in the UK if he reaches the required standard, on the basis that all other expenses are met from private funds."

"I am also at a loss, Yahya. I expect you're correct about the Ministry. Can you think of any other organisations or individuals that I could approach?"

"Not at the moment, Mrs Wankowski, but I shall give this careful thought. What Salah really needs is for someone, or a family, to adopt him although I am not at all sure how that could be arranged."

"Thanks, Yahya. I hope we can speak again soon."

"You're more than welcome, Mrs Wankowski."

As she was leaving, the word 'adopt' suddenly struck Mrs Wankowski like a bolt from the blue. For her, this was truly a Damascus moment. She felt the emotional impact in her stomach as if she had just narrowly avoided being hit by an express train – a strange mixture of panic and excitement.

Returning to her office to collect personal belongings and homework, Mrs Wankowski made her way to her car and drove home. She made herself a cup of tea and found a comfortable chair in which to unwind. She never knew exactly when Janek would arrive home. This wasn't a problem as she always had things to do, either her college-work or housework. Today she had no idea what they were going to eat for dinner.

She always heard him arriving home; first the electric gate rolled noisily along its track until it clanged open and then, when it closed, a car door slammed shut, then the key turned in the back door and Janek would come in and announce himself.

"I'm home."

"In the sitting room," she announced. "Would you like some tea?"

"OK, I'll make it; another cup?"

"No, thanks; I'm fine."

Mrs Wankowski let Janek have his tea and unwind, then they chatted about their day as usual. She updated him about Salah's moving to the Kuwaitis' villa in the morning. Janek hardly reacted to this news, just as he had accepted it when she phoned him to tell him she was coming home with Salah. Maria realised how lucky she was to be married to such an easy-going, accepting and laid-back husband.

"What are we having for dinner?"

"Sorry, I haven't figured that out yet, probably three jumps at the cupboard door."

"Well, as Salah is leaving us tomorrow why don't we all go to a restaurant? It will be good not to have to cook and wash up."

"That's a great idea, Jan; I expect he'll be here soon."

CHAPTER 2.7

Salah was navigating for Mrs Wankowski; he was sure they were in the correct street but not quite sure which villa he needed until he saw Khaled standing at the front door as they drove past. They reversed, electric gates opened slowly and Mrs Wankowski was able to drive in. She got out and said hello to Khaled who came over to help Salah unload. He and Salah carried the boxes and bags up the steps to the front door and thanked Mrs Wankowski. She left and Khaled ushered Salah into the villa.

He felt strange using the front door. Salah had been accustomed to using the back door where he lived before. He put his boxes and bags on the floor and looked around. His first impression was that it was much smaller and less grand than Sheikh Salem's villa. There was a door to his left and one to his right. Khaled explained these were designed to be separate entrances to the living rooms for males and females. Salah said he was aware of this tradition in Arab homes.

Ahead was a large entrance hall with a smallish open area to the right, a door in the far right corner and another in the far left corner with stairs leading off from the entrance hall. Khaled said the room to the right was his room and the one to the left was the kitchen. He helped Salah carry his things and led the way upstairs, a flight to the first floor with four more bedrooms, then a narrow stairway leading to a door opening onto the flat roof.

Once they reached the roof there were two more doors.

"The door on the right is the maid's room and on the left is your room."

They put Salah's boxes on the floor. There was a bed, a

tall cupboard, a smaller bedside cupboard with a lamp and a washbasin.

"It is very basic, but what do you think?"

"It's fine, Khaled, more than fine; actually, there's everything I need. With a few personal possessions here and there it will look homely and comfortable too. I am so grateful. Thank you again."

"It's very small and it's too hot during the hot months. I am sorry there's no air conditioning. You can always come into the house to cool down. The washbasin has hot and cold water but, as I am sure you know, all the water has to be delivered to the villas and stored in big tanks on the roofs. In the cooler months the cold water is never really cold and in the hot months both the cold and the hot are often too hot for comfort. It can be scalding hot, especially after the heat of the day. It's less of a problem first thing in the morning.

"There is a tap and a bucket just outside that you can fill when you want a shower. If you fill it before you need it and leave it in the shade or overnight it will be cool enough to pour over yourself. The maid does it all the time."

Salah felt a flutter of excitement at the thought of the maid taking a shower on the roof.

"We should set off for the College, Salah; I assume you'd like a lift."

"Thanks, Khaled. I don't know how I could ever repay your kindness."

The muezzin is reciting the call to Friday prayers; it's the Arab weekend. Mrs Wankowski was sitting with her laptop doing research into the adoption rules in the Emirates. Janek was at the gym with friends enjoying the exercise machines, the plunge pool, the sauna, the steam room, the swimming pool and Jacuzzi, as well as the occasional Thai massage.

The Wankowskis had neither wanted children nor *not* wanted them. As far as Mrs Wankowski could remember, there had never been any discussion with Janek around the subject. Both had been married before and their first marriages had been unhappy and childless. Both were divorced when they met. Their own marriage had been blissfully happy up to now and they hadn't felt they needed anyone else in their relationship.

Mrs Wankowski recently became aware that something new was happening to her. She had begun to realise she had been fretting about Salah moving out of their villa. She had encouraged him to move in with the Kuwaiti students for what she believed were the right reasons and had no regrets about the advice she'd given him, but she didn't anticipate that she would miss him when he left. She told him she would but thought it was out of respect, however, her recent upsurge of maternal feelings towards him surprised her.

She reasoned that these feelings were her response to the terrible misfortunes Salah had experienced, the same feelings any decent person would have in the same circumstances, nothing else. Otherwise she wouldn't feel any emotional attachment to him – but something had changed.

She had enjoyed Salah being in their villa and she began to wonder whether she had been in denial. Being helpful towards Salah when he was experiencing a crisis was one thing but perhaps helping Salah was also helping her to meet her own needs. If so, what were these needs; the need to be nice or nurturing, the need to be a good Christian, the need to be useful, valued, appreciated or just the need to be needed, or was it simply her maternal clock ticking away without her realising?

Mrs Wankowski hadn't yet told Janek about her conflicted feelings over Salah, neither about her most recent conversation with Yahya. She decided this could no longer be avoided; she must be completely honest with him. She wasn't looking forward to it, especially to raising the idea of adoption. She knew Janek so well and yet had no idea to how he would react. At least she could say that the idea had come from Yahya and that he was talking generally. He was not suggesting that they adopt Salah and hopefully this would lessen the bombshell effect on Janek.

Mrs Wankowski didn't have to wait long before Janek returned; he seemed in a good mood. He was pleased with his performance on the running machine and his efforts on some of the other exercise equipment. He'd enjoyed a relaxing sauna, which involved lots of male bonding and had finished with a short swim and a refreshing cold shower. Mrs Wankowski felt there might not be a better time to unburden herself.

"Jan, I have been meaning to tell you about my recent meeting with Yahya."

"Go ahead."

"Well, as we discussed, he is doing his best to trace Salah's mother and he has contacted one or two potentially useful people who are also working on it. There is nothing to report yet. Reading between the lines, I don't think Yahya is very optimistic but, as he said, it is still early days."

"OK, so—"

"Well, I told Yahya that finding Salah's mother wasn't the only issue. There is also the problem of how Salah is going to cope generally without parents and without even the small amount of financial support his mother provided. I am thinking about food and rent; how's he going to be able to eat? I'm sure the Kuwaitis will expect him to pay something. Then at some stage he will need books, transport, clothes, etc, and things will be even more difficult or even impossible if he makes it to the UK for the final year."

"Maria, you are absolutely right. I've already thought of some of these things; so what are we going to do? Putting him up for a couple of nights is clearly not enough. The way I see it we have two choices: either we congratulate ourselves for taking him off the streets for a couple of nights and let him sink or swim – he'll probably sink, or we find a way to be supportive in the medium to longer term and, with luck, he'll swim. We can afford to be more helpful. The question is: do we wish to and how do we do it?"

Maria was hugely relieved and more than a little surprised by Janek's response, so much so she felt emboldened.

"Jan, what Yahya actually said at one point was that Salah needs someone to adopt him. He was speaking generally, of course. He wasn't suggesting us necessarily."

"OK, fine, but it looks as if this is going to be difficult. To begin with, is Salah an Emirati? He seems to have an Indian mother and an Emirati father. Were his parents married?"

"I've discovered that a child of an Emirati father married to a non-Emirati woman has or can apply for Emirati nationality. As far as marriage is concerned, I believe that an Emirati man can legally marry a woman of a different nationality and religion. The marriage has to be registered with a Sharia court in Dubai. I think we can assume that these courts keep records."

"So we would have to check whether Salah is an Emirati and whether his mother was married to his father."

"I suppose so."

"Do you think Yahya would be willing to help us?"

"I expect he would but we can't expect him to take on a huge amount of extra work. He knows this country and could probably put us in touch with the right people. Perhaps we could meet him together just so he knows we are both on the same page."

"Maria, we must be careful not to get carried away. We haven't the first idea what Salah would think about our conversation today. What are we going to say to him? Our best efforts would come to nothing if he doesn't like the idea."

"True. Why don't I go back to Yahya to let him know what we have discussed? I can ask his advice on how to go about it if we do finally decide to adopt Salah, by which time we shall of course have spoken to Salah and we shall know whether he likes the idea."

"Sounds good to me, but would you like me to come too? I think he and I have met before."

"Why not?"

"If you let me know when Yahya is available, I'll try to free myself and join you."

"Thanks, Jan."

Maria and Janek spent the rest of the day feeling especially close together. Although they had been happily married for years they somehow felt as if they had been leading separate lives with separate careers, daily routines and social networks. Sometimes it seemed as if they only came together to eat and sleep.

Today was different. They were on the same page as far as

Salah was concerned. They were both conscious that they were embarking on a challenging joint project. There would be a great deal of work to do and many obstacles to be overcome. They would need all their individual energy as well as the synergy that would come from being absolutely together.

They went to the kitchen and prepared a light lunch and, whilst eating, discussed the fact that they had not been on holiday for a while. Maybe that was partly because they were living every day in one of the most iconic and sought-after holiday locations in the world. Where would they go to find better relaxation facilities and opportunities than on their doorstep? They agreed they couldn't possibly have a holiday until they knew what they were going to do about Salah and if they were going to adopt him it must be accepted by everyone concerned, most importantly, by Salah. Then they would treat themselves to a holiday.

After lunch they cleared up and decided on a drive, something they had not done for a while on a Friday afternoon. They got into their car and made for the Sharja-Kalba Road heading towards the Oman border. They ignored the turning off to Fujairah and followed the road to Hatta, passing through farming communities, with a backdrop of mountain landscapes. After about an hour they reached Hatta in the middle of the Al Hajar Mountains and close to Oman. They loved to go to Hatta, an historic sheikdom surrounded by heritage villages amid spectacular mountain scenery.

Finally they arrived at one of their all-time favourite destinations. They turned down the driveway to the JA Hatta Fort Hotel, a modern resort set amidst immaculately manicured green lawns and lush, green palm trees. They parked and went into the Café Gazebo, an all-day dining restaurant perched high above the chilled pool, with panoramic views of the mountains. They chatted about whether to stay in the temperature-controlled café shielded by shaded glass or go to the outside terrace overlooking the pool. They decided on the terrace, a perfect location from which to while away an afternoon sipping tea.

Maria and Janek were in their element until the afternoon

began to draw to a close. They calculated that if they left to go back to their villa within the next few minutes they should arrive home just ahead of sunset, followed by showers, supper, the TV news, a short read with a nightcap, bed and sleep. Not a bad day.

CHAPTER 2.8

September 20 2002

ENGLAND

Friday prayers begin at 1 pm; Salah and Khamis arrived at the mosque a few minutes before. It was the first time attending the local mosque for both of them and the first time Salah had attended Friday prayers anywhere. There was plenty of space in the very large car park. People were slowly making their way into the buildings and Salah and Khamis joined the queue.

Salah felt nervous about not having been to Friday prayers before and was unsure of what to expect. Initially, he was unnerved by the large number of other men, all in various styles of traditional Arab dress. They were strangers to Salah but apparently not to each other. In fact, everyone appeared to know everyone else, so they were probably mostly regular attendees. Salah wondered if Hani would also be there and regretted not asking him if he would like them to go together; he should have remembered, after all, he'd suggested it.

They found themselves within an attractive courtyard at the centre of which was a fountain with multiple washbasins. Salah realised this was the ablutions area. He knew it was necessary to be clean before attending prayers and had taken extra care with his morning shower. Nevertheless, he was happy to observe the custom of ritual washing. But the basins were all in use. Salah was concerned that if they waited for a basin to become free they would be late for prayers. Khamis said not to worry, as they would go to the restrooms to wash instead. Eventually it was their turn to go through the main door.

After removing their shoes and washing their feet they entered the Musallah and a door marked '*Prayer Hall*', right foot first, and sat down on the carpet facing the qibla indicating the direction towards Mecca. The hall was almost full but there was room for Salah and Khamis to sit at the back. Salah was happy to sit at the back because he wanted to be unnoticed and to be able to see everything that happened.

Khamis whispered that it was usual to offer a short personal prayer, like a prayer to greet the mosque. Salah did so. Other congregants arrived and filled up the remaining spaces. Salah and Khamis were now shoulder to shoulder on both sides. One congregant stood up and gave the call to prayer after which there was complete silence. The Imam stood up to begin his sermon.

"Bismillāh ir raḥmān ir raḥīm." (In the name of God, the gracious, the merciful).

"Our Muslim brothers and sisters are dying; not only of old age or poor health; they are being killed; killed by enemy action; fighting in wars; killed resisting occupation of their country; killed as a result of deprivation following expulsion from their homes and lands. They are being killed in their thousands, even millions; many for no reason other than being in the wrong place at the wrong time; ordinary people; killed by what is politely called collateral damage, the damage caused to non-combatants by every form of military violence and destruction known to humanity and these killings are occurring today in Palestine, Iraq, Afghanistan, Pakistan, Syria and elsewhere.

"The next Palestinian to be killed is likely to be aged 18 or even less. He will not die in combat; he is not allowed to join an army; his country is not allowed to have an army. He is a young civilian whose country is illegally occupied by an enemy, he will die protesting at the deprivation of all his human rights by the occupying power; his protest will be pathetically ineffective. He may have a handful of stones, a wooden implement or nothing at all. He may simply go to a so-called security fence and shout slogans or shake the wire. However he protests, however ineffective, he risks being killed.

"True, Muslims have sometimes been killed by other Muslims, but the common factor in these killings is the United States of America. It has been estimated that as many as 5,000,000 Palestinians have died since the creation of the State of Israel, although it's difficult to establish exact numbers. Israel could not have carried out its policies of ethnic cleansing and genocide against Palestinians without political and military support from the US. Neither would it have been able to persist in flouting international law and opinion.

"Since the end of the Second World War the US has invaded Korea, Vietnam, Iraq and Afghanistan. Other countries have also been caught up in these wars, for example, Pakistan, Yemen, and now Syria.

"Following the Second World War, Russian Communism was imposed in Europe with the Berlin Wall, the so-called Iron Curtain, resulting in the so-called Cold War. In China another Communist government appeared. US governments of the time argued that if communism wasn't contained other countries would also become Communist, the so-called domino theory.

"Korea had been a part of the Japanese empire until the defeat and withdrawal of Japan in August 1945 following the Second World War. The victors, Russia and the US, divided the Korean peninsula and occupied the north and south respectively. The Korean War began when the North Korean Communist army, supported by Russia and China, invaded the non-communist south and soon overran South Korea. The US came to South Korea's aid.

"In Korea, the US took sides in two competing popular visions of the kind of society that Koreans wanted. The North and South fought a bloody and frustrating war for the next three years; nearly 5,000,000 people died, more than half of these were civilian, about 10% of Korea's pre-war population. This war has still not ended; the most achieved was a ceasefire and a return to the status quo.

"This was soon repeated in Vietnam. Following the defeat and withdrawal of the French colonial power, Vietnam was split into two by international agreement. The partition was to be temporary and was followed by national elections to choose a leader for a unified Vietnam. When it looked as if the Communist leader, Ho Chi Minh, would be the winner, the leader of the

South, with US agreement, he decided to cancel the election.

"This was the beginning of a 20-year failed attempt to create an independent South Vietnam. The US fought against the Communist North, which was supported by Russia and China and against Communist guerrilla fighters in the South, known as Viet Cong, who were supported by the Communist North. The Viet Cong's objective was to undermine the government of the South and reunify Vietnam.

"Almost 60,000 US military were killed, with 300,000 injured. Between 200–250,000 South Vietnamese fighters were killed and 1.1 000,000 North Vietnamese and Viet Cong fighters were killed. In addition, 2,000,000 Vietnamese civilians were killed with 5.3 000,000 injured. The War ended with the Paris Peace Accords in January 1973. Saigon fell on 30 April 1975 and Vietnam was united as one country under Communist rule.

"The Vietnam War, as with the Korean War, was like a civil war with a nationwide struggle by Communist-led forces against the American-backed governments in the South. The US justified their involvement as preventing the spread of communism. They failed. The cost of this failure in human lives was enormous on all sides. The domino theory didn't happen. Communism collapsed in Russia and elsewhere, not because it was defeated militarily but because it was judged to be no longer fit for purpose and the spread of communism ceased to be an issue on the world's political stage.

"Not only did the US's attempt to halt the spread of communism fail spectacularly, the mission itself became discredited. The US needed another mantra to justify its military adventures and interventions in other countries. Then, in 1990, a new opportunity occurred. After decimating millions of Asians in the most barbaric fashion imaginable, it would now be the turn of Arabs to face US barbarism.

"In 1990, Iraq invaded Kuwait. The United Nations, including America, imposed economic sanctions against Iraq. These seriously worsened the quality of life for all Iraqis. Then, a coalition of 34 countries, led by the US, built up a huge military force to invade Kuwait and Iraq. One of the preparations for Desert Storm was to deploy American troops in Saudi Arabia ostensibly to defend Saudi Arabia. No doubt the real priority was to

protect the Saudi oil fields.

"Operation Desert Storm was a military success resulting in the defeat of Iraq and Iraq's withdrawal from Kuwait. But Saddam Hussein was left in power and this was disaster for the Iraqis. Dissident groups were encouraged by the US to rebel against Saddam Hussein but they were not supported. The rebel Kurds and Marsh Arabs were particularly betrayed by the US. Saddam was able to continue his ethnic cleansing of the Kurds in the North and purge the Marsh Arabs in the South.

"One and a half million Kurds had to escape from the towns to the mountains, to Iran and to Turkey. Thousands were gunned down daily in refugee columns strafed by helicopters. The Marsh Arabs were forced to flee to Iran after their marshes were drained by Hussein and their habitat deliberately destroyed. Those remaining were killed and their homes destroyed.

"Today's age of terror was partly shaped by this first Gulf War and its consequences. After Desert Storm, Osama bin Laden concluded that the US could not be successfully challenged on the battlefield but it could be confronted by deadly infiltrators, by a fifth column or simply by fear.

"He mobilised Al-Qaeda, which began as a response to the 1979 Soviet invasion of Afghanistan. Muslims throughout the world were shocked by Soviet aggression and roughly 20,000 foreign fighters arrived to help Afghans resist Soviet forces. After Desert Storm, one of the principal goals of Al-Qaeda was to drive the US armed forces out of the Saudi Arabian peninsula. Members of Al-Qaeda planned violent attacks and issued fatwas indicating that under Islamic Law such attacks were justified and necessary. Then, in 2001, Al-Qaeda attacked the US on its own soil. Their reasons: US support for Israel, US troops in Saudi Arabia and sanctions against Iraq. Now the US had its new mantra. The war on communism would be replaced by the War on Terror.

"In 2001, the US invaded Afghanistan supported by close allies. One aim was to remove the Taliban from power. The rise of the Taliban had occurred as a result of the civil war that followed the withdrawal of Soviet troops in 1989 when Pashtun forces from the South drove the Tajiks back to the North. Another aim was to dismantle Al-Qaeda and to deny it a safe

base in Afghanistan. The Taliban were sheltering Al-Qaeda's Osama bin Laden after the September 11 2001 attacks on the US.

"The war is still continuing and has cost the lives of more than 350,000 military and tens of thousands of Afghan civilians. The US built up a force of 100,000 troops as part of NATO[4] to hold land and establish a presence in Taliban valleys and villages. Millions of dollars were spent monthly to impress the Taliban with US resolve.

"But the policy was to last only until Afghan troops were trained ready to take over. The Afghan National Army increased in size and capability but could never have matched NATO nor hold the ground occupied by NATO forces. Corruption was another problem undermining its effectiveness.

"The Taliban simply waited while thousands more died or were injured, taking advantage of the weakness of the Afghan forces and taking back more and more territory. In spite of a new constitution and presidential elections, the insurgency and militancy continued and extended to Pakistan. NATO handed over security for the whole country to Afghan forces who soon lost more territory and incurred losses at an ever increasing rate. The Taliban insisted that all foreign troops leave Afghanistan while the US tried to oust the Taliban from Kabul.

"In fact, very little has been achieved by the war in Afghanistan. Al-Qaeda hid away in the eastern hills. Osama bin Laden was killed in Pakistan, not Afghanistan. The US is back to square one. It continues to struggle to deal with extremists and with helping to ensure that Afghanistan becomes a viable and secure country for its people. Even so, thousands of refugees are fleeing, many reaching Europe. The West is discredited throughout the country and ISIS[5] has emerged in Eastern Afghanistan as a radical alternative for those wanting to take the insurgency further and faster. ISIS captured large areas from the Taliban, as well as the mountain area of Tora Bora, formerly used by Al-Qaeda.

"With the possible exception of the First Gulf War, the wars I mentioned earlier produced few beneficial outcomes at enormous cost to human life, both military and civilian. In every case, the US failed to understand the

---

4. North Atlantic Treaty Organization
5. Islamic State of Iraq and Syria

countries it was invading and never won the hearts and minds of the people invaded. In many cases, the people the US was supposedly helping came to regard the US with contempt, not only because of the wrongheaded ways of the conflict itself, but because of the behaviour of the US military.

"The South Koreans didn't like their women being raped by US soldiers, nor by the way the US defended and protected the perpetrators. The Vietnamese will not forget the My Lai massacre where several hundred villagers were murdered by US soldiers, neither the slaughter of Vietnamese citizens on an industrial scale by US firepower. The US's uses of chemical weapons such as napalm, which caused painful deaths by burning, and dioxin, used in Agent Orange, which caused major health problems lasting until today, are unlikely ever to be forgotten. Neither is the lack of effort made to hold those responsible for war crimes accountable. Even worse, the soldier responsible for the My Lai massacre was actually pardoned by the US President at the time.

"The Afghans didn't like US soldiers burning copies of the Quran, urinating on dead Afghan bodies whilst being filmed or murdering innocent villagers. The Iraqis didn't like the widespread abuse of prisoners and detainees, some as young as 14 years old, nor did they like the many deaths in custody, some violent. Again, little action was taken against those responsible.

"Not surprisingly, anti-American feeling became more widespread around the world than ever before. People no longer believe that US wars were a valid response to communist aggression or helpful interventions in civil conflict. People are more likely to believe that the US has carried out colonial, even imperialist counter-revolutions to crush national movements perceived by the US, to be against its interests.

"The US has fostered the belief it is the only power that can bring peace and freedom to the world. But arrogant US unilateralism has certainly not brought peace. Neither has it helped other countries towards self-determination. On the contrary, the US has infuriated Muslims worldwide by using the language of liberation and reason whilst appointing itself judge and jury over the affairs of Muslim nations. As an invading power it has acted like God.

"The US says it is conducting a war against terror. But US foreign policy

has had the effect of increasing terror in the world, not reducing it. It has given the world global jihad. The language of jihad: fundamentalism, radicalisation, terrorism and asymmetric warfare are now on everyone's minds and lips.

"Members of Al-Qaeda believe that the killing of non-combatants is justified and acceptable within their religion and ignore those scriptures that have a different meaning. Al-Qaeda also wants all laws to be based strictly on Sharia law. US foreign policy has legitimised Al-Qaeda and created the suspicion that it is part of Christian Jewish conspiracy to undermine or even destroy Islam.

"ISIS grew out of Al-Qaeda in Iraq (AQI), which wanted to remove all foreign troops and establish a Sunni Islamist state and government. The Islamic State of Iraq (ISI) renamed itself Islamic State of Iraq and Syria (ISIS) when the civil war in Syria started and spread quickly throughout Iraq and Syria, declaring its territory a caliphate. ISIS ideology is a particularly brutal form of Islam, particularly their belief that those not sharing its world view should be killed. They see this as a cleansing process.

"ISIS has destroyed historic sites, carried out 'ethnic cleansing' of Yazidis and Assyrians, enslaved Yazidi women and executed foreign journalists and other workers. It has also carried out or sponsored many terrorist atrocities around the world. It has carried out terrorist attacks and executions in America, Britain, Egypt, France, Spain, Turkey, Syria, Bangladesh, Yemen and Libya (Christian Ethiopian migrant workers).

"US and Iraqi forces formed a large coalition including Iraqi, Kurdish, Turkish, other Arabic and European Forces to prevent ISIS from capturing Baghdad. Since then, ISIS's territorial gains have been significantly reversed and reduced, almost removing ISIS from Iraq. This effort to contain and eliminate ISIS will need to continue for some years."

The Imam sat down and offered silent prayers. Then he stood again and delivered a final summary.

"World leaders seem to have accepted, then and now, that the United

> *States is a great force for good in the world, wanting nothing for itself, only to defeat terror and bring peace. The evidence does not support this. The US exacerbates internal divisions and conflicts within countries and internationalises violence. US wars have not been well-intentioned but self-interested projections of imperial power. Meanwhile, the world at large continues to pay a heavy price for the direct and indirect consequences of US foreign policy. Millions of civilians have been killed or displaced and the rift between America and other countries widens everywhere."*

Another congregant gave a shorter call to prayer indicating that prayer was about to begin. Everyone stood shoulder to shoulder in straight lines facing the qibla. The congregants, including Khamis, followed the Imam in prayer, but Salah didn't feel able to join in. Then prayers came to an end and everyone shook hands with their neighbours. Khamis explained this was traditional. Everyone was expressing the hope that their prayers would be accepted by Allah.

A murmur of chatter became audible and grew louder as Salah and Khamis left the prayer hall. When they reached the courtyard the murmur was much louder and by the time they reached the outside of the mosque it was deafening. Clearly, something had aroused most if not all the worshippers, including Khamis and Salah.

"What the fuck was that, Salah?"

"I'm gobsmacked, Khamis."

"I had no idea. I used to think anti-American feeling was a bit hypocritical. I thought the Muslim's love-hate relationship with America was a kind of collective inferiority complex, hating America and other western countries because they are so much better off than Muslim countries. I thought they loved to hate America but at the same time they're jealous of American freedoms and material wealth. When the Imam began his sermon I was speculating that his children are probably studying at American universities and thoroughly enjoying the material benefits of American life."

"Surely not, Khamis, after all, his sermon was an unremitting attack on America; he sounded sincere enough to me. Actually, I already had some insight into some of this from Hani, a Jordanian I know on the same floor as me in Sharpe. His home has just been taken from his family by the Israeli occupying forces. He blames America for supporting Israel. What I didn't realise is that America has been committing atrocities in so many countries for such a long time."

"Well, you know now."

Khamis offered Salah a lift back to Sharpe. Walking back to the Pajero they noticed Majid in animated conversation with a group of congregants, waving his arms about and apparently shouting at the others.

Khamis and Salah were perplexed. They reached the Pajero.

"Majid didn't say he would be at the mosque; we could have come together or met up with him if we had known."

"Yeah, but what was he doing? Who was he with?"

"I have no idea, Salah. I'll ask him when I see him back at the house."

"It did look a bit odd."

"I agree."

They were almost at the University and Khamis turned into the University's main entrance.

"Sorry, Salah, I can't stop. We *do* need to discuss what just happened but not now, if that's OK. I'm meeting Reza."

"Who's Reza?"

"He's the Iranian in our house."

"OK, Khamis. If you let me out I can walk from here and thanks a lot for the lift. Have fun, see you soon."

"You too."

CHAPTER 2.9

Salah was almost halfway up the stairs to his room when a group of girls rushed out onto the second floor landing. They were loud, boisterously happy, excited, seductively dressed and seemingly already in a party mood. Salah found their cocktail of perfumes intoxicating and arousing; he wondered where the party was.

He watched the girls go down the stairs and out of the building. They headed towards the central area of the campus. It was almost dark even though the paths on the campus were well lit. Salah didn't feel like going far afield, but hearing the sound of music in the distance, he followed the girls a few steps behind. At first the music was faint but the farther he walked the louder it became. It didn't take him long to understand what was happening; of course, it was a Saturday, there was a disco going on.

He remembered there had been a disco in Freshers' Week and couldn't remember why he didn't go. The reason gradually came back to him; he vaguely thought it would be too noisy and sweaty and probably not a great place to meet people, meaning girls. Now, having seen some of the girls on their way to this disco he realised his earlier thinking on the subject may have been faulty. Far from being an unlikely place to meet girls, it was beginning to look like a great opportunity; he decided to go and try his luck.

Salah rushed to Sharpe to wash and change, hoping to avoid meeting Hani. It didn't feel right to be going to a disco so soon after he had shared Hani's troubles. Safely back in his room he decided to wear his new jeans with the trendiest top he could find. He didn't really do trendy so he settled for the Hard Rock Café Dubai T-shirt Maria and Janek bought him after a meal there. At least there wouldn't be many other people wearing one of those.

Stealthily, he left his room, quietly shutting his door, all the while hoping Hani wasn't in the kitchen where he could look through the window in the door and see Salah going down the stairs. He left the building and retraced his steps. There was no mistaking where the disco was taking place; the noise emanating from the students' union was deafening. He joined the crush of people trying to enter the building and, once inside, stayed close to those queuing to go into the main hall. The queue moved slowly.

From outside, the hall appeared to be in darkness. Inside was a different story. You could hardly see anything to begin with but there were intermittent beams of different coloured lights when vision was briefly possible. There was also a light show in time with the pace, mood and volume of the music. Salah was impressed and found it exciting; his eyes slowly adjusted and he began to make out various human shapes.

It was not always obvious to Salah which shapes were male and which female. He noticed several short skirts here and there but so many were wearing ripped jeans and had long hair, girls and boys. Salah made a note to self: be careful whom to chat up, it might be another male! He wondered if Samara and his other Dubai friends would be here; probably not Samara, it seemed unlikely this was her scene. He'd neglected to mention the disco to Khamis or Majid; maybe he would bump into them, not that he'd come to spend time with friends. He was here to make new friends, by which he meant girls.

A strobe light came on and Salah could see more of what was going on. Almost everyone was facing the disc jockey and jumping up and down to the music. For the most part he could only see people's backs except when occasionally they turned around. Moving forward into the crowd he joined in the action. Everyone was very friendly and he was soon accepted into several dancing groups, each one forming and reforming. Salah longed to have physical contact with one of the girls but it wasn't that kind of dancing as everyone more or less kept to themselves.

Then something strange happened. A rotating strobe light

suddenly illuminated the hair of a girl dancing some distance away. Salah was perplexed, as he couldn't see her face but her hair looked familiar; he didn't understand how he could recognise a girl here for he didn't know any girls.

He gradually moved through the crowd towards her as and when opportunity arose. It wasn't easy finding his way through the mass of gyrating bodies. He lost sight of the girl many times but each time the strobe light came around he caught sight of her again, in or near to the same place. He was determined to get closer to her to see her face. Eventually he made it. He was right; he *did* recognise her.

"Hi." Hayley didn't recognise him, seemed not to hear.

"Hi Hayley."

She looked puzzled, then, "Oh, hi."

"You won't remember me."

"I *do* remember you, you're Salah!"

"You remember my name?"

"It's such a nice name, unusual around here. Does it mean something?"

"It means righteous and also a messenger from Allah was named Saleh."

"Good to see you, Salah. Shall we dance?"

Salah couldn't believe his luck. Unsure what to do, he tried copying Hayley's moves. Then she offered her hand so he could help her turn. She turned and then he turned and they did the same again. He was thrilled when they touched.

"I could do with a break. It's already got very hot. Shall we have a drink?" Salah was delighted she had asked.

"OK with me."

Pulling him through the crowd, she led him towards an exit and to the bar. He asked her what she would like to drink.

"A Coke would be fine. I would prefer a proper drink but I am driving later."

Salah waited his turn at the bar. Hayley stayed close. He asked for a bottled beer (he hadn't yet discovered draught beer) and a Coke. They went to the side of the bar area and sat on stools around one of those small high tables.

"Thanks, Salah. Cheers."

At first, Salah didn't know what she meant. Then he remembered his time at the Wankowskis' house and raised his glass.

"Cheers, Hayley."

"Are you here with your friends?"

"No, I wasn't going to go to the disco so I never mentioned it to them. They may be around, but I doubt it."

"So, what made you change your mind?"

"I saw people from the hall going out, dressed up, laughing and joking and then I heard music in the distance and thought 'Why not? It could be fun; I might even meet someone nice'."

"And you did, so did I and here we are."

"Yeah! What brought you here, Hayley?"

"I thought I might meet someone nice."

"Really?"

"Well, I'm always hoping. Actually, I don't do discos much but I try to come to the one at the end of Freshers' Week or maybe the next one. Everyone's usually well-behaved early in the term; nobody gets too drunk, nobody gets into a fight and nobody is sexually assaulted. The discos during term time are different, more risky."

"I get it, would you like another drink or shall we go back to the dancing?"

"What would you like to do, Salah?"

"I don't mind, Hayley."

"Have you eaten?"

"Not for a while."

"If you would like to come back to my place I could get us something to eat."

"Are you sure?"

"I'm sure, I live close by and there is plenty of food. It's not a big deal."

For Salah it was most definitely a big deal. This lovely girl, whom he had only just met again for the second time, was inviting him into her home. The evening could hardly be going any better.

They walked to the multistorey car park and up the concrete steps to find her car. It was a second-hand Ford Fiesta.

"It's not much but it was cheap and OK for what I need."

"I like the gold colour, Hayley."

"It's not gold, it's Champagne."

Although he didn't know what Champagne was he said he liked it even more.

They drove to Hayley's flat, which was basically the ground floor of an old house, one of a row of old houses, not dissimilar to Khamis' house. They entered though the front door and down a long corridor that led to the other rooms. The conversion had blocked off the stairs, which had another door and led to the upper floors. Hayley guided Salah into the front room, switched on the lights, closed the long, heavy curtains and turned on the fire to a low setting.

"Please take a seat. Put the TV on if you like. I am going to see what's in the fridge."

The front room was spacious with a high ceiling and a large fireplace. Either side of the fireplace were shelves for books and ornaments. In front of the fireplace were a large rug and a modern sofa. There was also a gas fire giving the comforting effect of burning coals. A TV and a music centre were on a cabinet to the left of the fireplace.

In one corner of the room there was a round table with four chairs. In another was a tall uplighter producing a soft light reflected and diffused by the ceiling. There were pictures on the walls, books and family photos on the shelves and a table lamp on a small table next to the sofa.

Hayley returned.

"Salah, do you eat eggs?"

"Yeah, no problem."

"What about an omelette?"

"Sounds great."

"Come into the kitchen and you can tell me what to put in it. Do you like chillies?"

"Love them."

Hayley pan-fried some onions and whisked a few eggs in a bowl. Adding tomatoes, mushrooms and chopped chilli to the fried mixture she then poured in the whisked eggs followed by grated cheese and some pepper and salt. In hardly any time at all there were two omelettes on two plates. Salah was hugely impressed.

Hayley opened some wine and poured two glasses. Salah would have preferred beer but didn't like to ask. They ate their omelettes at the round table in the main room, Salah particularly appreciating eating spicy food for a change. They finished and cleared away. Salah offered to do the washing-up but Hayley pointed to a small dishwasher and then quickly washed the frying pan herself in the sink.

They went back into the main room and Hayley sat down on the sofa. Salah joined her. He was not used to drinking wine and it was beginning to affect him. He wanted to put his arm around her and kiss her but was unsure. He didn't want to take too much for granted and ruin everything. While he was thinking about it, Hayley got up to put some music on. Then, to Salah's astonishment and delight, she came back to the sofa, sat down again and leaned across his lap, resting her head and shoulders on his arm.

Salah could hardly contain his excitement. Surely it would be OK to stroke her hair and head. It was. She let him know she liked it. He carried on stroking her and reached across her body with his other hand to hold her. She put her hand on top of his. Just as he was thinking about being more ambitious she turned over towards him, put her hand behind his head and pulled him down. They kissed.

Salah was taken aback; it was only the second time he had kissed a girl. Jas had been great but this was definitely the real deal – the best kiss so far.

They held each other tighter and tighter until Salah found himself in an increasingly uncomfortable position. His back began to ache. He didn't want to let go of Hayley in case she thought he lacked passion or commitment. Luckily, she let go of him, they disentangled and she resumed her seat on the sofa.

"I'm tired, Salah, shall we go to bed?"

Salah couldn't believe it. Not at any time when he was thinking about how to get a girlfriend did it even occur to him that a girl might take the initiative.

"I'm tired too, Hayley, I think it's the wine. Are you sure? I can find my own way back to Sharpe."

"It's up to you. It's only a small bed but I am sure we can make it work. We'll have to cuddle up. How do you feel about that?"

"I feel great about that."

"Me too."

They got up from the sofa and Hayley led Salah into the bedroom. It was just big enough to accommodate a small double. After undressing and showering they got into bed, kissed, cuddled, began to explore each other's bodies and fell asleep.

When they had finished Hayley pushed Salah away and rolled out of bed. She opened the curtains; it looked pleasant enough. It was dry at least with the sun trying to make an appearance. She turned around, picked up the bedcovers on the floor and pulled what was left on the bed off of Salah. She grabbed his ankles and dragged him off the bed, his bottom hitting the floor with a gratifying thump.

"Ouch!"

"Come on, it's time to get up. Let's walk into town and grab a coffee."

"OK, anywhere in particular?"

"I like Coffee Plus."

Hayley went to the kitchen to make tea and toast whilst Salah was in the bathroom. They ate breakfast standing in the kitchen, Salah clearing away whilst Hayley used the bathroom. They dressed and left the flat.

CHAPTER 2.10

September 22 2002

Walking hand in hand they soon joined the main street; Salah began to recognise where he was because of his earlier visit with Khamis. They almost reached Coffee Plus when Salah saw Khamis on the other side of the street. He asked Hayley if it was OK with her to meet up with his friend; she didn't mind, so he called out.

"Khamis, fancy a coffee?"

Khamis turned to see who was calling his name. No longer looking ahead, he walked straight into a policeman. Salah and Hayley thought this hilarious but avoided laughing out loud. The policeman helped Khamis steady himself.

"Hi! OK, where?"

"Coffee Plus."

"I'll join you in a couple of minutes."

Salah and Hayley left Khamis apologising to the policeman, who didn't seem unhappy, and joined the queue in Coffee Plus. It was busy as usual for this time of day. As they reached the front of the queue, Khamis joined them and asked Salah for a large Americano, the seasonal blend with cold milk on the side. Hayley asked for a latte. Salah ordered a double espresso.

"Something to eat, anyone?"

"I recommend the chocolate caramel slice, fantastic."

"OK, Hayley; what about you, Khamis?"

"I really like the caramel cream tower."

Salah followed Khamis' advice and ordered two chocolate caramel slices and a caramel cream tower. Collecting their tray from the barista he moved to a vacant table. As soon as they sat with their coffees and cakes, Salah introduced Hayley, explaining that she worked in the Facilities Management department office. Khamis was very agreeable and courteous and explained to Hayley how he and Salah became friends. Hayley said she was pleased to meet one of Salah's friends and, guessing he was on the same course as Salah, promised to look out for him when he came into the department office. Khamis was more than intrigued and wondered how Salah had been able to act on his advice about getting a girlfriend so quickly; he thought Hayley very attractive and felt quite envious.

Whilst he was pondering this, Majid, who'd come into town with Khamis, came over and Khamis asked him to join them. Salah introduced Majid to Hayley who asked if he was on the same course as Salah and Khamis. Majid told her he was studying politics. Like Khamis, he found Hayley very attractive and couldn't stop staring at her, which made her and Salah feel uncomfortable. The tension was temporarily relieved when Majid left to get himself a coffee.

Then Reza appeared and sat down. He had already bought himself a coffee. Khamis introduced Reza to Hayley and Salah. Reza was similarly smitten and, after looking Hayley up and down several times, also became fixated. To relieve Hayley's embarrassment, Khamis explained that he was an Emirati, Majid was from Sudan, Reza from Iran and there were two others in the house, Bassam from Syria and Karim from Iraq.

"Sounds like a mini United Nations," she said.

Salah would confide in her later when they were alone that Arab boys are often a bit mixed up about girls, having been brought up with cultural attitudes regarding Western girls, often seeing them as easy prey because of their apparent sexual freedom and because they are not Muslims.

Majid returned with coffee. Khamis remembered he hadn't yet asked Majid what he was doing with a group of people after the Friday prayers' sermon.

"Majid, when Salah and I were leaving the mosque on Friday we saw you and several others talking, waving your arms about and looking very agitated. What was that about?"

"We were talking about the sermon and the proposed visit of an American to the mosque. Apparently he is a state guest and the elders have said they have no choice but to allow the visit, even welcome it. Most of those attending the mosque don't agree and want to stop the visit. I was expressing solidarity with them. Actually, I was urging them to protest, especially after that sermon.

"I would be willing to join a protest."

"Why's that, Salah?"

"I've got my own reasons to be against this visit. A Jordanian guy in Sharpe Hall has just been told by a relative that his family home in Nablus has been occupied by Israeli soldiers. His family have been evicted and nobody knows where they are. He is very upset and told me about the occupation saying that the Israelis wouldn't be able to do these terrible things if it were not for American backing. I would definitely, therefore, join a protest."

Reza joined in. "So would I. If you look at the history of my country you would have plenty of justification for being anti-American and protesting."

Hayley began to feel uncomfortable; she was unsure whether to say she heard talk in the office of an American being invited to visit the University, possibly to be awarded an honorary degree. Wondering if this could be true and whether it's the same American visiting the mosque, she anticipated that the majority of other students might hold the feelings amongst Salah and his friends and that there could be trouble. She had visions of mass student protests, anti-war slogans painted on the Vice-Chancellor's car and toilet roll streamers being thrown from the upper windows of the University's buildings at the honoured guest. She decided it best to tell them.

"You guys probably don't want to hear this but there may be an American visiting the University, perhaps to receive an honorary degree. It's only office chat but there may be something in it."

Nobody spoke for a while.

"If this is true and it's the same American, it could be big. We must win the argument at the mosque, get this visit cancelled and at the same time punish the University for endorsing a foreign power that kills Muslims whenever it feels like it."

"'Punish the University' sounds extreme, Majid. Isn't it enough to get the visit cancelled? The Student Islamic Society may be able to help deal with the University."

"You're joking. Student Islamic Societies are a waste of space; they're never going to stand up for murdered Muslims, they're too busy promoting Islam and multi-faith societies."

"What's wrong with that?"

"It has its place, Salah, but you can't win a war with brotherly love."

"Which war? You are sounding more and more like an extremist and a militant, Majid."

Khamis thought things were rapidly going downhill. He had his doubts about Majid, but this was neither the time nor the place for that conversation. Apart from everything else, other students were beginning to turn around to see why voices were being raised.

"OK, Majid, let's not forget why we all came, I thought it was for good old coffee and friendship."

Everyone agreed this was indeed why they had come together and the general tone of the conversation became more sociable.

Majid, however, had made them feel uneasy and provided them with food for thought to stick in their minds. Hayley looked at Salah and him at her. He thought she was trying to send him a signal but he couldn't work out what it meant. Then he got it – Hayley had had enough of his friends and wanted her and Salah to leave.

"Well, we must get going, this has been great – hope we can do it again sometime."

"Hope so too, Salah," said Khamis. "Bye."

"It was great meeting you all," said Hayley. "Bye."

Off they went, leaving the others still chatting. "That was getting a bit heavy, Salah."

"I know. I can't say I really enjoyed it, what with all the staring as well. Anyone would think they'd never seen a girl before and the politics looked as if it might get ugly."

"Right, perhaps I shouldn't have mentioned the American

thing."

"I don't see why not though."

They'd come out for coffee and done that, now what? They meandered aimlessly in and out of a few shops along the High Street and then stood still for a moment, realising they didn't know what to do next.

Would you like to see my room in Sharpe Hall?" Salah asked.

"Why not?"

"I've got some cooked chicken in the fridge. We could pick up some salad and call it lunch."

"Sounds good to me."

They crossed the road and went into Tesco. Salah knew his way around and quickly found a cucumber and some cherry tomatoes. Hayley grabbed a little gem lettuce and, on the way to the checkout, she noticed a box of chocolate éclairs in one of the chillers and pointed these out to Salah.

"What about these for dessert?"

"OK, go for it."

They paid, walked back towards the direction of Hayley's flat and jumped in her car. In a matter of minutes they were parked outside Sharpe Hall. In they went, up the stairs and into the kitchen where they put the shopping in Salah's fridge. Hayley was shocked to discover that every student had their own fridge and was greatly impressed by the kitchen facilities.

"Looks pretty good to me, Salah," she said as she entered his room."

"Can't complain."

He took hold of her and they kissed and kissed, almost falling on the bed together. They rolled around for a few minutes, enjoying their closeness and budding romance. Words seemed superfluous; Hayley swung her legs off the bed, sat up and looked around.

"It's a bit basic, Salah, but I suppose there is everything you need."

"Now, have a look in the bathroom."

"Amazing! How did they fit all that into such a small space?"

"How about that lunch?"

Back to the kitchen, Salah selected a few tomatoes and cut a length of cucumber, which Hayley washed and dried while Salah removed what was left of the chicken from the carcass. He hoped he hadn't kept it too long and they wouldn't get food poisoning. Salah plated up and they sat down at one of the long tables to eat.

"This is really nice, Salah."

"Thanks. You're very kind but it didn't exactly require a chef's skills."

"Perhaps cooking might be one of the nice things we do together, it's not much fun on your own. The planning, shopping, preparation and actual cooking feel such a chore. Even with eating, it is usually disappointing when you're on your own and then there's the clearing up. It would be so much more fun doing things together."

"Sounds good, Hayley; when shall we start?"

"Don't have much time during the week, probably the weekends are best."

"What about this evening?"

"Why not?"

"Do you fancy a curry? I've got some easy-cook rice and a jar of jalfrezi sauce."

"I'm not big on curry, Salah. I am willing to try but why don't I take the lead on this one? I've got stuff in the freezer. We can go back to my place, you can help me and we'll make a meal together."

"OK, but I shall most likely be pretty useless. Is there anything you need for the meal?"

"I think we're OK. You could get a bottle of wine, if you like."

Salah was used to drinking beer in small quantities but he remembered Hayley liked wine. He had tried it and wasn't sure he liked the effect it had on him. Maybe it would be good to try it again – even better – enjoy it. Top people drink wine, beer was for the masses. He needed to up his game.

"Red or white?"

"Red."

"Will do, the University Central Stores should be open if we go soon; I think they close early on a Sunday. Shall we go to your place via the shop?"

Hayley's Fiesta pulled up more or less outside her house. She made a comment about not being very good at parking, although as far as Salah could tell, she parked it perfectly.

Through the front door, down the corridor into the living room and then into the kitchen, they simultaneously felt a need to embrace. Salah made the most of the opportunity, kissing Hayley as passionately as he knew how, like in the movies when the actors look as if they are trying to eat each other. Hayley seemed to like it.

"If I don't find something that will defrost easily in the freezer, we shall starve. What about fishcakes? I can cook them from frozen."

"OK with me. Have you got tomato sauce?"

Hayley turned the oven on to a high temperature and took a flat pan and a saucepan from the cupboard under the sink. She placed the fishcakes on the pan, poured a small packet of peas into the saucepan and filled the kettle for the boiling water to cook the peas.

"Now, where were we?"

Salah moved towards her.

"Bad luck, Salah, we're not doing any more of that until you've peeled the potatoes. We're cooking together, remember?" Salah took out another saucepan whilst Hayley found the potatoes.

They poured two glasses of wine and sat down to their meal at the table in the living room. Salah majored on tomato sauce, something he'd recently discovered. Fortunately, Hayley had been able to produce a new bottle.

"I usually watch *Countryfile*; I find it interesting, beautiful and relaxing. Would you like to give it a try?"

"OK, it'll probably help me learn more about what England's like."

"There's stuff on Wales and Scotland too."

"Great."

They moved to the sofa. Salah liked the programme and understood what Hayley meant by relaxing, but he wasn't much in the mood for relaxing. He had other things on his mind, mainly the fact that he wanted to play with Hayley and finish what they had started together earlier. But she was engrossed in the programme and didn't seem in the mood, so Salah decided not to push his luck.

"I should probably be going back to Sharpe, Hayley. I'm not sure what I'm doing on the course tomorrow but I'd better have a good night's sleep."

"Really… what, now?"

"Well, after we've seen the rest of the programme."

"OK, but I can't give you a lift after drinking wine."

"Not a problem, I'm sure I can get a bus. If not, I'll walk; it will do me good."

There were only a few minutes left of *Countryfile* and then the closing credits began to roll.

"It's been great, Hayley. Thanks for the fishcakes; it's my turn to cook dinner next time."

"OK, Salah, perhaps not curry, but I promise I shall try it sometime."

"No hurry, Hayley, I'm sure I can think of something else."

He drew her to him and put his arms around her, stroking her hair, her back and her buttocks. He was tempted to change his mind but wasn't sure whether she wanted him to stay so, after lingering for a short while, he returned to the idea of leaving as probably the most sensible option.

CHAPTER 2.11

September 23 2002

Salah almost forgot he'd arranged with Khamis to meet for breakfast at the students' union cafeteria to discuss their Risk Assessment coursework. They'd agreed to work together as much as possible but submit their own individual coursework. They viewed this as a shared learning experience, not as cheating. After all, cooperative learning should be one of the main features of university education.

They helped themselves to breakfast, paid, and sat down with their trays. While they were eating, Salah asked Khamis if he remembered the five-step approach to risk assessment.

"I can remember the first step – Identify the hazards."

Salah was retrieving the previous term's notes from his rucksack.

"Is that all, Khamis?"

"Nobody likes a smart-arse, Salah, you've got last term's notes in front of you."

"OK, would you like me to tell you the other steps?"

"Of course."

"OK, Step 2 – Decide on who might be harmed; 3 – Evaluate the risks and devise precautions; 4 – Report and implement recommendations, and 5 – Review and adjust as needed."

"Thanks. There should be plenty of hazards around here, probably most of them in the kitchen areas."

"Sounds right, Khamis, I suppose we should speak to someone and ask if it's OK for us to do this."

They finished their breakfasts, stacked their trays and went looking for someone in authority. They asked around and eventually saw the assistant manager who was friendly and helpful.

Apparently, the cafeteria management was used to students doing surveys of one kind or another and welcomed them. They particularly valued recommendations in the area of health and safety.

Salah and Khamis felt pleased with themselves. They were well organised and ready to go. All they needed now was to do the work. As they were leaving the cafeteria, Khamis said he wanted to visit the library. Salah said he would return to Sharpe and asked Khamis if he would like to come over later in the morning for a coffee. Khamis declined politely and suggested they both go back to his place at lunchtime. Salah happily agreed. Khamis would pick him up later from the Sharpe student car park.

On arrival at his digs, Khamis offered to make tea or coffee and went straight to the kitchen. While he was away, Salah mooched about, leaving Khamis' room and wandered back into the hall. He noticed Majid's door ajar. He couldn't help pushing it further open, then pushing it again until he was able to lean into Majid's room. Everything looked more or less as expected.

Clearly, Majid was not a tidy person; his bed was unmade, his desk was covered with piles of books, pamphlets and papers and the floor was a repository for dirty laundry, shoes, food wrappers and dirty plates. What *was* unexpected was that on the mantelshelf above the fireplace was a copy of *BLEVE*. Salah just had to check to see if this was the missing University library copy. It was.

Salah just managed to get back into Khamis' room before he brought the tea. He must have looked guilty.

"Are you OK, Salah? You look worried."

"Yeah, Khamis, I'm sorry, but I just did something I shouldn't have. I snooped in Majid's room."

"Don't worry, it's no big deal, as they say."

They drank their tea. Salah wondered whether or not to share his concerns. After all, he didn't know Khamis that well."

"Khamis, how much do you know about Majid?" Khamis looked surprised.

"That's a funny question. About as much as you, I suppose."

"I don't know much."

"Neither do I. He's a mate, that's all." Khamis seemed OK with the topic of discussion so Salah decided to take the risk.

"I would like to share something with you in confidence, if that's OK with you. When I first arrived I had a quick look around the library. At first I was interested in comparing what they have here with what we had in the Dubai College. Then, as a test, I searched for a book that I had on loan from Dubai. The test was to see whether I could understand the classification system here. The book was called *BLEVE*. I found it in the library catalogue but I couldn't find it on the shelf where it was supposed to be. I asked at the issue desk and they looked to see if it had been issued. It hadn't. The best they could come up with was that someone had put it back in the wrong place."

"OK, but what does this have to do with Majid?"

"Right. When I was snooping in his room I noticed the same book on the shelf above the fireplace."

"Are you sure it's the same book?"

"Very sure; on the inside cover it has a sticker with this University's accession number, date of accession and sort code, etc."

"Maybe he steals books, so what?"

"Khamis, this book is about gas explosions." Salah could see that Khamis was on the point of getting the message.

"Oh, I see where this is going."

"Didn't you say to me one day that Majid is always on his mobile having private calls? You sounded at least a little suspicious."

"You're right, I did. Let's both have a look in his room."

"Are you sure?"

They went to Majid's room. Apart from seeing the book on the mantelpiece there wasn't much else of interest until they turned around to go back out. They had both noticed a large poster on the back of the door with the following message:

"Our words have no impact on you, therefore I am going to speak to you in a language you understand.

Our words are dead until we give them life with our blood... until you stop the bombing, gassing, torture and imprisonment of my people, we will not stop."

Siddique Khan – Al Jazeera video

They both stood still without speaking, staring at the poster and pondering the possible implications.

"We must avoid jumping to conclusions."

"I agree, Khamis, but you did sound suspicious of all these private calls to his mobile."

"True. I suppose the best thing is ask him what he's up to."

"I'm not sure, that could go very badly."

"What do you suggest, Salah?"

"I think we should try to avoid any kind of confrontation. I don't see the need to let him know what we've discovered straightaway. Why don't we just keep an eye on Majid for now?"

"Then we don't have to apologise for snooping in his room."

"Exactly."

"OK, sounds reasonable for now. Shall we get something to eat?"

"Why not?"

"There's Annie's round the corner if you fancy a box of falafel with other stuff you can choose. Are you interested?"

"Sounds great, Khamis. Last time I had extra salad and hummus. I love Annie's food, it's tasty and not too expensive either."

"Fine."

They walked down the road together. Salah was amazed at the row of identical houses. Some looked a mess.

"Probably occupied by students," said Khamis.

"So many still have their curtains shut," added Salah.

"Probably occupied by students," repeated Khamis.

They reached Annie's.

"Hello, what can I get for you two boys? As you know, everything is freshly made this morning."

"Can we both have some falafel and hummus, please?"

"Sure, shall I add some salad as well – no charge?" Annie knew the answer.

"Yes, please."

"Would you like to try my chicken shawarma? It's new. I have put it on to see if it sells."

"Yes, please."

She added the shawarma, then the plastic forks, closed the two boxes and handed them over. "I haven't charged for the shawarma this time. Please come back and tell me what you think of it."

"Will do, thanks Annie. Bye."

They walked back to Khamis' house, pleased with their boxes.

"Isn't she lovely?"

"A bit too old for you, Khamis?"

"She obviously loves food and cooking, reminds me of my mother."

Salah was quiet.

"I'm sorry, Salah. I didn't think."

"Not a problem, Khamis."

"No news, I suppose?"

"No, only 'leads' that lead nowhere," he replied, indicating the quote shapes with his hands.

Back in the house they decided to stay with the boxes and plastic forks, no washing-up required. The food was, as expected, authentic and delicious – much better than anything they had found in the University cafeteria. Salah told Khamis how lucky he was to have Annie's so near.

Just before they finished eating, Majid came through the front door, shouted 'Hi' through the open door to Khamis' room, went to his own room and shut the door. Very soon he could be heard speaking in a low voice on his mobile. Salah and Khamis looked at each other, each assuming they were having the same thought.

"Salah, let's go and see Majid. He doesn't know you're here."

"OK, let's." They knocked on Majid's door; he came to the door with his mobile in his hand and waved them in.

"Sorry, a visitor has just arrived; can we continue this another time? Thanks for calling. Al Hamdoolilla, *I'll call you later*, ma'a as salama." *Goodbye.*

"Sorry, Majid, we didn't know you were on the phone. Salah's with me, he wanted to touch base with you."

"Hi Salah, good to see you; have a seat, you too, Khamis, if you can find one."

Khamis and Salah dithered, then sat on the bed.

"What are you guys up to?"

"Oh just hanging out, you know." Salah got up and went to the mantelpiece and picked up the book. "What a coincidence, I know this book, Majid. I have one in my room from the Dubai College. I thought you were studying politics?"

"I am." Majid looked puzzled.

"What has this to do with politics?"

"Not a lot. I just like the colourful, dramatic picture on the front cover."

Salah wanted to ask 'Are you a terrorist?' then thought it would be going too far. Instead, he asked:

"But it's a picture of a gas tank exploding?"

Majid said nothing, but Khamis picked up the theme.

"You sound like a pyromaniac, Majid."

"You have no idea, Khamis."

"Are we supposed to understand that, Majid?"

"OK, I will tell you, in strictest confidence, of course. There's a new group. They're very secret, they don't like the word 'terrorist', they think of themselves as political activists. They regard the *countries* that have waged war against *Arabs* as terrorists. I have met some of them at the mosque. I like them. They're keen to do something meaningful to protest against the visit of the American politician. Some of them would like to cause an explosion. The problem is that they don't want to damage the mosque or hurt other Arabs.

"I have told them the University has also invited the American and it could be the focus of the protest rather than the mosque. They seemed to like the idea and they've gone away to think about it."

Salah was stunned by Majid's casual revelations; he was taking a big risk sharing this information. At the same time, Salah was excited. Very excited – this could be the opportunity to protest as he needed and he wanted to be involved.

Khamis was looking anxious and Salah was careful not to let him see his own reactions to what Majid was saying. Luckily, his mobile rang and created a distraction.

It was Hayley, she must have read his mind, wanted to know what he was doing and whether he fancied a drink after work.

"Any chance you could pick me up?"

"Maybe; where are you?"

Salah asked Khamis and replied, "83 Primrose Road."

"Oh, that's easy, I know where it is. See you later, bye."

"See you, bye."

"Majid, can we meet up sometime? I would like to discuss politics with you. I don't suppose you fancy coming over to Sharpe for a coffee any time soon?"

"Why not; tell me when?"

"I am not sure I have your mobile number." Majid reeled off his number and Salah then dialled it to make sure he'd got it right. Majid's mobile sprang into life – job done.

Salah became aware his mobile was vibrating. "Let me just see this." It was a text from one of the Pro-Vice-Chancellor's offices. "I am required to attend a meeting at 9.30 am on Monday. What could that be about?"

"Don't know, Salah, sounds bad news to me. Why don't you call me next week when you're free and we'll arrange to get together? It's easy for me to come to Sharpe if I am already on the campus. We can talk privately."

Salah was relieved Khamis wasn't paying attention to his conversation with Majid. He might have wanted to know what Salah was up to and why they needed to talk privately. Salah couldn't possibly come clean to Khamis, not yet anyway and perhaps not ever.

A car horn sounded in the road; Salah went outside to look, thinking it was Hayley. He was right. There was nowhere to park so he ran back into the house, said 'Ma'a as salama' to Khamis and Majid, then ran back outside to the car, jumping in as quickly as he could. Hayley wasn't holding anyone up but quickly sped off down the road anyway.

"Where are we going?"

"Good question. Let's go to your favourite place for a quiet drink?"

"I'm not sure I've got a favourite place."

"You know the area, Hayley. I don't, so I'm not much use. Sorry."

"There's quite a good-looking pub not far from my house. Shall we try it? If we don't like it we can go somewhere else or go to the off-licence and get something to drink at home."

"Sounds good."

The Bear pub was an imposing old building. A number of concealed floodlights made it look very attractive from the outside and it promised to be warm and inviting inside. They went in and immediately smelt wood smoke. Somewhere there was a real log fire. The weather had turned colder recently and being able to sit in front of an open fire was one of Hayley's favourite pastimes. For Salah it would be a new experience.

Sure enough, as they reached the bar area they could see a huge stone fireplace with a pile of burning logs in the hearth and a plume of smoke rising up the chimney. This was exactly the kind of cosy ambience Hayley had been hoping for. They ordered drinks and sat down in comfortable leather chairs as near as they could get to the fire. Salah had a bottled beer, Hayley a Coke, as she was driving.

For a while they stared at the flickering flames without feeling a need to speak. Salah said he had heard about cosy, hospitable, old-fashioned English country pubs, but this was his first experience of being in one. He might even try the proverbial warm beer sometime. Hayley said it was not really a country pub but a town pub trying to look like a country pub, but that she promised to introduce Salah to the real thing sometime.

"Hayley, there is something I have been meaning to ask you.

Now seems as good a time as any. I often feel like ringing you during the day, not for any reason, just to say 'Hi' and to hear your voice. I wanted to this morning after my session with the course leader. I didn't do it because I felt I shouldn't interrupt whatever you're doing at work. There's another reason – is it OK for you to be going out with a student or do we need to keep it a secret?"

"I suppose this was bound to come up sooner or later, Salah. I appreciate you not ringing me in the office, although I would always like to hear from you, of course. It could be awkward; I am not sure if there's a definite rule about University staff and students going out. I imagine it's probably frowned on as there's sometimes confidential work going on in the office, you know, stuff about assessments, student performance, etc. I guess the University wouldn't like it if they knew about it."

"So, what do we do?"

"I don't know. I'm happy as we are at the moment. Perhaps we should just carry on, be discreet, and keep going as long as we are both enjoying it and maybe stopping when either of us feels it's not working anymore. I'd prefer not to lose my job, but there are other jobs. I suppose what we do in the long term depends how much we mean to each other."

"OK, I can live with that, for now at least. I hope you didn't mind my bringing it up."

"I'm glad we talked about it. Perhaps we should just text each other during work time. Shall we have another drink? What about something to eat? There's a menu on the table."

Salah reached over for the menu, which they looked at together. Salah liked the idea of garlic mushrooms, Hayley chose lasagne.

"Garlic mushrooms will be tasty but not very filling, are you sure that's all you want?"

"What about sharing a portion of chips?"

"Fantastic – lasagne and chips, what's not to like?"

Salah went to the bar, ordered, paid, and then carried the drinks back to Hayley. The kitchen wasn't very busy and their food came quickly. Other customers must have been more interested in drinking than eating.

Salah was pleased with his choice, liking the mushrooms and enjoying dipping his chips in the creamy sauce. Hayley claimed that her chips elevated the lasagne from being a pleasant dish into a gourmet experience. Salah hadn't a clue what she was talking about. After they'd eaten they stayed close to the fire for a while, staring at the burning logs, enjoying the warmth and chatting occasionally.

"The way I see it, I can either give you a lift back to your room or we can go back to my place and finish what's left of a bottle of wine."

"The second sounds more attractive than the first. I can get a taxi back later."

"Or I could drop you off on my way to work in the morning; I usually reach the office around 8 am."

"Even better."

"Shall we go?"

CHAPTER 2.12

September 24 2002

Salah looked to see if anyone was looking, kissed Hayley and thanked her for the lift.

"It was very nice, Salah. Thank you for the drinks and the food. By the way, if you're going to stay regularly perhaps you could organise yourself a washbag, pyjamas and a change of clothing. Wouldn't that be sensible?"

"Good idea. Bye!"

Salah left Hayley in the staff car park and walked over to Sharpe. Whilst climbing the stairs he thought how amazing she was. She made everything so easy for him. After all the angst he'd experienced trying to find a girlfriend everything had suddenly fallen into his lap with almost no effort on his part. He couldn't believe his luck.

Back in his room, Salah opened his laptop to check his e-mails and, to his amazement, he noticed a message from Khaled. The subject was 'Fun in the Desert', photos were attached, the message itself…

'How's it going Salah? How are you enjoying the cold and the rain? Thought you'd like to see pics of our beautiful trip. There are more if you're interested. Don't forget, keep in touch.

Khaled'

Surprised and excited, Salah clicked through the photos, first forwards, then backwards, then forwards again. He began to relive the day he and the Kuwaitis visited the desert…

DUBAI – June 2002

Salah had been enjoying his morning showers. As long as he got up early before the heat of the day it was great to be on the roof with panoramic views over the tops of so many other villas. He could even see some of the world's most iconic high-rise buildings in the distance and beyond, as far as the sea. The water from the bucket was perfect, warm enough to be comfortable and cool enough to be refreshing.

He had yet to have the pleasure of watching the maid taking a shower. In fact, he hadn't seen her at all. Perhaps she'd stopped taking showers after he arrived for fear of being overlooked. Perhaps she was avoiding him altogether. She remained a fantasy, an enjoyable fantasy. For the time being, Salah was happy for this fantasy to continue as, for all he knew, reality may be a disappointment. Then he wouldn't have anything to fantasize about, except Samara, of course. Then there was Suhaila. But these had always seemed so distant and unattainable, whereas the maid was so closer by comparison.

The physical act of drying himself caused Salah to snap out of his daydream and return to his room. Salah had been looking forward to today. Although the College staff worked on Thursday mornings there were no classes or other student activities. This Thursday they had all been planning to drive into the desert and camp overnight. He dressed and went down to the kitchen to make breakfast.

Ali was in the kitchen at the fridge and he asked Salah if he wanted a juice or coffee.

"Coffee would be great if you are making some. Thanks, Ali."

Salah wasn't sure who else was up but someone must have been busy; as he came down the main stairs he noticed a large jumble of camping equipment in the hall including a tent, sleeping bags, blow-up mattresses and pillows, a kettle, a barbecue, a tow rope, several boxes and bags of charcoal, insect repellent, wipes and tissues, matches, rolls of bags for rubbish, maps and a GPS.

By the side of the kitchen sink, four large plastic containers were waiting to be filled with water and Ali was busy loading a cool box with ice and food. A note was attached to the fridge door in bold capital letters '**CHARGE MOBILES**'.

Ali said that they would be using his old Pajero. "It might look like a bit of a wreck and it rattles a lot but it is still a reliable workhorse and it has been serviced recently. We've all got 4 x 4s but, for some reason, the others didn't want to use their vehicles this time."

"Can I help you load up?"

"Thanks, Salah. We're not quite ready but, yes, I'll call you."

Khaled appeared and asked if anyone could provide a torch. He was unable to find his and thought they should have one on the trip.

"I've been looking at the map, guys. Why don't we drive out towards Hatta and the Oman border? We could make for the Big Red towards the village of Madam. This massive red dune is easy to spot from the road. It will, of course, be swarming with 4 x 4s and dune bashing bikes but we can find a quieter place to camp if we drive as far as the village of Madam and then make a turn at the roundabout back towards Dubai. There are several camel grids along that stretch and other places to go off-road. We can then pick our spot; if necessary we can stop at the shops in Madam if we need to or if we've forgotten anything."

"Sounds good, Khaled, presumably you have spoken with the Mohammeds?"

"Yeah, they're fine with it."

"OK, Salah and I will begin loading up in the next few minutes. When do you want to set off?"

"As soon as possible, I suppose. By the way, it's too much of a risk going off-road with one vehicle so I'll take my Toyota, just in case we get stuck in a dune or have some other emergency."

"Good idea, Khaled, I almost suggested it myself."

They loaded up and prepared to set off, Salah with Ali and the two Mohammeds with Khaled. Their convoy headed out of the city towards the Hatta Road and the village of Madam, as planned. For almost an hour the view from the vehicle windows was one of continuous rich red sand culminating in the appearance of the Big Red, the 100-metre-high red dune in the Rub' al Khali desert. They circumnavigated the roundabout and travelled back a short distance towards Dubai. After selecting an exit point they left the main road and entered the desert.

On the one hand, previous experience had taught them that the further anyone drives away from the roads and desert tracks the more likely they are to find a pleasant campsite; avoiding litter, burned out campfires and other evidence from previous campers. On the other hand, driving too far into the desert had other disadvantages; the desert is a dangerous place to be lost.

They were looking for a site that was accessible, previously unoccupied and lying between but not too close to two or three dunes. The dunes would give valuable protection from the wind but being too close might lead to an accident with dune bashers coming over the top at high speed, unable to avoid their camp.

They parked the vehicles and unloaded. The tent sprang into shape and was quickly secured with pegs in the sand. The equipment and other items were soon out of the vehicles and on the ground and a modest field kitchen was set up with the kettle heating to make a drink.

Mohammed K said there was no need to blow up the air beds. "Guys, I suggest we don't bother with the air beds. The most comfortable sleeping position comes from lying on the sand and rubbing and working your body into the sand; this creates a perfect sand mould for your body shape."

The others listened attentively without comment but were quietly sceptical that Mohammed had found the secret of the ultimate sleeping position. They decided to revisit the issue nearer to nightfall.

"Anyone for some dune bashing?"

Everyone jumped into action at Khaled's suggestion and assumed he would take the first turn at the wheel. They all got into the Toyota and set off up the nearest dune. The Toyota slithered and snaked from side to side, wheels spinning, engine roaring, whilst making only modest progress up the steep, soft, sand slope. Clouds of sand erupted and engulfed the vehicle, reducing visibility to zero from time to time. Eventually the engine revs and noise died down and the vehicle slowed and then paused. Visibility gradually returned and they could see, with a sense of relief, that they had reached the top.

They got out of the Toyota and stretched their legs. The sand was so hot it burned their feet, but the view was certainly worth the effort. A vast array of red sand and dunes stretched out in every direction. A few wisps of smoke could be seen, probably from other campers' campfires and, to everyone's delight, a few camels wandered around very slowly, no doubt having escaped temporarily from local farms.

During the ascent of the dune their thoughts had been focused on survival. Conversation was in short supply. Having survived they were now free to entertain other kinds of thoughts. Conversation began again cautiously at first as they were greatly in awe of their surroundings.

As most if not all those visiting the desert have done, they spoke of the vastness of the sands straddling several countries, the greatest expanse of sand on earth; they spoke of their isolation, the clarity and purity of the unpolluted air, the cloudless blue sky, the beauty and ferocity of the sun and the fact that the desert is continuously changing and evolving, reinventing itself and always different from one day to the next.

Unlike Khaled, Ali and the two Mohammeds who had camped in the desert on several previous occasions, this was a new experience for Salah. Initially, his thoughts were more about himself than about the desert. His first thought was how lucky he was to have met Khaled and the others and to have been able to join the trip. He was really enjoying himself. His second thought was realising why he was so lucky. It was because he had been unlucky to lose his father in very bad circumstances and unlucky his mother was missing. He thought of her and wondered where she was and if she was in trouble somewhere. This made him feel guilty about enjoying himself.

They drifted back together towards the Toyota as the sun

was beginning to set and the temperature began to drop. Khaled suggested they make their way back to the camp, light a fire and prepare food. Going down was without doubt less dramatic than going up, but the incline of the dune and the tilt of the vehicle when descending combined to create a fear of rolling over that increased their heart rates.

Returning to the camp, everyone except Salah seemed to know what to do and in no time a fire was going, which provided warmth and light as dusk crept over the desert. Salah, in an effort to make a contribution to the general good, offered to prepare and cook the evening meal. The others were delighted.

This was a bold move as Salah's experience of cooking was limited to watching his mother, but even then he hadn't always been attentive. He desperately tried to remember what the food served in the College looked like, particularly the salads. Perhaps he could imitate these.

The two Mohammeds brought out the big cool box from the tent and put it down near the cooking area. Ali brought the smaller cool box and handed everyone a chilled alcohol-free beer. Salah took the top off the large box to see what was inside. He began to feel a little more confident as he went through the contents. There was lamb, rice, onions, garlic, tomatoes, a cucumber, cooking oil, a couple of herbs, a tin of mixed spices, some hummus and pitta bread. Surely the application of common sense would be enough to produce an acceptable meal.

Salah lit one of the gas burners and heated some cooking oil in a saucepan. He tipped the lamb into the hot oil and sprinkled some spices from the tin, stirring the lamb as he did so. The smell was fantastic. He reduced the heat and left the meat cooking slowly. He then found another pan for the rice and filled the kettle with water. He lit the second burner and placed the kettle on it. He planned to hand everyone a plate with some hummus and ask them to toast their pitta bread to go with their hummus. However, the idea of toasting pitta bread gave him another idea. With the other salad items in the cool box he could make fattoush, the vegetable and croutons salad.

The kettle water was now boiling so he poured it on the rice and put the pan on the burner. He also poured some boiling water over the lamb and added a chopped onion. It smelled even better. He reached into the cool box and took out some tomatoes, the cucumber, salad onions, parsley, mint and oil. He chopped them all into bite-sized pieces and dressed them with oil and salt. He then toasted some pitta until it was crisp, broke it into small pieces and added these to the salad, which was now a fattoush.

Salah served some hummus and fattoush on each of the four plates and added pitta bread. He took the lid off the lamb pan to reduce the liquid and checked the rice, which was not quite ready. He called the others and told them dinner was ready. They were pleasantly surprised. Whilst Salah had been cooking, which seemed like no time at all, they had been organising sleeping arrangements, visiting the fire to keep warm and, with the exception of Mohammed K, blowing up their air beds.

Both the first course and the lamb and rice dish won high praise and they finished with coffee and dates. The upside was that Salah was thrilled with his newfound popularity and felt for the first time he was an equal member of the group. The downside for Salah was that the others now wanted him to cook for them back at the villa.

It was dark now except for the small light from the last few embers of the fire. Everyone was tired and looking forward to sleep. Khaled kicked sand over the remnants of the fire and went to his tent with the two Mohammeds while Salah and Ali went to theirs. Salah noticed that whilst he'd been cooking Ali had blown up his own air bed.

"Thanks, Ali."

"Layla sa'ida." *Good night.*

Salah went to bed thinking yet again about his good fortune with the Kuwaitis and, yet again, he wondered and worried about his mother. He felt he was getting used to life without her and this worried him too. Then he fell asleep.

He woke after a few hours and was surprised by the amount of light coming into the tent. In his dreamy state he imagined they had left the Toyota headlights on. He got up to have a look and saw the moon, which was the largest and brightest moon against the darkest sky he had ever seen. Also, the stars were clearer and brighter than ever and it was eerily quiet. No noise pollution here.

Salah felt small, very small, and alone, very alone in this desert wilderness, but he was not unhappy. On balance, he thought these feelings were good, that they helped declutter his mind and improve his understanding of his place in the world.

Whilst philosophizing and stargazing, he thought he saw a faint pinkness creeping into the sky. He waited. He wasn't wrong. It was definitely there and slowly spreading. Suddenly he realised he was going to see a desert sunrise. The pink gradually changed towards orange and then red and the colours became more and more intense until the first appearance of the sun itself, a ball of yellow fire surrounded by a red penumbra blazing on the horizon.

Salah didn't know whether or not to wake the others to see the sunrise; he reasoned they would have seen one during their previous camping trips so left them sleeping. He noticed how cold it was so he quietly went back into the tent to find more clothes. Ali stirred and then the other tent sprang into life.

Salah was the first to emerge so he began to organise breakfast. He found a tin of fava beans in the cool box, which he mixed and mashed with chopped onions, garlic, lemon zest and juice, parsley and oil to make ful medames. This was easy. He had seen his mother make it for the Sheikh. There was more pitta bread, some leftover hummus and cartons of different fruit juices. The others appeared one by one and helped themselves.

After breakfast they cleared away and packed up the tents and equipment until it was ready to be loaded into the vehicles. Ali asked if anyone would like to have a go at more dune bashing. They all agreed, piled into the Pajero and made for a different dune. Ali was more of a risk-taker than Khaled so the ascent was even more hair-raising, but then living dangerously seemed to be what dune bashing was all about. As before, they left the vehicle at the top of the dune and walked around, enjoying the views in all directions.

The morning seemed to go by quickly and they were soon down from the dune and back in camp. They checked to see that they hadn't left anything behind and that all their rubbish had been collected in the bags. Khaled suggested they drive back to Madam and go to the Arab World restaurant for lunch before driving home. The food was not very good, but it was cheap.

They set off back to the main road and travelled towards Dubai until they were able to make a U-turn and come back to Madam. As expected, the food at the Arab World was basic to say the least, and the Kuwaitis all complimented Salah again on his culinary efforts the previous night. After lunch, the journey back to their villa was uneventful and they all unloaded the vehicles and generally tidied up ready for college the next day.

They were also pleased to be able to take a shower and wash the sand out of their hair, from between their toes and from the other places where sand had accumulated. The water in the roof tank had been steadily heating up all day and was much too hot this time as they were taking showers so much later than usual. Salah refilled the bucket ready for the morning showers and was on his way back to his room, still towelling off, when a pretty girl came out of the room next-door.

"Hello, I'm Jas."

CHAPTER 2.13

Jas' unexpected appearance yesterday evening took Salah by surprise. His instinct was to say hello and perhaps shake her hand but he was frightened that if he reached out his towel would fall down. So he did nothing. Even worse, he said nothing and Jas walked straight past him to go downstairs.

Salah was furious with himself. He had allowed his embarrassment to ruin his opportunity to meet Jas, which had been a long time coming. He was also upset that, from her perspective, he must have looked like an incompetent idiot. Today was another day and he would somehow try to make amends.

He had awakened this morning to the sound of splashing water and recognised this as unusual, but it took a while to realise that it was probably Jas using the bucket for her morning shower. He leapt out of bed and then slowly, very slowly and as quietly as possible, pulled his door ajar to see if he could watch her through the gap.

No luck, there were two problems. Problem one: Salah had taken too long to come to his senses and get to his door; he was too late. Problem two: the gap was too narrow for a clear line of sight to the water tap and bucket.

Salah knew he couldn't open the door further without giving himself away. So, the most he could achieve was a fleeting glimpse of Jas coming back to her room tightly wrapped in a towel.

He looked at his clock and noted the time. Tomorrow he would get up earlier and wait until he heard Jas leave her room. He would then be better prepared and more likely to be a successful voyeur. Then something suddenly dawned on Salah. He hadn't heard Jas' door close when she returned to her room. Was it still open? He gently opened his door again. He could open it further this time because it wouldn't matter if Jas saw him leaving his room. She would think nothing of it.

Salah crept outside and looked to see if Jas' door was still open. There was a small gap. Salah couldn't see anything through the gap at first but he daren't try to open the door further in case it creaked. Then it happened. Jas came into view. Salah couldn't believe his luck. She had no clothes on. She appeared to be looking for something, turning this way and that, waving her arms about, thus enabling Salah to carry out a full body scan.

He no longer needed to try to imagine what Jas looked like underneath her clothes and he wasn't disappointed. He had liked her pretty face. Now he could also like her pretty shape and small but perfectly formed breasts, not to mention her shapely bottom. Salah was even keener to get to know Jas better and this he resolved to do as soon as possible.

He carried on with his normal morning routine and went over to the bucket, which was full as expected (the last person to use it always refilled it for the next person). He removed his clothes, lifted the bucket and poured the contents over himself. He then turned the tap on full, applied shampoo to his hair and rubbed soap over his body. Another bucketful washed most of the soap and shampoo away. The next and last bucket finished the job. He picked up his towel and made his way towards his room.

As he neared his door, Jas emerged and almost collided with him.

"Hello Jas."

"Hello."

He gripped his towel; he wasn't going to make a fool of himself this time.

"Nice to see you."

"Nice to see you, too."

Salah was standing in front of Jas, blocking her path, and showing no sign of moving out of the way to allow her to pass.

"We don't usually meet in the mornings, do we?"

"No. I think I must have overslept."

"Or perhaps I am up earlier than usual."

"Maybe; anyway, I must go and do my chores."

"What time do you finish work, Jas?"

"It depends, but I am mostly done by about 2 pm."

"Then what do you do?"

"I often have a sleep or, if I'm not too tired, I might get a bus to one of the malls for a wander around the shops. During the evening I sometimes meet a friend, then I get a bus back or, if I am with a friend, a taxi."

"I would like to do that; shall we go together one evening?"

"Why not? See you later, now let me go?"

He stepped aside and off she went downstairs to do her chores. Salah was still rooted to the spot. He could hardly contain his excitement, going over and over in his mind what had just happened. Did she just agree to a date? Did she realise she was agreeing to a date? What did she mean by 'see you later'? Does this mean that she likes him? Presumably, she doesn't *dis*like him.

Salah tried to dress quickly. "Shit," he didn't have any clean clothes, so he put on the same clothes as yesterday – he knew it was about time he learned how to use the washing machine. Up to now he'd managed by washing his clothes in a bucket of soapy water and rinsing them in clean water. They dried very quickly when laid out on the roof tiles outside his room. He could ask Jas to show him how to work the machine; he had seen her washing towels and clothes then hanging them up on lines to dry in bathrooms.

Downstairs, Khaled was waiting to give Salah a lift to the College as usual. Salah jumped in. Neither of them spoke for a while. Then Salah thought it wise to make use of the opportunity to check with Khaled about Jas.

"By the way, Khaled, is anybody in the villa interested in Jas?"

"What do you mean by 'interested'?"

"I mean, does anyone fancy her?"

"Not as far as I know. She keeps herself to herself in her room. Heaven only knows what she does up there. She must be so bored at times. Do you like her, then?"

"I think she is quite pretty. I met her this morning and we spoke briefly, I thought then how nice she is. We may go into the city centre together one evening and I wanted to be sure I wasn't going to upset you or one of the other guys."

"I don't think so, Salah, but be careful, you may find she's married – not that this needs to be an issue necessarily."

"Really, to someone in Dubai?"

"No, to someone in the Philippines."

Salah couldn't help feeling crestfallen. He didn't speak much for the rest of the journey and when he did they discussed the day ahead. They both had a Managing People Safely lecture first thing, then private study until lunchtime. In the afternoon they had Managing Physical Hazards again, followed by English. It was unusual for them to be together more or less all day; it would help the day go by pleasantly and they always enjoyed each other's company, although they were not close friends.

Salah couldn't help himself wondering whether this evening would be a good opportunity to continue the morning conversation with Jas. He decided to give it a try to see if she would like to go out together. He wouldn't be able to make tomorrow evening as he had agreed to go to the Wankowskis' for dinner.

Back at the villa, Salah reached the top of the stairs and went to his room. He paused outside Jas' door and listened for signs of life. Nothing. His room was very hot; he removed his rucksack, placed it on the floor, removed his top and lay on his bed. He was tired and hot and fell asleep. A few moments later he was awake again and realised he needed to wash some clothes, which he did, following his usual method.

With his laundry spread out on the hot tiles he decided that he had to be bold with Jas or nothing would happen. So he tapped lightly on her bedroom door. The door opened and there she was, standing in front of him wearing very short shorts and a tight top. She looked great.

"Hi Jas, hope I didn't disturb you."

"Hi Salah, no, I wasn't asleep. Actually, I finished a bit earlier today so I had an early sleep."

"Do you feel like going into the centre together like we spoke this morning?"

"OK… what, tonight?"

"Why not?"

"OK, if you like, but you'll have to give me half an hour to get ready."

"Fine."

Salah figured he needed time for his clothes to dry so half an hour was fine with him. He would also make use of the time to have a wash and make himself presentable.

The time went by quickly and they met up. Jas suggested they take a bus to the Dubai Mall. Salah was happy for Jas to take the lead as she had done this many times before and he had no particular plan in mind except to wander around the shops and, perhaps, visit the souk he'd heard about.

On arrival they left the bus and began to explore the downtown area. Salah had been aware of the massive building project over a long period but hadn't seen the finished product up close. They strolled towards the Burj Khalifa, the tallest building in the world, and its neighbour the Dubai Mall, and were amazed by the sight of the Burj Khalifa lit up at night. Jas pointed to the fountains saying she'd heard they put on a fantastic show dancing to music with special lighting effects. She'd like to see this sometime.

They found the entrance to the Dubai Mall and went inside to look for the store directory. Immediately, Salah felt overawed by the sheer number of stores, at least a thousand shops and restaurants. He asked Jas where she would like to go.

"I don't mind. I am not very familiar with this mall. It's very big; I usually just go round a few women's fashion outlets, but only window shopping."

"OK, let's do it."

They worked their way round level one, pausing here and there and occasionally going inside for Jas to look more closely at something or feel the material. Salah went into one or two gift shops but was dismayed by the prices so moved on quickly. He noticed a lift and stopped to look at the floor plan for the other levels. There was a McDonald's on level two.

"Jas, why don't we go to McDonald's for a drink?"

"If you'd like to, as long as it's not too expensive."

Salah had just enough money for both of them to have a burger and a Coke, so up they went. They eventually found McDonald's in the food court and joined the queue for ordering.

"What would you like, Jas?"

"What are you having?"

"I'm going to have a Big Mac, chips and a Coke."

Jas looked at the menu, apparently undecided, and then said, "I would like a McChicken meal with a thick shake, please."

Salah then asked Jas if she would like to get a table, some sauces and napkins while he ordered. When his tray of food and drink arrived he took it over to her and sat down. She was holding some cash and tried to hand it to Salah. He politely declined, Jas insisted, and he declined again saying it was his treat. They began to eat. Every time Salah looked up at Jas she was looking at him, but turned away quickly. They hardly spoke, perhaps because they were eating and drinking, perhaps because neither were relaxed and at ease with the situation.

When they finished, Jas thanked Salah several times and he said she was very welcome. As they left the table, Jas waited while Salah picked up the tray with their debris, took it to the disposal point and pushed it into the rubbish bin before stacking the tray.

He asked Jas if she would like to visit the nearby souk. They left the Mall and walked across the bridge over the Burj Lake to the souk. Along the way they realised that this bridge gave them the best view of the Burj and the fountains. Jas said they should come back another time to see the dancing fountains. Salah couldn't have been more pleased as Jas must be thinking of going out with him again.

They entered the souk and were impressed initially with the beauty of the building and the smart shops and food outlets, but this was not what they imagined a souk would be like. They were expecting a traditional collection of Arabic craftsmen and traders selling traditional wares from modest facilities. This souk was full of international brands and restaurants, hardly different from the Mall, albeit on a smaller scale, so they decided to leave and get a bus back to their villa.

They arrived back and climbed the stairs to the top of the villa and to their rooms. Salah began to feel awkward as he was unsure how to behave in this unfamiliar situation. He had enjoyed being with Jas and was sorry to be parting from her. He would like to show his feelings towards her. Could he put his arm around her as he said 'Good night'? He wanted to kiss her but if she didn't like it he would have spoilt everything. Shaking hands didn't seem right either. As Salah was thinking along these lines they arrived at their rooms together. Both hesitated and looked at each other for what seemed quite a long time but was probably only a couple of seconds.

"I really enjoyed this evening, Jas."

"So did I, Salah."

"I hope we can do it again."

"Why not? Good night."

"Good night, Jas."

Salah went to bed thinking the evening had gone as well as could be expected, although he would have liked to have been able to take things further – maybe next time.

CHAPTER 2.14

September 25 2002

ENGLAND

Salah entered the University Administration Building and asked the security guy for directions to the Vice-Chancellor's suite. On arrival, an eager bustling receptionist showed him to the conference room and left him outside the door. He paused, still wondering why he could possibly be required to attend a meeting in the Vice-Chancellor's offices figuring that, whatever the reason, it didn't bode well. Nervously, he knocked.

"Enter."

"Good morning. Are you Salah? Please take a seat. I expect you know Mr Russell. You can sit next to him; we're waiting for one more."

Salah's stress level increased rapidly. Was he told to sit next to Mr Russell because he might need the course leader's protection? Perhaps he might have accidentally plagiarised someone else's work and was about to be disciplined by the University's Unfair Means Committee. He might even be sacked, but what for? How would he explain this to the Wankowskis?

The clock was ticking and nothing happened.

"Whilst we're waiting, I'm Professor Kenneth Fage, I'm the Pro-Vice-Chancellor responsible for the University's security. Perhaps everyone else would like to introduce themselves; I suggest we begin on my right and then go around the table."

"I'm Jenny Bennett, Professor Fage's Secretary."

"I'm Superintendent Tom Sweeney, Police."

"I'm Joe Swift, Students' Union representative."

"Julie Jerrim, MI5. I'm with Government counterterrorism."

By this time Salah felt his heart pounding, beating so fast and so hard he thought it was trying to escape from his chest.

"I imagine it's become obvious by now what this meeting is about."

"Not really, Professor Fage."

Salah surprised himself, shocked himself actually, the fact that he'd spoken. He didn't mean to speak, it just happened. Everyone turned their heads and looked at him. They looked in surprise too, and why did he speak in such a pathetic whimpering voice? Now they were bound to think he was guilty of something, but of what?

"Well, let's try and make some progress for I am sure he won't be long; is that OK with everyone?"

"You are Salah Al Munairi from Dubai, Final Year Facilities Management, currently living in Sharpe Hall; is that correct?"

"That's correct, Professor."

"You attend the local mosque and have joined the Student Islamic Society, is this correct?"

"Yes."

"Would you describe yourself as a devout Muslim?"

"No, Professor."

"How would you describe yourself?"

Joe interjected with, "Professor, I am uneasy about this line of questioning."

"I understand, Joe; I think you'll feel better when you know where these questions are leading, Salah?"

"My mother was Hindu, my father Muslim and my adopted parents are Christian. I have come to Islam late and I am interested enough to want to pursue it. I am learning about the faith. My friends are helping, but I'm not devout."

Salah felt better after giving what he thought were good answers to the professor's questions. His jangling nerves were a little easier to handle, that is until there was a knock on the door and in walked Randy.

"Sorry everyone, the flight landed on time but we had to wait a while on the runway for an arrival gate."

"Welcome, Randy. Have you had some coffee?"

"Yes, thanks."

The professor asked Randy to introduce himself. While this was going on someone appeared wheeling a trolley with small plates of pastries and proceeded to push it towards the far wall.

Randy didn't give his surname and introduced himself as a consultant. After the introductions, Professor Fage suggested everyone help themselves to refreshments. Joe took the opportunity to be close to Salah to quietly tell him that he was not informed what the meeting was about, only to attend, adding that the students' union would 'watch Salah's back'.

Returning to the conference table with coffee and a muffin, Salah's palpitations were back with a vengeance. Why was Randy here? Why did the students' union need to watch his back? Why was he being asked personal questions about his religion? The feeling that he was in serious trouble wouldn't go away, but what sort of trouble?

"OK, let's get back to the meeting. Randy, do you have anything you wish to report?"

"Yes, but my report comes under 'Restricted', as usual."

"Understood." Professor Fage picked up his mobile and spoke to the receptionist.

"Could you look after our two students while we deal with Reserved Business? Thank you." The overeager receptionist arrived to collect Joe and Salah and take them to another room.

Those that remained in the conference room knew who Randy was and why he was there. He gave his report consisting of the results from yet another scan of the CIA database that confirmed suspicions that a potential terrorist incident was likely to take place somewhere in the University, in all probability as a protest at the invitation to the American Secretary of State to accept an honorary degree. A student from Sudan had been identified as needing to be closely watched.

Julie Jerrim added that the same person had been identified as a 'person of interest' by MI5. There was also a student from another university identified as a 'person of interest'; he had visited the local mosque and the University more than once. She said that Salah Al Munairi had met both students on more than one occasion and had been frequently in touch with them by telephone. For these reasons he should also be treated as a 'person of interest'.

"Thank you. I suggest we call the students back." He called the receptionist again. Joe and Salah were soon back and resumed their seats.

"I'm sorry, Salah, we have had rather a stop-go meeting. I think we now have everything we need to progress. Salah was saying that his friends were helping him to learn about Islam."

"Is that fair, Salah?"

"OK with me."

"Salah, my next question is about the University's invitation to an American Secretary of State to accept an honorary degree. Are you aware of this invitation?"

"I've heard about it, that's all." Salah felt in control.

"Are your friends talking about this?"

"I'm not sure what my friends are talking about when I am not with them."

"Are they talking about it when you *are* with them?"

"Yes, among many other things." Salah worried that he may have sounded evasive.

"Are other students talking about it?"

"I am not sure. I think so. It seems a lot of students are concerned about it."

"How do you know this?"

"They seem rather restless."

"Why do you think that might be?"

"I think there is a lot of anti-American feeling around."

"Is there? Do you know why?"

"I think so. I expect everyone around this table has some idea."

"Are you aware of any individual or group planning to make trouble?"

"I don't think it's fair to expect Salah to spy on his friends," interjected one of the others present.

"Fair enough, Joe, but I am not asking Salah about his friends now, I'm asking about students in general."

"Even so, I'm still not happy." Joe confirmed his unhappiness by looking very unhappy.

"OK, perhaps I can ask you about the mosque. You said you attend the mosque, right? I believe there's quite a rumpus going on about the Government's invitation for this American to visit the UK, particularly the suggestion he should visit the mosque."

"I am sure that's true, although I think the leaders of the mosque are mainly worried about demonstrations and causing local inconvenience, rather than the rights and wrongs of the invitation or international politics."

"You say that, Salah, but we have been advised by the intelligence services that some members of the mosque are members of a terrorist group."

"If that is so I don't know who they are, neither do I know anything about it."

As he spoke he couldn't help thinking of Majid's secret life.

"I'm sure you understand, Salah, that if anything like that spilled over into the University it would cause immense damage, maybe for a long time to come. We are looking to the Muslim community to help make sure that doesn't happen."

"I do understand, Professor. I am sure the Student Islamic Society will do the right thing and set a good example."

"Let's hope so. By the way, do you know Majid Qasim? He's studying Politics, I believe."

"Yes, he shares a house with my best friend, Khamis. I've only been there once or twice. He also joined us in the town for coffee the other day. Khamis and I have also seen him at the mosque. I wouldn't call him a friend."

Everything Salah said was true but he felt uneasy again and hoped it didn't show.

"Salah, I think we can let you go now. If you see or hear anything that might lead to trouble for the University, please let Mr Russell know immediately. Understand?"

"I shall, Professor."

"Thanks, Joe, for your help this morning; I hardly need add that the business of the meeting is totally confidential."

Joe nodded and followed Salah out of the conference room.

Professor Fage asked everyone for their observations and comments.

"Randy?"

"I met that boy; we sat together on the flight from Amsterdam when he came over to join the University. When his name came up in the current context I checked him out very thoroughly. I can't find anything specific.

"He's had a bad time recently. His mother was a housekeeper for a Sheikh. The Sheikh died and the family kicked the mother out and she disappeared without trace, making Salah for all practical purposes, an orphan. Two teachers at the University's partner college in Dubai adopted him. They look like solid citizens. He might have some kind of chip on his shoulder against the world but I don't think he fits our profile of a potential terrorist."

"Julie?"

"I'm inclined to agree. The problem with Salah is the company he keeps, for example, the Sudanese student we're interested in. We have reliable intelligence this individual has been fraternising with members of a new group of activists. We think he meets up with them on-line, in chat rooms and in the local mosque."

"Who are they?"

"Good question, we're not sure but we believe their membership is increasing. We think they see themselves as activists righting wrongs against Muslims."

"This sounds serious."

"I'm sure you're right, Professor. The good news is that we don't believe they have been responsible for any illegality up to now and they probably know they are being watched.

"The other guy we're interested in is a bit of a mystery. His name is Mubarak Al Munairi. You will recognise the family name as the same as Salah's. We think he is Salah's stepbrother. He's only come into the picture recently and he's not at this University, he's doing a higher degree somewhere in Business Studies by distance learning. He is not a regular at the local mosque but he flits in and out. He's visited Salah at this University; we cannot make out how well they know each other."

"Thank you, anyone else?" No one spoke.

"OK, well, thank you all for coming this morning and for your valuable contributions. Let's hope that our combined efforts will be sufficient for us to be able to keep on top of this. Needless to say, if there is any significant change in the situation, especially anything that increases risk, we shall need to get together again without delay. My guess is that the closest cooperation between the University and the various agencies and services is essential if we are to achieve success."

"Sorry to have the last word, Professor, but an unintended consequence of the increased surveillance is that we have found someone illegally downloading enormous quantities of films and other streamed material on their computer. We are almost sure the individual lives in Sharpe Hall and that the offending behaviour happens at night and into the early hours. Shall we act or not?"

"I'm sure the FBI would like to know about this."

"Isn't that a bit heavy, Randy? Might I suggest a warning first?"

"Tom, it's not too heavy if the downloads are terror related."

"I see your point, Randy, but let's not jump to conclusions. The individual concerned is breaking the law *and* the University regulations. I take this very seriously. However, I am happy for the police and the University to deal with it as Tom suggests. If the offences turn out to be more serious we shall take whatever further steps are necessary. OK, everybody?"

"As you wish, Professor."

Salah and Joe found their way out of the administration building and walked a short way together across the campus.

"Thanks for your support, Joe. Do you spend a lot of time in meetings like that?" he asked, aghast that he could be asked to attend such meetings.

"Not really. The responsibility to attend University meetings is shared between a group of students' union officials. That was quite an easy one."

"Really? I hated every minute of it."

"That's understandable, Salah. The worst for us are the disciplinary cases and the academic appeals. They are usually complicated, sometimes acrimonious and always sad. Our responsibility is huge because life-changing decisions are being made."

"Sure. I hope I don't get involved in either of those. By the way, does the students' union have a view about this invitation/honorary degree issue?"

"Not really. We would much rather it wasn't happening and we hope the University changes its mind. I suppose our current position could be described as 'watchful waiting'. We are not planning any sort of protest at the moment if that's what you mean." Joe moved away from Salah and indicated he was needed elsewhere.

"Bye."

"Thanks again, Joe." Salah understood that Joe needed to go in another direction and, having no other reason to be in the University himself, he returned to Sharpe where he made tea in the kitchen and took it to his room with a couple of leftover soggy biscuits.

Salah was soon paralysing himself with confusion and indecision. He concluded that what he *wanted* to do was not the same as what he *should* do and he'd no idea how this conflict could ever be resolved.

CHAPTER 2.15

September 26 2002

"Hello Salah, come in and take a seat. What did you want to see me about?"

"I'm not happy, Jack. I thought everything was going fine until yesterday's meeting with the Pro-Vice-Chancellor which, I must say, took me by surprise."

"It took me by surprise, too."

"Can I ask you what you thought about it?"

"Well, yes and no. Obviously I was present for the whole meeting, some of which was restricted and therefore confidential."

"I understand, but can you tell me who Randy is?"

"I don't see why not, he's a security expert helping the University. He comes and goes."

"I met Randy on the flight over. Actually, I sat next to him on the Dubai Schiphol flight. He was friendly and we got along fine; he worked on his laptop most of the time. I didn't see him on the Schiphol UK flight until after we all disembarked and I reached passport control. Everyone was being questioned and it was taking ages. The passport guy hardly looked at Randy's passport and waived him through quickly; then another uniformed guy saluted him. I couldn't understand why he was treated differently."

"Sorry, can't help you with that."

"Jack, is there any possibility my phone is being tapped?"

"I think it is possible; can't say more, I'm afraid."

"Who is allowed to do that and why would they do it?"

"I can only assume it would be the intelligence services, Salah. Why? Because this high-profile American VIP visitor is coming to the University. The University is worried about it because of the politics involved and has asked for help. The local police are also worried. This American has also been invited to visit the local mosque. They're worried too."

"OK, but what does this have to do with me?"

"Maybe nothing, Salah. I suggest you try not to worry yourself about it. My guess is that because there is some activism going on at the mosque, University students attending the mosque are being cleared for security purposes. Other than that you may have been seen or had phone contact with someone who has been identified as a 'person of interest' by the intelligence services."

"Have you heard the term 'racial profiling', Jack?"

"Yes, of course, Salah."

"Do you think that's what's happening to me now?"

"I can see why you would think that."

"I thought it wasn't supposed to happen anymore."

"Salah, the University has a lot of difficulty with students from the Middle East because of their names, family relationships, by which I mean fathers, sons, brothers and sisters, etc. Then there are problems with different spellings of names and a few cultural differences. I'm sorry to say there have been too many instances where students have used this confusion to plagiarise other people's work or even impersonate another person in some cases. As a result, universities are very wary."

"OK, I get it, so Arab students deserve to be profiled?"

"I didn't say that, Salah. Unfortunately, there is another issue – security – and we could add yet another – politics. I am sure you know we have just passed the anniversary of the attack on the Twin Towers in New York. People are more anxious and fearful nowadays and the University has to take security very seriously, hence the employment of experts as consultants."

"Jack, I understand what you have been saying and I appreciate your honesty."

"I may have said too much, Salah, so please keep our chat to yourself."

"I shall, Jack, thanks again."

Salah left Jack uneasy and wondering. This time Salah was

nothing like as self-assured as in their earlier meeting and he was clearly worried about the PVC[6] meeting. Jack wondered whether this was because Salah had felt offended by having been profiled or whether there might be a more sinister reason for his discomfort. Could it be, for example, that he was up to no good and fearful of being found out? Or maybe he was struggling with all the problems he's been having and things have begun to get on top of him. Jack wished he could persuade Salah to see a student counsellor.

Whilst he had been with Jack, Salah had a missed call on his mobile. It was from Majid, who also left a message:

'What about this morning? Tell me when you're free.'

He called Majid and arranged to meet him in the cafeteria for a drink. Then they would walk over to Sharpe together.

When Salah arrived, Majid was already in the cafeteria queuing. He asked Salah what he wanted to drink and suggested he find a table. After a while, Majid came over with a tray of tea, coffee and doughnuts. He refused Salah's offer to pay. They conversed briefly about non-controversial matters, stowed their tray with empty mugs and plates in the racks provided, and set off for Sharpe.

"So, what did you want to talk about, Salah?"

Salah tensed up. He was just about to conspire with someone to commit a crime. It wasn't as easy as he thought. He hoped he could trust Majid.

"Majid, I didn't want to say anything in front of Khamis the other day, but I felt very much on your wavelength when you were talking about political activism, protest, justice, righting wrongs and so on, and I was interested in your new group, you know, the people you meet up with in the mosque. I remember you saying they wanted to do something dramatic to protest against this ministerial invitation to a senior American politician to visit the mosque. You mentioned also the visit to the University and that you suggested making the University the target of the protest to protect the mosque."

"You've got a good memory, Salah. Go on."

"I wondered if you or they had made any progress." Majid

____

6. Pro-Vice-Chancellor

looked uneasy.

"Salah, you're a great guy but I think the fewer people who know anything about this the better."

"I agree. That's why I didn't want to say anything in front of Khamis. I am asking you because I would like to be involved. I want to help."

"How?"

"Majid, I'm not coming at this from an Islamic fundamentalist position. I am only just becoming committed to Islam. I haven't been radicalised. I'm coming at this from a humanitarian perspective. I have strong personal reasons for wanting to strike a blow against injustice and barbarism and I have ideas about how to do it. Unless you and your friends have got the whole thing planned I thought you might be interested in my ideas. And, if you are, I can help you carry them out."

"OK, Salah. You've got me interested."

"Good, so what's the answer to my question?"

"What was your question?"

"Have you made any progress?"

"Yes and no. We haven't settled on a target yet but we have purchased a stolen credit card on the Internet that we can use to buy anything we need or hire transport and there's no way the card could be traced to any of us."

"That's a start, I suppose. Would you like me to show you a possible target?"

"Is there any risk involved?"

"Not as far as I can tell. We should wear something with a hood."

"No problem. Let's go."

They left the room, went down the stairs and out of the building, trying to adopt as casual a manner as possible. They strolled down the path to the central area of the campus and pulled their hoods up. They joined the path leading to the lecture rooms and along the way came to a fenced enclosure on their left at the back of the Engineering Building. It was a boarded fence so they couldn't see inside. Salah pointed to the door that was of the same construction with a large padlock and attached to the door were two notices; one read 'DANGER KEEP OUT', the other 'HAZARDOUS CHEMICALS'.

They approached the door and Salah showed Majid the small crack between the door and doorframe with just enough room to look through and make out two large propane gas containers. Salah explained that in Dubai College these had been called gas bullets and they played a starring role in the videos showing BLEVES during the Fire Safety module. Majid had a good idea what a BLEVE was from the photograph on the front cover of the book currently on the mantelpiece in his room. Salah suggested it would look less suspicious if they retraced their steps one at a time, each taking a different route and meeting up again in Salah's room.

Back in Salah's room the two sat down and looked at each other. Neither spoke for several minutes.

"I assume you're suggesting we create an explosion."

"If it was done at night it would do a huge amount of damage without killing or hurting anyone."

"I see your point. Have you thought about how?"

"The bullets are mounted on brick pillars. We take a photo from one of the Engineering Building windows and count the number of courses of bricks. We can then calculate the height of the space under the bullets. We buy a garden barbecue and adapt it if necessary to make sure it's the right height to fit under the bullets and we buy a Camping Gaz cylinder. We cut the padlock with a hacksaw or strong wire cutters, install the barbecue and then turn on the gas and ignite it.

"The gas inside the bullets will overheat and then boil, which will produce an enormous explosion called a BLEVE. Have a look at the book you have on your mantelpiece. There's a picture of a BLEVE on the front cover."

"Sounds like a plan, Salah. When did you think of all that?"

"Several things have happened to me recently, prompting these ideas. Piece by piece they have been gradually taking hold in my mind. I just happened to see the fenced enclosure by chance the other day while walking away from a lecture. I took a closer look out of pure curiosity, nothing more. And then there was this strange meeting yesterday morning."

"I think the others will like the concept but I'm not sure they'll want you involved."

"Majid, don't you think it strange that I accidentally failed to return the *BLEVE* book to the Dubai College library, packed it and brought it to England by mistake and you took a copy out of the library here, purely because you liked the picture? It's as if we are being guided in some way."

"Maradona would have called it the 'hand of God'. Can you tell me about the meeting?"

"This morning I had to attend a meeting with one of the Pro-Vice-Chancellors. You remember? I got the message when we were with Khamis in your house. You described it as 'bad news'. The PVC said he is responsible for security. The local police were there, an American security consultant, a woman from counterterrorism, someone from the students' union and me, of course.

"They asked me loads of questions about my religion, about going to the mosque and about joining the Islamic Society. They asked about disturbances at the mosque and said that the intelligence services believe there is a terrorist group involved in the mosque. Did I know anything about it? They asked me about my friends and about what my friends thought of the University's invitation to the American politician.

"I think I handled it well. I can't imagine I said anything that was of any use to them. They asked specifically if I knew you. I said that I had met you only because you lived in the same house as my friend Khamis."

"Interesting; I wonder why they're asking questions about me."

"I think it's clear that the University is expecting trouble and that there is a huge amount of surveillance going on. We must be extremely careful, Majid. You are definitely on their radar. I suppose I must be too, although until today I have been totally innocent. Why else would they have chosen to interrogate me?"

"You're right, Salah. I think the biggest danger area is mobile phone calls, texts and e-mails. They are so easily traced. We must maintain mobile and cyber silence for the time being. Agreed?"

"Agreed."

"I hope this room isn't bugged. All our face to face communication from now on should be on open ground. Agreed?"

"Agreed."

"I shall talk to the others and see what they think, Salah, and let you know. We can probably arrange to meet through Khamis without him becoming suspicious."

"Good idea, Majid."

Majid got up to leave. "Remember: no texts, calls or e-mail messages and no talk except outside, away from any possible surveillance. I suppose nowadays we need to keep an eye out for drones as well."

"Got it." Salah felt nervous but excited. So many complained about the violence and injustices in the world but never thought to do anything about it. To be fair, few had any perception that they could do anything. He was different. He was fortunate. He had both motivation and opportunity.

Teamwork was going to be the key to success, even if all the members of the team never met each other. In fact, it would be better if they didn't, as long as every member of the team was committed to the plan and the goal – that's all that's needed for ultimate success. They would become a legend, an anonymous legend hopefully, but a legend nevertheless and they would be an example to others thinking of taking a stand against self-evidently immorally and wrong political decisions and actions. They might be doing wrong themselves but, for them, doing wrong was doing right, because it was in a good cause.

Salah decided to e-mail the Wankowskis again:

'Hello Janek and Maria

Thank you for your e-mail. Your message arrived on a very strange day. Do you remember me telling you that there was trouble at the mosque and that this could happen at the University too? This is all to do with the

Government's invitation to a US Under Secretary and their wish for him to visit the local mosque. This has inflamed anti-American sentiment among the mosque people. It seems the mosque leaders are not sure whether to cancel the invitation. The University has invited the same person to accept an honorary degree. They are worried about protests and demonstrations too.

Well, I was summoned to a meeting in a Pro-Vice-Chancellor's office. Also present were police, intelligence services, a security consultant, a students' union representative, etc. I was asked many questions about my religion, the mosque, my friends, about what people are saying about the visit, etc. One or two questions implied there is a terrorist group operating somewhere. Of course I knew nothing about that. I think I handled the situation well.

The following day I saw my course leader for a chat. I told him I was puzzled and a little unnerved by the PVC meeting. He told me not to worry and that nowadays universities carry out surveillance in this kind of situation and that, maybe, I had been in contact with someone they were interested in. He also said there were well-known issues with some Arab students that cause universities problems.

I don't think there is anything to worry about. I just thought you would like to know about this. I hope all is well with you. Will be in touch again soon…

Salah

P.S. You are always in my thoughts too!!'

This time, Salah sent the message with a guilty conscience. Although he was confident about his role in the plans he was making with Majid and others, which he felt was totally justified, he knew the Wankowskis would not approve. They had done so much to facilitate his current good fortune in being at a university in the UK. Although he felt disloyal and ungrateful he would still strike a blow for Hani and all those who had experienced similar atrocities and deprivations.

CHAPTER 2.16

June 2002

DUBAI

"Hello Mrs Wankowski. Good to see you again. Hello Janek. How are things? I expect you are wondering whether I've heard anything from Hilal about Aparna Malik."

"Good morning Yahya. If you have any news, of course we should like to hear it but actually we have come about another matter. We have been doing a great deal of soul-searching because of Salah's precarious situation. You mentioned that we could perhaps approach the Ministry of Higher Education to see if they can help him, maybe from a hardship fund or some such thing and then you said what Salah really needs is for some good people to adopt him.

"You cannot imagine the impact your suggestion has had on us. We've discussed this over and over again and have come to the conclusion that we would like to adopt Salah. Do you think you could help us with whatever process we have to go through? By the way, we've not mentioned this to Salah yet."

"I think both of you are very brave, unselfish and generous people, fully deserving of support. Of course, you will need to speak to Salah first. However, I must advise you that what you wish to do will not be easy. I understand Dubai has a large number of orphan children and I believe the principle of adoption is established and encouraged by the Government.

"As far as I know, all orphan children whatever their parents' nationality, must be treated as Emiratis and can only be adopted by Emiratis. To be successful in your plan to adopt Salah, I believe you would need to become Emirati nationals. I'm not sure whether you would be prepared to do this. I believe the rules for becoming an Emirati national are very demanding."

"We hear what you say, Yahya. We have done some research and have discovered that someone who is not an Emirati can apply for citizenship if they have legally lived in the Emirates for 30 years, legally earning a living, have a good reputation and can speak and understand basic Arabic. Obviously we cannot meet the residence requirement but it seems that for those living in Oman, Qatar or Bahrain, the period is only three years. Maybe there could be some wriggle room for us."

"I am not sure; are you aware dual nationality is not recognised by the Government here. How do you feel about giving up your British nationality?"

"Obviously, we would rather not have to do that but there could be a safety net for us if everything goes wrong. We understand it's possible for Emiratis to voluntarily give up Emirati citizenship if they wish to obtain another nationality; this might enable us to revert to British nationality if necessary."

"Then there's the problem of the residency requirement. However worthy your motives and intentions, I am not sure we could argue that you are a special case, an exception to the rule, if you like. I suggest we try to secure support from ministers. I expect the Minister for Nationality and Culture will make the final decision. I do know that one of the College owners is friendly with him, this might be helpful."

"That does sound very helpful, Yahya. Who is it?"

"The College owner is Sheikh Mohammed Al Balushi. The Minister of Nationality and Culture is His Excellency Ahmed Al-Mandhari."

"What about the Minister of Higher Education?"

"Good thought. I think we should definitely try to get her on our side. I suggest we send her a letter to begin with; it will be better not to spring this on her. If we write a letter explaining what we are trying to achieve she will probably ask us to go and see her and that will be our opportunity to win her over."

"Would you like us to draft something, Yahya? We can hardly expect you to do this."

"By all means, I shall give it some more thought as well and make a few notes. We can then put our heads together again and finalise the letter."

"We are so grateful to you for your willingness to be involved and for your help."

"Let me just check my e-mails. Up to yesterday there has been nothing. Oh! As luck would have it, there *is* a message from Hilal today. Let me just see what he says." After reading for a few moments, he continued, "OK, he has been told that if she's been returned to India it was not on a flight. The recent passenger lists have been checked; the Indian Embassy has no knowledge of her whereabouts and has expressed concern."

"Thanks for this morning's news; so the mystery deepens."

"Apparently so."

"Yahya, please call me Maria, and my husband Janek."

"I shall. Thank you both."

Maria and Janek left Yahya's office with handshakes in all directions and walked back outside to Janek's car. They agreed the meeting had been useful and productive and felt the adoption ball was now rolling, albeit very slowly. Janek needed to leave the College promptly to go back to work so they hugged and then parted reluctantly.

Maria went back to her office and sat down at her desk, deep in thought. There was a lot to think about and her thoughts began to multiply at a rate. She was becoming confused. When would be the right time to speak to Salah? Janek would want to be present, of course. This suggested they should meet up outside college hours. How could such a meeting be arranged without seeming too official and heavy-handed? It would surely be counterproductive to worry Salah unnecessarily at a time when he was facing the most difficult situation of his life.

Maria changed her thought subject and turned her attention to drafting the letter for the MoE. She began by making a list of what she thought were the main points:

1. The death of Sheikh Salem, Salah's father
2. The disappearance of Aparna, Salah's mother
3. Salah becomes an orphan
4. Lack of financial support locally and in UK
5. Progression to UK University for Final Year of the course, fees only paid by MoE – living expenses?
6. Possible withdrawal from higher education through poverty. She sent her first draft to Janek's laptop via e-mail. He must have been sitting at his desk as he replied quickly, suggesting two more points for possible inclusion:
7. *Salah's mental health, the need for a home life*
8. *The need for parental guidance until full independence.*

Maria sent another message…

> *Thanks for quick reply. Like your additions. Will do.*
> *When do you think we should speak to Salah xxx*

Janek replied immediately…

> *Not sure. We can discuss tonight. xxx*

Maria consolidated the list of points for the letter and began drafting it when she heard a knock on her door. It was Yahya.

"Hello Yahya. Come in and have a seat."

"Hello Maria, I have just received another e-mail from Hilal. I thought I should let you know straightaway. Hilal has just heard from the Indian Embassy who say they have no knowledge of the current whereabouts of Aparna Malik, neither have they any record of her status in Dubai or of anything at all, in fact. They have also said that they regard this situation as highly unsatisfactory although it is very common. Finally, they suggested contacting one or two Indian social workers who deal with this kind of thing and occasionally get results."

"I see, so she was not returned to India by air by her employer and has no status in Dubai as far as anyone knows. I assume the

Indian Embassy would have known had she married an Emirati. Officially, she is invisible. What a terrible thing and, even worse, this is a common problem."

"I think you have summarised the situation very well, Maria. I suggest for the time being we let Hilal do whatever he can with the social workers. I think it important too for us to be able to demonstrate we have left no stone unturned to find Salah's mother – this is important to our case."

"I agree, Yahya. Please thank Hilal on behalf of Janek and me. Shall I be the one to let Salah know?"

"I think that would be best, if you don't mind. You seem to have formed a relationship with him. That should be most helpful."

Yahya left and Maria pondered the latest news. Her immediate reaction was that it was now essential to meet Salah as soon as possible to let him know how things currently stood regarding his mother. Could this also be a good opportunity to introduce him to their idea of adopting him? Maria felt uncomfortable about this. On the one hand, it felt too manipulative, a bit like an ambush; on the other hand, it seemed there was no good time to bring up the subject.

Maria and Janek found their way quite easily to the Ministry of Higher Education building by following a local map. They stopped at the entrance and identified themselves to the man operating the barrier. He checked them against a list and let them pass. They parked their car and waited for Yahya to arrive. They were slightly early. Not having been to the Ministry before and being unsure of the way they had allowed plenty of time.

Yahya arrived in just enough time for them to collect their visitor badges from reception and travel up to the sixth floor in the lift as directed. They were amazed when the lift doors opened to find themselves walking on deep pile carpets among palatial furnishings and interior decorations. The Ministerial Offices were nothing short of magnificent. An immaculately attired aide greeted them ceremoniously, ushered them along a short corridor and knocked gently on the minister's door. The door was opened by another similarly attired aide on the other side of the door and they were ushered into an enormous room.

Immediately to their left was a large conference table with ten chairs. An elaborate floral display in a vase had been placed in the centre. In the distance against the far wall was a huge desk. Behind the desk sat Her Excellency Dr Farah Ahmadi. In front of the desk was a row of comfortable chairs and a coffee table. On the table at one end was a beautiful ceramic bowl of dates. At the other was an ornate box full of expensive looking chocolates.

"Hello Mrs Wankowski. I am afraid that long walk has been designed to make you feel nervous and me important. I am so sorry. Please take a seat. I assume this is your husband."

"Janek Wankowski, Your Excellency."

"I am pleased to meet you, Mr Wankowski; I see you are teaching at another one of our colleges." She didn't shake hands.

"That's correct, Your Excellency."

"And this is?"

"Yahya Al Maskari, Your Excellency – the College Personnel Manager. I have been advising and helping the Wankowskis with local laws, regulations, rules and customs."

"Welcome. Can I offer you tea or coffee, some dates maybe?"

They said no thank you to tea. The Wankowskis had been warned about Ministry tea, usually made by boiling teabags in a saucepan full of condensed milk for several hours. Arabic coffee was bearable but too spicy for the Wankowskis, but Yahya said yes to coffee. They liked the idea of dates but they looked under-ripe and, fearing they would be tasty but indigestible, they politely declined those too.

"Thank you for your letter. I've read it most carefully and I congratulate you on the way in which you have made a case for what you want to do. Regrettably, there are one or two stumbling blocks that will need to be overcome. I am sure Yahya has told you already so I shall not bore you by going through them all again now. Instead, I would like to concentrate on whatever I can do to help; I think it will help me most to help you if I ask you some questions. Do you mind?"

"Not at all."

She reeled them off one by one.

"First, Dubai does not recognise joint nationality. How do you feel about being required to become Emirati nationals in order to be able to adopt?

"Second, how good is your Arabic?

"Third, what are you going to say regarding the residential requirement for becoming an Emirati?

"Fourth, although your current expatriate employment contracts are renewable they are relatively short term, not permanent. Are you happy for your financial affairs to be looked into to establish that you have sufficient resources in the medium to longer term to adopt a young Emirati adult?"

"Your Excellency, we appreciate your having taken the time to study our letter and we thank you for your kind remarks. We, of course, understand that there are stumbling blocks. In answer to your questions…

"First, we are more than happy to apply for Emirati nationality.

"Second, we believe our Arabic is not currently at the standard that will be required. We are both willing to follow an intensive Arabic study programme prior to and beyond our application for Emirati nationality. We both have bilingual Arabic colleagues in our Colleges who would help us.

"Third, we understand that some nationalities are treated more leniently regarding the residential requirement and we would respectfully request that our present residential status of nine years is accepted as an exception to the general rule because of the importance of teaching and education in nation- building We would remain in Dubai for as long as the service we can provide is required.

"Fourth, we are willing to cooperate and comply with any financial investigations and requirements arising in connection with our application to adopt."

"Thank you, Mr Wankowski. That was very helpful. You do know, don't you, that there will also be a police check?"

"We have no worries about that, Your Excellency."

"It has just occurred to me that there is another argument. You mentioned nation-building. You could perhaps make more of the economic argument. When Salah graduates with a Facilities Management qualification he will be very useful. Every ministry and other government building needs at least one person with a Facilities Management qualification to manage the building and help maintain the Government estate. Currently, expatriates are carrying out the job. The Government wants to replace expats with nationals as soon as possible."

"Thank you, Your Excellency. We shall certainly include something along those lines. The Government has already invested in Salah's education. It would be very wasteful if he is unable to continue, for whatever reason."

"Exactly. I'm sure you're aware that HE the Minister for Culture and Nationality will deal with your case. I could pass your letter to him with a letter of support from me, or you can write to him directly and give my name as a kind of referee. This is up to you.

"I wouldn't want you to overestimate my influence with His Excellency. We have come a long way in the Emirates with gender equality but there is still a long way to go. Their Excellencies of the male gender are occasionally very traditional and not wholly in favour of females occupying senior positions in the Government.

"Unfortunately, I do not know His Excellency the Minister of Culture and Nationality personally, so I cannot be certain how he will react to my involvement. If you have any others who could help influence his decision I suggest you seriously consider asking them to help you."

"Your Excellency, I wish to say again how grateful we are for your advice and support. I am sure we all would wish to take advantage of your kind offer to forward our letter on to His Excellency with your recommendation. And on your last point, we shall definitely do everything we can to maximise influence on the decision, discreetly of course."

There was a natural pause and silence now. It seemed the right time to suggest closing the meeting and they wondered whether Dr Ahmadi was too polite to ask them to leave. So they suggested she must be very busy and offered to leave her. Dr Ahmadi thanked them for coming and wished them luck with the adoption. She asked to be kept informed.

The visitors retraced their steps, escorted by one of the ministerial aides, and handed back their badges. They were soon out of the building and on the way through the car park to their vehicles.

"What an impressive woman," uttered Janek to nobody in particular.

"That was a really positive meeting. Thank you Yahya for suggesting we involve her."

"I didn't know her before and I was not sure what to expect but I am very impressed and pleased to have met her. I think we need to go back and agree our strategy. See you back at the College."

Maria went straight to her office and sat at her desk. She wasn't sure what Yahya had meant by 'agree our strategy'. She thought their strategy was already agreed, except for the addition of Her Excellency's additional point about the value of a Facilities Management qualification to the Government. Or, perhaps Yahya was referring to the issue of whether to send the letter directly to HE the Minister for Culture and Nationality or via HE the Minister for Higher Education.

Maria believed herself to be in the lead for producing the letter. After all, she had already consulted Janek and he had approved her initial list of points and added a couple of his own. Surely he would expect her to finish the job. She decided she would go ahead and finalise the letter whilst everything was still fresh in her mind. She would check with Yahya and Janek to whom it should be sent later.

Somewhere among the assorted papers on her desk was her first draft and, although it was only a list of points, it seemed a good place to begin. She found it, added Janek's points, added Her Excellency's point and then began drafting.

After many reviews and revisions she produced the following letter:

'Your Excellency – with our highest respects and compliments

Permission to adopt – Salah Al Munairi

We are writing to request your approval for us to adopt the above-named who has recently become an orphan.

The recent death of Salah's father, Sheikh Salem Al Munairi, is a matter of public record. Following Sheikh Salem's death his family then dismissed Aparna Menon, Sheikh Salem's housekeeper, who is Salah's mother. Aparna Menon has disappeared without trace and all official and individual efforts to find her have been unsuccessful. It has been suggested that she may have become a victim of the illegal traffic in domestic staff.

Salah was raised by his mother who, although very poor herself, provided all the practical and emotional support Salah needed and as much financial support as she could afford. It follows that, without his mother, Salah no longer enjoys any of this support.

Salah is currently enrolled at one of the Dubai Colleges of Higher Education. His fees are paid by the Ministry of Higher Education. His other expenses have been met partly from his small savings, which are now exhausted, and from the kindness and generosity of friends and well-wishers. It goes without saying that Salah has needed to try to manage his life with insufficient resources. Equally, it is obvious that he could not afford to continue his studies in the UK where he needs to progress to complete the final year of his degree programme in Facilities Management.

We believe that by adopting him we can meet all of Salah's needs, including a stable and supportive home life, appropriate guidance as necessary in lieu of his parents, and all necessary financial resources. Further, we believe it would be a tragedy if Salah is forced to withdraw from higher education through poverty. By contrast, with our support he will graduate with a relevant qualification and become a valued citizen and contributor to Emirati society.

With highest respects and regards
Mrs Maria and Mr Janek Wankowski'

Maria then e-mailed the letter to Yahya and Janek with the following note:

> *'I believe this covers all the points we agreed. I suggest we keep this letter as brief as possible and don't go into further detail about the adoption process at this stage. I think the best option is for us to send this directly to HE the Minister for Culture and copy it to Dr Ahmadi at the Ministry for Higher Education requesting her support. What do you think?'*

She felt pleased with her efforts and left her office for an early finish and home. Surely she deserved a reward for her hard work. She had done her part and it was now up to the others. On the way out of the building she saw Salah coming towards her.

"Hello Mrs Wankowski. I saw you coming down the stairs; I only wanted to say hi!"

"Hello Salah. I hope you have been working hard at your English."

"I have, Mrs Wankowski. I am."

"Good, good, you must keep practising, Salah. Actually, there is something else I would like to talk to you about. I would prefer not to discuss it here at the College so I was wondering whether you could spare the time to come and have dinner with Jan and me; you know, nothing special, just something simple to eat and a bit of a chat, like we used to do when you stayed with us. Jan would be so pleased to see you again."

"I would like that, Mrs Wankowski, you are both so kind to me. Do you have an evening in mind?"

"I'd like to check with Janek first; can I put a note for you on the students' noticeboard tomorrow? Is that OK?"

"No problem, thanks again."

Maria was pleased with herself. She had thought up the dinner invitation on the spur of the moment and Salah seemed happy enough with the suggestion. This would be the perfect opportunity for her and Janek to ask Salah how he felt about their adoption hopes and plans.

She sent an e-mail to Janek at once and asked him to reply

quickly and suggest a date as soon as possible. She hoped he would also be pleased with her initiative!

As soon as she entered her villa, Maria switched on her laptop. She couldn't resist looking to see if Janek or Yahya had replied to her e-mail message. Of course, Janek may be waiting to discuss it at home. There was nothing so far, so she went and made some tea. When she came back with her mug of tea she saw that Yahya had now replied:

'Maria

Thanks. I think you have covered all the points we agreed. The letter is good. I agree with your suggestion for sending, etc. Please let me have a signed original, which I can send to Sheikh Al Balushi with a note from me requesting his support. I have spoken to him already and, as I thought, he knows HE Al Mandari personally. He said he would try to help. Let us hope for the best!'

Whilst she was reading Yahya's message an e-mail from Janek was arriving in her inbox. He must have thought she was still at the College otherwise he would have telephoned. It simply said…

'M

Good job. If Yahya likes it I suggest go ahead. We have still to talk to Salah but it makes sense to get ahead with the paperwork as it may take some time. See you later. J xxx'

Maria poured herself another mug of tea, sat down and reflected on the day's activities. It was a good day; a most helpful meeting with Her Excellency the Minister for Higher Education in the morning, the all-important letter to His Excellency the Minister for Culture now done, Yahya mobilising support from one of the College's owners and all that remained was to draft a covering letter to Dr Ahmadi. She would do this whilst awaiting Janek's return home.

'Your Excellency — with our highest respects and compliments

We are writing to thank you for meeting with us earlier today and for your kindness in allowing us to spend so much of your valuable time with you.

We have now finalised our request for permission to adopt Salah Al Munairi, which has been sent directly to His Excellency Ahmed Al Mandari, Minister for Nationality and Culture.

When we were together you kindly offered to support our application to the extent you are able. It would be enormously helpful if you would kindly let His Excellency know of your interest in this matter.

We have no illusions about the many obstacles and difficulties that may lie ahead and we remain absolutely committed to the course of action we propose.

With renewed thanks for your most helpful advice and suggestions,

Maria and Janek Wankowski'

CHAPTER 2.17

Dinner was over; Maria had left the table and was in the kitchen clearing away, putting the pans and plates in the dishwasher. Salah and Janek were still at the table finishing their drinks and chatting.

"Now Maria is back, Salah, there is something we would both like to ask you. I'm afraid there's nothing new we can say about the search for your mother. All the people working on this are still working hard and hoping for the best.

"I am sure you know, Maria and I are very concerned about your current situation without any family or other support and we would like to be more helpful. One of the ideas we have come up with is to ask you if you would like to become part of our family. That's one of the reasons we asked you to join us this evening." Now it was Maria's turn.

"Salah, we are sorry if this feels a bit like an ambush but we couldn't think of a more gentle way of letting you know our thinking. Janek and I realise this may be a shock for you and we don't expect you to say yes or no immediately, but we hope you will consider it in your own time and let us know when you are ready."

"Thank you both. This is totally unexpected. Actually, it's a shock. At the moment I don't think I understand what it means."

"It means we would like to adopt you as our son."

"What about my mother?"

"Your mother will always be your mother, this could never change and she is your biological parent. I would be your adoptive mother. It might seem strange but you would have two mothers. Jan would be your adoptive father. You would be our adoptive son." Then Janek continued again.

"Salah, the main benefit would be that it would give Maria and me a formal basis for caring and looking after you. We already have a personal wish to help you in whatever way we can. Adoption would give our helping relationship a legal basis. We would be more able to do all the things parents do for their children, or young adults, and everyone would be more able to understand."

"Would I have to live here with you?"

"No. At your age you can live wherever you like. Students mostly live away from home, but we could provide a home base for you with your own room to come and go as you please, like any other normal family, for as long as you need it or forever."

"I am beginning to get the idea but I'm still struggling to get my head around it. I suppose the question I want to ask, but am nervous about asking because I don't want to seem ungrateful, is why? Why you? Why me?"

"It's a good question, Salah. I am not sure either of us can answer it completely. Why us? We don't have children of our own but we have the ability and, luckily, the resources to help someone. You came into our lives and we like you enough to want you to be in our family. Why you? Because life has brought us together, it is as simple as that."

As they were leaving the dinner table, Salah began to look worried and anxious, even distressed, and it became obvious that something was troubling him.

"Thinking about your very kind proposal has caused me to have many negative thoughts."

Maria and Janek feared the worst, thinking Salah was upset and probably going to decline their offer.

"I have been living a lie since I lost my mother; actually, many lies. Your proposal has pricked my bubble and exposed my living lies. Some lies have given me comfort and made life more bearable. For example, I have been awaiting news of my mother hoping all the time that she will be found and that she and I will be reunited. This looks less and less likely – it's probably a lie. Other lies have simply covered up unpleasant truths. I don't have savings any more, I have almost no money to spend, I haven't paid any rent for my room, I cannot afford to go out or buy clothes and I can't see how I can possibly continue thinking I could go to the UK University to finish my degree."

"Salah, I am sorry that we've 'pricked your bubble', as you put it. But we all indulge in wishful thinking to some extent and many of us are unable to lead the kind of lives we would really like to lead. We all need a reality check occasionally. What is absolutely certain is that your difficult circumstances are not your fault. It was our hope that we could help you deal with these."

"I hope you can both understand that this situation feels strange to me and makes me feel nervous. It's hard to believe it's really happening. Although I've had little time to think about it I've already come to the conclusion that no amount of further thinking will help me overcome these feelings of strangeness and nervousness. I'm going to be thankful for the opportunity you are giving me and accept. I believe that only then will I know whether it's the right decision. It might turn out to be the best thing that ever happens to me but it's impossible for me to know that in advance."

Maria still didn't speak, trying not to feel disappointed, as this wasn't quite the positive response she'd hoped for, although it *was* a response and kind of positive. Realising she had underestimated the difficulty of the situation for Salah, she thought for a moment; of course he felt nervous, wouldn't anyone? After all, although for all practical purposes he is now an orphan there is no evidence so far that his mother is anything other than alive and well. He must be wondering what she would think of his being adopted.

"Salah, thank you for speaking so honestly and for the care and thoughtfulness you've given to our suggestion of adoption. Everything you've just said is completely understandable; I am sure Jan will say the same. Of course you are nervous about taking such a big step, now and for the future. It wouldn't be right to say that Jan and I are nervous, but I must agree with you that we cannot see into the future any more than you can and we can only hope we are all doing the right thing. If I am interpreting what you have said correctly I think you are telling me that you would like to go ahead but that you have some doubts. Is this correct?"

"You have put it very well, Mrs Wankowski. I am really grateful for your suggestion, I really am. I don't want either of you to think I don't appreciate your kindness. But even if my problems aren't my fault, perhaps there are too many of them even for you to deal with or for anyone to deal with?"

"Salah, I promise you Maria and I have thought about this very carefully. When you're part of a family there will be three people working together to try to solve these problems," explained Janek.

"We do understand your thinking and reservations, Salah, and appreciate we are asking you to place a lot of trust in us. At the same time we are happy beyond words at the prospect of us coming together as a family."

"Thank you both again for being so kind and understanding."

"Salah, we'll go ahead and formally approach the relevant authorities as there will be a long process to go through while they check that Maria and I would be suitable parents. If you would like to change your mind about anything at any time, please don't hesitate to let us know."

"What about an early night now? We can see how we all feel about things in the morning."

"Good idea, Maria."

CHAPTER 2.18

September 27 2002

ENGLAND

It was Friday again and, as usual, Salah joined Khamis for Friday prayers in the local mosque. This time he felt more confident because he was familiar with what goes on from his previous visit. Since then he had researched Islamic rituals on the Internet, which gave him a deeper understanding of Islamic faith, of the significance of prayer and, especially, of the importance of Fridays in bringing Muslims together.

This time the sermon was generally more anti-Western rather than anti-American, it wasn't as inflammatory as before but, nevertheless, Salah sensed an angry response from the congregants though not necessarily a militant one.

After the service congregants spilled out into the quadrangle and other open spaces forming into groups and engaging in animated discussion. The topic was the same as last week, the visit of the US dignitary. Salah was more receptive to the prevailing mood this time and thought of Hani's experience. For some reason, Hani had declined Salah's suggestion they go to the mosque together; he was obviously uneasy about it but didn't say why. Salah wondered why and thought of pursuing it further but decided to let it go.

Then there had been the discussion in Coffee Plus where he had signed up to becoming a protester. Since then Khamis had heard of a development.

"I heard from Majid that the elders may refuse to host the visit of the US politician because of the risk to safety in and around the mosque and elsewhere. It seems they are worried about widespread protests and demonstrations by Muslims angry about US military interventions in Muslim countries."

"Is that going to be enough for the hard-liners?"

"I've no idea, Salah; I expect they would rather have the protests and demonstrations."

"That's what I'm thinking. By the way, we haven't seen Majid. I wonder what he's up to. He's usually around somewhere."

Salah and Khamis attached themselves to a small group discussing the situation. One or two argued that if a person is a state guest they should be treated with respect and courtesy. This was not a popular view. Some more radical Islamists were even roused to anger. Most seemed to feel it was not enough simply to refuse the visit. There should be positive action of some sort.

Salah was reminded of his recent conversation with Majid and their secret plans for action. If the visit to the mosque was refused the activists would be even more likely to want to make the University their target. Salah was experiencing a feeling of excitement when he suddenly felt a tap on his shoulder.

He turned and couldn't believe his eyes. He found himself face to face with none other than Mubarak.

"Hi Salah, I thought I might find you here."

"Mubarak, what a surprise! I knew you were studying at a university somewhere in the UK, but–"

"To be precise, I was visiting a friend at your place; he has a flat in the town and he told me there's a bit of a fuss going on at the mosque and so I thought I would come and see for myself."

"What a surprise, indeed. It's good to see you; everything OK?"

"More or less; I've almost completed my Masters so I shall soon be going back home to help run the family businesses."

"If you are going to be around we could meet up for a chat." Salah amazed himself – in what universe would he want to spend time with Mubarak? Too late, the deed was done.

"Fine. Actually that would be good because I have something of yours."

Salah was mildly intrigued but didn't want to show too much interest. After all, what could Mubarak possibly have of his? It was hard to imagine it could be anything Salah needed or would ever want.

"We should exchange mobile numbers or, even better, why not come round tomorrow? It's the weekend. I am in Sharpe Hall, top floor. Not too early in the morning would be good – coffee time, perhaps?"

"OK, I'll be there. Give me your mobile number in case there's a problem." Salah gave Mubarak his number and Mubarak rang back to make sure he'd entered it in his address book correctly.

Realising he was still with Khamis, he said, "By the way, this is my friend, Khamis. We were at Dubai College together."

"Hi Khamis, I'm Mubarak. You look familiar; have I seen you around in Dubai?"

"I guess it's possible."

"Did you drive a silver Tiguan?"

"Yeah, that could have been me."

"Nice to meet you. Are you in Sharpe with Salah?"

"No, I'm sharing a house not far from the town centre. It's not as smart as Sharpe but it's cheaper and I like being close to the shops. Nice to meet you too."

Mubarak left them and went on his way. Salah explained briefly how he and Mubarak knew each other and why he had mixed feelings about seeing him again. Khamis didn't quite understand and would have liked to have known more but sensed it was not a good time to ask questions.

They rejoined the group they had been with and noticed that Majid had appeared while they had been talking to Mubarak. They found the same arguments taking place except that radical Islamist arguments now predominated. Salah could begin to see what the elders of the mosque were afraid of.

Majid sounded increasingly like one of the radicals. Salah was excited by their eloquence and was impressed by their conviction, especially their sense of needing to stand up against injustice. Thinking of Hani again he felt that, he too, should be proactive. He was more than happy to join a protest. He thought the effectiveness could be doubtful though and was ready to contemplate more extreme actions. He might even join a radical Islamic group although he believed his agenda was different to theirs.

Khamis was ready to go back home. He asked Majid if he wanted a lift but Majid declined. Salah phoned Hayley on the way back to tell her that he would have to be at Sharpe tomorrow because he had invited Mubarak over to visit for coffee, etc. She said she was fine with it and had nothing planned. He asked her when she was likely to leave work. She didn't know. He asked her if she would like to come over to Sharpe when she finished work. She said she wasn't sure she should. Salah felt crestfallen and hoped everything was OK between them.

Back in his room, Salah couldn't help fretting about Hayley. He thought she had been very evasive and wondered whether there was a problem. She said she was OK with him not seeing her on Saturday, but was she really? Had she become more anxious about dating a student? Perhaps someone had said something. Maybe she was thinking students are here today and gone tomorrow and that she was making a mistake with dating him.

He was tormenting himself with further questions, desperate to know the answers. He wanted to phone her again but he'd only just phoned her and she was still at work. He had told her he wouldn't ring her at work; she said she appreciated his thoughtfulness. He would look stupid if he went back on what he said and he definitely wouldn't do himself any favours by being too needy. She would soon get fed up with that.

He wavered and then decided to wait to see whether she phoned him after work. That would be the mature thing to do, but waiting for her to phone would be more torturous. If she phoned he would be able to tell whether everything was OK. If she didn't he would have to ring.

Meanwhile, he decided to review his notes from the first two lectures and maybe have a look at Dr Hunter's book on *Project Management*. Unsurprisingly, Salah found it difficult to concentrate on what he was doing. He put this down to feeling hungry, although it was likely to be more to do with his state of mind. He went to the kitchen to see if he could find something to eat.

The cupboards were sparse so he decided to go to the shop and buy food. The walk did him good. It could get a bit claustrophobic in a student bedsit. The University shop had everything he needed for a salad, some cold meat and chicken, bread for toast in the morning and a frozen vegetable korma with rice for his evening meal. At the last minute he added two bottles of beer to his basket to go with the curry and felt very pleased with himself.

Back at Sharpe he went to the kitchen, put his food away and made a quick salad, which he took back to his room to eat at his desk. It was a bit bland for his taste but was sensible, healthy, English food. He could look forward to stronger Middle Eastern flavours later, being a citizen of the world these days.

There was still some time to go before Hayley was likely to finish work. Being at a loose end, he needed to fill the time somehow and for some reason thought of the Wankowskis and wondered what they were doing. He calculated the time difference and gave this some thought. They wouldn't be at the College on a Friday for sure; more likely they were enjoying themselves at home, Maria reading the papers and Janek could be at the gym.

Thinking along these lines made him feel a little homesick, however, it made Salah realise he hadn't been in touch with the Wankowskis for a while and they would probably be pleased to hear from him. He sat in his easy chair with his laptop on his knees and wrote an e-mail message:

'Hello

I thought you would like to know how it's going here. I'm fine, no problems. Khamis and I have become close friends, the course got off to a good start, met a nice girl in one of the offices. She has a car which is good. We're all surprised at how much free time we have. I expect the workload will increase soon. Saw Mubarak Al Munairi at the mosque. I invited him over tomorrow. Should be interesting. He says he has something for me. Will tell you more after his visit.

Very best wishes

Salah'

He was pleased with this, it was short and sweet; nobody wanted to be bogged down with lengthy e-mails. 'It's the thought that counts' – that's what they said in England anyway. Although thinking about the wonderful Wankowskis in Dubai made him feel unsettled, it had at least distracted him from thinking so much about himself, which was probably a good thing, particularly while he was having dark thoughts about Hayley.

What's the time? Could she be finished? He would wait a bit longer – no point jumping the gun now after waiting this long. Then it happened, his mobile was vibrating on his desk. He picked it up in the nick of time before it fell. Hayley's name was on the screen.

"Hello Hayley."

"Hi Salah, I'm sorry if I was offhand when you rang, I wasn't expecting you to ring; you said you wouldn't."

"I'm so sorry, I forgot completely what we said about that."

"Don't worry, no harm done, it's just I felt that they were watching me in the office and listening and I got a bit self-conscious."

"I shouldn't have phoned, this is my fault."

"Salah, you're worrying too much. Of course you want to see your friends, you don't have to tell me what you're doing all the time. It's nice of you but it isn't necessary. I might want to spend time with *my* friends sometime, OK?"

"OK, I get it, Hayley. I just thought there might be a problem, that's all."

"Not that I know."

"Great, so are you coming round this evening?"

"I'd rather not this time. I absolutely have to do my washing or I'll have no clothes. Also, it's a bit public, don't you think? We said we would be discreet."

"You're right. OK, fair enough. I'll have to eat my vegetable korma on my own."

"You'd have to eat your vegetable korma on your own anyway even if I *did* come round, so you can stop the emotional blackmail."

"OK, Hayley, it was a joke, although I hope you'll try some

Indian food sometime. Have a good evening. Thanks for the call and see you soon. Bye."

"Bye."

The call ended well and he put the phone back on his desk. He was about to go to the kitchen to organise an early dinner when it vibrated again. It was Hayley. Perhaps she had changed her mind.

"Hi Salah, I meant to say I've got my period."

"OK, right. Love you, bye."

"Bye."

CHAPTER 2.19

September 28 2002

It was already a bright and sunny morning when Salah first opened his eyes and began following his usual Saturday routine of tea, bathroom, breakfast, make bed, tidy room, etc, when he remembered that yesterday he had asked Mubarak to come over. He had suggested Mubarak arrive around coffee time.

When he went to the fridge he realised he was short of milk so he had to go to the shop again. At the same time he could buy biscuits or something else to go with coffee.

On his return he noticed a strange car in the car park and wondered whether it could be Mubarak's. If so, he must have arrived early. Reaching the top of the stairs he first went into the kitchen to put the milk in his fridge and arrange a plate of biscuits, then back to his room; no sign of Mubarak. While he waited for a knock on the door he regretted inviting Mubarak and wondered how it would go, although they were brothers – kind of. He didn't need to wait long for the knock.

"Hi Mubarak, was that your Volkswagen in the car park?"

"Yes, I was a bit early and so I went for a short walk around the campus. It's impressive and the student accommodation looks great, very modern. Mine is historic and shabby."

"Tea or coffee?"

"Prefer tea, if that's OK with you."

"Fine, I've been drinking more tea since I have been in England. I'll just go and make it. Have a seat."

Mubarak sat down placing a large carrier bag on the floor next to him. Salah came back with mugs of tea and a plate of biscuits.

"Thanks, Salah."

"So, what do you make of what's going on at the mosque?"

"I doubt if the Elders have a problem with the American or the British minister who is organising the visit. I think they are genuinely concerned about the possible reaction and the impact on the community. The extent of anti-American feeling is such at the moment that there's bound to be violent protests, especially by aggrieved Muslims. There are people of all races and religions who don't like civilians being killed in wars of doubtful legality and, of course, there are those who don't like injustice – Guantanamo Bay, for instance."

"That's a lot of reasons to protest. I suppose what has happened to US Embassies around the world gives a clue as to what might happen."

"I guess so, Salah. There is no doubt there will be protests, of that I am certain. Whether they'll be violent I'm not sure. There could be peaceful marches, sit-ins and placards at one end of the spectrum or acts of violence and terror at the other.

"Of course, not all Muslims are potential terrorists or even potential protesters. Some actually know very little about Islam, but there are those who sit around watching videos of Muslims being ill-treated or killed and then they adopt a caricature of Islam emphasizing vengeance and violence. These are the people who are easily provoked and fired up.

"Others are motivated by feelings of humiliation and grievance over the apparent ascendancy of the West, which they believe is partly because of the exploitation of Muslim countries, particularly regarding oil. They tend to be ambivalent, willing to shout anti-American slogans but are secretly envious of American freedoms and quality of life.

"Others have been taught that Islam is superior to other religions and they look for opportunities to challenge those holding other religious beliefs. They like to demonstrate Islam's superiority.

"Then, of course, there's also the long-running conflict between Arab countries and Israel, supported by the US, not to mention Al-Qaeda and ISIS and the US War on Terror, so-called."

"Mubarak, you seem to know a lot about this. Are you suggesting any of the groups you just mentioned could be represented in the local mosque?"

"I don't see why not. I should think all of them could be. I don't really know much about communities in this part of the world. Your judgement is probably better than mine. Shall we leave politics for now and move on, Salah?"

"Why not?"

"I have something for you."

Mubarak reached into the carrier bag and took out a box carefully wrapped in paper with traditional Islamic motifs.

"This is for you."

Salah removed the paper carefully and folded it neatly. Inside was a box covered in red velvet, itself a thing of beauty; he opened the box and inside, resting on a white silk cushion, was a silver khanjar. It was a fine example of its kind.

"Do you recognise it?"

Salah took his time. He thought he recognised it but wasn't sure at first.

"Of course, it was displayed in a glass-fronted cabinet in the entrance hall of your family's villa. It was displayed in the middle of the middle shelf. I was always fascinated by it. It is so beautiful."

"Correct. After my father died the villa was sold and the contents either went to other family properties or were sold. When we removed the khanjar from the cabinet we found a note from my father inside the box. It said that, after his death, the khanjar should be given to you because you always admired it and because he was unable to leave you money or property."

"Mubarak, I don't know what to say."

"I'm sorry it has taken a long time to give it to you; unfortunately we've not exactly been in touch since the funeral."

"True. That was a terrible time for everybody."

At this point, Salah was thinking about his mother but he didn't know whether to say something or wait for Mubarak to mention it. He didn't. Salah wondered whether Mubarak was too embarrassed to mention her, too sorry or upset about her or whether he just didn't care. It was hard to tell. Salah couldn't help blurting it out…

"I don't suppose you know anything about my mother."

"Sorry, no."

Mubarak shifted uneasily in his chair, his body language said a lot.

"You might be surprised to learn that I didn't know Salem was my father until the day he died."

"I am surprised, although I must admit I never heard anyone speak about it."

"So, you knew?"

"My father told me *my* mother died when she was having me. I expect he was sad and lonely and reached out to Aparna. He told me he always liked her. Then you came along. Other family members were probably embarrassed, perhaps shocked. They probably expected Aparna to be sent back to wherever she came from. It was hardly ever spoken about."

"Did Salem marry Aparna?"

"I think so, but I'm not sure. Sorry, that was never spoken about either as far as I know and definitely not in my presence."

"Thank you for telling me, Mubarak. I'm sorry you lost your mother too."

"I'm sorry about what happened to *your* mother. I had nothing to do with it. I was very upset when my father died so suddenly; my uncle took over all my father's affairs after he died."

Salah thought Mubarak sounded genuinely sorry but it didn't help much. His feelings of bitterness and vengefulness towards the Al Munairi family surged. He looked again at the khanjar; it was very beautiful, impressive and probably valuable, but how could he possibly take or feel any pleasure owning it? It symbolised everything he hated about his life.

"Salah, I've done what I came to do and you have the khanjar. I'm glad we are at least on speaking terms. I suppose it is too much to hope that we could be friends. We are brothers; nothing can change that."

"I appreciate you bringing the khanjar, Mubarak, I am sure with the best of intentions, but I hope you will understand it reminds me of the worst time of my life. It's not that I could ever forget it but I was dealing with it. Now it has all come flooding back. That's how I feel. More than that I cannot say today."

"I understand, Salah. I'm very sorry, perhaps I should go now."

Mubarak hesitated. Salah said nothing. He sat motionless, staring without seeing, and then Mubarak left the room leaving Salah to reflect on what had just happened.

He decided to e-mail the Wankowskis and tell them everything, not that they could help in any way, but it felt good to share this with them as it felt even therapeutic in some way. He wrote:

'Hello again

As you know Mubarak visited today. We had a civilised chat and for a while I enjoyed his company. We talked about current things here in the UK, nothing about Dubai. Then he presented me with a khanjar from my father's villa. It seems he left a note that it was to be given to me after his death because I said I liked it and because he wasn't able to leave me any property or money. It's beautiful but I can't bring myself to appreciate it, too many bad memories. He said he had nothing to do with what happened to my mother and didn't know where she was. Hope you're both fine. How are things in Dubai?

Salah

P.S. There's trouble at the local mosque. Someone has invited a US politician to visit the UK and the University has made things worse by inviting him also. There may be trouble at the Uni as well.'

Salah was profoundly miserable. He felt sorry about so many things. He was sorry bad things happened in Dubai, sorry they had been resurrected by Mubarak's well-meaning gift, sorry about the way Mubarak left after what should have been a pleasant get-together, sorry that a rare opportunity to become friends with Mubarak had almost certainly been lost forever and he was sorry to have involved the Wankowskis because they would now be unhappy because *he* was unhappy.

Salah longed for someone to share all this with, but whom? He didn't want to bother Khamis with his misfortunes, although he would undoubtedly try to understand and be sympathetic. Even so, it was hard to imagine Khamis being able to cheer him up.

Hayley would want to be supportive but it would be difficult to explain everything to her and it would take so long, plus they would both become bogged down in his misery. This wouldn't be good for their relationship. Why would anyone want to date a basket case?

He was becoming increasingly morose when his mobile vibrated. He wouldn't have picked it up but if he didn't it would probably fall off his desk onto the floor again. He didn't recognise the number on the screen and switched it off. It vibrated again.

"Hello... hello... Oh, hi Mubarak."

"Salah, sorry to be a pain but I can't find my mobile anywhere. I am wondering if I could have left it in your room, in the building or in the car park."

"I haven't seen it, Mubarak, but I'll have a look around."

"Thanks." Mubarak waited and waited.

"I can't see it anywhere near to where you were sitting. I'll tell the senior resident and ask him to tell me if a mobile has been found and handed in. It may take some time, I'm afraid."

"OK, thanks for trying. If it turns up please e-mail me and I'll come and collect it. My address is malmunairi@yahoo.com."

"Will do."

"Don't stress. It's not the end of the world. I can make calls from my tablet if necessary or I can always Skype."

"OK, Mubarak, I won't stress, as you put it. Bye."

Mubarak ended the call. Salah put his mobile back on the desk thinking he must be fucking joking. *As if I am going to lose any sleep over his fucking mobile when I've got all the other fucking things to stress about. He can afford to buy a fucking drawer full of mobiles*, Salah thought to himself angrily.

It was unlike Salah to lose it and indulge in such language but he was frustrated and very angry. He couldn't remember if he had ever been so angry. Here he was, at the end of his emotional tether and Mubarak was bothering him about his mobile. 'Don't stress'? He must have had no understanding of what Salah was going through in trying to cope with his own problems!

He calmed down after a while and conjured up different thoughts. What happened to his mother may not have been Mubarak's fault and he had been very kind over the death of his father. He positively encouraged him to be involved in the funeral, which must have been difficult for him as Salah was an embarrassment to the family. And he was right to point out that it was one of his uncles who took over arrangements after his father's death.

But here and now Mubarak was the personification of the Al Munairi family and Salah couldn't help wanting to hit out. By hitting back at Mubarak, Salah would be hitting back at the Al Munairis. This felt good. It felt right and Salah began to feel better. He would find ways of hitting back hard and feel better still.

Salah's laptop screen caught his eye; it was showing his e-mail inbox and he noticed he had just received another message. He didn't think the Wankowskis would have replied so quickly…

'Hello Salah

Thanks for keeping us in the picture. Glad everything is OK with the University but sorry about the Mubarak business. What bad luck that he should suddenly reappear in your life? We are inclined to take a charitable view about the khanjar, but even if it is given with the best of intentions your feelings are all too real and very painful and upsetting. We DOOOOOO understand!!!!! Just try your best to rise above the hurt and the feeling of having been wronged. We wish we had news of your mother but all we can say is that people are still looking. You are always in our thoughts. Do keep in touch.

Maria

Salah re-read the message several times and asked himself whether he could 'rise above', as Maria suggested. His first thought was that he couldn't because his desire for revenge was much stronger than his desire to 'rise above'. He'd heard that 'turning the other cheek' was part of Christian philosophy; he'd also heard of 'an eye for an eye', which is the Arab way, although Islam teaches that forgiveness is preferable to revenge because revenge makes problems worse. His current feeling was that his plans for retribution were fully justified and that it was too late to turn back. He followed up with:

'Dear Maria

I appreciate your kind and helpful comments. I shall of course try to follow your advice to 'rise above' but it will be difficult.

Salah'

CHAPTER 2.20

September 29 2002

"Open the door – police! Open the door! Now! Police! Open the door – police!"

Salah turned over and reached for his mobile. It was 4.30 am. There must be a fire in the building. The shouting continued. It sounded as if it was coming from down the corridor several rooms away. Salah was tempted to open his door and have a look but lost his nerve.

Initially, he was alarmed and in a panic but once various possible explanations came into his mind he became less worried. The presence of the police suggested some sort of criminal activity. A student had either stolen something or assaulted someone. Maybe he had a car accident and didn't stop. Perhaps he'd got drunk and disgraced himself in some way, like being caught by the security people pissing into the flowers outside the Vice-Chancellor's house. He could even have been identified as a potential terrorist. Salah decided he wasn't going to find out any time soon, if at all, so he went back to bed and pulled the duvet up around his ears.

It was time to get up, not that Salah felt like getting up, but the bed was now an uncomfortable mess. The disturbance in the early hours had played hell with his sleep; the evidence of his restlessness was everywhere with the screwed up bottom sheet and other bedding on the floor. Leaving his room to get a hot drink, he met Hani who was also on the way to the kitchen.

"Hi Hani. Kayf haalek?"

"Hi Salah. Tamam." Hani followed Salah into the kitchen.

"Did you hear all that shouting and door banging last night?"

"Yes, of course, Salah, it woke me up."

"I don't suppose you know what it was about."

"I do, it was Sebastian; he's an idiot. He has been illegally downloading huge quantities of movies and other media, probably porn. He does this night after night until the early hours of the morning. He's been caught by the police; they turned up with someone from the University. It seems what he's been doing is not only illegal, but is also breaking the University's regulations. I believe he got away with a warning but if he does it again his computer will be confiscated. He may even be arrested."

"Are you surprised?"

"Not really. I had my suspicions because he always stayed up so late."

"What a twit; just goes to show though, someone *is* watching us."

Salah privately reflected on his meetings with the Pro-Vice-Chancellor and Jack. Perhaps Sebastian had been unlucky getting caught because of all the other intelligence gathering and surveillance going on."

"Hani, how are things at home? Is there any news of your family?"

"Thanks for asking, Salah. There is some. One of my uncles managed to locate my parents and brothers. They were staying with one of my cousins. They're safe but terribly upset, of course. I am hoping the whole extended family will pull together and help them. At least in our culture families do try to look after each other."

"I am happy for you, Hani, it must be a big relief."

"Thanks, it is. I can concentrate on my work better now. Glad I bumped into you, Salah, I'll leave you to your breakfast."

"Are you enjoying the course?"

"Yeah, so far it's great. Bye."

Hani finished getting his breakfast and went back to his room. Salah followed him out of the kitchen, taking his tea and a bowl of cereal with him. After breakfasting at his desk he reluctantly accepted he needed to do something about the shambles that was his bed.

He pulled the bed away from the wall so as to be able to straighten the mattress cover and tuck in the bottom sheet. The cover was soon in place and the sheet draped over the bed, ready for tucking in. He was putting his hand down the side of the bed next to the wall ready to tuck the sheet between the mattress and the base when it happened. A solid object fell to the floor. He leaned over further and stretched his arm out to pick it up. Feeling it, but not seeing it, he wondered what it could be. It was Mubarak's mobile.

All his negative feelings about the Al Munairis came back to him with a vengeance. Why should he trouble himself to return the phone? Mubarak said he could manage without it, including the 'Don't stress' comment. He began to play with it and he soon found the mobile wasn't locked. He explored the address book, which was extensive. His own mobile number was there, of course.

Salah stared at the mobile, wondering if he could make use of it in some way. This didn't make much sense as he had his own mobile. Then he wondered if he could use Mubarak's mobile when he didn't want to use his own. This didn't make a lot of sense either, but it caused Salah to become inspired.

He wanted to hit back at the Al Munairis, so why not put incriminating material on Mubarak's mobile and then hand it in to the police? If he could inflict serious damage on the Al Munairis' golden boy it would badly affect the family and avenge his mother for the terrible treatment she had received.

At this point he received even more inspiration. He would use Mubarak's mobile to take pictures of the gas bullets, to contact BLEVE sites and bomb-making sites and then give the mobile to Majid to be used for whatever procurement was necessary for their project. Without going into too much detail he would ask Majid to make sure the police find it. That should be enough to incriminate him.

Fate had created an opportunity to kill two birds with one stone – to get his own back on the Al Munairis and to protest in the strongest possible terms against American war crimes. The opportunity to do these two things was too good to miss. After all, he was only planning to destroy property. It wasn't as though people would be harmed. He couldn't be doing with that.

Salah added the finishing touches to his bed pillows and cushions and then removed his showerproof and wind-proof outdoor jacket, the one with the hood, from the peg on his door. He put Mubarak's mobile in his pocket and left Sharpe for the Engineering Building for he was sure he'd seen windows on the first floor overlooking the bullets.

Doing his best to look casual and relaxed he strolled along the path towards the centre of the campus, apparently without a care in the world, keeping his hood up, his head down and his hands in his pockets. If it weren't for his jaunty manner he might have seemed evasive, but the last thing he wanted was to catch someone's eye or become involved in conversation. He was on a mission.

Arriving at the entrance to the Faculty of Engineering Building, he hoped he would be able to find what he was looking for without going anywhere near the Department of Built Environment. Seeing Hayley coming or going would be awkward as he had no convincing explanation as for why he was there. He was bound to look guilty if he tried to make up lies on the spot and she would notice and start asking questions.

The task was more difficult than he had supposed. The Civil Engineering and Mechanical Engineering Labs were vast, cavernous spaces with high ceilings taking up both the ground and upper floors. Their windows weren't accessible. Salah could see from the floor plans in the entrance area that there was little first floor accommodation in the part of the building he needed to get to but there were rooms used for storage and services.

He noticed a diagrammatic representation of a stairway in a corner of the ground floor map and decided to try his luck there. Seeing a door he thought would lead to the stairs, he entered a long passage with pipes and conduits running along the walls at the end of which, sure enough, he found the stairwell. He began to climb; it didn't take long to reach the first floor and a door that opened easily. He took one or two exploratory steps, trying not to look furtive.

Ahead was a corridor with doors on both sides. Being disoriented after his wanderings down the passage and around corners, he wasn't sure which side of the building he needed to be able to see the bullets. He tried the first door on the left. It was locked. He tried the second on the left, also locked. He tried the second door on the right, which opened. The small room had no windows. He walked further along the corridor intending to try more doors when he noticed a door at the end. He assumed this would lead to another stairwell, opened it, and found stairs leading up, not down.

Salah realised these stairs must be leading to the roof. He expected the door to the roof to be locked but climbed up anyway. Luckily, it wasn't and he emerged into daylight to see a variety of small- and medium-sized towers presumably containing air conditioning units and other equipment of some sort.

There were walkways crisscrossing the length and breadth of the roof, which Salah assumed were for maintenance purposes. He walked along one of these to get a better view of the surrounding campus buildings so that he could orientate himself and move to the right side of the building. To get nearer to the edge of the roof he had to step off the walkway. This made him extremely nervous because at the edge there was a sheer drop to the ground.

He saw the bullets and moved slowly into the best position to photograph them. This involved lying on his stomach whilst inching forward until he could see over the edge. He was not just nervous now, he was terrified. His forearms were waving in mid-air beyond the roof edge as he was taking the shots. His legs were shaking. He kept telling himself that if his body was flat on the roof and only his arms were over the edge he couldn't fall.

After taking several pictures he inched back to safer ground. If they weren't good enough it was tough because nothing would ever persuade him to go through all that again. Salah wanted to study the pictures closely but the priority was to get down off the roof and out of the building, preferably without being seen. He had been lucky so far and hoped his luck would last.

He carefully retraced his steps off the roof, down the stairs along the corridor of small rooms, down the main stairwell and along the passages to the ground floor entrance area. The only person he saw along the way was a cleaner who was very obviously foreign and unable to speak English. Good, he wouldn't make much of a witness.

Salah left the building and increased his step until he realised it was still important to look casual. He wasn't aware of any CCTV cameras, but there could be some in the vicinity and it would be foolish to attract attention at this late stage by looking suspicious.

It seemed to take an age to get back to his room. It didn't, of course; Salah's misjudgement was the result of his high level of anxiety. He sat in his easy chair and calmed down whilst scrolling through the pictures. The results were fairly satisfactory although the high camera angle was far from ideal.

With careful manipulation of the camera's enlargement function, the brick pillars supporting the bullets were just clear enough to be able to count the individual courses. He thought of transferring the pictures to his computer, which had a programme capable of carrying out a whole range of functions and adjustments to improve picture quality, but decided it was too risky. He'd heard from someone somewhere sometime that even deleted material can be recovered from a computer hard drive with the right forensic skills.

Salah counted 15 courses of bricks. The bricks looked very much like everyday standard house bricks. He found on the Internet that a standard brick was 65 mm thick. Allowing 10 mm for each mortar join, the height of the pillars must be about 65 mm, plus 10 mm, times 15, which equals 1,125 mm, or 44.29 inches or 3'7" high.

Feeling pleased with himself he now needed to see Majid. Meanwhile, he applied himself to creating more problems for Mubarak. Using Mubarak's mobile he began searching the Internet for BLEVE and bomb-making sites, also sites supplying garden barbecue equipment by mail order. The next step was to search for local car hire companies. If he could ensure the mobile got into the hands of the police or intelligence people, Mubarak would certainly come under suspicion, have 'questions to answer' and possibly be arrested.

Salah and Majid had agreed to maintain telephone and cyber silence and to make use of Khamis as a go-between, so Salah rang Khamis and pretended it was just for a friendly chat. Khamis seemed happy to reciprocate and, after a while, Salah asked him if Majid was there.

"I think he's in his room. Do you want to speak to him?"

"No, no, but perhaps you could give him a message. Please tell him I shall be in the University tomorrow morning and happy to meet him for coffee as we discussed."

"Will do, Salah, no problem. Thanks for ringing, see you soon."

Of course, they had discussed no such thing. Salah hoped Majid would realise he was speaking in code because he didn't have a lecture tomorrow and would be happy to sit in the cafeteria reading or working on his laptop until Majid turned up.

Salah's thoughts turned to Hayley. He hadn't seen her for several days and there was quite a lot to tell her like the meetings with the Pro-Vice-Chancellor and with Jack Russell, also the funny things going on at Sharpe, which he thought she would find amusing.

He really wanted to tell her about his special project with Majid and the others, but of course he couldn't for so many reasons. First, he wasn't at all sure what she would think about it and, second, it would be wrong to involve her in case it all went pear-shaped – the less she knew, the better. Third, it would break the commitment to secrecy, which was supposed to keep them everyone safe. Finally, and on the one hand, he wasn't proud of the way he was exacting revenge on Mubarak and she might think less of him if she knew about it. On the other hand, he felt a strong impulse to be honest with Hayley. Reluctantly, he accepted that he couldn't, at least not for now.

CHAPTER 2.21

July 2002

DUBAI

"Hello Maria. You won't believe it but I was just thinking of you. It was about Salah, of course. He suddenly came into my mind and I couldn't think why to begin with. Then I realised. We haven't heard anything for a while. I should ring Hilal to see if there is any news."

"That would be very helpful, Yahya. Actually, I came to tell you that Janek and I had Salah to dinner the other evening and we put the idea of adoption to him. He gave us the go-ahead. He had some mixed feelings about it but that is only to be expected, don't you think?"

"That's good news. I'm very pleased for you all. Would you like to wait while I telephone Hilal?"

"Why not?"

Yahya scrolled through the addresses on his mobile phone and picked up his College telephone.

"Sabaah alkhair, *good morning*, as-salaam alaykum… *may I speak with* Hilal Al Farsi, please? Thank you… OK, I shall be in my office, ma'a as salama, *goodbye*. Shukran." *Thank you.*

Yahya explained that Hilal had someone with him and he would ring back as soon as possible.

A short while later the telephone rang.

"Sabaah al noor." *Good morning.*

Hello Hilal, thank you for ringing back. Hilal, I have a colleague with me, the one who is trying to help Salah, you remember? We are both wondering whether there's any progress with the search for the boy's mother. We're thinking probably not or you would have been in touch."

Hilal spoke to Yahya for several minutes. Mrs Wankowski could not hear what was being said so she watched Yahya's facial expression for clues. She saw nothing hopeful and assumed the worst.

"Hilal was grateful for my call as it was on his mind to ring me. He was sorry to say he is unaware of any positive developments or news of any kind. He has made various enquiries among those who have been trying to help and has drawn a blank everywhere. He believes the Indian Embassy is unlikely to drop the matter, but it seems they are not staffed sufficiently to deal with all the problems that come to their notice. He advises us to go forward on the basis that it is unlikely we are going to have a good outcome. He cannot think of anything else to do and he's very sorry."

"So, the search is being discontinued, is that it?"

"Hilal was very careful not to say that, he said a missing person is just that – missing. It doesn't mean they're gone forever or that they cannot reappear sometime somewhere."

"I think we must be careful not to mislead Salah with false hopes."

"I agree, Maria; I think that is what Hilal is trying to say, in his own way."

"Yahya, may I ask a favour, a big favour?"

"Of course."

"If I bring Salah to see you, could you possibly explain to him everything that has been done to try to find his mother and convey to him the gist of what we have learned today? I am worried that if I try to do this it will get tangled up with the adoption business, which is at a sensitive stage at the moment."

"OK, I shall do my best."

"Thank you so much, it would help me a lot."

Maria drifted in and out of consciousness as she gradually realised it was a new day. As happened most mornings these days, she sat up in bed and began to wonder whether it could be 'the' day.

She got up and went to the kitchen for a drink and then to the bathroom for a shower. The water was too hot for comfort this morning. She and Janek were used to there being no mains water after so many years in the Emirates, relying on desalinated water delivered by a bowser and pumped up to a large tank on the roof.

Running out of water caused huge problems but, fortunately, the delivery system rarely failed. This was the time of year when the shower water coming from the roof tank was almost too hot to bear. During the rest of the year the water was just pleasantly warm. She towelled off, sat at her dressing table and followed her usual hair and cosmetic routine before choosing clothes appropriate for another day of glorious Gulf weather.

She locked up, left the house and got into the car as quickly as possible to avoid sweating. She started the engine and felt the benefit of the car's air conditioning almost immediately. She pressed the remote control and waited for the gate to roll away before reversing into the road and setting off for the College.

Maria decided to collect the College post on the way to work. As one of the longest serving staff she was entrusted with a key to the College's post office box. Keyholders took it in turns to empty the box and bring the post back to the College. There was neither a rota nor any other formal system and an arrangement based on felt-need seemed to work reasonably well.

She always enjoyed visits to the post office to collect the mail. For one reason, the local post office always reminded her of her brother because the building itself, which was a typical off-white Arabic-style building standing more or less on its own surrounded by desert, looked so much like the fort in *Luck of the Legion*, the cartoon in the *Eagle*, her brother's comic. The French Foreign Legion occupied the fort and they both used to read the *Eagle* when they were kids.

The second reason was that the post office provided occasional entertainment. There was always a chance when she opened her PO Box door she would see a face at the other side of the box. This happened when the boxes were open on the inside of the post office while the staff stuffed the mail in. It was an opportunity for a friendly greeting and for Maria to practice her very limited Arabic.

There was no one the other side of the box today so she collected the post, returned to her car, glad to be back in the cool, stretching an elastic band around the envelopes, before setting off back across the desert track for the main road to the College. Along the way she saw a Bedouin man walking with a goat and reflected that this must have been happening since biblical times, possibly along the exact same track. This thought made her feel connected with the past and, as a consequence, she experienced a calming sense of timelessness.

Arriving at the College, Maria removed the elastic band and shuffled the envelopes to see if there was any personal mail. Noticing a Government logo on one of the envelopes, she became excited to see if it was addressed to her. It was and she kept it; perhaps this *would* be 'the day'. The others she handed in at reception for distribution as she passed by.

She arrived at her office, sat at her desk and opened her letter with high hopes that it contained what she had been waiting for.

'Dear Mr and Mrs Wankowski

Permission to Adopt – Salah Al Munairi

I am writing to acknowledge receipt of your letter regarding the above request.

Whilst I acknowledge your good intentions I regret to say that there are many difficulties for me in agreeing your request. I am sure you are aware the Emirates Government has ruled that only Emirati citizens may adopt orphans, whatever their nationality, and for adoption purposes all orphans are treated as if they are Emirati citizens. In your case you are not Emirati citizens, neither do you appear to be able to meet the Government's requirements for becoming Emirati citizens.

On the evidence of the case before me my initial reaction is to deny your request for permission to adopt the above named. However, I have been impressed by the strong representations made to me supporting your case and I am therefore prepared to exercise my limited discretion in this matter.

You have resided in Dubai for 12 years. The residential requirement for becoming an Emirati citizen is 30 years. I am prepared to reduce this from 30 years to 20 years on the clear understanding that you remain in Dubai for a further 8 years. This will need to be formally agreed and legally binding.

I regard the requirement that you both have a working knowledge of Arabic as essential to your ability to perform your role as adoptive parents. However, I am prepared to allow you to proceed with your adoption provided that you either achieve the required standard at the appropriate time or, if you do not, you remain on an intensive Arabic speaking course until such time as you do reach the required standard. You are both language specialists and this should be helpful to you in learning Arabic.

I believe these concessions will greatly assist you in your application to become adoptive parents in Dubai. In all other respects you must adhere in full to the internationally recognised adoption process determined by the Emirate of Dubai, which includes a self-study, police check, preparation of a file of specified essential documents, home visit and final interview, before a decision can be made.

In proposing these arrangements I have had regard not only to the representations made to me on your behalf but also to the valuable service you have provided to the Emirates over many years. It is my hope that you will be able to continue to do so as Emirati citizens.

Ahmed Al Mandari

Minister for Nationality and Culture'

Maria was taken aback and reread the letter, hardly believing their astonishing good luck with the Minister, clearly going out of his way to be helpful. Who else had been making representation on their behalf apart from Dr Ahmadi who they already knew about? It seemed these representations had made all the difference.

Maybe the College owner mentioned by Yahya had also put in a good word. Yahya might know.

Maria wanted to ring Janek immediately and read the letter to him but he was away in the UK on a course about the latest developments in teaching English as a foreign language. She would have to wait because of the time difference. If she woke him too early he might not be in a good mood. Years of mostly happy marriage had taught Maria that Janek was not a morning person and she was keen to maximise the likelihood of his being receptive to her good news. After all, he would realise at once that after receiving permission to go ahead they would both be committing themselves to a huge amount of extra work and, probably, expense.

Being unable to contact Janek for now, Maria decided to see if Yahya was in his office; he had been so helpful at every stage and deserved to be one of the first to know the outcome of all their efforts. She was certain he would share her feelings of relief and joy and she got up and left the office. On her way downstairs she saw Yahya arriving via the main entrance and followed him to his office, which they entered together much to Yahya's surprise. He only just had time to put his briefcase down and walk to his desk when, visibly excited, Maria handed him the letter. Neither spoke. Yahya read the letter and looked up at her. He then read the letter again.

"Mabrook." *Congratulations.*

"Thank you, Yahya. I cannot thank you enough for everything you've done to help us. We couldn't have got this far without your help."

"You are very welcome. It always seemed a worthy cause to me. Salah deserves a break after what happened to him. I wouldn't be surprised if His Excellency instructed some of his staff to make enquiries about this case. If so, I am sure he would have been embarrassed that one of the Emirate's best known families had behaved so callously after Sheikh Salem's death. Maybe this also influenced his decision."

"Do you think so?"

"I think it's very likely. By the way, Sheikh Al Balushi rang about the copy of your letter I sent him. We spoke at length and he was wholly supportive and promised to speak to the Minister. They know each other."

"Should I write and thank him?"

"I don't think that's necessary, Mrs Wankowski. On one hand, I can give him a call and convey your appreciation with mine. On the other hand, it might be a good idea to let Dr Ahmadi know the outcome of your application. I am sure she would like to be kept informed and you could pass on all our thanks at the same time."

"Will do, thanks again, Yahya. By the way, please call me Maria. I must go now. Jan is in the UK at the moment on a course. He should be awake now so I am going to ring him and read the letter to him."

Maria returned to her office and telephoned Janek. He was already awake, standing and looking out of the window of his room while the kettle boiled for his morning tea and biscuit. He was staying in a student halls of residence for the duration of the course. The room itself was small and typical of its kind, better than the room he had lived in when *he* was a student. It even had an en suite WC, washbasin and shower and a tiny cubicle that was a masterpiece of design and space management. In the old days he had to walk down a long corridor to a shared bathroom and hope there was a vacancy for the particular bathroom facility he needed.

Janek was pouring tea when his mobile started vibrating.

"Hi Maria."

"Hello darling."

"Nice to hear your voice."

"Nice to hear your voice too; I'm not too early, am I?"

"Not at all, just making some tea."

"Well, I would have waited until we speak this evening as usual, but I have great news and I want you to know straightaway."

"Go on."

"We have had a reply from the Minister; let me read it to you." She read it slowly.

"Oh my God, what have we got ourselves into?"

"I thought you might say something like that. I'm not sure how to interpret your reaction. Can you help me?"

"Would you mind reading it once more?"

"Not a bit. I had to read it twice myself when I opened the letter."

She read it a little faster this time, emphasising key points.

"Thanks. I always understood that adopting Salah would be a big deal. I'm only just realising what a massive life-changing experience it's going to be for us. It may take me a little time to get my head around all of it."

"I confess I was rather taken aback to begin with; then when I remembered how much support we've received and how helpful the Minister has been, I felt re-motivated."

"I have no problem with the adoption process itself. It's this having to become an Emirati that makes me a little uneasy, especially having to give up our British nationality. Do we really want to stay here for another eight years?"

"I know what you mean. But the first 12 years seem to have gone quite quickly, would you agree?"

"I suppose so. By the way, I've got the perfect guy for the Arabic tuition; a while ago he offered to help us Brits in my College learn some Arabic on an informal basis and it was good fun. We all made some progress but didn't keep it going. I am sure he will be up for getting us both up to standard. We should pay him, of course."

"That's great, Jan."

Maria was much relieved. Janek had turned a corner. He had just gone from a focus on problems to a focus on solutions. This was the story of her life. He could find it difficult to come to terms with new ideas and situations initially, but, if she was patient and pointed him in the direction she wanted him to go, he would usually do whatever was required. Maria judged this was the moment to change the subject. They agreed to go though the letter again when Janek returned to Dubai.

CHAPTER 2.22

The door chimes rang. Maria was in the kitchen and Janek answered the door.

"Hello Salah." Welcome. Good to see you again. Come into the living room. Maria's cooking, she won't be long."

"Hello Janek, thanks; good to see you too."

Salah realised he'd just called Janek by his first name. He had sometimes referred to Mr Wankowski as Janek when talking with Mrs Wankowski, but this was something new. It came so naturally. It wasn't going to come naturally to call Mrs Wankowski, Maria. He might have to ask her which she preferred.

"How did you get here?"

"I used the bus, there's a short walk to and from."

"By the way, congratulations on your exam results! So, now you're all set for life in the UK?"

"I suppose so – nearly – a few more things need to fall into place first, I guess."

"Of course, actually we've come up with a few ideas to help you on your way. Is this a good time to tell you what we have discussed?"

Salah agreed it was as good a time as any.

"First, we think you need a mobile phone. You probably know they're called GSMs in this part of the world. We happen to have a spare so I have obtained a new SIM card and swapped it over. It's registered in your name so the mobile is now yours. Your bills will be charged against your bank account.

"Which brings me to the next matter; we've opened a bank account for you here in Dubai, an HSBC current account – they call it a Flexi Account. We think this seems most suitable for your needs. There is no minimum balance required, you can bank on-line 24/7, or do mobile banking or phone banking, and you can earn 2% per annum interest on current balances. We have deposited 2,500 dirhams to start you off."

"It sounds amazing; I don't know what to say, Janek."

"For your time in the UK we would like to open an HSBC Student Bank Account. This account is specially designed for students and allows you to have an overdraft of up to £1,000 without fees or interest should you run out of money. You will also receive an £80 Amazon gift card and 12 months of Prime Student when you open an HSBC Student Account. We will transfer enough money to you monthly to cover your living expenses in the UK. You will need to let us know how much you need."

Maria joined them.

"Hello Mrs Wankowski. I hope I have timed it right."

"Perfect, Salah, lovely to see you. Have you been having a good chat with Jan?"

"We haven't exactly been chatting, but Janek has been telling me about all the wonderful things you are doing for me. Truthfully, it all seems too good to be true."

"Jan, shall we all have a drink? My usual, please."

"Salah?"

"Any fruit juice would be great. Thank you."

"Regarding your adoption, I think I told you Jan and I had a very helpful letter from the Minister of Culture. It is going to be hard meeting all the adoption requirements, but thanks to the Minister and to those who have supported us, it is now looking very positive.

"The main requirement is that you have to be an Emirati yourself to adopt an Emirati. You are classed as an Emirati because, officially, you are an orphan. The residential requirement to become an Emirati is 30 years, which we could not possibly have met. The Minister has shortened this to 20 years, which we would be able to meet if we stayed here for another eight years. We didn't have any plans to leave so that shouldn't be difficult.

"The rest of it is all about learning Arabic, which we wanted to do anyway and we should have made much more effort whilst we've been here; also, it's about not having a criminal record, which we haven't of course and about having sufficient financial resources, which we have. We shall need to undergo various investigations and interviews, etc, which we are sure we can cope with.

"So that is where we are, Salah."

Janek handed round the drinks.

"Cheers!" they all cried in unison.

"I do feel extraordinarily lucky."

"That's nice of you to say. Before, you were extraordinarily *un*lucky, so maybe things have evened up a bit."

"Only because of all your kindness, Mrs Wankowski."

"Salah, I think the time has come for you to call me Maria, although perhaps not at the College."

"If you are happy, Maria, I certainly shall."

"I think the main thing we wanted to talk to you about today, Salah, is that we can't wait until all the adoption formalities are sorted out before we start helping you with such things as having phone contact and your finances."

"I have been explaining to Salah what we have in mind," said Janek.

"Oh. You've covered the GSM and the bank accounts? What about my laptop?"

"I thought you would like to deal with that."

"OK. Salah, I am buying myself a new laptop computer and I wondered whether you might like my old one. It's a Sony VAIO. It is not the latest technology or software but it still works for all the basics such as word processing, Internet and so on. It should be good enough until you can afford a better, more up-to-date system. Would you like to see it?"

"Please."

Maria left the room and soon returned carrying a case, which she placed on Salah's lap. She pulled the zip to open it and inside was a Sony VAIO.

"You can keep the case, of course; why don't you start it?"

Salah had used the College's computers enough to know his way around the keyboard. He turned the laptop on and the desktop screen appeared with the usual icons for programmes, anti-virus software, e-mail, Internet, battery and so on. Maria pointed out the Yahoo! icon and said that she and Janek had been happy with Yahoo! and had never used any other e-mail service providers. She suggested Salah open his own Yahoo! account to familiarise himself with how it works, then send Janek a test message. When Maria had her new laptop they could also exchange messages.

"So we shall have telephone contact and e-mail contact in future, Salah. You might even like to try Skype when you are in the UK, then we should be able to see each other as well as chat. Sometimes either the image or the sound is unsatisfactory, occasionally both, but it is great when it works."

By this time the smell from the kitchen had become stronger and was very appetising.

"I haven't tried to make Indian food this time, Salah. I hope you don't mind. I felt a bit out of my depth last time, actually."

"Maybe we could make a curry together, Maria. I only know what I saw my mother doing when she was cooking, I'm not an expert."

"That would be such fun, Salah, let's do it. This evening I made a lasagne. I discovered Italian food myself when I was a student. The popular dishes are very easy to make and lend themselves to batch cooking and freezing, which is more convenient and economical for students. You are most welcome to try out some recipes in our kitchen before you go to the UK if you like."

"Thanks, Maria; sounds fun."

They all ate their dinner of lasagne with garlic bread and a simple pudding of caramelised oranges, which Salah thought was fantastic, so much so that Maria put the leftover lasagne and oranges in plastic containers for him to take away.

Salah had said he wouldn't stay the night on this occasion. He said he thought the Kuwaitis would be going back to Kuwait soon and he would be looking for somewhere else to live. He remembered that previously Maria and Janek had said he could have a room with them and he hoped by mentioning the Kuwaitis he may have prompted them into confirming this. They did.

"Oh, that's an easy one, Salah. You must come here as soon as you need to leave your villa. Just let us know if you need any help moving your things."

"That's great, Janek. So, perhaps I could leave the laptop here for the time being."

"No problem."

"Thank you both so much for everything, for all your kindness and generosity and for another most enjoyable evening."

"You're very welcome. See you soon."

CHAPTER 2.23

Salah arrived back at the villa. It was shrouded in darkness and very quiet. The Kuwaitis must either be asleep in their rooms or out somewhere enjoying themselves. Probably the latter; he didn't think to look to see if there were any cars in the carport.

Salah climbed the stairs up to the roof, opened his room door and put the light on. He quickly turned it off. To his amazement, Jas was lying on his bed in her underwear, fast asleep. He hesitated, then undressed and slid onto the bed beside her. Pulling up a sheet he turned towards her and gently put his arm around her. There was just enough room for two if they stayed close and, with something soft and warm under his hand, Salah realised he had never been happier.

He reflected on what an amazing day it had been and felt for the first time that the future was going to be something he could look forward to with optimism and enthusiasm. He and Jas fell happily asleep.

Salah awoke in a state of moderate confusion having slept more deeply and longer than usual. He remembered he didn't have to go to the College so he didn't hurry to get out of bed. Then the fog gradually cleared and a picture of Jas emerged, a picture of Jas lying on his bed.

Slowly coming to his senses, he belatedly realised that Jas must have had to get up as usual and begin work on her daily chores. He rolled out of bed and went out to the bucket for his usual shower and, after drying himself, put on the clothes he had worn the previous evening. Unusually, he tidied the bed. Then he went downstairs to look for something for breakfast.

Salah was hoping to see Jas on his way downstairs but this didn't happen. In the fridge he found dates, laban and pitta bread. He dipped broken pieces of pitta bread into the laban and ate these with the dates. He didn't linger as he was anxious to find Jas, so he cleared away, washed and dried up, and went looking for her.

He began on the ground floor. In the past he had caught sight of her cleaning and tidying through half-open doors, but today all the doors were shut. He quietly went from door to door listening outside. He didn't want to open any doors and risk the embarrassment of going into one of his friend's bedrooms. How would he explain himself? Then his luck changed.

He heard a noise, which sounded like a handle clanging against a metal bucket. Beginning to walk upstairs he heard the sound again. He guessed that Jas was working her way down from the top, washing and drying the marble stairs as she went. He continued upwards.

"Hi Jas, OK?"

"OK, Salah, thanks."

"I am wondering when you finish work today and whether we could go into the centre again."

"About 2 o'clock, I think. Yes that would be nice."

"We could be back in time for me to go out to dinner later?"

"No problem."

"Unless you would like to go shopping, shall we try one of the adventure parks?"

"Why not?"

Jas and Salah walked to the nearest tram station and bought tickets. The tram lines were all in one zone so they could travel anywhere they wished. The ride itself was pleasant enough; sightseeing in Dubai. On the downside, the tram made painfully slow progress through the proverbially congested Dubai traffic.

At least there was plenty of time to talk about where they wanted to go. Jas liked Salah's idea of going to an attraction and veered between various watery options, especially Dolphin

Bay, Aquaventure or the Aquarium. Salah was thinking of other possibilities but happy to let Jas choose. They realised eventually there wasn't enough time to make it worthwhile going to some of the attractions and cost was an issue, as ever.

The tram reached the end of its route at the Dubai Marina. Salah and Jas got off and decided to explore the Marina Walk, a long pedestrianised walkway. As it would take a whole day to walk all the way, Salah and Jas contented themselves with strolling together for as long as time would allow.

They loved the beautiful beachfront paved area overlooking Jumeira Beach with great scenic views of the Arabian Gulf. Having not eaten lunch they were pleased to find a variety of restaurants catering to all cuisines and tastes. They browsed, looking carefully at prices before committing.

They also saw some of the many outlets along the walk. Roughly halfway along they came across the Covent Garden Market, a seafront location with an extensive range of covered stalls selling clothing, jewellery, sweets, gifts and souvenirs. Many items were made locally. Street entertainers were providing entertainment.

Moving along, Jas spotted a McDonald's. She felt comfortable in a McDonald's. She knew what she would have to spend and she knew she would be able to afford it. They were both hungry and went inside. Jas ordered a Happy Meal with chicken nuggets, fries, orange juice and apple bites for dessert. Salah had a Coke and a doughnut saying he didn't want to spoil his appetite for later. He paid. Jas tried to give him money.

"I can do this, thanks."

They found a table.

"We must be careful not to fall in love, Salah."

Salah was taken aback.

"Why?"

"You are very nice, Salah, and I like you a lot. But I know I can't choose you."

"Why?"

"It's complicated."

"Why?" He had nothing but questions.

Jas had a mouthful of nuggets and couldn't speak for a while.

"Because I'm married."

"OK. But why are you not with your husband?"

"He doesn't like to work. He likes to stay with his friends in the Philippines taking drugs and gambling. In any case, he doesn't speak English so he wouldn't get a job here in Dubai, probably not in the Gulf anyway."

"Why don't you divorce him?"

"He would never agree."

"Why?" That question again.

"Because of the money I send home."

"Why do you send him money?"

"I don't send him money. I send it to my mum who is looking after my daughter. But he keeps begging for money and if she doesn't give it he threatens her and the child."

"What a terrible story. So, you have a daughter. How old is she?"

"She's five."

"What's her name?"

"Angel. She's lovely."

"I expect she is if she's anything like you."

Although Salah was surprised and saddened by Jas' story, Khaled had warned him a while ago when they were in his car together that she might be married. Perhaps he should have taken more notice. Even if he had, what could he have done with this information? It's doubtful whether he could have prevented this afternoon turning into something very different from what he had imagined and not at all to his liking.

He and Jas retraced their steps and boarded the tram. On the way back they were both conscious of unfinished business and would have liked to continue their conversation. But the tram was almost full and others would overhear what they were saying. Instead, they held hands out of sight of everyone, neither certain of the rules in Dubai, but they had been led to believe open displays of affection could get you into trouble.

They left the tram after travelling back in silence, walked the rest of the way to the villa and then to the top of the stairs to the roof. They hugged and kissed outside their rooms.

"Don't be sad, Salah. You will be going away to another country soon to finish your studies and you will forget all about me in no time."

Salah felt tearful. He overcame the urge to say he would never forget her. He was worried it wouldn't sound sincere. No words came and they went to their rooms. Salah sat on his bed and thought how much wiser Jas was than he.

Salah went downstairs. The two Mohammeds and Ali were in the kitchen getting ready to go out. When Salah arrived there were congratulations and high fives in all directions. Everyone was pleased with their exam results and in good spirits. They talked about booking a taxi rather than risk being caught out by the drink- driving laws. They waited to see what Khaled would say.

They arrived at 'The Mexican', as it was known. Salah had been once before with the Wankowskis. For the others it was a new experience. They entered through the ornately carved wooden doors. Inside, the decor was predictably Mexican with vibrantly coloured pottery adorning walls and traditional artefacts carefully placed on shelves.

The attempt to create an authentic ambience, with one exception, didn't extend to the staff, who were all Indian migrant workers suitably dressed up for the occasion with leather covered carafes of tequila hanging from their belts. The exception was the proprietor and head chef who was a real Mexican.

Miguel appeared at Salah's table and introduced himself. He was friendly, welcoming and huge. He may have caught Salah and his friends looking at the size of his stomach.

"You've come to the best place to eat. Look what a great advertisement I am for Mexican food. You should be deeply suspicious if a chef is thin. Never eat in a restaurant where the chef is thin."

Miguel returned to his kitchen and a waiter arrived to take an order for drinks. The friends were thinking Cokes, but Ali stopped a waiter who was passing by carrying large jugs of something.

"Excuse me. What's in the jugs?"

"Margarita, a traditional tequila-based Mexican cocktail."

None of them knew anything about cocktails but they were sold on the idea of a traditional Mexican drink and ordered a jug each. Whilst they were looking at their menus and waiting for the jugs to arrive, another waiter passed them carrying a tray of food sizzling and letting off steam. Mohammed K asked another waiter about it.

"Chicken fajitas."

Mohammed S said he had eaten a fajita before and explained to the others how to roll the meat in flour tortillas with accompaniments of guacamole and sour cream. They found fajitas on their menus. They weren't too expensive and so they decided to order them.

The jugs of margarita arrived. The waiter poured a glass each. They sipped and glugged and were not disappointed. Khaled was slightly anxious because he wasn't sure how much alcohol was in the drink. He vaguely remembered cocktails were small, strong drinks. This felt like a large, strong drink that did nothing to relieve his anxiety. In no time, all four were in high spirits enjoying themselves so much he stopped worrying. After all, they were making use of a taxi, so what was the problem?

The fajitas arrived sizzling and smoking accompanied by bowls of guacamole, sour cream and grated hard cheese. They enjoyed the drama and congratulated themselves on their choice of food, which looked great and smelt even better. They tried to follow Mohammed S's instructions but only Salah managed to prevent the chicken filling from dropping out of the tortilla wraps. Slippery fingers were the main problem, particularly those attached to hands covered with various quantities of guacamole and cream.

They finished the jugs of margarita. Nobody had room to eat a pudding. The food and drink had been so good they wondered why they hadn't been to the Mexican before. They all agreed they had depended too much on Indian and Chinese takeaways. The

Mexican didn't provide takeaways or deliveries but it was not far from their villa and taxis were not expensive, as long as you didn't use them too often.

They paid their bills and gave a small tip. A taxi was waiting for them as they came out rather unsteadily into the hot night air. During the ride home they said they would like to go to the Mexican again but that, sadly, time was running out and they would have to be back in Kuwait soon. Salah wasn't sure which of them was planning to go on to a university and, if so, where. All being well he would be in the UK soon and, whilst he was excited by the prospect, he felt sad that he and the Kuwaitis would soon be going their separate ways. They had been such good friends and he would miss them.

They paid the driver, entered the villa – still in alcohol-enhanced high spirits – and went to their rooms. Salah climbed up to his room and opened the door without switching the light on. He was right not to put the light on. Jas was lying on his bed as before. He joined her as quietly as possible and covered them both. She stirred a little and whispered…

"We may as well enjoy being with each other for as long as we can."

Salah was already feeling sad about the Kuwaitis, even sadder now at the thought of also having to leave Jas. He would miss her too!

ACT THREE

CHAPTER 3.1

September 30 2002

ENGLAND

Salah and Samara arrived at the same time for the first lecture on the Asset Management module. They were looking forward to finding out what it was going to be about. Salah was always pleased to see Samara; this morning she seemed pleased to see him too.

"Where shall we sit?"

Samara liked to sit somewhere near the middle of a row and about halfway up the tiers.

"Thank you for asking me to join you yesterday; I really enjoyed the company and the food was great.

"Me, too; we should hang out together more often."

"I would like that, but are you sure you'll have time, Salah? You'll be spending more time with your girlfriend."

"Her name's Hayley," he told Samara with evident pride.

"That's a nice name."

"I'm sure there will be enough time for everything, Samara."

The lecturer arrived waving his notes and stood behind the lectern in the corner. He looked across the room, his eyes ranging from top to bottom and side to side.

"Good morning. I believe you've already been given an introduction to the FM programme and you're familiar with the modular structure. I'm Dr Hunter and I shall be with you for the Asset Management module. The module is in four sections. These are Project Management, Strategic Planning, Capital Planning and Construction.

"We shall begin this morning with Project Management. I am sure you are already aware that the dominant issues in any project for all the stakeholders are cost, quality and time. It follows that project managers need to acquire or develop a project administration system that deals with these issues, as well as other important matters such as resource allocation, change management, documentation and review.

"Fortunately, with the advent of computers, various kinds of software have been developed that enable project managers to perform their role. These may be desktop based or, more recently, Internet based. The best software provides an interface for multiple users to make contact with their project management tool via their mobiles 24/7, whenever they need and from wherever they are. One such system is called 'Basecamp' and it's very popular. We'll come back to Basecamp and look at it in detail."

Salah had a vision of himself working on a major construction site, wearing a hard hat and a high visibility tabard, communing with 'Basecamp' on his mobile and providing all the answers to all the questions all the people on the site might wish to ask.

The lecturer then asked a question unexpectedly and Salah snapped out of his reverie.

"Has anyone had any experience of project management?"

Silence – no response.

"Has no one ever planned a family holiday, moved house, bought a car or organised a party, a celebration or an anniversary?"

One or two hands were raised, slowly and nervously.

"There's no need to be shy; I'm not going to stand here and talk *at* you all the time; I need you to be engaged with the subject. It's your turn to do some work."

Several more arms went up, one at a time, still tentatively.

"Now, I want you all to work in pairs, maybe a threesome if we don't have even numbers, and identify something you have been involved in that could be loosely called a project. Then consider what steps, processes, actions and factors were involved in going from the starting point to a successful outcome. Go. I shall give you a time check periodically."

Although the lecturer had suddenly turned the tables on them, so that *they* were now under pressure and not *him*, they were mostly happy with the task. The buzz of chatter indicated they'd accepted the challenge and were busily engaged in the task. After about 20 minutes the lecturer told them they should make a short note of what they had come up with and be ready to report back to the whole group in ten minutes.

"Time's up." He picked out a male student in the middle of the back row on his left and asked him what he and the others had written down.

"Leadership, planning, resource allocation and monitoring, especially time."

"Thank you, that's a great start."

"You, next." He pointed to a girl near the front on his right.

"Planning, quality assurance, realistic achievable goals, communication."

"Also very good; notice how some activities are coming up more than once. For example, I expect you all mentioned 'planning' even if you didn't write it down."

"Next, over there to my left, the person fourth row back on the end, in the middle."

"We had leadership, communication, review, risk assessment and we thought it important to celebrate success."

The lecturer had written all these down on the whiteboard. "Good point about celebrating success, I like that."

"OK, the lady eight rows back, five seats in from the central aisle."

"We had several of those you already wrote down, plus teamwork, performance monitoring and closure."

"Good, thank you. So you can see from the whiteboard that some of your everyday experiences have already taught you the basics of project management. We can see also that some aspects of managing a project came up more than once. We can probably infer this is because they are important to every single project.

"You will gather that project management is potentially a large, wide-ranging subject. I am going to go further and suggest that anything and everything that has ever been discovered about management is potentially relevant to managing projects. So, the task we have now is to narrow down the field, increase the focus and create a logical framework for the main essential elements, which we can then explore further in more detail. I suggest we begin by considering the issue of leadership."

The lecture continued in this vein until the end of the session. There were no more student tasks as such but the style was relaxed and participative with students having opportunities for as much or as little involvement as they wished. The session concluded with the distribution of a reading list. Students were impressed when they discovered that one of the recommended books had been written by Dr Hunter himself.

After the lecture, Salah asked Samara if she would like a coffee. She declined politely, so Salah set off towards the cafeteria and joined the queue. He looked around for familiar faces. No such luck today; he wondered about Khamis, he hadn't seen him all morning. With a coffee and a doughnut he looked for a table, which were few and far between, but luckily, people were leaving as others were arriving and he was soon able to sit down. Majid joined the queue; Salah waved but couldn't catch his eye and so he went over.

"Hi Majid, I'm over by the noticeboard if you would like to join me."

"Hi Salah, OK, I shall… Won't be long."

Majid brought his tea over and joined Salah. He'd just been to a 'boring' lecture on geopolitics; he was not only bored but offended as well.

"How can you call it geopolitics when everything said about the Middle East is based on seeing the world through Western eyes?"

"That must have been very frustrating, Majid," agreed Salah, wanting to show interest although not quite understanding what Majid was talking about.

"Will you be going to the mosque this week?"

"Of course, I never miss Friday prayers. Any reason for asking?"

"I wondered whether you might find out from your friends

whether their ideas have crystallised at all."

"I don't think we should be discussing that here, Salah."

"Sorry, you're right, of course. I should have realised; maybe I shall see you at the mosque."

"OK, but I've got something on after with another Sudanese guy – should be fun – there aren't many of us around. He says he has some Sudanese coffee. What about tomorrow sometime?"

"Fine with me, we could meet up again here mid-morning."

"OK, Salah, done. See you tomorrow."

They parted company and Salah set off back to Sharpe. Nearer to the hall he came across Hani heading in the same direction. They walked together without much to say other than a friendly greeting and they went inside.

They reached the top of the stairs and were beginning to walk down the corridor to their rooms when they saw Sebastian in the distance standing outside his room with his hand in his pocket, apparently looking for his keys. As soon as he found them and turned the key in the lock, the door fell inwards, hitting the floor of his room with an almighty crash. Sebastian himself was dragged into his room on top of his door.

Hani and Salah went to help and found him flailing around trying to get back up on his feet. This required several attempts owing to the slippery, varnished surface of the door. Hani put his hand out to steady him but he was in no mood to be helped.

"What the fuck?"

"There are eight screws on your desk, Sebastian. It looks as if they've been taken out of your doorframe, so there was nothing holding the door in place except the lock, until you opened it, that is."

"Thank you, Salah. I suppose you think it's funny."

"Come on, Sebastian, from our position at the end of the corridor the sight of your legs flying through mid-air into your room *was* hysterical!"

"Are you hurt?" asked Hani, belatedly, trying to sound as if he cared.

"Has anyone got a screwdriver?" asked Sebastian, trying to

recover some dignity.

"Not me," replied Hani. "Sorry."

"Sorry, Sebastian, me neither. We could use a knife from the kitchen for now, put the screws back in their hole and tighten them later. Someone must have a screwdriver."

Salah came back from the kitchen with a stainless steel knife.

"Thanks, Salah. I suppose it was only a joke. It was a hell of a shock though, I can tell you. I don't suppose you know who did it?"

"Not a clue. I am sure it was not meant to be malicious. So, would you like to get your own back?"

"Not really; can't be bothered, actually."

Sebastian had passed quickly through several reactions including shock, anger, revenge and finally, grudging acceptance. Now he was thinking damage control, damage to the door, damage to his pride and potential damage to fraternal relations if he overreacted.

Hani and Salah left Sebastian to his own devices after helping to put the door back in place and being as supportive as they could. They couldn't be sure whether someone, or some group, was just having a laugh or whether it was more serious. Not knowing much about Sebastian they hoped he wasn't being bullied and that it was only a student prank. It was certainly very funny.

CHAPTER 3.2

October 1 2002

Salah awoke to the sound of birdsong; it was the sound of a new alarm he'd selected from his mobile, very realistic and hardly distinguishable from the real thing. He loved it but there was a problem. Salah found it so beautiful he was apt to listen to it for too long and allow himself to be lulled back to sleep. If he didn't remember to press the snooze option the birds would carry on chirruping and he'd oversleep.

No chance of oversleeping today for today was going to be a big day – he'd arranged to meet Majid. He had no idea when Majid would arrive at the cafeteria so he needed to be there early in case Majid was an early riser.

Whilst in the shower he heard his mobile vibrating on the bed. Whoever it was would have to wait. He came back into the bedroom to dress, picking up his pants with one hand and his mobile with the other. He quickly learned that putting on underpants is a two-handed operation. By performing an unusual dance and at the same time fumbling with his phone, he checked his missed calls. It was Samara.

"Hello Samara."

"Sorry to miss you, you're up early today."

"Hi Salah, I'm always up at this time. I promised to tell you when the Islamic Society is meeting; they're having a meeting at 4.30 pm today. I'm sorry it's such short notice but I've only just found out about it."

"Thanks, Samara, good of you to let me know. I'll be there if I can. Thanks again, have a good day."

"You too, Salah, hope to see you."

Salah expected to meet Majid sometime during the morning so figured he could probably make the IS meeting later, no problem. If not, Samara would be happy to tell him about it.

Grabbing his coat, Salah went down the stairs two at a time until he met some second-floor girls going down more slowly. They were unusually friendly and he chatted to one of them as they went down the stairs together. She was nice, very nice and very pretty. Perhaps there were possibilities here after all. He reminded himself he was happy with Hayley, he didn't need more than one girlfriend and, should this happen by some extraordinary accident, he probably wouldn't be able to cope.

He walked quickly and soon reached the cafeteria, checking his pockets to make sure he brought the camera, and queued with the others looking for breakfast food. When his turn came he bought tea for two and a packet of biscuits (Majid paid the previous time). If the tea was cold when Majid arrived he would just have to get another pot.

Salah opened his laptop and began to do more work on the Risk Management module. As the lecturer had outlined, the module consisted of four main areas, two of which included Security and Emergency Management. Salah couldn't help thinking of the irony of the situation. Here was the University teaching him about security whilst he was making plans to teach the University a lesson about security. It was the same for Emergency Management; thanks to Salah, Majid and his mates, the University's emergency management arrangements would be tested to the limit and probably beyond. A smile crept across Salah's face; he didn't have long to dwell on these thoughts as Majid arrived and came straight over.

"Hi Salah, what's up?"

"Take a seat, Majid."

Majid pulled a seat out; Salah poured another tea.

"Is the tea OK, is it still hot?"

"Could you put some more tea in please, there's a bit too much milk; that'll warm it up as well."

"Have a biscuit. Thanks, that's fine now."

"We need to talk. I've made some progress, Majid. Let's have the tea and head off."

"Great."

At this stage, Salah was still not quite sure whether he and Majid were on the same page. All would become clear.

They left the cafeteria and wandered around the campus avoiding the main areas and looking for an open space. When he felt they were alone, Salah took Mubarak's mobile out of his pocket and handed it to Majid who immediately put it in one of his jacket pockets and zipped it up. Salah said he had wiped it carefully to remove any fingerprints and Majid should be careful to do the same.

"I found that mobile, Majid, and I used it to photograph the bullets. It wasn't easy; I had to climb onto the roof of the Engineering Building. You can just see the courses of bricks in the pictures. I counted them and, based on the size of a standard brick, the bullets are just over 1 metre above the ground. If we go ahead with my plan, the barbecue would need to fit within that height under the bullets."

"The others are impressed with your plan, Salah, but I am not sure if they are fully on board with the idea of attacking the University. I am not even sure how they're organised. They may operate within some kind of command structure and have to get approval for something like this."

"You said they had bought a stolen credit card, doesn't that imply that they intend to do something?"

"True, they're definitely going to do something and they're very upset with the mosque."

"If you give them the mobile they can use it to buy the barbecue, the gas, maybe car hire or tools, without any fear of being traced." Majid looked anxious.

"Are you sure about this mobile?" Salah didn't want to tell Majid any more than he had to about finding the mobile.

"Very sure; very, very sure. Trust me." Salah hoped Majid was convinced.

"OK, if you say so."

"Have you got a map of the campus to give them? They'll need one unless you or I are involved. Also, they'll need to know the timings of the security patrols – I assume if anything happens it will be at night."

"I am sure I have. This is beginning to sound very real, Salah. We are rapidly reaching the point when we'll be unable to turn back. I'll let you know what happens, if they tell me, that is."

"Majid, if you or they want to abort, it's OK with me."

"I didn't say I wanted to abort, did I?" said Majid as he walked away.

Salah felt more than a tingle of excitement. He thought about nothing else as he made his way back to his room and wondered if Majid was having second thoughts. Could they be making any stupid mistakes that would give them away? Back in Sharpe he hung his coat on the door peg, dropped his rucksack on his bed and went to the kitchen.

Lunch options weren't great. He warmed a piece of dry pitta bread, which softened a little and he split it open to form a pouch. Shredding the remains of an old lettuce, he stuffed it in with some leftover cold chicken and chilli mayonnaise. The general effect was better than he expected. After eating he lay on his bed and closed his eyes.

The Islamic Society meeting was at the same location as the first meeting Salah attended. This one looked even more popular. He couldn't find a seat and then spotted Samara with an empty seat beside her.

"Hi Samara, is this for your boyfriend or are you keeping it for me?"

"It's for you, dummy; I don't have a boyfriend and, guess what? I don't *need* a boyfriend and, guess what again? I don't *want* a boyfriend."

"Anyway, thanks for the heads-up and thanks for keeping me a seat." Salah hoped she wasn't offended by his silly boyfriend joke. "They've taken a long time to get around to this meeting, don't you think?"

"I know what you mean, they'll probably tell us why."

The IS Committee members gradually assembled and sat on the chairs arranged for them. The President arrived last and stepped forward to the microphone centre stage.

"I know you've all been waiting to hear what we have to say about our Deputy Prime Minister's invitation to the US Under Secretary of State for International Affairs to visit his constituency, including a visit to our local mosque. No doubt the Government thought this would be a diplomatic triumph, but it's turning out to be a PR disaster. Unfortunately, our University has followed suit with its own invitation to visit. We understand the purpose of this visit is to award the Under Secretary an honorary doctorate.

"Of course, we would like to have been able to meet you all before now but we've been waiting for the mosque's decision on this. Meanwhile, we understand the Government is considering cancelling the visit because of the threat of anti-war protests.

"The general consensus among leaders of the mosque is that the invitation should be withdrawn, but they have insisted they have nothing against the Under Secretary. On the contrary, many at the mosque argued the visit should go ahead. What seems to have decided the matter is that large numbers of Muslims have threatened to attend the mosque around the time the visitors were due to be present, thus paralysing the mosque and creating a security nightmare.

"An outspoken member of the Council of Mosques has said he was always against the visit because of American unilateral foreign policies and militarism, but he acknowledged that there were two valid competing arguments involved.

"The first, cancelling the visit creates a lost opportunity to show the world that the mosque consists of model citizens who respect others' beliefs and build bridges internationally to improve mutual understanding. In other words, it would have been better for Muslims who are aggrieved and others against US wars to put their case face to face.

"The second argument is that Muslim issues and anti-war issues are already familiar to and well understood by all concerned, but nobody is listening or showing the slightest inclination to change their prejudiced views. Therefore, the argument says there is no point in meetings of this kind; they simply give legitimacy to wrongdoers.

"It seems some of those in the mosque held both these views but found they were unable to go ahead with their invitation. One senior figure said that Muslims should always welcome visitors and that it was very disappointing and upsetting not to be able to welcome the American.

"Now we come to the University's invitation. We have been asked by so many Muslim and non-Muslim brothers how we should respond to this affront to Muslim sensibilities. We in the IS Committee believe we can learn from the outcome of the situation at the mosque. The feelings amongst the faithful are very strong and they are willing to take a stand to make their feelings felt, even as far as making the visit a practical impossibility. We also learn that they chose a non-violent way of protesting even though we understand some hold radical fundamentalist views.

"After much careful thought we recommend we follow their example by doing our best to persuade the University to change its mind. If necessary we can, of course, organise a peaceful mass protest. I believe this would be well-supported by our non-Muslim brothers. We are not aware of any radical or fundamentalist groups within the University student population. Nevertheless, we strongly advise against any disproportionate action or any action that damages the public image of Muslims.

"Are there any questions?"

Salah wondered what Majid would have thought of the presentation. No doubt he would have anticipated the Islamic Society would adopt a conciliatory position.

There were a few questions, all timid and predictable. Samara sensed Salah's restlessness. At the end of the meeting, on the way out of the hall, she asked...

"What did you think of that, Salah?"

"I thought it was disappointing. Nobody challenged the logic of the IS Committee's recommendation; nobody asked how the IS

Committee thought it could change the University's mind or what they would do if the University declined to do so; nobody asked what form a mass protest could or would take or how it would be organised. Sadly, I think the IS Committee will have taken the response from the floor as agreement with their analysis, whereas I am sure a significant number would disagree."

"Wow! You could have said something yourself…"

CHAPTER 3.3

October 4th 2002

His first waking thought was that his mobile alarm was tweeting and chirruping. The birds weren't charming him this morning, they were deafening; he must have changed the volume by mistake. He was fumbling in an uncoordinated attempt to rectify this when his phone began to vibrate.

"Hello Khamis," he answered, sounding groggy.

"Hi Salah, sorry if I woke you, I just wanted to know if you are coming to Friday prayers."

"I suppose so. I mean, yes, of course," he replied, sounding a little more alert.

"I need to go to the library first thing so I could give you a lift, if you like. No sweat, I shall be in the University anyway."

"Yes please, Khamis. Thanks, you're a good friend. See you."

"Bye."

Salah got out of bed, went to the bathroom for a pee and then to the kitchen. As usual it wasn't busy this early, with only one other student reaching into a cupboard. They exchanged hellos; neither knew the other's name.

He felt like eating toast this morning and luckily there was still some sliced bread. By the time he'd prepared a toasted peanut butter sandwich the kettle had boiled and he'd made tea. As usual, he took his breakfast back to his room.

When he'd finished he washed and dried his buttery, toasty fingers and switched on his laptop thinking there might be another e-mail from the Wankowskis. There was; it said:

'Hello Salah

Thanks for your latest message. Oh dear, this is worrying. You told us about the mosque, which didn't worry us too much, but we didn't realise it could affect the University. The meeting with the PVC sounds ominous. Is it possible one or more of your friends has been up to something they shouldn't? You say you don't think there is anything to be worried about. We ARE worried, Salah. We don't want anything to spoil your time at uni. Hopefully you've heard the end of it. If not, please tell us at once. We may be able to help in some way, even from a distance.

Maria and Jan'

Salah wished he hadn't told them now; he didn't need to worry them. He decided to respond straightaway:

'Hi

Thanks for your message. Sorry to have worried you. Everything's fine at the moment. I am sure my friends (I only have one or two) are OK. Will let you know if there are any more problems. Off to the mosque with Khamis now for Friday prayers.

Salah'

Salah's mobile vibrated in his pocket again. It was a text message from Khamis:

'I'll pick you up in the Sharpe car park at 11.15'

They arrived at the mosque and went straight to the ablutions area to wash before entering the prayer hall. The mosque was not as busy as it had been recently and the general atmosphere seemed more relaxed. Apparently, there wouldn't be a sermon from a visiting Imam this week but the resident Imam would give a short address.

After leading prayers, the Imam said it had been decided the invitation for the American to visit the mosque would be withdrawn, although he may meet the American briefly when he visits the town. He congratulated everyone involved on having reached a compromise and a peaceful resolution of the problem. He said he understood those who wanted positive action against the visit but added that Muslims need to be especially careful of the reputation of Islam following the London bombings, particularly as the British were now aware that they were growing their own terrorists.

Khamis and Salah filed out of the prayer hall with the others and saw Majid waiting for them outside.

"Hi Majid. Not with your usual friends today?"

"Hi Khamis, they're not friends but I know who you mean. I haven't seen them; I don't think they're here." Majid looked around as if to confirm their absence.

"Hi Majid, everyone seems more relaxed today and there are fewer people."

"Hi Salah, it's probably because word has got out that the invitation is going to be withdrawn."

"Very likely. It's good there's not going to be any trouble." Salah gave Majid a knowing look when Khamis wasn't looking.

"What shall we do now, guys?" Khamis suggested various possibilities such as going back to the University, going to his house, going to Annie's for food, going into town, etc. No one wanted to go back to the University as they didn't have a lecture and it was Friday afternoon, almost the weekend.

They jumped in Khamis' car and drove to Primrose Road. Parking was difficult as usual but Khamis managed to find a space in the next street, which, as it happened, was nearer to Annie's.

Annie began with her usual repertoire. "Hello boys, have you come back for more of my tasty food..?"

"Hello Annie, what's new?"

"Have you tried my shawarma?

"Yes, we have; you gave us some to taste last time. We loved it."

"Good, I'm glad you liked it. Well, if you want more you'll have to pay for it this time." Khamis and Salah laughed. Annie was pleased with her little joke.

"Sure, are you still doing falafel, hummus and fattoush?"

"Yes, I've got those. Today's special is baba ghanoush if you like aubergine – you'll love it. I can give you some pitta bread to go with it."

Salah and Majid were making up their minds while Khamis was talking to Annie.

Salah ordered. "Shawarma and fattoush for me, please."

"Falafel and hummus, please, Annie," requested Khamis. "Do you remember Majid?"

"Hello Majid."

"I'm going to try the baba ghanoush, Annie. Some pitta also would be good."

"Would you like some salad as well, no charge?"

"That will be great."

Annie arranged three boxes on top of the chiller and filled them generously, giving everyone a plastic fork and a napkin. They each paid and walked to their house in Primrose Road where they sat in Khamis' room and raided their boxes. As usual, conversation was in short supply for a while. When they finished, Majid spoke for all, full of praise for Annie.

"Great food and good value. Thanks, guys."

Khamis gathered up the debris after lunch and binned it. They talked for a while and then Salah excused himself saying he needed to go into town to shop for some food items. He was thinking of Hayley, having not having seen her recently, and he was evolving a plan. She knew he was hoping she would try Indian food sometime; his big idea was to offer to cook her dinner tonight. He would choose carefully, it needed to be something English people generally like, tasty but not too spicy and definitely not too hot. The answer must be chicken tikka masala. He'd heard this was the most popular choice among English people in Indian restaurants and takeaways.

Walking to the High Street, he went into Tesco and picked up a basket. He soon found the chicken and picked a packet of breast fillets, then he located the yoghurt, lemon juice, ginger, garlic, coriander and chilli powder. He knew what was needed for an authentic marinade from his research on the Internet. He decided to take it easy with the sauce by buying a jar of ready-made masala sauce and a small carton of cream. Finally, he found garlic naan bread and added wine and beer to his basket. He checked out and paid, then waited for a bus to the campus.

Back in the kitchen at Sharpe, he put the chicken fillets and yogurt in his fridge and the rest of his shopping in his cupboard next to the easy-cook rice before texting Hayley:

'How about I cook dinner for us this evening, fancy some Indian food?'

After a while…

'Why not? But if I don't like it you'll have to buy me fish and chips. See you in the Staff Car Park at 5pm we usually finish a bit earlier on Fridays.'

He replied…

'Done see you later.'

So far, so good, it was working; she even agreed to try the Indian food.

Salah had reached the staff car park and was looking for Hayley's car when she appeared and pointed to where she'd left it. They both got in without demonstrations of affection, hoping that nobody would put two and two together. He liked being driven by Hayley for she was a careful, steady driver –, very different to Khamis. He would like to be able to drive and Janek had offered to arrange lessons but, for some reason, it hadn't happened. Perhaps Hayley would be willing to get him started and then he could pay for a few lessons.

As soon as they arrived at Hayley's, Salah took his ingredients to the kitchen as if to begin work on the meal, but he thought he'd better check with Hayley first.

"Is it OK if I do some food preparation?" It was her kitchen after all.

"Knock yourself out; I'm going for a shower."

First, Salah put the wine and beer in the fridge and then he opened and closed a few cupboards and drawers until he found the equipment he needed. He cut the chicken into pieces and put them in a glass bowl before adding the other marinade ingredients and gave it all a big stir. The smell was wonderful; at least that's what he thought. It had probably reached Hayley in the shower by now and, so far, he heard no complaints.

He found a saucepan and opened the jar of masala sauce, emptying it into the pan and putting a lid on it. He would add the cream at the last minute. Removing the wrapper from the garlic naan bread, he re-wrapped it in foil, ready to be warmed in the oven. Job done. There was nothing more to do by way of preparation except measure out the rice. All he had to do nearer the time for dinner was to cook the rice and put the chicken under the grill, then add it to the sauce and warm it through, possibly adding a little cream if required.

Hayley emerged from the bedroom in home clothes with wet hair. They came together and hugged each other. She smelt wonderful. It was unlikely she had used perfume; it must be something to do with her hair. Whatever it was, Salah found it arousing. By contrast, he probably smelt of spices and doubted if Hayley was similarly aroused.

"Shall we have a glass of wine?" Hayley placed two wine glasses on the kitchen worktop.

"Can I have a beer instead?" It was a bit early to be drinking wine for Salah. He still wasn't quite used to it.

Hayley reached for another glass. "Perhaps you would like to pour it." They took their drinks to the living room and sat on the sofa.

"It's nice to be together again, Hayley, I've missed you this week."

"I assumed you were very busy." Salah noticed she didn't say she had missed him too.

"Actually, a lot has happened. Some of it's very odd, actually.

I've been looking forward to telling you about it." Salah began with the Pro-Vice-Chancellor meeting, which he recounted in some detail.

Hayley didn't like the sound of it at all saying that during her years at the University she had never heard any rumours or been aware of any suspicions about terrorist activity or even about discontent among Muslim students. As far as she knew, the University didn't have any security problems. She found Salah's story very worrying.

Salah said that he had never been aware of these things either but the world was changing. He could see why the University might be concerned, particularly with what was going on in the mosque over the American visitor. He then went on to tell Hayley about how Sebastian had been caught out by the increased surveillance and exposed over his late-night illegal downloads of porn movies. She found that highly amusing.

"Shall I cook the chicken now? We can have another drink and keep talking in the kitchen."

"Good idea. I prefer not to eat too late. I'll pour us another drink. By the way, the food smells lovely." Salah was more than a little relieved it was going well.

As soon as the chicken was cooked, Salah tipped it into the sauce warming in the saucepan. The rice was ready and the naan warm. Salah took it out of the oven, removed the foil and tore it in half, putting each half on a plate. Finally, he served the rice, chicken and sauce and brought the plates to the table where Hayley was sitting, having laid it herself. The plates looked good, smelt good and, he hoped, would taste good.

Hayley gently waved her hand to waft the spicy aroma towards her face.

"I know I am going to enjoy this, Salah, because it smells incredible."

"This is a very popular dish among English people. I do hope you enjoy it." Salah began to use small pieces of naan to mop up the sauce. Hayley did the same, which pleased him; she was eating Indian food like a native.

Hayley topped up their glasses and soon they were looking at empty plates.

"That was great, Salah, you can do that again any time you like. I'll clear up."

"We can do it together."

Back in the living room they sat on the sofa. Hayley picked up a magazine, one of those with a guide to TV programmes. "There's not usually much of interest on Fridays."

They looked at each other and he put his arm around her. She leaned over and kissed him. It wasn't only a peck on his cheek; it was a full-blown tongue-tingling, wet, lingering kiss.

He pulled her across him so she was lying over his lap, her head resting on his arm. He slid his hand under her skirt and stroked her legs; she seemed happy. His hand crept up and up as far as her stomach, which was warm and soft. He was enjoying stroking her stomach when he brushed against the elastic top of her knickers. Instinctively, he slid his hand under the elastic and felt her legs move apart slightly as she guided his hand to where she wanted it.

"Shall we go to bed?"

"You bet."

CHAPTER 3.4

October 5 2002

They were sleeping late as usual on a Saturday. They would have slept even later had Hayley's telephone not rung at 11 am. It wasn't her mobile it was her house phone and she had to get out of bed to answer this. Sliding out from under the duvet as quickly and quietly as possible, trying not to disturb Salah (he stirred anyway), she tiptoed to the telephone in the sitting room.

"Hello… Hello Mum." Hayley spoke quietly.

"Hello Hayley, what's the matter? Are you OK?" Her mum sounded anxious.

"Fine, thanks; why do you ask?" she asked, still speaking quietly.

"You sound a bit off and I can hardly hear you."

"To be honest, I was asleep having a lazy Saturday morning, you know, after a busy week. You know the kind of thing – you've been there."

She spoke a little louder, still afraid that Salah would wake up and make a noise. She was cool about having a man in her bed but she wasn't sure her mother would be and it would lead to questions such as how old, or how tall he was and what he was like, and so on. She couldn't be doing with an inquisition, not this morning.

"Sorry, I didn't mean to wake you, I just wanted to ask what sort of time you think you'll be here."

Hayley hesitated and then the feeling of panic swept over her. She had completely forgotten her promise to go home this weekend. Her grandparents were coming to stay and, apart from the fact they always wanted to see Hayley who they doted on, her mother had asked her to help with the visit.

"Would sometime in the early afternoon be OK with you?"

"I suppose so. If you leave it any later it'll hardly be worth it. I thought you would be coming this weekend anyway, we haven't seen you for ages."

"That's not quite true, Mum. Anyway, I'll be there. Would you like me to bring anything?"

"I've got all the main stuff but something for tea today would be nice."

"OK, if you think of anything else you can always ring me on my mobile."

"I'll do that. Drive carefully, darling; a driver got crushed to death by a falling tree the other day."

"Thanks, Mum." Hayley's mum always had a motoring horror story ready whenever she was about to drive somewhere.

Salah didn't wake up, having rolled over and pulled the covers up. She wasn't sure whether to wake him or quietly get ready to leave the flat. She made tea, went to have a shower, dried herself and poured a second mug of tea (which she left on Salah's bedside table), dressed and then sat at her dressing table to dry her hair and do her make-up.

Salah woke up. "What's going on?" The noise of the hairdryer must have woken him.

Hayley saw him in the mirror looking straight at her and she turned the hairdryer off.

"There's some tea for you there."

"Thanks." Salah reached for the mug.

"Have some tea and I'll explain."

"Explain what?"

Hayley got up and sat at the foot of the bed. "Salah. I've boobed. I was so excited about seeing you last night I forgot I'd promised to go home this weekend. My grandparents have come to stay. They're very old and not very well and my mum finds them a bit of a handful. I said I'd help her this weekend."

"OK." Salah was expecting Hayley to say more.

"Luckily, she just rang up to ask when I was planning to arrive. If she hadn't I would have forgotten all about it."

"It's not the end of the world, we'll cope."

"I'm so sorry, Salah. Are you ready to meet my parents?"

"Ehm…, ehm…, not really."

"That's what I thought. Not this time then. I need to get petrol and do a small shop, so I'd better be on my way. Why don't you stay as long as you like and we'll catch up asap?"

He got out of bed and gave her a kiss and a hug, being careful not to spoil her hair or make-up. "See you soon, then. Be careful."

"Will do." Hayley picked up her car keys and left.

To say Salah was disappointed would be an understatement. This was not the way he thought he would be starting the weekend. He got back into bed and looked around soon realising that if Hayley wasn't there he didn't want to be there either. If he was going to be lonely he'd rather be lonely somewhere else.

He decided to find out what Khamis was doing, so he got up and looked for his mobile, not sure where he left it. As soon as he had the phone in his hand it pinged. It was a text message from Hayley:

'Please make sure you lock the front door if you leave the flat. xxx'

Salah then called Khamis who picked up straightaway. "Hi Salah?"

"Hi Khamis. I'm at Hayley's. She's just gone to her parents for the weekend so I'm on my own. Any chance of meeting up in town for a coffee?"

"Majid and I were just talking about doing that. Coffee Plus, as usual? We like the cakes there. They're doing a new cheesecake."

"So do I. I'm not showered yet, see you there, maybe in an hour or so if I walk?"

"OK, we'll likely be there by then. See ya!"

Salah was pleased. He had order and meaning in his life again after being left in the lurch by Hayley's abrupt departure. After making another mug of tea he went to the shower. He had no choice but to wear the same clothes as yesterday and thought again about Hayley's idea of keeping a change of clothes at her flat.

He realised the reason he hadn't taken up her suggestion of meeting her parents was not because it was a bad idea – on the contrary – it was because it made him uneasy. Deep down and on one hand, Salah felt it a step too far, like getting married, as they had only known each other for a few days. On the other hand, this morning it would have been good to have a change of clothes. He would keep the idea under review.

He enjoyed the walk and reached Coffee Plus in less than an hour. Majid and Khamis were comfortably ensconced on sofas either side of a low table with plenty of room for Salah to join them. Salah waved and joined the queue, ordering a large Americano with the new blend and a triple chocolate cupcake. He sat down next to Khamis facing Majid; they seemed pleased to see him.

Majid was extolling the superior virtues of Sudanese coffee as usual and appeared not to have a care in the world. Salah wondered what was going through his mind and what was happening with their plans but, of course, he couldn't ask. Khamis was his usual self, complaining this time about the near impossibility of parking his vehicle close to where he lives on any day of the week.

Salah explained how he came to be on his own and gave a glowing account of his chicken tikka masala, including how Hayley had been wooed by the culinary magic of his spicing. No one asked if he used a jar of sauce. Maybe they weren't interested or were just being tactful. Khamis politely reminded Salah he promised some while ago to invite him to Sharpe and cook him a jalfrezi dinner. This had not happened. Salah squirmed a little, adopted an apologetic manner and said he hadn't forgotten. It was a lie. They knew.

Salah was keen to change the subject and moved the conversation on to something else. They compared notes on teaching styles and standards, workload, coursework, assessments and, naturally, girls. Seemingly, none of the girls on their courses were fanciable and so they had to look elsewhere. They were both unsuccessful so far. Salah didn't mention Hayley, nor did the others.

Salah and Khamis said they were reasonably satisfied with their course; only Majid was critical of his, the Politics course. He was more and more annoyed about what he considered to be Western bias in the University's political coverage of world affairs and events. He thought the University should be above reproach in this respect and he was exasperated that no one seemed to mind the US continuing to 'act like God on Earth'. Salah nodded his head but said nothing, feeling that he was on the same page as Majid. Khamis didn't react at all, no doubt feeling this was Majid on his hobbyhorse again.

Salah was hoping one or both of them had some sort of plan for the rest of the weekend, but this was looking unlikely.

"What are you guys up to this weekend, anything interesting?" He meant, of course, 'anything interesting that I could join?' but didn't want to show he was completely at a loose end. Neither had much to say; at least, nothing of interest to Salah. Majid was meeting up with some Sudanese students for an evening meal of Sudanese food. Khamis was going to tidy up, do his laundry and clean his car.

Salah realised he, too, had chores; his bed needed changing, his room could do with a clean, his laundry was overdue and he had very little food in his cupboards or fridge. He had assumed he and Hayley would be doing something together this weekend. Reluctantly, he parted company with Khamis and Majid and set off for Tesco.

He took his time walking up and down the aisles hoping for inspiration, but ended up with the same boring items in his basket. Suddenly he remembered he needed to buy another jar of jalfrezi for the dinner he'd promised Khamis. This time he decided prawns would be a good choice so he searched the freezers until he found some. He liked the sound of 'king prawns' and put a box in his basket.

Walking past the rice (he still had some easy-rice back at Sharpe), he noticed a jar of lime pickle that looked worth a try. The jars had slightly different labels; it took him a while to notice the small print, which was very small. The greenish label described the contents as medium hot and the reddish label as very hot. He wasn't sure which Khamis would prefer but he guessed medium hot would be safer; very hot might even spoil the whole meal.

Having decided on the pickle he thought about vegetables

and found a korma in the vegetable freezer. On the way to the checkout he picked up some naan bread and then, realising he had overlooked something to drink, he doubled back, grabbed a four-pack of beers, dropped them in his basket and went to pay.

Salah reached the bus stop in the nick of time, just catching the next bus to the University. After getting off the bus he walked across the campus to Sharpe and up the stairs; he was glad to reach the kitchen, the beers had made his bag heavy. He soon put everything away and felt pleased to have a few food items to keep him going and with the food in the freezer he could easily put something together when Khamis came for dinner.

Doing the shopping, getting back to Sharpe and unloading and putting away his purchases had used up a couple of hours or so. Now he was back in his room, on his own, miserable and lonely again. This happened occasionally and he didn't handle it well. Of course, there were the chores. He didn't feel like doing the chores having procrastinated already – what difference would another day make? Or two, even?

He tried to think of pleasant distractions. He could ring Hayley. He would like that but she might find it awkward, especially if she had not told her parents about him. Anyhow, he didn't have much to say and she might realise he only rang because he was bored. Salah hated the idea she might think him needy. Or he could make a short call later to say 'Goodnight'. That would work.

He thought of wandering down the corridor and knocking on Hani's door. He liked Hani, they got on well enough and he might be feeling sociable, but Hani was depressed because he was going through a terrible time and, whilst Salah was full of sympathy and wanted to be supportive, Hani wasn't exactly a bundle of laughs. In fact, he was probably the least likely person to cheer Salah up.

Rather in desperation and without expectations of improving his mood, Salah decided to visit the TV and games room in the next block. Thus far he hadn't made any use of this facility. When he arrived, several rows of chairs were occupied by noisy supporters of a football team who were in the final stage of their match. The result was close and tensions were high. Salah had heard about the English love of football but had not experienced it at firsthand until now. He decided to move on and found himself in a side room that was altogether more relaxing with subdued lighting and a floodlit snooker table with green baize. Salah found the overall effect calming. There was only one other person there, standing close to the table, chalking the tip of his cue.

"Fancy a game?" The guy had a strange accent.

"I don't really play." Salah wasn't being modest.

"There's nothing to it. All you have to do is knock the balls into the pockets."

Salah more or less understood the rules of the game having watched snooker on television, but he'd only held a cue in his hand once before and feared he was about to make a fool of himself.

"Why don't you do a few warm-up shots?"

Salah picked up a cue and struck the white against a red. The red dropped nicely into one of the middle pockets. The green was now the easiest to pot so he had a go. He did a miscue and the white, after failing to connect with the green, disturbed nearly all the other red balls.

"Don't worry. We all do it. I'm Janos, by the way. Let me help with your bridge." Janos took Salah's left hand, placed it on the green baize and spread his fingers and thumb to form a bridge for his cue. Salah positioned his cue in the 'V' shape between his fingers and thumb and moved it back and forward while Janos adjusted the position of his right wrist and elbow. Salah could feel the difference immediately and was beginning to enjoy himself.

"Thanks, Janos. I'm Salah."

"Hello Salah. Are you from India?"

"Actually, I'm from Dubai. Where are you from?"

"I'm Hungarian."

"Good to meet you, Janos. Shall we try a game then?"

Janos set up the balls and invited Salah to go first. Salah played the first shot enjoying his new cueing action. The white just nudged the reds. Janos played a safety shot. Salah opened up the reds and had a lucky pot. He chose the blue next and it dropped into a middle pocket. A red hovered over a pocket but Salah missed it.

Janos potted the red and then the brown. They continued in this fashion with Salah's score always slightly ahead. Salah potted the last red and missed the black. Then Janos potted every colour one after the other, winning the game by a small margin.

Salah realised he had never really been ahead with the score. Janos had been playing with him in more than one sense. The way the colours dropped into the pots one after another at the end clearly showed the highest level of skill.

"Where did you learn to play like that, Janos?"

"I used to work as a hotel kitchen porter to earn pocket money. The chef was a brilliant snooker player and we used to play every night after service until the early hours. He said he was glad of the practice. I learned a hell of a lot and got better and better."

"Shall we go for a drink?"

"Good idea."

They went to the bar in the students' union and chatted over a couple of beers. They agreed to play again tomorrow and Salah felt as if he was making a new friend in Janos. Going to the games room had enabled him to forget all the negative thinking that had been bogging him down and he walked back to Sharpe in good spirits, looking forward to a quick call to Hayley to say 'Goodnight'.

CHAPTER 3.5

October 6 2002

For everyone there must be a nanosecond during the transition from sleep to wakefulness when they are both asleep and awake at the same time. For Salah, that was when the explosion occurred. Although it awakened him, in the sense that he must have been asleep when it took place, he still felt he had experienced the whole thing: the shattering noise, the shaking building, the tinkling of broken glass and the rattling sound of debris falling onto roofs and vehicles. It was 3 am and pitch-black on a Sunday morning.

The noise was a mixture of thunder with the roar of a huge jet aircraft taking off. His first reaction was to be terrified for his own safety, then, a few seconds later, after he realised what had happened, he was terrified for the safety of others. He hadn't often prayed during his life but today he said aloud, "Oh God, I hope no one was killed."

He switched on his light. It worked. He was up; so was everyone else. Girls on the floor below were screaming, probably thinking a bomb had gone off close by. He imagined them clinging to each other. Boys were different; they wanted to find out what was going on. He heard his neighbours open their doors and go into the corridor. He joined them, some were still in their pyjamas; most had pulled on tracksuit bottoms and trainers.

Salah and the others noticed as they left the building that all the cars in the Sharpe car park were covered in a thick layer of dust and most of their alarms were going off. Along the way everyone was walking on rubble and dust rather than on the campus path itself. Some of the pieces of rubble were quite large. They stepped carefully on their way towards the central campus where the smoke-filled sky was lit up by red and orange flames. Salah imagined that these were what were left of the original fireball.

Successively more two-tone sirens could be heard, as well as police vehicles, fire engines and ambulances, all arriving with their flashing blue lights adding more colour to the night sky, now a strange mixture of red, orange and blue. Yet more police arrived spilling out of their transports and, although they had no idea what had happened or where, they began to restrict the movement of onlookers who were headed where the flames were still burning.

Only Salah knew where he was going and what to look for. When he reached the Engineering Building the scene was one of utter devastation – the propane gas bullets had completely disappeared and the brick pillars had been reduced to dust. There was a hole in the ground ten feet deep where the bullets had been and the nearest wall of the Engineering Building had been reduced to a pile of individual bricks and shards of mortar.

There was brick dust, cement dust and broken glass everywhere as several windows in adjoining buildings had been smashed by the blast. Salah learned later that fragments of the fencing forming the enclosure around the bullets had travelled up to 800 metres and had landed all over the campus. The end section of one of the bullets had done the same.

Salah noticed two white cat's paws on the ground near the Engineering Building. There was no trace of the cat's head or body, but a furry ear and several fragments of entrails were hanging like fridge magnets on a nearby wall; the cat's insides eviscerated by the blast's shrapnel.

Salah continued his walkabout. The first three floors of the Faculty of Commerce Building had no windows. They had been blown in or perhaps out by the blast wave from the explosion. Small fires continued to burn from flaming propane gas sprayed by the explosion and falling debris from the fireball had ignited combustible material throughout the campus. Hoses were everywhere as firefighters unrolled them, ready to pump water and foam on the fires.

It became increasingly obvious to Salah that the emergency

services were gradually putting two and two together and focusing on the scene at the back of the Engineering Building as the likely source of all the problems. Police with dogs, police in forensic suits and fire investigators in special protective clothing began to appear, all working slowly and meticulously. Senior members of the University were visiting the area where the bullets used to be and were going from building to building asking questions and surveying the damage.

Further floodlighting and generators appeared in order to help the emergency services and Salah suddenly found himself illuminated. He wasn't the only one, but it caused him to panic and worry that he was drawing attention to himself by showing too much interest. Moving steadily away from the scene and stealthily retreating into the shadows, he found a way through the darkness and the rubble back to Sharpe. It was still only 4.30 am.

Salah felt much safer back in his room. He didn't realise but he was almost certainly suffering from shock. He may have recovered from being violently woken up but now he was experiencing a second shock wave, this time delayed action shock. His mind was in a chaotic state. A major contributor was that he had no idea whether Majid's friends had caused the explosion or not. He hadn't expected anything to happen so soon. Then there was the effect of the BLEVE itself. Although he had studied BLEVES and watched videos of them in Dubai, he hadn't realised the scale of the devastation caused by exploding bullets would be so huge.

Salah reflected on how he had reached this point. He had taken the *BLEVE* book off the Dubai College library shelf only so he could go to the issue desk and be close to Suhaila while she stamped the book. He had no interest in the subject matter whatsoever; the book was a pretext so that he could flirt with her. Neither did he have any reason for packing the book in his luggage while he was getting ready to travel to the UK; it was an accident – a mistake.

Even more extraordinary was the fact that he couldn't find *BLEVE* on the shelves of the University library and Majid had the book all the time. Majid didn't have any interest in BLEVES either; he simply liked the picture on the front cover and perhaps the idea of blowing something up. How did all these unintended actions come together to produce what happened in the early hours of this morning?

Part of the answer may include other contributory factors such as the unrest at the mosque over the invitation to a US Under Secretary to visit. This had led to Majid's involvement with hard-line Islamic activists whose beliefs that fighting back against American brutality was not only necessary, but a duty.

Majid had then influenced Salah, who was primed to take on similar beliefs because of Hani's story and the similarities to his own experience of losing his family and home. Hani had blamed the US for supporting Israel's ruthless imperial ambitions. Salah had been moved by what happened to Hani's family and then outraged by the Imam's relentless anti-American sermon at the mosque. He became a fully-fledged anti-American activist.

Then there was the University's invitation for the same US Under Secretary to receive an honorary degree. This fed straight into Salah's new anti-American agenda. When the mosque withdrew its invitation the University became the focus and battleground of Islamic righteous indignation and anti-American sentiment.

Finally, there was his mother and the khanjar. If Mubarak hadn't turned up out of the blue and given Salah his late father's khanjar, Salah would not have resurrected his feelings of bitterness towards the Al Munairi family, nor his long suppressed desire for revenge over the treatment of his mother. Furthermore, Mubarak actually facilitated Salah's revenge by virtually gifting him his mobile phone.

Salah paused as it slowly dawned on him that he had just been trying to rewrite history in order to exonerate himself from responsibility for what had happened. It was as if he was trying to convince himself that the BLEVE at the University was pre-ordained in some way, like an act of God. He began to feel uncomfortable about this version of events. Salah didn't want to be a coward; he was going to accept responsibility for his involvement, which had been freely entered into for good reasons. He should be proud of himself and celebrating, not making excuses.

At this point his mobile vibrated. It was Hayley.

"Hello Hayley; you're up early today."

"Hello Salah, so are you. A friend in the office has just rung me to tell me she received a text saying the University is closed until further notice and not to go into work. I've just looked at my mobile and I've got the same message. Do you know anything about it?"

"Hayley, there's been a big explosion in the centre of the campus. It woke us all with a huge bang at about 3 am this morning. Most of the male students went out to have a look. There were fires burning, walls down and windows broken. It's a bad scene."

"God, what happened?"

"I'm not sure, Hayley." Salah was trying not to sound too knowledgeable or excited.

"Hey, wait a minute; I'm watching the early morning news… There's a video of a massive fireball rising hundreds of feet into the air. They're interviewing a baker… He says he's always up at the crack of dawn to turn his ovens on for the morning bake, he heard the bang, saw the flames and caught it on his mobile… Now they're talking to a policeman… He is saying it is early days but at the moment there are no suspicious circumstances. It looks like an industrial accident," she reported, having listened carefully at the same time.

"Thanks, Hayley. Let me know if there are any more details. I don't suppose the papers had time to cover it; the first editions would already have been printed."

"OK, Salah, but what are we all going to do?"

"Good question; we could meet up?"

"Why not? I doubt if I'll be able to drive into the University at the moment; you could meet me at the main gate, if you like?"

"Great. Shall we say in an hour? There's no point hurrying; nothing will be open if we're looking for coffee shops, or anything, actually."

"See ya."

Salah's stress level was coming down. Biometrically, he was still recovering. His heart rate and blood pressure were normalising, he wasn't sweating as much and his hands were no longer shaking. He felt much better after speaking to Hayley. Meeting up with her would be an excellent way of continuing his recovery. Meanwhile, he would pop over to the recreation room in the next block to see if the TV was on. It would be great to see the fireball.

Salah was a few minutes early and waited at the main gate for Hayley to arrive. During this time a steady stream of ambulances left the campus, presumably having turned out according to their major disaster plan and found they weren't needed. On the one hand, Salah obviously hoped this meant good news and that there hadn't been any casualties. On the other hand, police and fire appliances came and went in both directions, probably relief crews arriving to replace the first responders.

Hayley arrived, Salah got in her car; Hayley looked at her watch.

"It's still only around 6.50 am."

"I doubt anything will be open until 8 am at the earliest."

"We could go back to my place, I'll make us a nice coffee."

"That would be great, Hayley."

Hayley's coffee used to be terrible but since she had met Salah she had abandoned instant coffee and now used freshly ground coffee, putting a heaped measure in the cafetière and allowing more time for the coffee to brew. Her coffee was now very good.

As soon as they were inside Hayley's flat she put on the TV again before going to the kitchen. The main TV stations were all running the same loop with the baker and the policeman. There was nothing new so Salah pressed the mute button. Hayley appeared with a tray of coffee and some small cakes she'd made at her mum's the day before.

Salah cleared away, took the tray to the kitchen and then washed up, hoping Hayley would be impressed; he didn't want her to think he was one of those men who expected the little woman to do all the chores, because he wasn't like that. He resumed his seat next to her on the sofa; the same loop was still running; she held his hand and thanked him for washing-up.

"It's still early. Shall we go back to bed and try to get some more sleep?"

"Why not?" Salah didn't hesitate.

Salah woke up at 10.33 am and Hayley a few seconds later. It took both of them a minute or so to figure out why they were together in her flat at this time on a Sunday morning. Hayley got out of bed first and went to the kitchen to make a drink. Salah looked at his mobile; there were several texts:

Khamis*'What the fuck?'*

Hani*'Did you hear the bang? There really is a god!'*

Samara*'Something terrible has happened, I hope there aren't any Muslims involved.'*

Hayley returned with mugs of tea, then Salah got out of bed and they went into the living room. Hayley turned on the TV. The main channels were still covering the explosion, but no one was speaking. There was new footage, including aerial shots of the part of the campus nearest the explosion site, which must have been taken from a drone, interspersed with wider shots showing how far debris from the explosion had travelled over the campus. The tape at the foot of the screen now read…

'University explosion – Arson not ruled out'

Salah felt a powerful urge to speak with Majid but couldn't think how best to make this happen. He asked Hayley what she wanted to do.

"I don't mind. What would you like to do?"

"I don't mind, either. We could go for a walk and get some fresh air. How about meeting up with Khamis and Majid? I could give Khamis a ring."

"OK with me." Hayley sounded less than enthusiastic.

Salah dialled Khamis' mobile.

"Hi Salah. Did you get my text? What the hell?"

"Yeah, sorry I haven't replied, I was asleep."

"Never mind; what's your take on it?"

"Not sure, it's hard to know what's going on. According to the TV they think it might be arson. Are you at home?"

"Yeah, do you want to come over?"

"That would be great. I'm with Hayley."

"So bring her with you. Majid will be pleased, he likes Hayley." Salah was pleased to learn Majid was also at home but he hoped he wouldn't stare at Hayley so much this time.

"Will do, we'll be walking so we'll take a few minutes, maybe half an hour."

"OK, I'll tell Majid you're coming."

Hayley put two and two together from what she overheard and began to get ready to leave the flat. Salah did the same and they set off on foot for Primrose Road.

"Hi Salah, Hi Hayley, come in – welcome." Khamis ushered them in and steered them towards his room. Hayley asked for the bathroom so he directed her to the room in the corner of the hall.

"Majid's just coming."

Hayley rejoined Salah and Khamis, then Majid appeared.

"Hello Salah, Hayley." Majid sounded as if he was in a good mood.

"Hello Majid," Salah and Hayley responded in unison.

"So, what are we going to do with all this free time while the University is not open for business?"

"Good question, Majid; any ideas?"

"I suppose it rather depends on how long it takes for the University to reopen – days, weeks, months? If it's a long time I may go back to Sudan for a while."

"Really? Surely it won't be closed long enough for that. If it is I suppose I might consider a trip home to Dubai." Khamis spoke in haste, he didn't really mean it.

"I won't be going anywhere, that's definite. How can you guys afford it?"

Salah certainly couldn't afford to go anywhere.

"So, what do we know?" They all took it in turns to say what happened from their perspective.

"Not much; we heard the bang here because it woke everyone

in the house." Salah thought Majid must have known a lot more but wasn't letting on.

"I bet it was a lot louder in Sharpe. I didn't only hear it, I experienced it. Believe me, it wasn't just the explosion that was terrifying, there was also a lot of noise after the explosion such as stuff raining down on roofs and vehicles, etc."

"The first I knew was when someone in the office rang me to tell me not to come to work because the University was closed. I rang Salah to ask what was happening and whilst I was talking to him I saw the explosion on the morning news. A baker had filmed it on his mobile as he was going to his bakery."

"I think we've all seen that bit of video now. So, what caused it?" Khamis clearly had no idea.

"They thought it was an industrial accident at first, but now they think it may be arson," explained Salah, trying hard to sound as if he wouldn't know anything about it were it not for the media.

"It couldn't be anything to do with the University's invitation to the American, could it? It was very unpopular among students and there was already a lot of anti-Americanism about. I believe the mosque cancelled their invitation because they thought there would be bad stuff. Perhaps someone or some group had a grievance against the University. There was quite a lot of unrest among students, wasn't there? Perhaps the student anti-war brigade is responsible."

"Perhaps, Khamis." Majid got up to leave saying he was expecting a phone call and would take it in his room.

Salah got up too, saying he needed the 'loo'.

Khamis said he would take orders for tea and coffee. Hayley offered to help and they both went to the kitchen.

Salah didn't need the bathroom; he sensed an opportunity to speak to Majid alone. Quickly leaving the bathroom, he sneaked into Majid's room. Majid was fully aware of what was going on and put his second finger to his lips. He mouthed the word 'bugs'. Salah picked up a piece of paper from Majid's desk and wrote 'Did you expect this to happen so soon?' Majid wrote 'No'. Salah next wrote 'Can we speak soon?' Majid wrote 'We need to make up an excuse to meet', then Salah replied 'I'll think of something and ring you'. Majid nodded and mouthed 'OK'. They heard the others coming back next-door with drinks.

Majid and Salah rejoined Khamis and Hayley. While they were all chatting, Khamis switched on his small TV and surfed the channels for news. Not finding anything he settled on the local channel and pressed the mute button.

Majid thanked Khamis for the drink, announced he was going to meet up with some Sudanese friends and left. "Sorry to abandon you, guys. It was good to see you again, Hayley." Hayley simply smiled and waved.

Salah looked at Hayley to see if she, too, wished to leave. On this occasion he was unable to read her mind. She seemed settled enough so he asked her if she would like to try some Arabic food. Khamis could see where this was leading and joined in with persuading her.

"Hayley, there's a great little takeaway just around the corner. Would you like to give it a try? We go there often and recommend it."

"I've just started eating Indian food so I suppose I may as well try Arabic food." Hayley sounded cautious but willing.

Off they went down the road to Annie's, enjoying the walk and glad of a break from their preoccupations over what was happening at the University. It felt as if they were resuming normal life for a while.

Annie was her usual welcoming self; Khamis asked what was on offer today.

"Oh, all the usual things," she responded. "I think you boys know my menu pretty well now."

"This is Hayley. Perhaps you could help her choose something."

"Hello dear, what would you like?"

"I'm not sure. I haven't eaten Arabic food before."

"No problem, dear. If you would like to point to something I'll tell you what it is or these two can. If you like I can give you a taste of everything to try."

Hayley spotted the hummus; she knew about hummus because

she'd seen it in supermarkets. She figured if it's generally available it must be popular so it's probably OK.

"I'd like some hummus, please, Annie."

"Homemade, dear; I'm going to give you a taste of my chicken shawarma and a little salad – no charge. Would you like some Arabic bread to go with it?"

"Yes, please. Thank you very much."

Khamis and Salah had falafel and shawarma with salad. Annie filled their three boxes, Salah paid, and off they returned to Primrose Road.

As usual they ate from the boxes using the plastic forks provided. Hayley enjoyed the hummus, salad and bread, but was doubtful about the shawarma, which she found 'a little spicy'. Khamis collected the empty boxes and used forks and went to the kitchen to dispose of them.

They noticed something about the University on the TV and pressed the button for sound. The footage was still the same as shown earlier, with the same tape running along the bottom of the screen:

'University explosion – Arson not ruled out'

There was also new footage showing the clean-up operation. The commentary didn't add anything much, no one felt any wiser and the TV was switched off.

Salah looked at Hayley, willing her to suggest they leave. After a while it worked and she got the message.

"Khamis, it's been lovely seeing you again. Thank you so much for your kind hospitality. I enjoyed Annie's lunch and I'll probably try some more Arabic food sometime. I tried Indian food the other day. Salah's chicken tikka masala was very good; you must come to my place and have a meal with us."

"That will be great, Hayley. If you tell me what's cooking I'll bring something nice to drink."

"And we'll all have a party?"

"Yeah."

CHAPTER 3.6

October 7 2002

Salah didn't sleep at all well. Hayley kept asking him if anything was wrong. He said 'he couldn't think of anything'. He didn't like lying to her but it couldn't be helped. After waking up almost every hour he went to the bathroom for a pee at 2 am. Usually he managed to do this and get back into bed without waking Hayley so, hoping for the best, he crept into the living room and switched on the TV to see if they were still running the same loop.

It looked as if things had moved on. One of the University's security guys was being interviewed saying he'd heard a hissing sound when he was out on a routine patrol near the Engineering Building and radioed his mate because it was unusual. By the time his mate arrived the hiss had turned into a whistle. They both decided there must be a leak of something, possibly gas and that it might be dangerous and so they decided to go back to their office to phone the fire brigade. On their way back the whistle turned into a roar, 'like a jet engine' he said, so they turned round and looked behind them to see what it was. He described what they saw as 'a giant blowtorch lighting up the campus and the night sky'.

Salah broke into a cold sweat at the thought that one or two security staff could easily have been killed. At the same time he noticed that the tape running along the bottom of the screen still read…

'University explosion – Arson not ruled out'

"Are you OK? You look very pale." Salah jumped. Hayley was

standing behind him; he hadn't heard her come in.

"Hello Hayley. I couldn't sleep. I had to get up to go to the bathroom anyway so I thought I'd see if there was any more news about the University."

"Would you like a drink?"

"No, thanks; shall we go back to bed?"

Hayley seemed satisfied with Salah's explanation; she pulled the duvet up and over them, then turned and kissed him. He hugged her tightly.

Some hours later Hayley got up. Salah was still making up for the sleep he missed during the night. She quietly poured herself a mug of tea and went to sit on the sofa. She switched on the TV.

The tape now read…

'University explosion – it was NOT an accident – foul play suspected'

A reporter was explaining how the police had been carrying out a thorough fingertip search of the University campus and that a police statement was expected in the next few minutes. She pressed the mute button and waited.

A senior police officer appeared on the screen sitting at a table alongside a fire officer and someone in civilian clothes. She pressed the button again and raised the volume slightly…

"Good morning,

We were called to a large explosion at the University just after 3 am yesterday morning. This appears to have been caused by two large propane gas bullets. Early signs are that the bullets or pipe work had malfunctioned in some way causing gas to escape and catch fire. Two security guards reported seeing a gas flame just before the explosion. The signs are of an accident on an industrial scale. Fortunately, as far as we know, there have been no casualties. We secured the site and began a thorough search. This is still progressing. So far we have found a twisted metal frame that appears to have been subjected to intense heat. It was found partially submerged in the University pond several hundred metres from the crater caused by the explosion. We have also found a deformed patio gas canister buried in the roof of the University Medical Centre, again some distance from the crater, but in the opposite direction. These are the main finds. So far there are numerous smaller items being found all over the site. We now believe the explosion may have been caused deliberately. We don't know why or how but foul play is suspected. If anyone has any information relevant to this incident please contact your local police force. There will be further statements in due course."

Hayley heard the lavatory flush in the bathroom; Salah must be up. She went to the kitchen to make him tea.

"Good morning Salah. They've found some twisted metal and a patio gas canister."

"Really… is that significant?" Salah tried hard to sound surprised.

"They don't know but they're fairly sure foul play is involved."

"I wonder what makes them think that." He hated being so dishonest with Hayley.

"They didn't say."

"Thanks for the tea."

"You're very welcome."

"Shall we go into town and buy some newspapers? Then we could have coffee and read about the explosion."

"Fine with me; shall we have breakfast first?"

"I think I'll just have something with my coffee."

"OK, I'll do the same." Hayley was pleased not to have the bother of getting breakfast for them both.

They showered, dressed and went to the front door to see what the weather was doing. It looked OK; it wasn't raining, at least, and the sky looked mostly clear, so they decided to walk. They found a newsagent on the way to the High Street and bought copies of the local *Herald* and a couple of national dailies. Continuing to the High Street they went into Coffee Plus, ordered coffees and croissants. They took a table for four with enough space to spread out their papers. Salah gave Hayley the *Post* and *Echo* and kept the

Herald and the *Journal* for himself.

The *Herald* carried the following headline on its front page:

EXPLOSION AT UNIVERSITY

There was also a picture of a huge fireball reaching up into the night sky. It said the photograph was taken by a baker using his mobile phone on his way to work. According to the article the cause of the explosion is thought to be a leak from the gas supply to the University Faculty of Engineering Building. Police and fire investigation teams are at work to establish the exact cause and, until such time as this work is completed, the University will remain closed.

The article was short on detail so Salah moved to the *Journal*, which carried the following headline:

UNIVERSITY FEARED ATTACK

For some reason the *Journal* was majoring on conspiracy theories. The journalist must have interviewed University staff who were open about the surveillance that had been going on, as well as their concerns the University might face protests over their invitation to the American Under Secretary to accept a higher degree. They were also worried about the unrest at the mosque for the same reason and feared that this could impact on the University's Muslim population. The article stated that the explosions may have been arson or even a terror attack and that nobody or any group had claimed responsibility.

Salah was more than a little disconcerted that the *Journal* had put two and two together so well and so soon and because the University must also be thinking along these lines now.

The *Post* covered the explosion on page three, beginning with the small headline:

BLEVE AT UNIVERSITY

"What does 'BLEVE' mean?" asked Hayley.

"Boiling Liquid Expanding Vapour Explosion," explained Salah with authority. "Why do you ask?" he said as if he didn't know why. He felt like a shit again.

"The *Post* believes the cause of the explosion was a BLEVE. I've never heard the word before. How do *you* know about BLEVES?"

"We studied BLEVES as part of fire safety during the course in Dubai. Do you want to know what happens?"

"Yes, but please keep it simple."

"You know there's gas in storage cylinders called bullets?"

"OK, yep."

"The trouble begins when the pressure of the gas inside the bullets increases. This normally happens when the bullets get hot. The bullets are very strong but, even so, if the pressure gets too high they can split. To stop this, when the pressure gets too high a relief valve lets off small quantities of gas to reduce the pressure inside. So far so good, but the gas is heavier than air and forms a cloud that floats around until it reaches ground level. The slightest spark can cause the cloud to catch fire and/or explode. This creates more heat on the bullets, which further overheats the gas inside. If the gas pressure rises too much the casing splits and large quantities of gas are released, which also explodes in the form of a fireball."

"I get it. But how did the gas in the bullets get hot in the middle of the night and how did anything catch alight? Surely this has got to be suspicious, hasn't it?"

"The way you put it, Hayley, yes. May I see the *Post*, please?"

Hayley handed Salah the *Post* and picked up the *Echo*.

The *Echo* article speculated on whether the explosion was directly related to the Deputy Prime Minister's invitation for the American Under Secretary to visit his hometown and local mosque, which had been controversial from the start and had turned into a spectacular foot shooting PR disaster:

'The University had innocently climbed on the bandwagon by offering the American a higher degree, apparently unaware of the anti-American feeling in the community and among its students. Massive protests and civil disobedience were predicted until the invitation to visit the Mosque was withdrawn. The invitation to visit the University was not withdrawn. Was that why the University became a target? The proponents of these goodwill gestures seemed to have been fatally unaware either of the fact that anti-American feeling is at an all-time high, particularly among Muslims, and that Muslim sentiment was already inflamed by American military adventures in Islamic Countries. The investigation has already revealed foul play was likely. Experience suggests it is unlikely this arson, or terror, attack was carried out by a single aggrieved individual. So far, no organisation has claimed responsibility. It is possible, therefore, we may never have a full explanation of what happened and why.'

Hayley passed the *Echo* to Salah who seemed delighted with the article, which he considered provided a convincing rationale for the attack on the University that could attract public support. He made a note to self to be careful not to show any enthusiasm for this view, which could be perceived by some as incriminating.

Salah was beginning to feel overwhelmed by newsprint and decided he'd had enough so he went to get more coffees. When he got back Hayley was still reading the *Herald*, which she found not very informative.

"It's hard to believe that any one could feel so strongly about something that they would blow up the University."

"Hayley, I don't have any difficulty believing it. People don't hate the University but a lot of people *do* hate America, not Americans themselves, but American bullying and warmongering."

"I never thought I would be so close to a possible terrorist incident."

Salah realised for the first time that the explosion happened close to Hayley's office. The plan was always going to be carried out at night and the offices would be empty but, even so, Hayley was right to say it had been close. Salah experienced another cold sweat at the very idea he could have endangered her. They finished their coffees and walked back to Hayley's flat.

Salah was feeling anxious. He liked being with Hayley but the more they spoke about the explosion the more worried he became he might reveal too much or say the wrong thing.

He also wanted to speak to Majid as soon as possible, so he decided to make an excuse to go back to his room. He told Hayley he needed to get in touch with the Wankowskis. If they heard about the explosion or saw it on the international news they would be very worried. She understood and it was a very rational explanation.

Hayley offered to make a sandwich so that they could have an early lunch before he left, so she went to the kitchen. Salah went to the living room and switched on the TV.

The tape now read:

'University explosion
– Hire car found abandoned on campus'

A reporter was explaining that a car hired several days ago was not returned on time and reported missing. It had now been found during the search of the campus in one of the student car parks. A mobile phone was also found, inside the car under one of the front seats. The car and the mobile were being taken away by police for forensic examination. A further statement from the police was expected soon.

Hayley came in with tea and cheese and pickle sandwiches. Salah updated her on the latest news whilst devouring the sandwiches.

"Is it possible the car stuff is connected with the explosion?"

"I have no idea, Hayley; time will tell." Hayley's questions were becoming increasingly unnerving. He needed a break. Salah thanked her for lunch and helped her clear away – she washed, he dried. He gave her a big hug and said he was sorry he had to go. She said she understood and offered to drive him back to the University. He declined saying the walk would do him good.

After putting some distance between himself and Hayley's flat, he rang Majid.

"Hi Majid. Good to see you yesterday. I've found the book on

Dubai we were talking about. You're very welcome to borrow it if you think it could be helpful. We could meet up for a drink somewhere or you could collect it if you can come round to Sharpe?"

"Hi Salah, where are you now?"

"Not far from the town centre, walking back to Sharpe."

"I'm walking into town, just left Primrose Road; do you have the book with you?"

"Yeah, I meant to give it to you yesterday, it's still in my rucksack."

"Where shall we meet?"

"What about the little café in Waitrose?"

"See you there; I reckon you'll be there first."

"Hello Salah. I must say, Hayley is a very attractive young lady and very sweet; you're very lucky."

"Hi Majid. Yes, she is and, yes, I am. Shall we stay here and chat over a drink or shall we go for a walk?"

"Better go for a walk."

They left Waitrose and walked towards the recreation ground where there was a vast amount of open space and no one within earshot. Neither of them imagined that Waitrose could be bugged but there was nothing like an open space for privacy, unless there were drones around, of course.

"I must say I was shocked when it happened. Actually, shocked is an understatement."

"So was I, Salah. I knew we had given them everything they needed, that they had done some reconnaissance and trial runs and that they were raring to go, but it still took me by surprise."

"Will they claim responsibility, do you think?"

"I have no idea. They may think there's no point in drawing attention to themselves. They may even be out of the country by now."

"Do you feel vulnerable, personally?"

"Not really. I think there was enough separation between us and them for us to feel safe."

"Did I ever tell you I was summoned to a meeting one day by one of the Pro-Vice-Chancellors and asked a lot of questions about my religion, my friends, about students' reactions to the University's invitation to the American Under Secretary and so on? He is responsible for security. He mentioned your name and asked if you were one of my friends."

"You did mention that."

"I think both of us must have been on their radar at sometime. I didn't see it as something to worry about at the time. Now I'm not so sure."

"That's why we must continue to be careful."

"Yeah."

They sat on a bench for a few moments without speaking, just watching a man kicking a football around with a young boy. A woman appeared elsewhere pushing a pram. Salah and Majid both had the same thought. How shocked and frightened these people would be if they knew they were almost in touching distance of two international terrorists.

They decided enough was enough and it was time to go their separate ways.

"No doubt we shall bump into each other in Coffee Plus, at Friday prayers or on the campus if they get it cleared up, unless you are going back to Sudan?"

"Probably not, Salah. We'll see how long it takes to reopen the University. Let's keep in touch."

"Will do, Majid. All the best."

Salah retraced his steps and walked back to Sharpe, glad to have touched base with Majid, especially as he seemed to think there was nothing to worry about. Salah found this reassuring but deep down he was still apprehensive.

When he reached the University he noticed the campus looked less like a bombsite. For example, the pathway across campus to Sharpe had already been cleared and looked almost normal. On his way past the games room he called in to see if there were any developments on the TV. It looked much the same so he didn't linger.

Back in his room he switched on his laptop and was astonished to find when he reached the Yahoo! home page that one of the trending items was the explosion at the University. He hoped that Maria and Janek hadn't seen it and he began drafting a message.

CHAPTER 3.7

October 8 2002

Although the University was slowly getting back to normal the area around the Engineering Building where the explosion took place was still fenced off; it was impossible to see what was going on. The rest of the campus was still being cleaned up in many areas but most of the debris had been removed.

Lectures resumed as normal for Salah in the lecture room block which, although close to the Engineering Building, was unaffected by the explosion. Nevertheless, the first three floors of the Faculty of Social Sciences Building, which was one of the worst affected by the explosion, were still closed while the large number of broken windows were replaced. Lectures in this Faculty's departments were relocated to several different buildings around the campus, much to the annoyance of the Faculty's staff and students.

The Medical Centre roof had been repaired and medical services were back to normal. The social areas frequented by students were hardly affected and the all-important student union building and its facilities were up and running more or less as before.

Recent TV coverage and press releases hadn't given out much detailed information about the explosion recently and no one was sure what had happened, how it happened or why. The word on the street was that the explosion was now being treated as a terrorist incident and that someone had stolen a car and used it to bring a barbecue onto the campus, which was then placed underneath the gas bullets and ignited. The reason was supposed to be a protest about the University's endorsement of American foreign policy by inviting a senior member of the US Administration to visit the

University and accept an honorary degree.

Salah was sitting at his desk working on his sustainability assignment. It wasn't going well and he was on the point of abandoning it when there was a knock. Having a perfect excuse to stop work, he got up to open the door expecting to see Khamis, perhaps Hani or possibly Majid.

Instead he was astonished, and this is a huge understatement, to see Maria and Janek standing in the corridor outside his room, smiling at him. He stood there for several seconds unable to speak, rooted to the spot, with words failing him.

Janek was the first to break the spell.

"Hello Salah – surprised?"

"*Surprised*? I can't *believe* it!" Salah was mentally pinching himself. It wasn't a dream.

"We got your e-mail," began Maria, "but we had already seen the news and thought it important enough to come and see for ourselves. Shall we come in?"

"Of course… I'm so sorry, come in. We're a bit short of chairs. If Jan could take the desk chair and you have the easy chair, Maria, I'll sit on the bed."

"This is such a nice room, Salah; does that door lead to a bathroom?" Maria got up to use the bathroom.

"Yes, it's very comfortable. I'm very lucky, all thanks to both of you," said Salah, beginning to find his voice and get into his stride. Are you in England for a visit?"

"We've come to see *you*, Salah. Actually, we have a surprise for you too."

"This is a *wonderful* surprise."

"Yes, but we have an even *bigger* surprise," said Maria, returning from the bathroom and nodding knowingly.

"Really?" There was another knock.

"Excuse me, I expect this will be one of my friends."

Salah opened the door and, to his total bewilderment, in walked his mother closely followed by Randy.

Although disoriented, Salah instinctively wrapped his arms around his mother and hugged her in a mutual embrace lasting several minutes. Both cried tears of relief and joy.

Janek moved to the bed and gave Randy the desk chair. Randy chatted with Maria and Janek whilst Salah and his mother clung to each other. When they disentangled themselves, Janek gestured to Aparna to sit next to him. Randy got up to shake Salah's hand and Salah reached out to Randy, although he was nervous of Randy because of what happened at the meeting with the Pro-Vice-Chancellor.

Salah said he would try to borrow another chair from next-door. Luckily, a neighbouring student obliged and Salah returned with another chair so he could also sit down in what was now a crowded room.

"Salah, the person we have to thank for finding Aparna is Randy. He came to see us in Dubai and told us he had been asked by the University to carry out security checks on a group of overseas students. He said there were political issues with potential security implications troubling the University. Obviously we were worried, but understood how this could happen, and gave him our full cooperation. In the process we told him why we adopted you and that's how he found out about your mother. Before leaving he said he would ask his colleagues in the region to see what they could find out.

"To be honest, we didn't have high hopes but, after a while, Randy phoned us and told us she had been found. We were ecstatic of course to learn she was working for a family in Qatar. With the information Randy gave us we were able to contact the family who happily released Aparna when they were made aware of the circumstances. They also offered to take her back after she had been reunited with her son if she so wished.

"Aparna has been staying with us. We came as soon as we could organise flights and accommodation. Happily, Randy is in the University again today and able to join us. We all owe him a very great debt."

By now, Salah had tears streaming down his face and then Aparna began to cry, then Maria and then Janek. Salah got up to shake Randy's hand again but changed his mind at the last minute and gave him a hug. Randy was huge and Salah was only just able to get his arms around him but, fortunately, Randy reciprocated, which made hugging much easier.

Randy, who was also visibly moved, said he was pleased the routine work of the CIA had produced such a happy outcome, adding he was glad to have been able to help.

"So, you're CIA, Randy," said Salah, feeling even more nervous.

"Yes, Sir."

"Is that how you were able to come straight through passport control after we arrived in the UK?"

"Yes, Sir. I have a CIA stamp in my passport and those of us working in law enforcement are usually courteous and helpful towards each other."

"From what I saw you were treated as a VIP."

"The Brits are great, Salah."

"So, what exactly have you been doing with the University?"

"Actually, I have been working with several universities, Salah. Generally, they have asked for our help to vet students from parts of the world where there is a perceived security risk. Sometimes it is just a question of checking and verifying identity. UK universities are having a lot of trouble with the names of Arab students and their families. The CIA can usually help because we have built up a massive database as a result of our military presence in the Middle East."

"I see. I don't suppose you know how the investigation into the explosion is going?"

"The police and intelligence services are handling it; I've only given advice here and there. I believe they've got it worked out. It seems a car was hired using a stolen credit card and a barbecue purchased and set up under the bullets. The barbecue was probably ignited using a gas cylinder. It's not clear how they made their escape as the hire car was left behind on the campus. One of the clinching bits of evidence was a small metal badge with the word 'OUTBACK' stamped on it. It was found during the clear-up near the outskirts of the campus with its rivets still attached. OUTBACK is a brand of garden barbecue and one was purchased locally using the stolen credit card shortly before the explosion."

"Who do the authorities think was responsible?" asked Janek.

"The University doesn't think it was any of their students, more likely a political activist or terrorist group, possibly connected to the mosque or to a fundamentalist religious group. It's very likely more than one person was involved. A mobile phone used to purchase the barbecue and hire car was found underneath one of the car seats; apparently it contains incriminating material and the owner has been arrested, but there is still a long way to go to complete the case for a prosecution."

"Really... that's quick work. Is anything known about the person arrested?" Salah could hardly contain his excitement.

"I believe he's an Emirati studying at another university not far away."

"It's a pity he's an Emirati; but it's good they've caught someone. I don't suppose anyone knows the motive."

"Sorry, Maria."

Salah noticed that Randy was becoming impatient with the number of questions, but Salah didn't want him to leave; an idea had just come into his head.

"Randy, you found my mother. It's hard for me to find the right words to show you how grateful I am." Salah faltered and became choked. "You have given me the most wonderful, most amazing gift. I doubt there is anything I could give you in return that would be enough. I know I can never repay your kindness but it would make me very happy if you would accept a small gift."

"That's very kind of you, Salah, but it isn't necessary and, in any case, we are not allowed to accept gifts."

Salah went to his cupboard and took out the bag with the khanjar in it. He slid it out of the bag, opened the red velvet box and presented it to Randy. Randy took hold of the box and examined the khanjar from every angle. He lifted it slowly, ran his fingers over the intricate silver design and stroked the silk cushion before returning the khanjar back to its box.

"It's for you, Randy. Perhaps you could think of it as a souvenir rather than a gift."

"Thank you very much, Salah, that's exactly what I'm going to do. Can you tell me more about it?"

"I don't know the history. Obviously it's very old, the silver is the best quality, the craftsmanship is superb and very traditional and it may even be quite valuable. When my father died a note was found saying that I should be given the khanjar, as he couldn't leave me money or property."

"But surely it must be of enormous sentimental value to you?"

"Yes, but it makes me both happy and sad in equal measure. If I explained all the circumstances, Randy, I am sure you would understand. Please believe I am very, very happy for you to have it."

"Thank you, then I shall accept it and treat it with great respect. It will be one of my most prized possessions. Now it's time for this family to be together again and to try to make up for lost time. I wish you all the very best and will take my leave. Thanks again, Salah, for the 'souvenir'."

Randy opened the door and was gone.

CHAPTER 3.8

No one spoke for a while. There was still a lot of emotional tension in the room. Salah was beginning to wonder what was going to happen next.

"How long are you staying?"

"I'm sorry, Salah, we can't stay. We'd like to, but we have both taken compassionate leave and have to get back to our teaching. Aparna is going to stay with us for a while. She said she'd like to help us around the house and I'd like her to teach me how to cook Indian food. Why don't you come home for your vacation and spend some time with your mother?"

"That's a great idea but surely you could stay long enough for us all to have a meal together?"

"Actually, we need to go soon so we can deliver our hire car back to the airport and catch the flight back to Dubai. I'm so sorry it's such a rush; I promise we'll do all those things when you come home, Salah. We've got time for a cup of tea if that's OK?"

"OK Jan, I understand." Salah got up to go to the kitchen.

"Would you like to see the kitchen while I make some tea?" They all followed Salah out of his room, along the corridor and into the kitchen. They were amazed at the size and at the facilities. Salah filled a kettle. Whilst waiting for the water to boil he found a clean mug and washed up three more. He knew from past experience how everyone liked their tea so he filled their mugs and they all returned to his room.

Aparna looked relaxed but a little bewildered. She couldn't take her eyes off Salah. She probably noticed a big difference; the last time she saw him he was an awkward teenager. Now he was a self-confident adult. She gazed lovingly at Maria and Janek, no doubt grateful for their very existence bearing in mind all they were doing for Salah and now for her.

Maria and Janek finished their tea and looked at Salah as if to say 'Sorry, but we've got to go'. They got up and helped Aparna to her feet. She went over to Salah and hugged him again. He hugged her back; their hugging took some time. Maria and Janek understood, not showing any impatience. When they finished, Salah hugged Maria and Janek in turn and asked Maria if she would kindly return the *BLEVE* book to the College library with his apologies and, if necessary, pay the fine.

"No trouble, Salah; I think we really shall have to leave you now."

They all filed out of the room and made their way down the stairs to the car park. They opened the doors of the hire car but dithered and dallied; no one was in a hurry to leave. Salah hugged the others again and thanked them for coming. He said he would definitely return to Dubai in the vacation.

They got into the car, Janek started the engine and the wheels began to roll. Everyone inside waved through open windows. Salah waved back, more and more vigorously as the tears came into his eyes. The car became smaller and smaller, the waving stopped, the windows went back up and they disappeared from view.

Salah stayed where he was for a while, looking for the car that was no longer there. He was inclined to feel lonely from time to time but now he felt more lonely than at any other time in his life. Almost in desperation he decided to go back to his room and ring Khamis.

"Hi Salah, what's up?"

"Khamis, can you come over? I'm making a prawn jalfrezi. Sorry it's such short notice."

"Yeah, why not? When do you want me?"

"Any time, Khamis, as soon as you like."

"OK, I'll be a few minutes, see ya."

Salah couldn't wait to tell Khamis his news. He went to the kitchen and began to find the pans and assemble the ingredients for his prawn jalfrezi. Then he made sure the beers were chilling in the fridge. After experiencing a slight loss of confidence he went back to his room to find the recipe on his laptop.

There was a knock on the door and Salah was surprised Khamis had arrived so soon.

"Sorry to bother you, Sir. We're interviewing Mubarak Al Munairi in connection with the explosion here at the University. He is insisting he lost his mobile phone during a visit to see you. Do you have any recollection of that?"

"No. I'm afraid not."

"He says he rang you to ask you to look for it?"

"I don't think so. He may have phoned me but not about his mobile. If he did I don't remember. Sorry, is this important in some way?"

"It is, Sir. Mr Munairi's mobile was found in the hire car left on the campus after the explosion. We believe it was used for research and reconnaissance, also to purchase the barbecue and the hire car used by those involved in the explosion at the University. I assume he *did* visit you?"

"Oh yes, he's my half-brother. We're not close and I didn't know he was in the UK until I met him by chance at the mosque recently. We chatted and I invited him for coffee, then he came here. He didn't stay long."

"Don't worry, Sir. You're confirming what we thought. He's just trying to create some kind of alibi. He's pretending he lost his mobile because he knows it's been found and provides incriminating evidence suggesting he's up to his neck in the conspiracy to cause the explosion at the University."

"Really? I'm shocked. I'm so sorry; I wish I could be more helpful."

"Actually, you've been very helpful, Sir. Please let us know if you change your address in case we need to talk to you again or take a statement and be sure to let us know if you plan to leave the UK."

"OK. I will, for sure. Bye now."

ARABIC – ENGLISH DICTIONARY

Afwan	You're welcome
Asalaam alaykum	Peace be with you
Alaykum as salaam	And with you peace
Al hamdoolilla	Thanks be to God
Fattoush	Vegetable and bread salad
Ful mesdames	Fava bean stew
Kayf haalek	How are you?
Inshaa Allah	If God wills
Laban	Middle Eastern yogurt
Layla sa'ida	Good night
Ma'a as salama	Goodbye
Mabrook	Congratulations
Mafi mishkila	No problem
Makdous	Stuffed pickled aubergine
Muezzin	Crier calling Muslims to prayer
Musallah	Prayer hall
Sabaah al khair	Good morning

Sabaah al noor	Good morning (reply)
Shukran	Thank you
Tamam	I'm fine/OK
Quibla	Direction of Mecca
Wa inta	And you

ACKNOWLEDGEMENTS

This novel would not exist in its present form without the involvement of people to whom I owe a debt of heartfelt gratitude.

After producing a draft of *Khanjar*, my wife kindly read it to check for errors (I'd in mind typos, spelling, etc). As well as finding typographical errors, she also highlighted passages of questionable meaning, judgement and taste.

After correcting these I thought I was all set until my daughter, an accomplished writer, expressed her interest and began raising more and more issues, some of which were fundamental. For example, she suggested the novel should begin in the UK and not in Dubai where it was originally set. Alarmed at the amount of extra work involved I resisted for as long as possible before producing yet another draft based on a complete restructure of the story. The many ideas and suggestions from my wife and daughter proved invaluable when producing the new draft, which was unquestionably superior to earlier versions.

Khanjar was further corrected and improved by Caroline Ahern's excellent editing from which I learned so much; I am hugely grateful. Thanks also to Ginevra Picani for the excellent review she kindly sent to me at a time when I needed a morale boost.

The self-publishing process was a complete mystery to me, even more so after a great deal of Internet research. Then I came across Spiffing Covers. Thank you James, Joe, Stefan and Gabriel, a dream team, whose collective wisdom, technical knowledge, creativity and patience are truly remarkable. By working collaboratively they have produced what I believe is a beautiful product, which speaks volumes for their creativity, artistry, technical skill and discernment.